THE GIRL SHE WANTED

BOOKS BY K.L. SLATER

Safe with Me
Blink
Liar
The Mistake
The Visitor
The Secret
Closer
Finding Grace
The Silent Ones
Single
Little Whispers

THE GIRL SHE WANTED

K.L. SLATER

bookouture

Published by Bookouture in 2020

An imprint of Storyfire Ltd.
Carmelite House
50 Victoria Embankment
London EC4Y 0DZ

www.bookouture.com

ISBN: 978-1-83888-932-6
eBook ISBN: 978-1-83888-931-9

To my daughter, Francesca Kim x

PROLOGUE

Sunday 12 April

Angus Titchford felt cheered when he pulled open his bedroom curtains at precisely 6.10 a.m.

He sat on the edge of the bed to watch the glorious sunrise and realised with pleasure that it was going to be the perfect day. He'd been waiting in anticipation for weeks to sow the vegetable seeds in his freshly raked small allotment patch. The beetroot, carrots and leeks would provide him with tasty meals in the summer months, and he'd be able to feed Josh and Jemima with home-grown goodness when they came to visit.

It was Easter Sunday too, he suddenly remembered. Beth had popped round yesterday with the Troublesome Twins, as he fondly called his five-year-old grandchildren, and they'd bought him a Lindt chocolate rabbit as a treat.

'You're not allowed to eat it until tomorrow, Grandad,' Jemima had told him firmly.

'Because you might be sick,' Josh added gravely.

'Oh, I see.' Angus frowned. 'Well that's a bit disappointing.'

'That rule only applies to you two,' Beth laughed. 'Grandad's a grown-up, and besides, he isn't working his way through a dozen Easter eggs like you are.'

Angus had ruffled their hair and marvelled, as he often did, how forty-odd years could have flown past so quickly. He could remember quite clearly when Beth, a small child herself, had raced around this very garden clutching her Easter basket and searching high and low for the eggs her mother had hidden amongst the shrubs and flowers.

His heart squeezed as he thought of Sandy, his dear departed wife. Four years he'd been without her now. Since she'd been gone, he'd felt as though he was just going through the motions. But over the last eighteen months, he'd perked up a bit, started enjoying life again. Pottering around the garden, spending time with the Troublesome Twins, and then he'd taken up bowls, joined the club a couple of streets away. He'd met new people who lived locally, and his game was improving too.

'Dad … are you feeling OK?' Beth's concerned voice had brought him back to the moment.

He'd blinked his moist eyes. 'Aye, I'm champion, love. Just thinking about you running up and down the garden on one of your mum's Easter egg hunts.'

She smiled, laid her hand on his arm. 'We can do a hunt for these two next year, Dad, how about that? I'm sure you'll manage to out-fox them with your chocolatey hidey-holes.'

Angus had nodded and smiled. 'You're on. I like that idea.'

When the sun had risen fully, he stood up from the bed, grimacing as his joints creaked and grumbled. The first ten minutes were the worst, until his body managed to somehow crank itself into order. The old rack was hardly a finely oiled machine these days, but he couldn't complain. Apart from the usual aches and pains that came with wear and tear, he was relatively healthy, and had so far miraculously managed to avoid the diabetes, ticker trouble and breathing difficulties that many of his bowls club acquaintances had to put up with.

Downstairs, he made a cup of nice strong Yorkshire tea, put his egg on to boil and buttered his toast soldiers for dipping into the soft yolk.

Sandy's voice rang in his ears, as it did regularly throughout the day now. 'A few grapes and a sliced banana to go towards your five-a-day.'

'Yes, dear. I shall do it now,' he said mildly.

Despite often speaking to himself out loud, Angus hadn't lost his marbles – far from it. He still had all his wits about him, otherwise how was he able to finish the *Times* crossword every day? He spoke to Sandy because he liked doing it, simple as that. It comforted him to continue the routines they'd shared for forty-five years.

Sadly, the habit was set to be his demise on that Easter morning.

Heading for the fridge to get the grapes, he slipped on a wet patch of floor, and the next thing he knew he was lying flat on his back with a breathtaking pain shooting through his hip and leg.

His first thought was for the egg bobbing away in the pan on the hob. What would happen if the pan boiled dry? His second thought was one of pure annoyance at himself. Only a couple of months ago he'd scathingly waved away Beth's idea to get a panic alarm installed for emergency situations just like this one.

He had fallen once before. Sprained his wrist and got away lightly. But now … now this. It was a bad one, he could feel it.

Very slowly and painfully, he managed to shuffle a few inches at a time towards the hallway, where the phone sat tantalisingly on a small table. It took him nearly fifteen minutes to get there, by which time his forehead was spotted with sweat and he felt nauseous from the pain radiating from his left hip.

He used his right foot to kick the flimsy leg of the hall table, and the cordless phone tumbled out of its charging base.

*

Thirty minutes later, Angus was safely in an ambulance heading for King's Mill Hospital in the next town. He might be getting on a bit, but he had lots to live for: his garden, his loving daughter and his beautiful grandchildren. Silently he thanked his lucky stars that he'd managed to summon help.

It was going to be OK now, he felt absolutely sure of that.

1

King's Mill Hospital, Nottinghamshire

Dr Nathan Mosley groaned as his pager trilled again. He was in the last thirty minutes of yet another gruelling twelve-hour shift. You never knew what you were going to encounter when that pager went off. Could be a two-minute signing of paperwork for a routine discharge, or the start of an intense two-hour treatment and monitoring of a patient.

There was just no telling until you got there.

Nathan was twenty-nine years old and had almost completed his final year as a medical intern and junior doctor in the accident and emergency department at King's Mill Hospital in Sutton-in-Ashfield, part of the Sherwood Forest Health Trust.

He loved the buzz and pace of the emergency wards. Every day felt like he was at the sharp end of saving lives. He could never have envisaged opting for a GP role in a sleepy village like the one he'd grown up in. No, his job here had it all: unlimited adrenaline, an unrivalled sense of daily unpredictability, and many satisfying moments over the course of every shift. His duties could range from giving someone the good news that they wouldn't lose their badly crushed finger, to spotting a serious medical problem when the patient arrived for some unconnected ailment and referring them for what he knew would be life-saving treatment.

He'd clawed his way up from humble beginnings and a few of life's obstacles to get here. Now, he told anyone who would listen that he loved his job. But boy, was it tiring. The A&E department gave new meaning to the word. He was dog-tired most of the time these days, even on his day off. Exhaustion was like a fusty smell that clung to his clothes no matter how often he washed them. It was always there.

During training, they'd constantly been warned of the toll the shifts took on new doctors, but Nathan could never have imagined just how tired it was possible to get and still carry on working. Not to mention making crucially important decisions that affected hundreds of people's lives every month.

He silenced the pager and strode through the waiting area, his eyes scanning the hopeful but weary rows of patients, some of whom looked at him pleadingly, as if he might be here for them. All the usual sights were present: a hastily bandaged arm, a blood-stained rag held up to an eye, a crying child cradled in a mother's arms, and numerous worried and desperate-looking relatives of the ill and injured. The smell of antiseptic perked him up a bit, at least, and he pushed his light-brown curls out of his eyes as he fixed his gaze on the opposite side of the room to discourage any of the patients from speaking to him, and whooshed through the swinging double doors that led to the emergency wards, his open white coat billowing behind his lanky frame like a magician's cloak.

The A&E department was classed as one ward for the purposes of internal organisation, but in actual fact it was split into four arms of patient beds – one male and one female section, and two mixed – that ran from the central nurses' station. Instantly alert and focused, he saw the point of interest immediately over in Section 2, where a cluster of nurses and auxiliary staff buzzed around a bed at the far end.

Someone announced his arrival, and Carrie Parsons, the A&E ward manager, rushed towards him, her face tight with concern and tension.

'What have we got here?' he barked, not yet breaking his stride.

'Male, eighty-two years old, admitted this morning following a fall. Hip fracture, mild concussion. Patient stabilised and monitored ready for transfer to a ward. He's just gone into cardiac arrest.'

He remembered Angus Titchford's admission onto the ward earlier. The supervising clinician had reported that there was no great concern over his condition, but Nathan had looked in on him a couple of times anyway. He was a plucky old chap, self-deprecating about his own clumsiness. He'd rather reminded Nathan of his grandfather, who'd passed away when Nathan had been just twelve years old.

Nathan had seen the patient just one more time to view his X-ray. Carrie Parsons had assured him she was happy to take over the supervision of Angus's care until his transfer to another area of the hospital had been completed.

Nathan stood next to Carrie now and watched the resuscitation team at work, applying the cardiac charges to the patient's bare chest and then standing back to wait for the shock. A growing discomfort moved up from his solar plexus and lodged itself firmly in his chest. Something wasn't right here, but he couldn't put his finger on exactly what.

He glanced at Carrie, trying to gauge if she too seemed concerned. But her expression was bland as a mask, as if she was simply observing a routine daily procedure. Maybe she had become accustomed to this sort of thing happening.

Yet this was the second case in the last few months where a patient admitted to the emergency ward with a seemingly fairly minor condition had deteriorated dramatically.

Nathan recalled the six-month-old baby girl who'd been admitted with a high temperature and vomiting – a suspected nasty viral infection. Following a period of intravenous rehydration, the child had appeared to be recovering; then, completely without warning, her condition had rapidly declined. Urgent tests had shown the rapid onset of respiratory failure and she had died.

And now Angus Titchford was fighting for his life even though his initial prognosis had been perfectly routine. It was unusual and troubling. Very troubling indeed.

While the resuscitation team battled to save the elderly man, Nathan plucked the clipboard displaying his information from the bottom rail of the bed. His eyes slid expertly across the myriad of readings and particulars recorded since the patient's admission. Finally, he found what he was looking for: the heart rate variability chart.

There had been a worrying ramping up of the heart rate, and palpitations had started, for no apparent reason, less than an hour ago. It was puzzling, because there was no trace of this anomaly when the patient had been admitted, nor was any history of the problem recorded in the notes. Mr Titchford had been treated with appropriate beta blocker medication and the symptoms had initially settled down again. Then, out of nowhere, there had been another massive spike, and now here he was in full cardiac arrest.

It was unusual, even in an eighty-two-year-old after the shock of a fall. The other case, a few months ago, had been remarkably similar in that serious symptoms had suddenly appeared as if from nowhere, resulting in an irreversible and tragic outcome.

Nathan knew how carefully the hospital trust protected its reputation. Although transparent policies and procedures were in place encouraging staff to speak up if they witnessed any wrongdoing, he'd heard unofficial stories from other hospitals of how careers could mysteriously stall if people dared to do so.

He was just six months away from achieving his lifelong dream of qualifying as a full-time A&E doctor. It had been a long, long road and his achievement would taste all the sweeter for the struggle. He'd already booked a dream trip to Santorini with his fiancée, Suzy, to celebrate both this milestone and his thirtieth birthday. She didn't know yet but he planned to use the holiday to scout for possible wedding venues. Life was good and full of promise, but Nathan couldn't fully enjoy it with guilt twisting in his guts, lethal as razor blades.

He had to do something.

The medical team leader stood back and raised his hand for the activity to cease. The faces around Nathan faded out. It was possible the feeling he had in his chest right now was just his imagination, but he seriously doubted it. Something was wrong. He could feel anxiety pulsing and expanding inside him.

First, do no harm. The Hippocratic oath he'd pledged echoed once again in his ears.

If he spoke up and raised the alarm, then his colleagues' jobs could be at stake. An unpleasant inquiry might ensue, and there was no guarantee he would be proven right. There might be no wrongdoing to be found and he'd be left a leper amongst his own team.

And yet the feeling in his chest grew stronger, like a bad case of indigestion. He knew he couldn't live with himself if he just stood by and watched another patient die. Whatever the cost to his own career might be, he had to take action.

He took a deep breath in and released the air slowly before turning on his heel and leaving the ward. He ignored Carrie Parsons calling out his name, asking him to return.

He took long, determined strides until he reached the swing doors at the end of the ward. No matter what disruption it caused to the rest of the ward staff, it was time to do the right thing.

2

Alexa

I'm walking back from the ice cream van with our 99 cones when I see my sister is on the phone.

She's tucked my one-year-old daughter, Florence, into one of the park's baby swings and I wave the ice creams to get their attention. My smile quickly fades when I realise that Carrie isn't giving Florence her full attention. She's pushing her swing but is talking animatedly, the phone trapped awkwardly between her ear and her shoulder.

My throat turns dry and I pick up my pace. It's the perfect set-up for an accident waiting to happen.

As I get closer, I see that Florence is squealing with pleasure. She bangs her podgy little gloved hands on the swing's security rail in front of her, and I have to admit she looks happy enough, her springy blonde curls breaking free of her bobble hat.

Carrie sees my approach, clocks my panicked expression. She holds up a hand as if to repeat her usual refrain, 'Alexa, everything's fine. Stop fretting!' and stops pushing Florence so I can take over. I watch as her expression changes to an irritated frown as she focuses on whatever it is the caller is saying. She turns away and her voice ramps up an octave.

I stand by my daughter and steady the swing so it's barely moving as I listen to Carrie's conversation.

'I understand that, but does it have to be today?' She's objecting quite strongly, obviously irked. But then the person on the other end says something else, and she sighs, as if in defeat. 'OK, that's fine then. No, no, if it has to be today then it has to be today. Yes, bye.'

She looks a little troubled as she puts the phone in her pocket, but tries to cover it with an eye roll.

'Is everything OK?' I ask, handing her a cone.

She ignores the ice cream and stares over my shoulder at the copse of silver birches behind me.

'Not really. That was the PA to the senior head of nursing at King's Mill Hospital.' She screws up her face and mimics the caller as she recites the job title. 'There's been some kind of incident and they need me to go back in this afternoon.'

Ice cream has started to drip down the sides of her cone, and Florence is reaching up and squealing for it.

'Has there been a big car crash or something?' In all the years Carrie has worked at King's Mill Hospital, I've only known the senior management call the staff in at short notice once or twice at the most. It's usually only if they're overwhelmed by something like a multiple-vehicle pile-up or, as happened once, a terrible fire in a local nursing home. But my sister has worked the last six days straight and she badly needs her two days off. She still gets easily stressed since her marriage to Cameron ended so badly.

Silently I hand her both ice creams to hold while I attempt to wrestle a squirming Florence out of the swing.

'It's not an influx of patients that's the problem,' Carrie says, staring into the trees again. 'A situation has kicked off inside the hospital and they need all the staff to go in for some kind of urgent briefing.'

She sighs heavily with the inconvenience of it all and hands me back my cone.

'Typical,' I say, just as Florence buries her face in the side of my ice cream and emerges covered in vanilla goo. 'Not fair, really, on your day off. We were looking forward to Auntie Carrie playing with us, weren't we, sweetie?' I reach inside the changing bag and pull out a wipe. Florence wriggles in my arms and bats her little arms around in protest. 'You can stay here with us for another half an hour, though, can't you? I mean, you don't have to go into work right away, surely?'

Carrie looks at me directly. I know she's picking up on my anxious response, and she puts her hand on my arm in reassurance.

'This is a really good opportunity for you to be out with Florence on your own.' She looks around the park. 'It's perfectly safe here and there are plenty of people around. I'd stay if I could, but they're insisting I go in.'

'It's fine,' I say brightly, ignoring my tight chest. 'We'll be fine.'

Carrie studies me a moment. 'I can give you a lift home first, if you'd feel better?'

I shake my head and steel myself. 'You get off. The fresh air will do Florence good now she's over her cold. We'll stay a bit longer and then head back. See you back at home for dinner, yes?'

She nods. 'Shouldn't take long.'

Like Carrie says, it's not as if we're here at the park on our own. If I got into any kind of trouble, it wouldn't be like before. There'd be someone around to help this time. Almost without realising it, I've come to rely on my sister's company whenever I'm out of the house. I even organise Florence's appointments and activities around Carrie's shifts at the hospital so I know she'll be able to come with us. Most of the time I try not to think about it.

Carrie tosses her untouched ice cream in a nearby bin and hitches her handbag further onto her shoulder. 'See you later, then.' She turns and walks away from us, so deep in thought she forgets to say goodbye to her beloved Florence, so I know she must have an awful lot on her mind.

Carrie has worked at the hospital for the last ten years; before that, she was at the Queen's Medical Centre, in Nottingham. Her career has been her life, particularly after her marriage to Cameron broke down a year ago. She ran into hard times financially after discovering Cameron had left her in a lot of credit card debt as a result of his personal spending, and so came to live with us about eight months ago. It caused some tension between me and my husband, Perry, at the time, but that's behind us now. The three of us have found a way to amicably co-exist, and as I keep telling him, it won't be forever.

'Hey, Carrie?' I call after her.

She turns and starts to walk backwards so she can keep moving and look at me at the same time.

'Smile … it can't be that bad!' It's an inside joke; something she often says to me.

She raises a hand and gives me a weak smile. Florence lets out an ear-piercing squawk and waves frantically to her auntie, but Carrie has turned away and doesn't look back at us again.

It's like she's screened herself off and stepped into a world of her own.

3

Perry's face brightens when Florence and I arrive home.

'You two been out on your own?'

'We've been at the park,' I say brightly, even though I feel a bit shaky being out alone with Florence. 'Just for a little while.'

He smiles and I can tell he sees it as a big step forward.

'Just the three of us for dinner, then?' He looks up from chopping tomatoes. 'I'm making a ragù sauce for the pasta and it takes ages to cook, so I started early.'

'Sounds lovely,' I say, slipping off Florence's hat, scarf and coat as Perry blows raspberries at her, making her chuckle. 'Carrie will be back later, so make enough for her too.'

His face drops. 'I thought she'd moved out at last.' He winks at me to show he's just teasing, but I know full well there's an element of truth behind it and I can't really blame him. Most men would've baulked at their sister-in-law moving into their family's small three-bed semi even if it was only temporary.

But Carrie was in a desperate situation and was about to be evicted, so Perry did the right thing. I'm proud to say that's the kind of man my husband is. On top of that, he's hard-working – toiling on an oil rig in the North Sea two to three weeks at a time – and he's also a great daddy to Florence. We just need to recapture a bit of closeness, make the effort in our busy lives to get some time together.

'Carrie's been called back in to work,' I say, pushing a glass under the fridge water dispenser. 'Some kind of crisis meeting at the hospital, apparently.'

Perry pulls down the corners of his mouth. 'Sounds messy. Fancy a glass of red?'

I glance at the clock and take a sip of ice-cool water, willing myself to relax now we're home. 'It's a bit early, isn't it? Drinking at five in the afternoon. I haven't fed Florence yet.'

'She doesn't need you to, Alexa.' He raises an eyebrow. 'We've talked about this. She's a year old now; she can sit at the table with us and feed herself. Will she have some pasta and ragù?'

I shake my head. 'I made a fresh batch of sweet potato and courgette mash yesterday. It's in the freezer.'

He's not giving up. 'I can chop the pasta up finely for her?'

I put my water down and trace a line through the condensation on the side of the glass.

'She can't chew our food properly yet,' I say. 'That's how babies end up choking.'

'It's also how they learn,' Perry says lightly, winking at Florence. 'Isn't it, princess?'

She rocks back and forth in delight and squeals her agreement.

We've been through all this before and I don't want it all again now. Perry's away working so much, I wish he'd just leave Florence's food entirely to me. I know what's best for her and I actually have a weaning spreadsheet all planned out.

'Well, have a glass of wine at least, eh? I reckon it will do you good to live a little dangerously.' He grins and puts down the chopping knife, wiping his hands on a tea towel before planting a kiss on my cheek, not seeming to realise how tense the conversation has made me.

He travels across the room making strange ape-like moves that soon have Florence squealing again, this time in mock terror because she knows she'll be in for a tummy tickle when Daddy reaches her bouncy chair.

I watch the two of them larking around together and smile. I can't deny it is lovely, just the three of us at home again. But I love my sister, and she has been a real rock for me in the past. She supported me through my own nightmare, which is thankfully behind us now. Staying on with Florence at the park today on our own was a bit of a milestone and proves just how far I've come, even if it gave me palpitations.

Usually when Carrie and I are chatting in the kitchen before dinner, Perry tends to stay well out of the way. He'll watch television or read one of his fitness magazines in the living room. He's never explicitly told me he's sick of having her around, but I can tell he's been getting a bit restless, probably wondering if and when she's going to get her own place again.

I do want to raise the subject of moving out with Carrie, but I've cried off until now because I just don't know where to start. The last thing I want to do is make her feel she isn't wanted, particularly after she found out just a few months ago that Cameron, the rat, is getting married again, to someone Carrie actually went to school with. She knew he'd been cheating but the identity of the woman has seemed to add insult to injury.

I walk over to the counter and pick up a small piece of chopped tomato. Seeds and red flesh ooze over my fingers as I pop it into my mouth.

I *will* talk to Carrie about her plans for the future.

It's just a matter of waiting for the right moment.

With the sauce now done and the pan of boiling water waiting for the pasta, Perry starts pacing up and down the kitchen, looking at the wall clock every few seconds.

'I thought you said she'd be back?' He frowns. 'It's going to be too late for us to eat soon.'

Florence lets out a yelp and bangs the tray of her high chair with her plastic cutlery as if she agrees.

'We'll have ours now then,' I say, too tired to argue. It's only six o'clock, hardly late, even though we do tend to eat earlier now we have Florence. Funny how our entire lives have been bent around our tiny bundle of love and happiness.

I know he's being difficult though. Would it really be so terrible to delay dinner by another half an hour so Carrie can eat with us? Perry is just making one of his points again, although he'll deny it if I accuse him of doing so. I hate feeling pulled both ways like this, and it seems to be happening more and more.

Still, he goes back to work again in a couple of days, so at least I won't have to put up with it for the next three weeks.

He wordlessly places the pasta in the boiling water and slides the slices of garlic bread under the grill. I take a small plastic container of Florence's food out of the freezer, ready to defrost in the microwave. Perry doesn't comment, and I relax a little. I pour us another small glass of wine each and top up Florence's free-flow cup with water.

I sip my wine and stare out of the window at the drizzling rain blurring my view of the big oak tree at the bottom of the garden, and find myself wondering what's keeping Carrie so long at the hospital. It's only a ten-minute drive away.

She's been gone quite a while.

4

King's Mill Hospital

It was 6 p.m. by the time the accident and emergency ward staff had gathered in the lecture theatre. There were about forty of them in total.

Carrie stood with Marcia Hunt, her deputy ward manager, and Roisin Kenny, the senior shift nurse. The three women had worked together for years and felt a natural kinship under any kind of duress.

'I wonder if the rumours are true,' Roisin whispered hoarsely. 'Unexplained deaths on the ward.'

'I don't know, but it makes you feel worthless, doesn't it? As if we're not doing our jobs right.' Marcia frowned. 'It's a hospital and sometimes people die. That's just a sad fact of the business we're in, I'm afraid. It's nobody's fault, but these days it seems people are always looking for someone to blame.'

Carrie pursed her lips and nodded. Everyone she'd spoken to since her arrival seemed to be thinking along the same lines.

The other staff members immediately in their vicinity were distracted from their own conversations by the arrival of A&E's junior doctor, Nathan Mosley. He'd slipped in at the last minute and stood shiftily beside the theatre doors as if he might be considering making a quick escape.

Rumour had it that this shitstorm was all Mosley's doing. He'd apparently been the whistle-blower who'd shafted his colleagues and gone directly to the senior management, leapfrogging his own supervising consultant. Like Roisin, for the last couple of days Carrie had heard whispers on the hospital grapevine that there was big trouble brewing in the A&E department. Even so, when she'd received the call at the park, it had been a nasty shock. She had immediately decided not to give Alexa any inkling that she might know what it was all about.

Alexa was a natural worrier and Carrie knew she was still extremely fragile from events a couple of years earlier, which she always avoided talking about. She'd become more and more reliant on Carrie; wouldn't take a step outside the house without her. She'd even refused to take Florence to playgroup a few weeks ago when Carrie had a chest infection.

'This is getting out of control, Alexa.' Whether or not her sister was angry with her as a result of her directness, it had needed saying. 'You've got to do more on your own. Baby steps at first and then—'

'Don't say anything to Perry,' Alexa had blurted out. Perry had been due home that afternoon.' I don't need him going on at me.'

Perry wasn't stupid; he was aware that Alexa had a bit of a problem. He just didn't realise how bad it was, what with him spending chunks of time away working. When he came home, he made an effort to do lots with Florence and Alexa, so that when Carrie took a step back, her sister had someone with her.

It was a worry and she wasn't sure what to do about it. She hadn't quite got the type of relationship with Perry that meant she could confide in him. Understatement of the year.

She broke from her thoughts when the suit at the front of the room cleared his throat and everyone fell quiet.

'I'm Jeff Cottonwood, and these are my colleagues …' Carrie tuned his droning voice out as he introduced the three other smartly dressed people standing with him: two men and a woman, with their clipboards and their regulation concerned faces.

These people represented the top tier of the hospital staff. They were members of the board of trustees, senior players who made all the important decisions. Decisions that were often grounded in popular opinion and budgetary constraints rather than what might be best for the patients and staff.

Carrie hadn't seen any of this lot in the flesh before, although she recognised one or two of them from their glossy photographs on the new hospital website that had recently been launched with the help of an expensive London-based PR company. Yet another executive decision made possible by a sudden pocket of funding springing up that could have been better spent on patient care.

Yes, she thought irritably, these were the sort of people who were so important they never made themselves known or approachable to the staff. They wouldn't dream of inconveniencing themselves on the front line to meet people like her, the foot soldiers who dealt directly with the patients.

She felt a familiar bitter curl of resentment towards each and every one of them and was glad they looked uncomfortable. They deserved to feel the pressure.

'Thank you for coming today,' Cottonwood continued, as if he were reading from a script.

'As if we had a choice in the matter,' Roisin muttered under her breath.

'We appreciate that for some of you, this is your day off, but we have something to announce that simply cannot wait.'

A tall blonde woman in a navy skirt suit and high nude heels stepped forward. 'I'm sorry to tell you we have received a serious complaint, a *concern*, from a member of the hospital staff.'

Everyone's eyes drifted surreptitiously towards the doors, where Nathan Mosley stood with his arms folded. Carrie watched as he fronted it out, ignoring the hostile glances and keeping his focus firmly on what was being said at the front of the room.

Ironically, Carrie had always rather liked Nathan. He seemed interested in her professional opinion and wasn't as stuffy as some of the other doctors; he was efficient and smart but not too stuck up to have the odd laugh. When they'd worked last August bank holiday, he'd brought doughnuts in for the whole shift. Some of the younger nurses swooned a bit in his presence, called him 'Poldark' on account of his messy curls and olive complexion.

'There have been two fatalities over the past four months in the accident and emergency department. These deaths are currently being fully investigated in line with the hospital's internal inquiry process. We will be ensuring our official procedure is stringently followed.' The woman paused for a moment, scanning the room. 'I want to reassure everyone here that this is not a witch hunt. We're certain that everyone here fully respects that we must remain accountable to the public and are seen to be fully cooperative and transparent by the governing bodies of our profession.'

Muted murmurs of discontent rippled through the room. The woman glanced at Cottonwood, who recognised his cue to take centre stage again.

'We are expecting the details of the inquiry to break in local news outlets at any time. Because of the seriousness of this issue, national press coverage is bound to follow quickly. So we ask that when you leave this building, please do *not* discuss any details of what has been said here today. This includes the nature of this meeting and the procedures mentioned. It is essential that we maintain full confidentiality at all times.'

'Does that mean we can go now?' Marcia whispered.

'We need each person present here to speak with a member of the inquiry team before leaving. They will take your particulars and ask you a few questions; we anticipate that it should take no more than fifteen minutes. After that, you can leave the premises.'

There was an audible groan from some members of staff.

'Any questions?' Cottonwood asked, glancing at his watch.

A man called from the back of the room, 'Are we getting paid extra for this?'

'I can confirm you will be reimbursed for your time today, yes,' Cottonwood answered curtly.

'What about travel time, plus the fact that our day off has been ruined?' the man asked. This time, he was ignored.

'As a follow-up to today's interviews, some staff may need to be interviewed further by the police,' Cottonwood said.

Again concerned voices began to buzz, and Cottonwood raised his hand.

'If you are one of those the police need to speak to, please don't draw hasty conclusions. More than likely they will simply need to confirm certain details pertinent to the inquiry.'

'Are you going to find a scapegoat? Some poor sod who'll take the rap for these deaths that were probably caused by underfunding?' someone in close proximity to Carrie called out.

'Most certainly not.' Cottonwood sniffed in distaste. 'Our priority is to uphold the hospital's excellent patient care record and to protect staff and patients alike. Nobody wants to work in the stressful environment of an inquiry and we'll endeavour to get the matter cleared up as quickly as possible. If everyone cooperates, that should help hasten our progress.'

'We have staff ready to take your name and tell you which inquiry team you need to speak to,' the woman added. 'Thanks to everyone for your time.'

'Great. I'm going to have to call Pete,' Marcia grumbled. 'There's no way I'll get back in time to pick the twins up from football practice now we have to stay for questioning.'

'Tell me about it,' Roisin fumed. 'My book club starts at seven and it's a twenty-minute drive. Not worth my while going when I finish here.'

Carrie nodded sympathetically at them both but didn't say anything.

If she did, she might just throw up. Right here in front of everyone.

5

Carrie queued up with her colleagues and was handed a slip confirming that her interview with a member of the inquiry team would take place in thirty minutes, at 6.15. Marcia's interview was at 6.00 and Roisin's at 6.30.

'As if we've nothing better to do than hang around waiting to be accused of all sorts of evil misdemeanours!' Marcia raged. 'It's such an insult; the blood, sweat and tears we willingly give every single day to keep our patients safe.'

'And look who's done a disappearing act,' Carrie added scathingly. 'Our snake-in-the-grass junior doctor.'

They all glanced towards the doors. Dr Mosley was no longer standing there.

'Hey, don't look so concerned, Carrie, love,' Marcia said. 'None of us have anything to worry about. They'll soon realise there were perfectly good reasons for those awful deaths. It's always sad when someone passes on our watch, but I'm convinced it's all just a horrible coincidence.'

'Ten years of giving our all, and this is the thanks we get,' Carrie said, chewing on a nail. 'Treated like common criminals.'

'They can't force us to stay, you know,' Roisin said, suddenly militant. 'We could walk out right now and they couldn't do a thing about it.'

'Wouldn't look good, though, would it? Might seem as if you're trying to hide something.' Marcia pulled a face. 'I'm staying. I'll answer their questions just to get it out of the way. But they'd better apologise for dragging us through the mud when they find out the deaths were explainable after all.'

'We can do without the media putting a spin on it, that's for sure,' Carrie remarked. 'Everyone on our street knows I work in A&E at King's Mill, and trust me, it doesn't take much to set their tongues wagging.'

'Hopefully it'll all blow over in a few days.' Marcia frowned. 'Half our village knows I work here too. Guilty by association and all that. It could get very unpleasant.'

'I worry about somebody saying something nasty to my sister. She's still really nervous, I don't want it to cause another setback.' Carrie chewed her thumbnail.

'She doesn't work here though, does she?' Roisin remarked. 'It's worse for us that do.'

Carrie shot her a look. She'd been friends with Roisin a long time now, but she could be hard at times.

'Poor Alexa,' Marcia said softly. 'Is she doing better now? It must be so difficult to bounce back after what she's been through.'

Carrie silently reprimanded herself for bringing Alexa's name into it. She was thinking out loud; it was a bad habit of hers. Marcia was a nice enough colleague to work with, but she could be a nosy so-and-so. Alexa was so insular these days, she'd hate to think Carrie was discussing her private business with her workmates.

'She's getting there,' she said, turning to Roisin to deflect. 'How's little Jay doing?'

If you wanted to zone out for ten minutes, the best way to do it was to encourage Roisin to talk about her seven-year-old nephew, Jay. Today was no different, hospital inquiry or not. She was off like a racehorse, babbling on, and Marcia caught Carrie's eye knowingly.

Carrie pulled out her phone, nodding here and there in Roisin's account of Jay's incredible technical skills on the football pitch. She opened up her text messages and tapped a quick line to Alexa.

Got held up here. Should be back by 7.

Alexa's reply pinged back in seconds.

7?? That's late, what's happening?

Carrie's heart sank. Alexa would expect a full explanation when she got back, and all she wanted to do after this was go upstairs to bed and shut the world out.

Nothing to worry about. See you soon.

She turned her phone to silent and pushed it back into her pocket. She had to take a pragmatic view about what was happening. She'd get the interview out of the way and then pull herself together before driving home and putting a brave face on it. Especially if Perry was there, still trying to pretend she didn't live with them.

As far as Carrie was concerned, the sooner this nightmare at the hospital was over, the better. She told herself again she had nothing to worry about. Her paperwork was all up to date and she always made a point of covering herself for every eventuality.

Ward manager or not, she'd no intention of taking the rap for this.

Her inquiry officer, as they were calling the officials asking the questions, was a young woman who looked fresh out of university. She had short dark hair and sallow skin, and when Carrie tapped on the door and walked in, she glanced up from her paperwork but didn't smile. They didn't seem to train them much in the art of communication these days.

'I'm Zoe Johnson from the Sherwood Forest Health Trust, and you are' – she consulted her list – 'Carrie Parsons, the A&E ward manager. Is that correct?'

'Yes.'

'Thanks for coming in, Carrie. I just have a few questions to go through with you, and I'll need to check the current details we hold for you are correct, if that's OK.'

Carrie didn't respond. Zoe had an unfortunate condescending manner and she willed herself to ignore it and not make a fuss.

She was asked to confirm various details from a printed HR personnel sheet.

Age: 42
Current address: 102 Lindrick Road, Kirkby-in-Ashfield
Year first employed by the trust: 2010
Time working at King's Mill Hospital: 10 years

After each of her answers, Zoe ticked a box on the sheet with a pencil.

'Can I confirm you were on duty and working on the A&E ward on both of the following dates.' Zoe checked another sheet of paper. 'The twenty-seventh of December and the twelfth of April.'

Carrie looked at her blankly. 'Yes, I was working on both days the patients died but surely you have the shift rotas to confirm it?'

'Yes, we do have those.'

'So, if the rota says I was in on those days, then you can be sure I was in.'

Zoe bit her lip. 'I need you to confirm it verbally before I can tick the box.' She shuffled her paperwork. 'Now. Are you available tomorrow if the police need to speak with you?'

'I didn't realise it was a definite thing.' Carrie swallowed. 'That the police would need to speak to everyone.'

'That's correct. They won't be speaking to everyone, but should they ask to see you, would you be available in the morning? I know it's a little difficult, as we don't have timings yet. The detectives have already said they can conduct home visits if necessary, if people have children or elderly—'

'No. That's fine. If they need to speak to me, I'll come in.' She couldn't bear to think of Alexa's panicky reaction if the police turned up at the house.

Zoe's face brightened a touch. 'Perfect. We'll be contacting the members of staff affected either later today or first thing, and of course, you'll get some notice.'

When Carrie left the office, she bumped into Roisin, who was arriving for her own appointment.

'I've a good mind to go in there and tell them what I think about this … this foolishness.' Roisin threw her hands up in the air.

'I wouldn't waste your breath,' Carrie replied dully. 'I just answered her questions and got out of there as quickly as I could. They're determined to see this through, make a thing out of it to publicly show their transparency.'

'Ridiculous! I mean, the old fella who died was eighty-two. Hello? The body does some strange things at that age. He'd had a good innings, I'm sure. What good can come of all this interrogation? Sadly, it won't bring him or anyone else back, that's for sure.'

Carrie shrugged. 'I don't think they look at it like that. I've been told the police will be speaking to selected individuals tomorrow.'

Roisin shook her head in frustration and went on her way, still mumbling to herself.

Carrie headed for the exit and tried to reframe her own negative thoughts. Maybe she wouldn't be one of the members of staff the police wanted to speak to. There were lots of people on her shift. Lots of people who might be looked on with suspicion, who didn't have the benefit of a perfect patient-care record behind them like she did.

Carrie always did everything by the book when it came to her admin duties, dotting the i's and crossing the t's. Whilst others would wait until the next day and sometimes even forget, she always ensured she got every official sheet and form countersigned as per the official policy.

On paper, she had never put a foot wrong.

She'd always made sure of that.

6

The police station

As DI Adam Partridge sauntered back down the street towards the station, enjoying the fresh air, his phone rang. Balancing his Greggs BLT, bag of crisps and pastry under his arm and swapping his takeout coffee to the other hand, he answered it.

'Hello?' he said hopefully, wondering if Saskia had forgiven him yet.

'Partridge?' the detective superintendent barked. 'Where are you?'

'I'm … I've just popped out for a sandwich, ma'am, but I'm nearly back now.'

What was it about this job that meant you felt guilty not being at the station even when you'd skipped lunch and had nipped out for a bit of tea?

'Can you come up?'

The sandwich and other items slipped out from under his arm. He jerked his other arm to try and catch them, and spilt coffee down his right trouser leg. 'Damn it!'

He looked down forlornly. Bread, filling and the most delectable apricot turnover were now casualties on the pavement.

'What was that, Partridge?' his superior snapped.

'Sorry, ma'am, coffee spill. I'm on my way. Has there been a—'

'Fill you in when you get here. Quick as you can, mind.' The line went dead.

Adam dithered for a moment. He was ravenous! Should he go back to the shop and get another sandwich and a pastry? Or make do with a bag of crisps and half a cup of coffee?

He sighed and dumped the spoiled food in a nearby bin, then walked the remaining few yards and climbed the steps to the station entrance. A decent meal would just have to wait.

His day was about to get worse. Up on the top floor, one of the other DIs exited the superintendent's office and gave a smirk. 'Hope you've got no holidays booked for the next few months, Adam. Sounds like she's got a corker with your name all over it.'

'Bloody great,' he muttered, and tapped on the office door.

Detective Superintendent Della Grey was in her mid fifties, slim, with short silver hair and angular features. She had a way of moving in sharp, cautious bursts that reminded Adam of a nervous bird.

'You wanted to see me, ma'am?' He stepped inside the sparsely furnished office. 'Sorry about my trousers; I had a disagreement with a coffee.'

'Take a seat, Adam. How are you with hospitals?'

'Sorry?'

'Hospitals, Adam. Places of illness, recovery and sometimes death. Some people have rather an aversion to them.'

'I'm pleased to say I haven't had many dealings with them so far, but I—'

'Good. Well there's something very nasty kicking off at King's Mill Hospital. Junior doctor has reported a couple of unusual deaths. They're in the throes of interviewing all the A&E staff.'

'Unusual deaths?'

'Unnatural, unexplained. Might be nothing, but then again might be something. Might be the tip of the iceberg, if you get my drift, and then we'll be looking at quite a stint in there.' She hesitated, her hand making a quick movement across her desk.

'So you want me to look into it?'

She gave a curt nod and pushed a slim brown folder over to him. Inside were three sheets of A4 paper with sparse notes.

'That's all we have so far, I'm afraid. I want you to take DS Tremaine and find out what the hell is going on. Get the overview from the people in the know. Stay as long as it takes.'

Adam swallowed, racking his brains for what Grey might consider a reasonable excuse. Saskia would have him by the balls if he wasn't ready to go out at seven tonight. One cancelled meal with her boss was serious; two and it would be curtains for him.

Grey fixed him with those beady avian eyes of hers. 'Is there a problem with that, Partridge?'

'No, ma'am.' He coughed. 'No problem at all.'

'Pleased to hear it. There are going to be some long days ahead, Adam. We can't afford to lose public confidence by dragging our feet with this. There's enough concern from the hospital management that the chief superintendent has asked us to look into it to see whether any criminal offences may have been committed, although there appears to be next to no evidence at the moment. We must be seen to be doing the right thing, nice and thorough, leave no stone unturned. Even if the deaths are proven to be natural. Let me have an update first thing tomorrow morning.'

She picked up a hardback journal on her desk and he considered himself dismissed. He scooped up the folder and stood, moving towards the door. 'I'll get right on to it.'

'Oh, and Adam?'

He turned around.

'Just so you know, you've got coffee on your shirt as well.'

7

Alexa

It's almost 7 p.m. when Carrie finally gets back home from the hospital. Florence is tucked up safely in bed and we're sitting watching television with a glass of wine.

'We saved you some pasta,' I say, jumping up to get Carrie's food while a previously jolly Perry now sits stony-faced, his eyes glued to a TV show about renovating properties abroad.

Carrie puts her hand up. 'No, honestly, don't bother. I grabbed something while I was out, thanks. You sit down and watch your programme.'

'How did it go at the hospital?' I ask her, slumping back onto the sofa and picking up my wine glass.

'Shh,' Perry interrupts rudely. 'This is the important bit; they're going to offer them less than the asking price.'

I ignore him. 'Is everything OK, Carrie? You were gone ages.'

'Fine. It was something and nothing, a storm in a teacup as always,' she says dismissively, ducking out of the room. 'I'm shattered and going straight up to bed. I'll tell you all about it tomorrow. Night, you two.'

'Night!' I say, nudging Perry.

'Night,' he calls blankly.

Despite Perry's protests that I should stay and watch the programme with him, I get up from my seat and follow Carrie upstairs. I know my sister and can see through her casual replies. It's clear from her rigid posture and flushed face that she's stressed about something.

'Carrie?' I get to the top of the stairs just as she's about to disappear into her bedroom.

Her hand flies to her chest. 'You startled me! Have you come up to check on Florence?'

'I came up to check on *you*,' I say, stepping closer to her. 'You're a bit jumpy. Are you sure you're OK? I mean, you'd say if something was wrong, wouldn't you?'

She laughs, and it sounds tinny on the quiet landing. 'Like what?'

'Well, if something's happened at work, for instance,' I press her. 'You just don't seem yourself.'

'You worry too much. I'm fine.' She touches my arm to show there are no hard feelings. 'Thanks for asking, but it's just red tape. Nothing's wrong, OK?'

'OK.' I smile, thinking she must just be tired. 'Just checking up on my big sis, that's all. Hey, let's look in on the little munchkin together, shall we?'

We creep into Florence's room and stand by her cot, watching her tiny chest rising and falling, one arm thrown back, one relaxed down by her side.

'She's so perfect,' Carrie breathes. 'I love her so much.'

Something in her tone makes me glance at her face, and I'm touched to see her eyes glistening. Carrie would have loved kids with Cameron but it just never happened for her. She worships Florence as if she were her own.

'*So* perfect,' I agree, sliding my arm around her shoulders. 'Especially when she's fast asleep, eh?'

'Bless her! I'm saving all this up to tell her when she's older, you know,' Carrie teases, and we giggle quietly together. I touch

Florence's flushed cheek gently and Carrie blows her a kiss before we tiptoe out of the bedroom.

Back out on the landing, her phone buzzes and she glances at it, swallowing before pushing it hastily back into her pocket.

'Night,' she says, and turns to open her door. Then she stops, looking back at me. 'I care about you and Florence more than you could ever know. Always remember that.' And before I can quiz her further on why she felt the need to say such a thing, she disappears into her bedroom, leaving me alone on the landing.

There's a five-year gap between me and Carrie. Growing up as the younger sister, I never thought about careers – other than being a Disney princess, of course – but Carrie was always adamant she was going to be a doctor. She hated any kind of schoolwork, though, and Mum used to say to her, 'If becoming a doctor proves out of your reach, there's always nursing, love. That's a very worthwhile career.'

Carrie wouldn't be discouraged, and focused instead on her practical skills. I remember once when I fell over and gashed my knee, she was first on the scene as usual with her medical box, but even at my young age, I recognised that her bedside manner needed some work. She had a macabre interest in all sorts of injuries and illnesses, things that terrified me, made me queasy.

'Stop wriggling, Alexa, I've got to clean it properly. I read about someone who hurt their knee just like this. The cut got infected and she had to have her leg taken off.'

Funny now, but not so amusing when you're just seven and believe everything your big sister tells you. I started to whimper.

'I'll save your leg, don't worry,' she said confidently, reaching for a tube of antiseptic cream. 'Dr Carrie to the rescue yet again.'

That hospital means everything to her. I hope to God everything is OK there.

8

King's Mill Hospital

The next morning, Carrie was back at the hospital at 9.30. Her appointment with the police was scheduled for 10.30, but she'd deliberately arrived early, mainly because she wanted to get out of the house.

The text confirming they wanted to speak to her had come last night just as she'd left Florence's room with Alexa. It had unnerved her. It felt as if events at the hospital were spiralling out of control, bleeding into the home life she loved. Luckily, Alexa hadn't asked who the text was from, otherwise, in that moment of weakness, she might've just broken down there and then and told her sister everything.

On the way to the cafeteria, Carrie bumped into Roisin.

'I've just been in there,' Roisin said a little breathlessly. 'Boy, am I glad *that's* over!'

Carrie's heartbeat quickened. 'What did they ask you?'

'They just confirmed a lot of information, like the shift dates I'd worked and the patients I'd had contact with, that sort of thing.'

'That's it?'

Roisin nodded. 'I was in there about twenty minutes.'

'Did you deal with both the patients who died?'

'I did.' She rolled her eyes. 'Means you will have done too, seeing as you oversee all my ward cases. Just our luck, eh?'

'Listen, Roisin, maybe we should meet up for a coffee, have a chat, you know?' Carrie looked at her meaningfully, but Roisin made some excuse about having to pick her nephew up and went on her way.

Carrie turned the corner at the end of the corridor and saw that a young uniformed officer stood outside the door of the room she had been instructed to report to. The officer consulted a list when she approached, asked her to take a seat, then disappeared through the door for a few moments.

'They'll see you now,' she said when she came out again.

Carrie walked into the small room, usually used as a consultant's office. She'd been in here several times as part of her ward manager role. The leafy plants and wall pictures remained, but the consultant's family photographs had been removed from the desk.

Her insides were squirming, but she made an effort to appear calm and unruffled as she walked confidently over to the desk.

The male detective stood up. He was in his mid thirties and wore a trendy petrol-blue suit. He had constructed an impressive quiff with his hair, held in place with a hefty dollop of product, unless she was mistaken. He looked too fresh and stylish to be a detective; the only ones Carrie had ever seen on TV were overweight and jaded.

'Thanks for coming, Ms Parsons,' he said. 'May I call you Carrie?'

She nodded and sat down on the chair he indicated and glanced at the female officer. She looked to be in her late twenties and had short red hair and a pale, freckled complexion.

'I'm DI Adam Partridge and this is DS Nell Tremaine. We have some questions to ask you following on from the information you gave the hospital inquiry officer yesterday afternoon, if that's all right.'

Carrie nodded. Without further ado, Tremaine began, asking her virtually identical questions to the ones the inquiry officer had asked yesterday. Carrie gave the same answers, but now added, 'I've double-checked the dates in my diary and I did work both those shifts.'

'Excellent.' Tremaine nodded, writing something down. 'That helps, thank you.'

Carrie breathed a little easier and massaged the back of her neck while the two detectives shuffled their paperwork.

Partridge leaned forward, a piece of paper in his hand.

'We've been interviewing your colleagues, Carrie, trying to build up a picture of what happened on those key dates when two patients unfortunately died. Let's start with the twelfth of April, shall we?' He consulted his sheet. 'That was when eighty-two-year-old Angus Titchford was admitted to the ward. Can you tell us what you remember about that day?'

'There was nothing unusual about Mr Titchford's case, as I recall,' Carrie said, looking at a copy of her own ward report that Partridge had slid across the table. 'Like it says here, he'd been admitted by ambulance staff so he'd skipped triage and come directly to the ward to be assessed and X-rayed, and then to wait for a bed to come free on the general ward.'

'I would assume it became clear quite quickly that Mr Titchford had broken his hip?' Partridge asked.

Carrie nodded. 'It was obvious given the circumstances of his fall and the location of the pain. He seemed disorientated for a short time and had mild concussion. Dr Mosley examined him initially and ordered an X-ray, but said he was fairly certain the hip was broken.'

Partridge nodded, watching her. 'We've already spoken to Dr Mosley.'

I bet you have, Carrie fumed silently. She might've known that sneaky rat would have got his two penn'orth in right away. He'd always seemed so nice, so genuine, when in fact he was the worst kind of snake in the grass. Not content with reporting his own colleagues for supposed unexplained deaths, it seemed he'd then gone on to given a few individuals' names for good measure, including her own.

Partridge continued. 'So Mr Titchford was then left in your capable hands, as ward manager, to organise the X-ray and to administer medication, including appropriate pain relief.'

Carrie nodded. 'The usual arrangements. Yes.'

'What happened next?' Tremaine asked. 'Did you carry out these procedures yourself?'

'I usually delegate patient care to one of the nurses or health assistants, depending on the patient's requirements.' Carrie looked at the ward case sheet again for effect, though she didn't need to. Every stage of the Angus Titchford admission was perfectly clear in her mind. 'I asked one of my nurses, Roisin Kenny, to take care of Mr Titchford. Marcia Hunt was her line manager.'

Carrie watched as Tremaine scribbled down copious notes. She was left-handed and held the pen a little awkwardly.

'So what did you do after passing on the case?'

Carrie looked at her. 'I moved on to the next patient. Admissions are pretty constant, all day, every day. You deal with one and then go to the next, revisiting cases as necessary. No time for a cup of tea and a biscuit in between patients, sadly.'

Partridge nodded, ignoring her sarcasm. 'And did you revisit Mr Titchford?'

'Roisin let me know the X-ray had confirmed his hip was broken, so no surprise there.'

'Approximately what time period had elapsed at this point?' Tremaine asked.

Carrie shrugged. 'I'd say about an hour and a half. The report details the timings.' She scoured the sheet in front of her, making a tremendous effort to keep the irritation off her face. She'd like to see this pair of jokers on an A&E ward, where the hours flew by like minutes, the patients arriving in a relentless stream. No time to sit around and ask people lazy questions, like these two were doing, when the information was readily available elsewhere.

'He came back down onto the ward after his X-ray?'

'Yes, so that Dr Mosley could complete his case notes and determine where Mr Titchford was to go next.'

'And were you involved with this process at all? Did you have any interaction with the patient again?'

'Yes, I checked in with Roisin. We carried out Mr Titchford's observations together and I had a quick look at the X-ray report to see the findings for myself. Then I asked Roisin to page Dr Mosley to get him back to the ward to see the patient.'

Partridge pursed his lips. 'And how did Mr Titchford seem at this point?'

'Well, he was in a lot of pain, as you might expect. Nurse Kenny had administered ibuprofen to help with the inflammation, but nothing stronger could be given until the doctor had sight of a list of his current medication and the X-ray report.'

'It must be distressing to see an elderly man in pain like that,' Tremaine remarked.

Carrie looked at her. It was a stupid comment specifically designed to draw out some sort of self-damning comment from her. 'Nobody likes to see any patient in pain, but it invariably happens. We have to be certain of the details before pumping them full of morphine.'

Tremaine raised an eyebrow and Partridge shot her a look before asking, 'Carrie, were you alone with Mr Titchford at any point in this process?'

'Do you know how busy the emergency wards are, and how short-staffed we are? Sometimes I have no choice but to deal with patients on an individual basis.'

'I understand,' Partridge said in a patronising voice. 'So is that a yes? You were alone with Mr Titchford?'

'Possibly. Probably … I can't say for certain. If I was, it would have been perfectly normal practice.'

'So you waited for the doctor to come back to complete his assessment,' Tremaine repeated. 'What happened next?'

'Not long after that, the emergency siren sounded in the nurses' room and we rushed to the patient.'

'And what did you find when you got there?'

'Mr Titchford was fighting for his life. He'd gone into cardiac arrest. We called for the resus team, but sadly they weren't able to save the patient. It must have been the shock of the fall. He was eighty-two years old after all.'

'Maybe so, but you wouldn't necessarily expect him to appear stable and then suddenly suffer a heart attack, would you?' Partridge said smoothly.

'In twenty-odd years of nursing I've seen all sorts, and nothing surprises me any more.' Carrie sniffed. 'Apart from the lengths the authorities are prepared to go to in order to find a scapegoat, that is.'

9

Alexa

When Carrie gets home from the hospital in the early afternoon, I can only describe her mood as odd.

By the time she's parked her small red Corsa on the driveway behind my car, I have coffee waiting. I plan to start by asking what is happening at work, and perhaps, if it feels right, seamlessly work around to when she envisages getting her own place.

She comes through the front door and walks straight into the kitchen. She looks, I don't know, sort of flustered.

'Are you OK?' I ask, adding milk to our coffee. 'You've been gone a while again.'

'I'm fine, I sat in the canteen a bit before coming home,' she says, walking over to Florence in her walker. 'Come here, little one, Auntie Carrie needs a big cuddle.' She plucks her out of the walker and holds her close. After tolerating this for a couple of seconds, Florence objects, squealing and squirming in her arms.

Carrie grins and set her back down again, pushing her legs gently into the walker.

I hand her a mug and she takes it gratefully. 'This smells good; just what I need.'

'So,' I say after a few moments, when she doesn't volunteer any information, 'what's the deal with work calling you in two days in a row?'

'Oh, it's just a bit of a reorganisation,' she says smoothly. 'New rota system, new this, new that. I feel worn out with it all.'

'You look it.'

'Oh, cheers,' she laughs.

'Seriously, you do look tired, Carrie. I don't see why they have to change this stuff on your day off. Can't it wait until you're next in?'

'Tell me about it. It's just our shift that's affected, though, so we drew the short straw and had to go in.'

I offer her the biscuit tin but she passes.

'Anyway, how are you?' she says. 'Is everything OK with you and Perry? You seemed a bit fraught last night.'

'We're fine,' I say too quickly. I knew she'd noticed the tense atmosphere when she got home from the hospital last night. 'Mostly fine, anyway. You know how it is; he gets grumpy when Aberdeen is looming again.'

She watches me and nods slowly. 'He's going back to the rig tomorrow, isn't he?'

I nod, feeling suddenly miserable. Despite Perry's grumbles, I now wish he wasn't going. I hate it when there's an unresolved issue between us and then he has to disappear for another two or three weeks.

'Listen, why don't you two go out tonight? I'll look after Florence; it'll do you both good.'

I wonder why I didn't think of that. It seems like a great idea to get things back on a good footing with Perry before he leaves for Aberdeen, although he's probably still got lots to do before his trip.

'I don't mean a boozy late night,' she continues. 'Just go out for tea or something. A couple of hours to yourselves will do you good. The offer's there, anyway. It's up to you.'

'I appreciate it – thanks, Carrie,' I say. 'I'll have a word with Perry, but it would be nice, I think.'

She swallows down the last of her coffee. 'Well, just let me know.'

Before I can ask her anything else about work or even broach the subject of her moving out, she disappears upstairs.

When Perry gets back from the gym, I wait until he's put his training gear away and has come into the living room before telling him the good news.

'Carrie's offered to babysit for us. Just a couple of hours, so it's not a late night for your early start in the morning.'

A slight frown crosses his face. 'I've still got stuff to do.'

'Like what?'

'There's still quite a bit of packing.' He registers my deflated expression. 'But yeah, OK, that sounds great. Be nice to have a bit of time together before I go, and I'll be able to finish packing when we get back.'

We decide on tea at Rosso's Brasserie on Nottingham Road, which is just a ten-minute drive from our house.

'I'll take the car,' Perry says. 'The last thing I want is a thick head accompanying me back to Aberdeen in the morning.'

We kiss Florence goodbye, but she barely notices, so rapt is she in Carrie's pat-a-cake game.

A couple of hours whizzes by very pleasantly while we enjoy a bottle of wine – of which Perry will only drink a glass – and a couple of steaks and house salads.

'We should do this more often,' I murmur, my whole body warm from the smooth Rioja. I reach across the table and lightly trace my finger over his hand. 'Now that Florence is a little older, we could do a regular date night when you're home. I'm sure Carrie wouldn't mind watching her for us.'

Perry frowns. 'I love the idea, but Carrie's probably not going to be around when I'm next home in three weeks' time, is she? At least I hope not.'

'She can still come over and babysit now and again,' I say, placing my hand back down on the table. 'She'll always be a big part of my life, Perry. She's my sister and Florence's aunt.'

'I know that, but it will be a more *normal* relationship between the two of you. Where you'll arrange to meet up with her, I mean, instead of her living upstairs in our house.'

I grit my teeth. It's natural that I feel defensive about Carrie. She's always been there for me. She used to look out for me at school, checking on me in the playground to make sure nobody was leaving me out or upsetting me. I was only fifteen when Mum died of a heart attack. Carrie, twenty by then, still lived at home and she barely moved from my side, taking Mum's place as my guardian. Even more importantly, she helped me get through the worst time in my life. I thank my lucky stars I had both my husband and my sister for support back then, but when Perry had to go back to work, Carrie was left to cope alone with my instability. He seems to have conveniently forgotten about that.

'Anyway, I wanted to ask if you're all ready for work. Your big promotion, I mean!'

He pulls a face but I can see he's pleased. 'I don't know about a big promotion; big headache more like. Let's hope I'm up to it, eh?'

'You'll be brilliant, I know it. And you deserve it, Perry. You work hard and finally you've got just reward for your experience and skills.'

He laughs. 'I think you're a bit biased, but I'll take it. Thanks.'

'Just speaking the truth.'

'What are you and Florence planning on getting up to while I'm away? Anything exciting?'

'There are a few birthday parties, people at playgroup who've invited us. I was going to ask Carrie if she fancied coming with us to Ducklings, the new swimming club at the leisure centre pool.'

Perry reaches for the water jug. 'You know, it would be nice for Florence if it was just you and her sometimes.'

'Florence loves Carrie, you know she does!'

'Of course I know that.' He pours the water too quickly and it splashes onto the table. 'I just think you rely on her a bit too much. You and Florence only seem to go out when she's not working.'

I feel both furious and embarrassed that he's noticed more than I've assumed. But I don't say anything as I don't want to argue the night before he goes away.

'Maybe I'll take her on my own,' I say easily. 'There are other activity clubs I'm looking at too, so we'll keep ourselves busy, though we'll be counting the days until Daddy gets home.'

Perry launches into a diatribe about the politics of the rig and which teams like working together and why, and I sip my wine and zone his voice out a bit, smiling and nodding enough to keep him unaware.

I'd never admit it, but the mere thought of attending Florence's various clubs and events without Carrie unnerves me. I feel so flaky and inadequate as a mother so much of the time these days.

The waiter brings our desserts and we relax again into light conversation about possible holiday destinations next year, and whether Perry should cancel his gym membership now his stretches away from home are likely to be longer.

Afterwards, he drives us home. When he pulls up on the drive and I reach for the door handle, he touches my arm to stop me and covers my hand with his own.

'Look, I just wanted to say before we go back in that I don't want to pressure you, Alexa. I know you want it to be just the three of us again as much as I do.' He sighs and squeezes my fingers. 'Just talk to her, OK? I'll be gone three weeks this time, so you can pick your moment. Carrie's great, but she has to rebuild her life after Cameron dumped her in the dark and smelly. It's not good for her or for us as a family unit. We all need our space again. You and I need to reconnect, and we can't do that with a third person continually present.'

I shift uncomfortably and reach for the door handle again. I know he's right; it just makes my stomach roil to think of hurting Carrie's feelings. The last thing I want is for her to feel lonely or pushed out. And frankly, I can't imagine life without her now.

10

The next morning, Perry's colleague Dermott picks him up as arranged at 6 a.m. ready for their long drive up to Scotland.

We hug and kiss before he leaves and I feel glad I held back my feelings last night so that we're parting on amicable terms. I go out to the car to say hi to Dermott. He's a short man, thickset body with no neck. Sitting there in the car, he looks squat and sort of wedged in, a little odd really. But Perry says he's a good friend on the rig and a good driving partner. As soon as the two of them met and realised they lived within ten miles of each other, they arranged to car-share to Aberdeen and back again. They've been doing it for three years now, and it works well. 'It'll save us travel costs and means we can also share the driving so it's a bit less tiring,' Perry explained at the time. Unsurprisingly, after spending all that time together at work and in the car, they hardly see each other during their time off between jobs.

'How's Zara?' I ask after Dermott's wife, who I usually get to see once a year when we all go out for a drink at Christmas.

'Ah, she's grand, thanks for asking, Alexa.' Dermott nods, tapping the steering wheel and obviously itching to get on the road.

I wave them off and make myself a cup of tea. While I wait for the kettle to boil, I feel my shoulders drop a little, the tendons in my neck softening. I love Perry and I do want to work on our stale relationship, but him being at home with Carrie around makes me feel increasingly tense. I'm always worrying he'll overstep the mark and say something about it being time for her to get her own place. Thankfully, he always seems to stop short of confronting her himself. It's always possible she'll overhear one of his thoughtless remarks to me, though.

I take my tea upstairs and get back into bed, praying that Florence stays asleep a little while longer so I can snatch a bit more rest. Alas, she wakes up grizzling a few minutes later, so I bring her into bed with me.

Instantly calmed, she lies on her back next to me, gently tapping her fingertips together in front of her face and singing her wonderfully soft baby nonsense. I stare at her perfect shell-pink fingernails, her flawless peachy skin and the wild blonde curls that consistently refuse to be tamed by the comb and that have old ladies stopping in their tracks to admire her whenever we're out shopping. I can't believe how lucky I am to have her. Every day I thank my lucky stars and renew my silent pledge to always keep her safe, whatever it takes.

'I'll always look after you … I promise,' I whisper.

We both doze off again. We must have only been asleep for about an hour when the doorbell rings. I glance over at Florence and she stirs.

My first thought is to check my phone, but there are no messages or missed calls from Perry to warn me he's forgotten something and is coming back for it. I pull on my dressing gown and, scooping a still sleepy Florence up in my arms, walk out of the bedroom. Carrie's door is still closed, with no sign she's heard the bell.

When I get to the front door, I don't even look through the spyhole, so sure am I that it's Perry. Then the bell's shrill call sounds again, making me jump. It's only at the very last second, as I'm opening up, that I realise Perry would've used his key.

A man and a woman are standing there, both wearing suits. The man is quite groomed, and I get the impression he fancies himself a bit in a cocky way; the woman is small and neat with short red hair and lots of freckles. The man smiles at Florence and holds up his ID.

'Good morning, madam. I'm DI Adam Partridge and this is DS Nell Tremaine, from Nottinghamshire Police. We're looking for Carrie Parsons.'

My hand flies to my mouth. 'Is everything all right?' Bizarrely, the first thought I have is that Carrie left the house without me hearing and something has happened to her. Then I come to my senses. 'Carrie's my sister. She's upstairs, in bed.'

'We'll come in and wait while you tell her we're here, if that's all right, Mrs …?'

'Ford. Alexa Ford.' I step back into the hallway, signalling for them to come in, then close the front door and lead them through to the living room.

'This is your house and you're Carrie Parsons' sister?' Partridge confirms.

'That's right … but what's happened?' Florence's fingers tangle around my hair and she tugs gently.

'I'm sorry, we're not able to divulge that information at the moment. But it's very important that we speak to Carrie.'

Heart pounding, I take Florence upstairs. I tap on Carrie's door and tiptoe into the dim room. The curtains are still closed, but daylight is flooding in around the edges of the fabric now. Florence immediately strains towards her auntie for a cuddle.

'Alexa? What's wrong?' Carrie sits bolt upright, looking startled.

'There are two detectives downstairs!' I hiss, feeling like I might throw up. 'They want to speak to you but they won't tell me why.'

Florence lets out a squawk of impatience and reaches towards Carrie again. I jiggle her in my arms to placate her.

I don't know what I expect from Carrie – shock, denial, nervousness at what they want, perhaps? She displays none of that. Quite calmly, and ignoring Florence's continuing efforts to win her attention, she swings her legs out of bed and reaches for her jogging bottoms and T-shirt.

'Stay up here with Florence,' she says as she shrugs her clothes on. 'I know what this is about. There's been a mix-up at work, that's all. I'll sort it out and get rid of them.'

'A mix-up at work? What's it all about, Carrie? Why do the police want to speak to you?' I follow her to the door, talking to her back until she turns to face me.

'There's no time to explain now. But whatever happens, I give you my word I'll sort it out. However bad it seems.'

However bad it seems?

I grab her arm, my chest tightening. 'Carrie! What do you mean? Sort what out?' She hasn't mentioned anything about a disagreement with a colleague at work or any other problems at the hospital. Maybe a patient has assaulted a member of staff – it does happen from time to time – but in that case why not just say so?

'Believe in me, Alexa,' she says softly, her face pale and doughy in the dim light. 'That's all I ask.'

'You know I'll always stand by you,' I say frantically as she slips on her training shoes and descends the staircase. 'Whatever's happened, Carrie, I'm here for you.'

In that moment, I mean every single word I say. I don't care what's happened at the hospital. She's my sister. And that means everything.

I set Florence down on the floor next to me where she immediately pulls herself up to standing against the bannister rods.

'What's all this about?' I crane over the rail and see Carrie standing in the hallway, facing the two of them.

The female detective steps forward.

'Carrie Parsons, I am arresting you on suspicion of causing the unnatural deaths of Samina Khalil and Angus Titchford …'

I grab on to the handrail to keep myself upright, their voices beginning to fade out before I force myself to listen again.

'…but it may harm your defence if you do not mention when questioned something you later rely on in court. Anything you do say may be given in evidence.'

'I'll call you soon as I can, Alexa,' my sister calls over her shoulder. Her voice sounds high-pitched and strained.

'Carrie!' I cry out but as they lead her out of the front door, she grabs her warm jacket from the coat stand and doesn't look back again.

11

Barely an hour has passed since Carrie was arrested and left with the police, but I'm beside myself worrying about what might be happening to her.

It all kicked off so quickly. The strange look on her face and, when I woke her up, the odd things she was saying before going downstairs unnerved me.

I sit on the living room floor with Florence now and get out her Noah's ark. I spread out the animals in front of her and start her favourite game.

'What does a lion say?' I hold up the bulky orange plastic lion, satisfyingly large and completely safe for Florence to play with. I've screened every single one of her toys to ensure none is small enough for her to choke on. 'What does he say, the lion?'

Florence squeals and snatches up an elephant.

'A lion says *grrr*!' I growl and make to tickle her belly, and she rocks back and forth on her bottom gleefully, her curls bouncing.

We carry on like this for a while and I feel grateful Florence is absorbed in the game, as I haven't got the energy to play chase from dawn until dusk like usual. She started crawling a couple of months ago, first tentatively plodding along in between toppling over and sitting still. Then overnight she seemed to stabilise and speed up, pulling herself up on the furniture to standing, and now … even though she's not yet properly walking, she can move like lightning and reach a hundred places she couldn't manage before. I literally can't take my eyes off her for a moment. It's exhausting, but thankfully she's stationary for now at least.

I pick up the elephant and Florence claps in anticipation of my next noise. I just wish I could share the burden of worry with someone, get another adult's perspective on the situation. I can't call Perry; he's still in the car on his way to Aberdeen with Dermott on his seven-hour journey. He won't be able to speak freely or confidentially for a good few hours yet. Besides, what can he do to help, really? This is his big chance to show his worth since his promotion, and he can hardly turn back home now and delay both of them.

There are a couple of other mums Carrie and I sit with and chat to at the local mother-and-toddler group that I could maybe contact. But I don't know them *really* well as we don't go every week, only when Carrie's shift pattern allows it. Anyway, at this early stage, I might well regret speaking to someone else about it. It could – theoretically – be something and nothing. But who are the people they named when they arrested her? I rub my temples, trying to ease the knots of pressure I can feel building there. My heart aches for Mum, the one person who was always there for us through thick and thin. The person who could somehow sort out anything with her reassuring manner and a cup of tea. I miss her so much.

I can't admit this to anyone, but in my heart, I feel like Carrie's arrest might not be a mistake. Now that I'm analysing things with new eyes, I remember that Carrie has been a bit off for the last couple of days in a way I couldn't quite put my finger on. I noticed it but never suspected it might be something serious. We're all allowed to have off days and it's so irritating when someone badgers you about it when you just want to be left alone. So I didn't try and get her to talk.

Now, when I take the time to break it down, I realise she has been antsy ever since we were at the park and she got the call to go into work. She also hasn't spent much time downstairs with us like she normally does.

I have an idea. I reach for my phone and open up the *Notts Sentinel* news website. I don't have to look far. There at the top of the page, emblazoned in bold lettering, is the headline: *Unexplained Deaths at Local Hospital*. Feeling instantly queasy, I read on.

King's Mill Hospital, part of the Sherwood Forest Health Trust, has launched an internal inquiry in connection with two unexplained deaths in its accident and emergency department.

Over a period of four months, two patients have died after being admitted to the hospital's A&E ward with unrelated fairly minor conditions that a hospital source tells us 'should not have resulted in death'.

Our source, currently working at the hospital, told the *Sentinel*, 'A member of the senior staff turned whistle-blower to initially raise the alarm. Now a formal internal inquiry is under way.'

The *Sentinel* contacted the hospital press office, but they have declined to comment at this stage.

For more news as we get it, sign up for our story alerts on the *Notts Sentinel* website.

My hands start to shake as I place the phone back down on the worktop.

They think Carrie killed those poor patients. This internal inquiry is obviously the 'mix-up at work' she mentioned in passing.

Carrie is friendly with a few of her colleagues, two in particular: Marcia Hunt, the assistant ward manager, and Roisin Kenny, a senior nurse. They've worked together for years and used to enjoy occasional nights out, although they haven't done that for a while.

As the A&E ward manager, I know Carrie couldn't fail to know about these two unexplained deaths and yet she's never mentioned them. The more I think about her mood and behaviour over the past couple of days, the more I realise she was perhaps trying to work out how to tell me that something was wrong.

On the afternoon of the hospital meeting she was suddenly summoned to attend, she came home and went directly to her room. That's unusual for Carrie. She likes to sit and eat and talk. It's just the way she is. I often have to encourage her to go up to bed instead of falling asleep in front of the television. The next morning, she was up early getting ready to go to the hospital again, even though it wasn't a work day. I heard the shower and her padding around up there, but she didn't come into the kitchen for coffee or a slice of toast as per her usual routine. She just called out that she wouldn't be gone long before she left the house and I heard the front door close.

When she got back home, she waved away my questions and made some vague remark about a rota reorganisation. I thought at the time that it seemed a weak excuse to call her into work for that on her day off but now that I've seen the news article … well, now I know for certain that wasn't the truth.

And now it's not just an internal inquiry. The police are obviously involved too and they seem certain enough about what's happened to arrest Carrie.

I have this creeping dread that things are going to get rapidly worse at the police station and I feel sick when I think that Perry is completely unaware of what's happening back here at home. There's nothing I can do about it. I can only wait until Carrie gets back.

Surely to God, this has all got to be a mistake or a terrible coincidence that has nothing to do with her. Still, I can't get over the fact she hasn't said a word about the deaths. My sister, who usually tells me everything.

It's easy to jump to conclusions in a serious case like this. Panicky staff members pointing the finger of blame at one another … targeting Carrie, being the person in charge of the ward. A flicker of warmth surges in my chest as I start to feel a real conviction that they'll bring her home soon, full of grovelling apologies. She's so competent, so conscientious at doing her job. She's been practising a long time.

I remember when I was nine years old, I woke up in the middle of the night with terrible stomach pains. I lay there for a while, afraid to call out, afraid to get up. Making a fuss would only make pain worse, Mum had always taught us if ever we'd hurt ourselves. I decided I'd rather wait until the pain went away. But eventually I could stand it no more and cried out.

A moment later, my sister was there, as always, by my side.

'It's my tummy,' I whined. 'It *really* hurts.'

Carrie fetched Mum and then asked me to point out exactly where the pain was. I touched my lower right-hand abdomen. 'It was in the middle first, and now it's moved to this bit of my tummy.'

'That's not your tummy,' Carrie said immediately. 'Look at her face, Mum, she has a high temperature. I think it might be appendicitis.'

Appendicitis sounded a very big and worrying word to me. I started to cry and Mum held me while Carrie rang for the ambulance. Twenty minutes later, I was rushed into hospital after the paramedics had agreed with Carrie's diagnosis.

'You've got yourself a proper little Florence Nightingale here, Mrs Parsons,' the tall paramedic told Mum. 'We'll be seeing her working with us in a couple of years.'

'I want to be a proper doctor, not a paramedic.' Carrie scowled, but underneath, I knew she was proud of herself for helping out.

All she's ever wanted to do is to help people.

I decide that the best thing to do – the *only* thing I can really do – is to carry on as normally as possible. It's too early in the day for me to be able to talk to anyone at the hospital, and there's nobody else around to discuss it with.

I'll get Florence ready and we'll go for a little walk, get some fresh air. My stomach twists at the thought of going without Carrie or Perry. Perhaps I'll spread some sheets of newspaper on the kitchen floor and get out the finger paints instead. We haven't done that for ages. The last thing I want is for Florence to pick up on my tension, although that might be difficult to avoid until I know for sure that Carrie has nothing to do with this horrible scenario.

I need to be strong. Whatever happens, I will be there for Carrie.

12

Carrie's been gone a couple of hours now and I'm beside myself.

I look down at the newspaper spread at my feet, spattered with finger paints, and I feel so utterly useless and on edge, my nerves jangling like crazy. I know Florence has picked up on it because she's whining and needy and nothing I seem to do, whether it's playing with her or making her a healthy snack, is appeasing her.

But what *do* I do? Without Perry or Carrie around, I'm stuck here. Unless I take Florence out alone … I feel more anxious than usual about this prospect. And yet when Carrie does get back, I've nothing in to cook for her. She's bound to be exhausted and in need of a decent meal. We're also out of milk and bread and I need more fresh ingredients to make the next batch of food to freeze for Florence's healthy meals.

There's a local grocery store about a ten-minute walk away. It's cloudy and cold but dry outside and I feel like we'll benefit from a brisk stroll in the fresh air rather than bundling Florence in the car and driving to the big superstore in town. A local shop will be quieter, and I could be there and back within the hour.

I'm doing it again … overthinking the situation. I pick a newly dressed Florence up and bounce her in my arms.

'Shall we go and get some goodies to have when Auntie Carrie gets home?' I ask her. Usually she beams at the mention of Carrie's name, but now she screws her face up and rubs her eyes. Of course, it's nearly time for her nap. It totally slipped my mind, what with everything that's happening. I ought to take her upstairs now, but I can't bear to be stuck in here a moment longer, held hostage by the stuff playing out about Carrie in my head.

I decide we'll walk to the shop and then Florence will fall asleep in her pushchair. As soon as I make the decision to leave the house with her on my own, I feel the beginnings of a dull thud in my head. Awful possibilities start to present themselves, visual snatches of the things that could happen: a car mounting the pavement, a terrible and sudden storm with lightning that might strike us. The worst pictures involve other people. A youth out of his skull on drugs, a group of rowdy teenagers surrounding Florence's pushchair and keeping me away from her. A crazed woman who hits me on the head with something heavy and wrenches Florence from my arms.

I turn on the radio and increase the volume to take up space in my mind.

It's OK. Everything is fine. You and Florence are perfectly safe.

I hear Carrie's soothing voice in my head. She says it every time we go out somewhere new, and so far she's been right. That's got to count for something.

Florence is far from happy at the prospect of being strapped in, but I wrap her up nice and warm and tuck her into her pushchair with a blanket, gloves and hat. She squirms and puts up a bit of a fight as I pull on my own jacket and grab my handbag, making sure I have my phone, and by the time we get to the front gate, she's stopped grumbling.

'This is nice, isn't it, pumpkin? Just the two of us,' I say brightly as we walk along, my heart hammering in my chest. 'We're going on a little walk to get something tasty for our tea.'

There's no response from Florence, who I suspect may already be dozing, but I carry on regardless.

'Maybe we'll get a chocolate cake, what do you say, Florence? A nice sticky slice of chocolate cake to celebrate Auntie Carrie being back home and all this nastiness behind us.' I keep rattling on, talking nonsense, and it calms me down a bit, keeps the negative images from taking hold.

'When me and Auntie Carrie were little, we made a chocolate cake once. Did I tell you about that? We made a cake for your granny's birthday and it looked beautiful, but when we tasted it we were nearly sick. Auntie Carrie had used salt instead of sugar. Can you believe it?' I laugh and stop pushing, then bend forward and gently ease her hat back. As I suspected, she's fast asleep.

I check my phone to see if there are any messages. I have one notification and my heart leaps but then I see it's from Perry.

Just stopped at services for a McDonald's brekkie. Journey going well. Hope you and Flo good. Rig ETA currently 2 pm. Text later.

Nothing at all from Carrie.

They arrested Carrie and took her to the police station two and a half hours ago. They're treating her like a full-blown criminal even though they didn't even ask her any questions before hauling her away.

What am I going to tell Perry? What will he say when he finds out about the patient deaths … and that they've arrested Carrie for it? Surely he'll be as aghast as I am.

I find I can't move. I just stand there, in the middle of the street. People driving by turn to look at me inquisitively as I pull the pushchair close and press my back into the brick wall behind me. I'm halfway between home and the shop, but I can't move one way or the other. I feel suddenly immobilised with shock.

I'm arresting you on suspicion of causing the unnatural deaths of … The detective had said two names that I can't remember now. She'd reeled the words off as easily as if she was telling Carrie what day it was. My sister, arrested for the deaths of patients in her care … it's unthinkable! Mum will be turning in her grave.

I can feel my breathing becoming more and more shallow. Thank goodness Florence is asleep; I'd hate her to see me like this. She might not be talking yet, but she's so sensitive to what's happening around her. She picks up on my mood really quickly and can get distressed if she senses I'm upset.

'Are you OK, lovey?' A middle-aged woman in a brown coat and carrying a bulging canvas shopping bag stops next to me. She tips her head to one side and looks at me with concern.

'Yes, I'm fine. Thanks.'

I shrink back further against the unforgiving wall. Although she clearly means well, I find myself hoping she just goes away.

'You look very pale.' She takes a couple of steps forward and peers at Florence in the pushchair.

'She's fine, she's sleeping,' I manage, trying to regulate my ragged breathing but not wanting her anywhere near my baby. 'I'm OK. I just had some bad news, that's all.'

'Oh dear, I'm sorry to hear that.' She glances at Florence again and then back at me. 'Sure you're all right? There's nobody I can contact for you?'

I shake my head. 'Thanks. I'm just taking a couple of moments before I go home.'

I wait for her to walk away, then let my breath out with relief. I can't risk anyone else stopping to question me, so I grasp the handles of the pushchair, swing it around and walk off in the other direction, back towards the safety of home.

13

The police station

DI Adam Partridge took a seat next to DS Tremaine in the small, airless interview room. Opposite him, Carrie Parsons and the duty solicitor, Mark Bolton, were whispering together.

Adam had worked with Bolton on numerous occasions. He was a weedy little man with bad skin. Shrewd enough in an interview situation, but with an unfortunate manner about him. He had trouble getting his words out or selecting the correct words, resulting in him stopping and starting each time he began to speak. Adam had seen plenty of suspects get annoyed with him before, and he wondered if the no-nonsense Carrie Parsons would be the same.

While they all shuffled in their seats and Tremaine collated her notes, Adam turned his attention to Carrie. To all intents and purposes she appeared calm and unruffled. Her body language was open – none of the usual folded arms or clamped jaw with this one – but the eyes, as always, were the giveaway. For all she'd clearly worked on her relaxed demeanour, her gaze was slightly wild, skirting around the walls and purposely avoiding Partridge's incisive stare. He knew people often judged him by his dapper suits and fashionable haircut, but there wasn't much that evaded him, although he'd never be so arrogant as to let down his guard.

His late father, a DCI with a lengthy career as a detective himself for forty-two years, had always told him to view his interactions with suspects as a metaphorical boxing match. 'Never underestimate your opponent' had been his favourite piece of advice for the interview room. He'd been an older dad when his second wife had given birth to Adam, and a consequence of that was that Adam had witnessed, at a young age, the final stages of the dementia that had taken hold of him. Towards the end, his dad had repeated the 'boxing match' theory several times a day. It was true that the concept of the suspect being an opponent and someone he had to beat was outdated now, but the old adage still contained some valuable truth. Adam always looked deeper than the shallow indications first on show, and it had stood him in good stead. He had reached the heady heights of detective inspector rank in record time.

The more he got involved in the King's Mill Hospital case, the more he realised that if the deaths were proved to be unnatural, it would be a massive story garnering a lot of attention. It could well be the case that made his career. All detectives looked out for a case like that, and they were liars if they denied it. The last thing Adam would want was for innocent people to die in order for him to get a promotion, but neither was he foolish enough not to recognise the opportunity when it presented itself.

While Tremaine fiddled with the recording equipment and the duty solicitor continued to speak in indiscernible tones, Adam tried to imagine how Carrie Parsons might be feeling right at this moment.

This morning she'd woken in her own bed at home, wondering what the next twenty-four hours might bring after the previous day's interviews at the hospital. She'd known there would probably be more questions about the unexplained deaths, but this? Detectives coming to her home to arrest and haul her off to the police station?

Staring straight ahead as if her head were spinning, she'd clearly been numb with shock as the custody officer booked her in and explained her rights. That had been before she'd managed to construct the calmer facade on display here in the interview room. Adam had a hunch that she was scared and shocked but also angry. It wasn't a bad thing if that was the case. Annoyed suspects often made mistakes, said more than they meant to.

He'd watched with interest as she looked scathingly around the small windowless room where they'd left her to wait for the duty solicitor. It wasn't a cell exactly, but it wasn't pleasant. It might have been his imagination, but despite her benign expression, he felt sure he could detect hostile vibes rolling off her. There was more to Miss Carrie Parsons than first met the eye, of that he felt convinced. Of course, he knew that justice for the two victims and their families would only be reached by establishing concrete facts and solid evidence. Hunches made compelling viewing on a TV cop show, but they didn't cut it when it came to bringing real criminals to justice.

A female officer came in and offered Carrie an unappealing plastic beaker of water.

She'd been stuck at the station for nearly three hours now, most of it in the same poky interview room. Apart from when she'd had her fingerprints digitally scanned and her photograph taken, and had provided a sample of her DNA, that was. She was getting tired and frustrated. Adam could understand that and it suited his purposes perfectly.

She thought they had nothing solid but she didn't know about the circumstantial evidence. She didn't know some of the things her own colleagues had intimated about her. They'd be giving her a harder time here than she could imagine.

Nell nodded to him to signal they were ready to start.

'The interview today will be audio- and video-recorded,' she said, cataloguing the names of those present for the record. 'You do not have to say anything but it may harm your defence …' Adam watched Carrie carefully as Nell cautioned her before questioning. '… Anything you do say may be given in evidence. Do you understand?'

'Yes.'

Adam spoke next. 'Carrie, you've answered some of our questions at the hospital and you have confirmed you were working on the accident and emergency ward when the deaths of Samina Khalil and Angus Titchford occurred. Agreed?'

Carrie Parsons nodded.

'Speak up for the tape, please,' Tremaine interjected.

'Yes,' Parsons said curtly.

'We want to take you through events for each of the victims,' Partridge said, consulting his notes. 'On the twenty-seventh of December, a six-month-old baby girl, Samina Khalil, was admitted with a suspected serious viral infection. Can you tell us what you remember about that day and the patient?'

Parsons thought for a moment, then began to speak in a clear, unemotional voice.

'The child's mother brought her in, as I remember. The baby was in some distress, so we arranged for them to skip triage and come straight through to the ward. It became apparent quite quickly that the child had a nasty viral infection and was dehydrated. We hooked her up to a drip and the doctor ordered further tests to establish whether it was norovirus.'

'And at that stage treatment was, would you say, straightforward and uncomplicated?'

Parsons gave a single nod. 'We get a lot of babies in with the same symptoms. It only takes a short period of sickness and diarrhoea to dehydrate them.'

'Because they're so small?'

'Yes,' she replied.

Tremaine spoke up. 'I'd imagine it was quite distressing for you, seeing a tiny baby in that state.'

Parsons shrugged. 'It's part of the job. We don't enjoy seeing any patient suffering, regardless of age.'

'Some of your colleagues have suggested you can be quite cold and indifferent to patients on the ward, Carrie. What do you say to that?' Tremaine pressed her.

'She's already … she's answered your question in regards to her feelings already,' Bolton managed.

'Who said that?' Parsons snapped, ignoring her brief's raised hand, a signal to stay quiet.

Adam perked up. The suspect's eyes were sparking. She didn't like the thought of her colleagues speaking out of turn, saw it as a betrayal. He knew then that that would be their way in.

'Are you a popular member of the ward staff, would you say?' he asked casually.

She pursed her lips as if she didn't care one way or the other. 'I have plenty of support from colleagues at work, if that's what you mean.'

'That's not quite what I meant.' Adam gave a thin, disingenuous smile. 'You're the ward manager after all. I'd expect your own staff to appear supportive on the surface. But do you think they approve of your … shall we say rather *cold* manner at times towards your patients?'

'It's not a crime to carry out one's job in a professional manner,' the duty solicitor said.

'Of course it's not,' Partridge agreed. 'It's just that one or two of your colleagues' comments led us to believe that they think your … bedside manner could do with a bit of work. These are the people you see on every shift.'

'Who said that about me?' Parsons demanded again. 'I have a right to know.'

'Sadly we can't divulge that information,' Tremaine said smoothly.

'I do my job and I do it well. It doesn't do to get too friendly with the patients.'

'Why's that?' Adam asked, appearing puzzled.

'You don't have to answer,' Bolton interrupted, but to Adam's relief, Parsons ignored him.

She held the detective's gaze. 'Because it's not professional. And you never know what might happen to a patient, so it's best to keep your distance emotionally.'

'When you say "what might happen", what do you mean exactly?' Adam responded.

'I mean that they might die,' Parsons clarified coldly as her brief let out a heavy sigh and closed his notebook with a snap.

14

Alexa

When we get back from our disastrous walk, Florence is still asleep, so I loosen the straps, slip off her hat and gloves and unzip her coat. I leave her in her pushchair while I sit quietly in the kitchen and try to recover from the ordeal. I'm grateful for the space to just breathe and take the time to think through what might be happening to Carrie without passers-by in the street having the opportunity to scrutinise my expression.

Despite my sister's assurances that she'd be in touch as soon as she could from the police station, I've heard nothing at all from her. It sounds stupid, but I even called her phone while I was out, hoping beyond hope that she might be on a comfort break or something. But I suppose it was no surprise that her phone was turned off. It's probably lying in a sealed evidence bag somewhere at the police station.

I'm alternating between feeling hot and cold, exhausted and hyperactive. I wish I could settle, wish I knew she was OK. That would allow me to relax a little. I can't afford to break down. With Perry away for three weeks and Carrie stuck at the police station for goodness knows how long, my daughter has only me to take care of her.

One thing is certain: I just can't just sit here doing nothing. I can't speak to Carrie, Perry will be on the road for a good few hours yet, and the police aren't going to tell me what's happening and why they've arrested my sister. But there must be *something* I can do to help matters. It occurs to me that if I could speak to someone at the hospital, someone who *does* know what's happening, maybe they could shed some light on this whole troubling mystery.

After checking that Florence is still out for the count, I call King's Mill Hospital. I have to google the main number, as usually I just text or ring Carrie's mobile if I need to speak to her. I'm taken through an irritating automated call-sifting system and keep holding past all the options until finally a real person answers.

'Good morning, King's Mill Hospital, how may I help?'

'Hi, I'm a relative of a senior staff member and I'd like to speak to someone about the accident and emergency ward case that's being investigated at the moment, please.'

The receptionist is as helpful as a brick wall. 'Sorry, madam, we aren't giving out information about any ongoing cases at the moment,' is the most she will say. Her bored tone suggests she's already said the same thing on a number of occasions already this morning. I didn't really expect anything more, I suppose, but I had to at least try.

I haven't got the personal mobile numbers for Roisin or Marcia, the two colleagues Carrie mentions in conversation the most. Her phone containing all her contacts is with her at the police station, turned off. She has a laptop that's still in my car boot from when she took it in to PC World for a new CD disk drive last week, but I'd feel a bit weird looking through her emails and personal documents when she'll probably be home later.

I feel so helpless and decide that maybe I should try the hospital again, in the hope that I get a more helpful receptionist.

I've just pressed redial when the doorbell rings. I glance at Florence, who's beginning to stir, then run to the living room window, which gives a clear view of the front of the house.

I can see figures at the windows of a couple of houses opposite, straining to see our house, and my new next-door neighbour appears to have decided to trim the exact stretch of hedge she trimmed just last week, a task that affords her an excellent vantage point. There's also a woman in her twenties hovering at the gate, thin and pale with long, stringy brown hair that looks like it needs a good wash. When she sees me at the window, she half raises her hand, as if I might call her over for a better look. My house is suddenly the centre for local entertainment, it seems.

There are two police cars parked outside, and I can see at least three uniformed police officers at my front door. Blood rushes to my head and I'm momentarily dizzy.

I give myself a couple of moments and open the side window, just in time to see the neighbour crane her neck. I speak in a low voice out of the window. 'We've just got back from a walk so I'll need to get my daughter out of her pushchair. I'll open the door in a moment.'

One of the officers nods and they begin talking amongst themselves. It occurs to me that there might have been a mix-up in communications. Maybe they don't realise Carrie is already at the police station and they've come here to the house to arrest her. How many officers does it take to do *that* though?

Florence gives me a gummy smile when I appear in the kitchen doorway. She's got three teeth – two at the top and one at the bottom – and judging by the restless nights she's had for the past week, more are on their way.

I unbuckle her and slip her out of her warm outdoor jacket.

My heart is racing, but I feel odd, sort of detached from the craziness of what's happening here. So much has gone wrong in the past couple of days, nothing really surprises me any more.

There are police officers outside and no doubt the neighbours are putting two and two together and making six. The lump in my throat seems to swell further when I think of Perry's reaction when he finds out what's going on. It occurs to me he might well be annoyed I didn't get in touch sooner.

Holding a grumbling, hungry Florence, I open the front door to the officers.

'Mrs Alexa Ford? We're here to carry out a Section 18 search at this address in connection with the arrest of a Miss Carrie Parsons.'

I step back in horror at this most unwelcome development. Then I take a breath and push my fear down.

'This is not Carrie's house. I'm the owner,' I say firmly even though my knees are trembling.

The lead officer hands me a paper. 'I believe this is her main residence and as such, we're exercising the Section 18 search.'

'But she hasn't been charged with anything,' I say faintly.

The officer is undaunted. 'She's been arrested pending further investigation, madam, and that has given us the right to search her home.'

Five minutes later, my house is full of police officers. They're everywhere, all at once. Upstairs, downstairs … one officer even asks me for the key to the garden shed. I show them Carrie's bedroom, and the lead officer looks up and down the small landing. If I don't sit down in a moment, I'm going to collapse.

'We'll need to check out the other rooms too,' he says regretfully.

Perry's furious face flashes into my mind and I feel like crying. 'But why? Carrie doesn't even come into our bedroom! What is it exactly you're looking for?' It feels like such a violation.

'Sorry, madam, I'm not at liberty to say.' He looks as if he doesn't mean a word of it and turns away.

Florence looks around at the officers and starts to bawl. Without doubt she knows something is very wrong. She's hungry and she needs changing. I can't stay up here arguing when I know it's a losing game, especially when my daughter is clearly picking up on my stress. They clearly have the right to do this and there's nothing I can do about it. I have to minimise the disruption for Florence and that means leaving them to it and removing myself from what's happening. The thought of them going through our things fills me with dread, shame and fury, but I resolve to push it away and pretend they aren't violating my home, my safe space.

Downstairs, I decide Florence's nappy can wait another ten minutes and strap her into her high chair. Sitting down, I try to breathe a little deeper. I cut a slice of apple, peel it carefully and give Florence one small piece so I can keep track on it while I prepare her lunch. You can't be too careful … small bits of food are a well-known a choking hazard.

Upstairs, heavy boots clomp around and my head starts to pound. I take one of the frozen pods of food from the freezer and pop it in the microwave. As I wait for it to heat up, I stare out of the window at the trees blowing. Watching a blackbird foraging for worms on the lawn and massaging my temples with two fingers, it strikes me how everything looks so normal and yet nothing is.

I turn around as a figure appears in the doorway.

'I'll make you a cuppa,' a young female officer says, making me start. It's not really an offer; she just walks in and heads for the kettle. She's quite short, with a round face and the sort of ruddy cheeks that never fade.

'I'm PC Dawn Butler,' she says cheerfully.

The microwave beeps and saves me having to speak to her. I don't want her in here. I'm trying to keep a space free from the police, a little area that's a refuge for Florence and a balm to the anxiety currently whirling like a typhoon in my chest.

I take out the food pod and, using a teaspoon, scoop out the lukewarm contents – sweet potato and courgette that I prepared a few days ago when this nightmare was non-existent – into Florence's orange plastic bowl.

PC Butler reaches for the kettle and shakes it. Deciding there's enough water in there already, she flicks the switch to set it boiling.

'Doesn't seem two minutes since my little boy was that age.' She watches Florence as I set the bowl before her and wedge the fat plastic spoon into her clutching hand. 'Need a cleaning company round after they've finished, but they soon get really good at feeding themselves. Brandon is two and a half now. What's her name?'

'Florence.' I keep my tone pleasant enough but not friendly. I don't feel like talking. She seems young to have a little boy. She looks to be in her early to mid twenties; she could be eight or nine years younger than me, and yet she's got a career, she's a mother and she obviously has bags of confidence.

'Florence? Lovely, that. The old-fashioned names are popular again now, aren't they? My friend called her son Arthur.'

I nod and give a weak smile, helping Florence to load her spoon with food.

Butler turns her back and opens a couple of cupboard doors until she finds the clean mugs, setting them down on the worktop as the kettle clicks. I feel like a stranger in my own kitchen.

'Do you go out to work?' she asks, her back still to me.

'Not any more,' I say. 'I stopped working when … a couple of years ago.'

'You're so lucky. Don't get me wrong, I love my job, but I worry I'm missing out, you know? I'm a single mum and Brandon's growing up so fast. He's started to dress himself now and he can catch a ball.' She reaches for the tea canister and turns around to me, holding it. 'I'm lucky, though, my mum looks after him, so I know he's in the best hands. Nice when they can stay with family.'

She's so personable it's hard not to warm to her.

'My mum died when I was fifteen, sadly. But my sister …' I swallow, realising that Carrie is the reason they're here. But why shouldn't they know how close she is to her niece? It can only help matters. 'Carrie, my sister, is like Florence's second mum. They adore each other. That's why all this' – I look up to the ceiling with disdain – 'is so upsetting. The three of us are very close.'

She nods before turning back round to finish making the tea. Steam rises up around her head.

'I suppose your sister living here is a bit like having a resident babysitter.' She puts my mug down on the table. 'Is your husband a hands-on dad?'

'He's great with Florence but he works on an oil rig in Aberdeen. He just left this morning for another three-week stint.'

'I guess your sister is a big help to you then.'

I nod. 'I don't know what I'd do without her.'

She hesitates before speaking again. 'It must have been quite a shock … finding out what happened at the hospital, I mean.'

I reach for my mug. 'You can say that again. We were at the park when Carrie got the call to say she had to go into work for a meeting. She hadn't a clue what it was about and now, two days later, they're accusing her of such terrible things.'

It's not quite true. I know now that Carrie must have been aware of the deaths, but still. She doesn't deserve to be hounded like this.

We drink our tea in silence and watch Florence's impressive efforts at feeding herself.

There's an almighty bang upstairs and Florence looks startled.

'What exactly are they doing up there?' I frown. 'Sounds like they're knocking the walls down.'

'They'll try their best not to make a mess,' Butler says easily.

'But what is it they're hoping to find?'

'I'm not party to the details. The guys upstairs will have been given a brief and it'll be connected to your sister's case.' She puts down her mug. 'How's your husband taking Carrie's arrest?'

'He doesn't know!' I blurt out before thinking better of it. 'I mean, I haven't had a chance to tell him yet. He won't arrive in Aberdeen until mid afternoon.'

'So while he's working away, it's just you and Florence here?'

'Yes. Me, Florence and Carrie.'

'I see,' she says quietly.

15

The officer is still talking to me, asking inane things about Carrie and our home life, but I can't seem to focus on what she's saying any longer.

Upstairs the police are moving systematically through the rooms. I can tell exactly where they are and what they're doing by the noises filtering downstairs. Someone just opened the disorganised cupboard at the top of the stairs where I shove anything that hasn't got a home, and I've just heard the telltale squeak of my bedroom door opening.

I flood with heat. It's not that we have anything to hide; it's just the fact of a complete stranger entering your home and delving into everything: cupboards, the wardrobe. I even hear the drawers under the bed being pulled out.

'What *are* they looking for?' I say, gritting my teeth. 'How can those hospital deaths possibly have anything to do with our house?'

Butler leans across and jiggles Florence's hand. My daughter looks at her suspiciously. I know how she feels. The woman might be a police officer, but I don't like her touching Florence without asking. I'm glad my daughter is wary of strangers and I want to keep it that way.

'I'm sure it'll all become apparent,' she says cryptically. 'It's unusual, I suppose, for Carrie to be living here. If I lived with my sister, I think we'd just wind each other up.'

'Not a problem for us,' I say, taking my mug over to the sink. 'Carrie and I have always been really close. It's only temporary anyway.'

She raises an eyebrow. 'Is she planning on moving out?'

'No, no. Not yet,' I say quickly. It's important they know Carrie has a stable home life and a family who care about her. That could be important if things … progress. 'She's got a home with us as long as she wants it.'

'She's lucky to have a sister like you.'

'She'd do the same for me,' I say. 'It's not her fault she's here; it's that rat of a husband who did the dirty on her.'

Butler shakes her head slowly, as if she sympathises with Carrie's plight. 'Bloody men, eh? My friend, Arthur's mum, her partner dumped her a month before he was born. Nearly killed her, it did.'

The old fury still burns inside me on behalf of my sister for what Cameron did to her. Before I know it, I'm raging out loud. 'Cameron liked the good life even though they couldn't really afford it. He left her in a load of debt and ran off with an old school friend of hers who had plenty of money. Carrie was devastated when she lost the house; that's when she moved in with us.'

Butler looks shocked. 'Sounds as if she's really been through it.'

I'm in my stride now. This could help them see that Carrie is just an ordinary woman who gives her all to her job at the hospital.

'She went from being outgoing and confident to having nothing in her life but work,' I say. 'I'm not sure she'll trust anyone again.'

'Understandable,' she murmurs. 'How long ago was this?'

'She's been living here about eight months but she only found out in December that the woman he left her for was her friend,' I say. 'As far as I'm concerned she can stay another eight months if she needs to.'

She brushes down her uniform with her hands. 'Does your husband feel the same?'

'I don't care what Perry thinks,' I say shortly. 'She's my sister and I'll stand by her, whatever happens, whatever you lot say. She's a good person.'

She nods slowly and heads for the door. When she reaches it, she hesitates and takes a business card out of her top pocket.

'This investigation might take a while,' she says quietly, placing the card on the side. 'If things start to get on top of you, give me a call. We might be able to arrange some counselling support.'

When she leaves the kitchen, I sit down at the table and cover my face with my hands.

16

The police station

The interview with Carrie Parsons was ticking along. They were clarifying certain points and progressing in a fashion, but after thirty minutes of chatting it was time to turn up the heat.

'Let's move on,' Adam said, glancing at his colleague. The phrase had been agreed between the detectives as the sign to ramp up the pressure. He watched as Nell Tremaine pressed a button on her laptop and turned it ninety degrees so the suspect could see the screen.

'Carrie, you've told us you went for a break mid morning on the twenty-seventh of December at approximately 11.10,' she said. 'That would be around an hour after Samina Khalil was first admitted onto the ward.'

'Yes,' Carrie said. 'Sounds about right.'

'This is CCTV footage we've obtained from hospital security.' A grainy image suddenly flashed into full-colour footage. A nurse appeared from a side door in the ward entrance and began walking towards the patient area. As she approached the camera, the image was clear enough to see that it was Carrie Parsons. 'You appeared to leave the ward at 11.12 a.m., presumably for your break, and yet …' Tremaine tapped the keyboard again, 'here you are re-entering the ward at 11.13.'

Adam watched the ward manager's face visibly pale. She squinted at the laptop screen as if she was trying to make sense of what she was looking at. He suspected he knew exactly why she was puzzled.

'You seem surprised to see this footage, Miss Parsons,' he said.

'No, I … I must've forgotten something.' She hesitated. 'It's just … I was under the impression the CCTV was still out of action on that date. They'd upgraded the system over the Christmas break and there had been unforeseen delays.'

'Yes, we were told the same, but apparently the new equipment was in fact functional and test recording had started that very morning,' Adam said brightly. 'Fortunately, the very helpful security manager found she still had that test footage.'

Carrie's face remained hard to read, but the nail of her index finger carved into the webbed skin at the base of her thumb.

'In addition, we have a statement from one of your colleagues detailing the unusually high number of times you visited the drugs room that morning,' Nell added.

'I had stuff on my mind and had to go back twice for some medication,' Carrie said, her words clipped and resentful. 'That's hardly a crime.'

Adam could almost see the cogs turning furiously in her head, trying to work out which colleague had dobbed her in.

'What sort of stuff had you got on your mind?' Tremaine enquired.

'Well, I'd just found out my husband is getting married to someone who used to be a friend, for one thing.'

Tremaine consulted her notes. 'Cameron Kingsley, your ex-husband. Is that right?'

'Yes.' Carrie winced as if hearing his name in full still pained her.

Partridge said, 'So that morning, having found out what Cameron had been up to, would you say you were feeling … upset? Furious, perhaps?'

'Both! I used to go to school with that … that *cow*.' Carrie swallowed and looked at the two detectives as though nervous she'd gone too far. She continued in a more measured tone. 'I felt betrayed, angry, devastated. I can't let it go. All completely normal reactions in my opinion.'

'Absolutely,' Tremaine said emphatically.

'And I'd imagine the last place you wanted to be was on the ward,' Adam added.

Carrie looked at him, tipping her head to one side. 'I was glad of it, actually. Work has really helped to keep my mind off it all. I'm the sort of person who likes to be busy, so it was just like any other day in terms of doing my job.'

Adam watched as she shifted uncomfortably in her chair and pulled at the neck of her T-shirt in an effort to get some air.

'Back to the medication cabinet,' Tremaine said. 'Did you get any of the patients' drugs mixed up that day, with everything that was on your mind?'

'Is that what someone's told you? Because if so, they're wrong.' Carrie's eyes flashed. 'I forgot a couple of patients' medication and had to go back, that's all.'

'You forgot *two* patients' medication?'

Carrie shrugged. 'It was a busy shift. It happens. We only give out one patient's medication at a time so there's never any mix-up between them.'

'And one nurse can administer medication with no counter-checks?' Adam asked.

'If the medication is insulin or morphine-based then that's a two-nurse check,' Carrie said without elaborating further.

'Was one of the patients whose drugs you forgot the baby girl who died, Samina Khalil?'

'No!' Carrie closed her eyes briefly before speaking again, calmer this time. 'No. It wasn't her medication. I can't recall the names of the patients; it was months ago. I'd have to check the log.'

'Yet you seem to know for certain that it wasn't Samina.' Adam made a note on the sheet in front of him. 'I have a statement here from another member of the ward staff. There are a couple of lines that trouble me, frankly.' He leafed through a few pages of typed notes. 'Here we are. Your colleague said, "I was about to do the checks on Samina Khalil just after lunch when the ward manager, Carrie Parsons, asked me to swap to medication trolley duty. She said she'd take over monitoring Samina." Is that what happened?'

Carrie's pale cheeks flushed pink. 'I don't remember off-hand. It wasn't unusual, if so. We often swap duties to fit in with the patients' needs.'

'Do you remember carrying out the monitoring checks on Samina yourself?'

'No. I mean, I remember doing various things for Samina that day, but I don't specifically recall taking someone off the checks so I could do them myself. I'm constantly shuffling duties, especially when we're understaffed.'

'What sort of other things did you do for her?' Partridge asked.

Carrie hitched up her shoulders. 'I would've taken her oxygen levels, I suppose.'

'Is that standard practice?' Tremaine interjected. 'Taking a patient's oxygen levels, I mean?'

Carrie rubbed her chin. 'Can be. I'd noticed her breathing had become a little erratic. It's normal procedure to check oxygen levels in those sorts of circumstances.'

'After you'd taken her oxygen levels, I expect you alerted the ward doctor of your concerns right away,' Tremaine said.

'Well, her levels weren't too worrying, so no, I didn't. I thought I'd keep a close eye on her myself.'

'A six-month-old child with a severe viral infection who seemed to be developing breathing difficulties wasn't enough of a concern for you to speak to a doctor?'

Tremaine was on to something here and Adam waited with bated breath for Carrie's reply. They'd bombarded her with CCTV images of the ward and a statement from a colleague, along with facts about the patients who had died, demanding information from her she could not recall under duress. Now Nell had her pinned down about her lack of reporting to the ward doctor. Adam's experience told him this was the optimum time for her resolve to crack. He bit his tongue and sat back.

'On reflection, I wish I had spoken to someone, yes.' Carrie looked down at the table. 'But the doctors are always incredibly busy. So rightly or wrongly, I made the decision to wait and see how she was rather than page someone unnecessarily.'

'I think we can safely say now that it was most definitely the *wrong* decision,' Adam said grimly.

Carrie Parsons was a hard nut to crack, but she hadn't managed to completely sustain her cool and collected demeanour. It had long been Adam's approach to bide his time in interrogations, keeping the pressure on until he recognised what he labelled the 'twitchy and itchy' state, when the suspect realised that, despite their best efforts to evade the police, they'd been backed into a corner with no way of getting out. Parsons was displaying the classic symptoms now, nervously shifting in her seat, nibbling her nails and compulsively scratching her scalp and the back of her neck.

Adam took out his phone and appeared to check it before placing it face down, leaning forward on the table and lacing his fingers together.

'Good news. We've just had word that the search is in progress at your home address,' he remarked.

'The *what*?' Carrie sat bolt upright in her seat and Bolton laid a calming hand on her arm. 'You're searching my sister's house?'

'Your home address, yes,' Adam confirmed.

'They can't do that. Can they?' She glared at her solicitor, her voice rising. 'They have to get my permission, right?'

Bolton shook his head. 'Not if you've been arrested and they have a Section 18.'

'And you *have* been arrested and we *do* have a Section 18,' Adam confirmed before standing up and stretching. 'Time for a short break, I think. Unless you have anything you'd like to tell us in which case we could stop the search immediately and avoid all that unpleasantness and upheaval for your sister?'

She looked him straight in the eye. 'Do your worst, DI Partridge. I haven't done anything wrong.'

Adam held her stare. 'Do the honours please, DS Tremaine.'

Nell paused the recording and they left the room to let Carrie Parsons sweat it out for another twenty minutes or so.

'We've nothing else to throw at her at this point,' Adam said back in the incident room as he drained the last terrible dregs of the station's machine coffee from his cup. 'Our time is best spent continuing with the investigation now and seeing what the house search throws up.'

'I'm gutted there's still not enough to charge her.' Nell stood up and pushed her hands into the small of her back. 'I'll tell the desk to call her sister.'

'Your sister's on her way over to take you home,' Nell said after Carrie had signed all the paperwork.

'That's it?' Carrie's face flooded with relief. 'I'm free to go?'

'For now.' Adam tapped the desk with his fingers. 'No doubt we'll need to speak to you again. We'll be in touch.'

He watched as the corners of her mouth twitched up. She sighed and relaxed back into her seat. Her solicitor leaned towards her, speaking in little more than a whisper.

Adam rubbed his forehead and looked away. Sometimes this bloody job could be so frustrating.

17

Alexa

I enter the Oxclose Lane police station reception with Florence clinging to me like a little koala. She fell asleep during the twenty-five-minute drive to Arnold and is still slightly groggy, but she quickly realises we're somewhere new that she hasn't seen before, and I feel her perk up, becoming more alert.

I hate bringing her here with every fibre of my body, but I had no choice. There was nobody to leave her with. Overriding this feeling, though, is a strong inclination to be by Carrie's side every step of the way on this horrific journey that has blighted our lives, seemingly out of nowhere.

The desk officer asks me to wait, but I can't bring myself to sit down on one of the grubby plastic seats covered in marks and ingrained muck.

It's a blessing when, a few minutes later, a door clicks open and an officer escorts my sister out into the reception area. We both stand rooted to the spot, looking at each other.

On the drive over here, I imagined Carrie looking her normal self. Tired, of course, but normal. Certainly not like *this*. She looks ten years older, her face grey and sagging.

Florence begins to wriggle around in my arms and reaches out to her.

'Yes, it's Auntie Carrie, isn't it?' I say excitedly in what Perry calls my 'Florence voice'. But my forced jolly tone sounds incongruous in the grim surroundings.

Carrie rushes forward and wraps us both in a big bear hug. She's hot and smells strange, which is no surprise now that I've seen the run-down surroundings here at the station.

'Have they charged you with anything?' I gulp, unable to function until I know the truth. When she shakes her head, I feel like punching the air. They've done their level best to pin blame on her, but the truth has obviously won out. As I knew all along, she had nothing to do with those awful deaths. Nothing at all.

'Let's get you home,' I whisper in her ear, and I feel her slump slightly against me with relief.

Outside, the air is cool and fresh. Carrie hesitates for a moment when she steps out of the building, turning her face up to the weak sunlight seeping from behind thick pale grey cloud cover.

'I've managed to park close, just down here,' I say, and lead her towards the car, which is on a side street, a stone's throw away from the station entrance. When I open the back door to strap Florence into her car seat, I see Carrie just standing watching us as if she's in some strange kind of trance.

When I'm satisfied Florence is secure, I turn to my sister and lay a hand on her arm. That breaks the spell, and she looks at me, startled.

'He said they've searched the house.' Her voice sounds so thin and weak.

I nod but don't comment. 'Come on,' I say gently. 'Let's go home. I'll make us a nice cuppa and then we can talk properly.'

On the way back to the house, Carrie sits in the back with Florence, singing songs and making up for the last few days, when she's been unavailable both emotionally and physically. I want to ask her about what's happened but I stay quiet. I can talk when we get home and it's better for Florence we keep the mood light.

Although I feel more relaxed now than I've been all day, my mind drifts and I spend a lot of the journey cringing at the thought of our neighbours twitching their curtains when we return home. I don't know how much they know, but everyone locally must be aware of the deaths at the hospital now, and most of our street know that Carrie is a ward manager in A&E.

It's fallen quiet in the back, and when I peek into the rear-view mirror, I see that Florence is dropping off to sleep again and Carrie is resting her head against the car window, her eyes closed. She must be exhausted.

After I had my appendix out when I was nine, Carrie was like a mother hen, fussing around, constantly attending to me, and in particular to my wound. I remember I liked the attention, and even more, I loved the fact that Carrie said I was helping to make her a brilliant doctor in the future.

One night I woke up, my wound aching. I couldn't sleep so I went downstairs into the living room and carried out the procedure Carrie had taught me to do.

In the middle of it, the living room door opened and Mum appeared.

'What on earth are you doing down here, Alexa? Can't you—' She gasped when she saw that my nightdress was pulled up and the surgical dressing removed.

Using tweezers, I was plucking haphazardly at the neat stitches. There were gaping wet red slashes on my belly where I had pulled them out far too early.

'What the hell are you doing, you silly girl?' Mum flew across the room and snatched the tweezers from my hand. 'Your wound is going to get infected if you mess about with it like that.'

'Carrie will make it better, Mum,' I said simply, sticking the large white piece of gauze back on my pale stomach. 'She says medicine is boring when it goes to plan, so I'm helping her practise for when she's a proper doctor.'

Even back then, I'd do anything to help my sister. Now, of course, I can see it would have been more than a little disturbing for Mum and perhaps a strange thing for Carrie to have asked me to do. But we were both still kids back then; it's got no bearing on the terrible things Carrie has been accused of.

Where the hell should I start when it comes to explaining to Perry the horrendous mess Carrie has found herself in? I'm relieved she hasn't been charged, but she has been arrested, and that's serious enough.

Whatever's happened, Carrie, I'm here for you.

My last words to her before she left with the detectives this morning echo in my head. I meant everything I said, but following up on it is going to be tricky once Perry gets wind of Carrie's arrest.

I feel so relieved he's back in Scotland. At least Carrie and I won't have to deal with his sidelong glances and heavy sighs. Even though it will be a shock when I tell him, I'm praying that Perry will understand when I fully explain the situation.

For now, I just feel grateful that Carrie is back home and I'm no longer completely alone.

18

When we get back, I give Florence a bottle of milk and set her down in her cot for a sleep. I'm grateful when she snuggles down happily with her beloved Benjy Bunny. Her normal routine is a bit out of kilter, but needs must today. It's important that Carrie and I can talk freely without worrying about Florence picking up on the stress of it all.

If anything, Carrie looks even more dishevelled and exhausted than she did at the police station. Her eyes are red-rimmed and there's an unhealthy pallor about her face. I feel almost guilty for initiating this talk, but it has to be done.

'Carrie … why didn't you tell me about the deaths at the hospital? You tell me lots of stuff about work and yet you've never mentioned this.'

'It happened so quickly, I—'

'I heard the reason they'd arrested you and I had to find out the details online! How do you think that made me feel?' I take a breath, try and keep my voice level. 'That phone call you got at the park … you knew back then the meeting was about the patient deaths, didn't you? As ward manager you must've realised you'd be implicated and yet you never said a word to warn me.'

'Forgive me, Alexa, but I haven't had a chance to consider how *you're* feeling.'

Her cool words are a slap in the face, but I'm not going to let her brow-beat me. She *should* have told me. She lives here. I should have heard what was happening from her, not from an online report, the way everyone else found out.

'I've had half a dozen burly police officers searching every inch of this house. They've even been through my bedroom with a fine-tooth comb. I can't begin to tell you the humiliation I'm feeling about that.'

Her head drops then. 'I'm … I'm so sorry, Alexa, really I am. I had no clue they'd do that. Is it a bomb site upstairs?'

'They've rifled through everything but they haven't trashed the place, thank goodness.' I press the heel of my hand into my forehead and close my eyes. 'I still feel like burning everything they've touched.'

'I'm sorry,' she whispers, and touches my hand.

I open my eyes. 'What were they looking for? They wouldn't tell me, but they took a couple of bin bags away with them. They left a list of what they've taken, but nothing means anything to me: some clothing, paperwork, that kind of thing.'

'Did they take my laptop?'

'Your laptop's still in my boot. They didn't ask for it, and anyway, I didn't want my car taken to pieces.' I look at her. 'There's nothing on there they'd be interested in, is there?'

'Course not. I'm just thinking of obvious things they'd take if they were looking for non-existent evidence.'

'So what's the next stage? Have they finished with you now?'

'They gave me a proper grilling but didn't get anywhere because there's nothing to find out. But …' She hesitates. 'I've had an email. The hospital have suspended me on full pay.'

'What?' My hand flies to my mouth.

'Hopefully it won't be long until they realise their mistake.'

'Have they suspended anyone else?'

'Nope. Just yours truly.' She clamps her mouth closed before continuing. 'Guess that's the thanks I get for all these years of loyal service.'

'This is terrible,' I say faintly, thinking about what Perry's going to say when I have to tell him what both the hospital and the police are accusing her of.

She stands up and rubs at her red-rimmed eyes. 'Listen, I think I'm going to go up and have a lie-down, if that's OK with you.'

'I know you're tired, but we have a lot to discuss before you disappear, Carrie.' My throat feels like sandpaper and there's nothing more I'd love than a lie-down myself. But I can't let this thing roll on; I need some answers. 'You have to level with me, starting right from the beginning. What exactly happened on that ward?'

I expect her to put up a fight, but she looks beaten. Resigned to the fact that I'm not going to let this go. We sit down in the living room to talk, and I pray Florence stays asleep for a little while longer.

Without preamble, Carrie tells me in a rather disturbingly matter-of-fact manner about the deaths of two patients on the ward she manages. 'There was a six-month-old baby at the end of December and then an elderly man on Easter Sunday. I had some interaction with both of them but I wasn't the only one on the ward who attended to them. Lots of staff had contact.'

'But the authorities seem to have made their minds up that you're the one to blame,' I say gently. However much I believe she's innocent, the hospital and the police have targeted her for some reason. They don't just pull a name out of a hat and run with it.

'Well they would, wouldn't they? I'm the ward manager and that makes me an easy target. Plus we don't know what the blabbermouth junior doctor's been saying.'

'But why would he accuse you, if there's no evidence to find? And I still can't understand why you never mentioned the deaths to me. Not a word,' I say faintly.

'Who knows what he did and didn't say …' She stares at the wall before looking at me. 'Look, Alexa. You have to understand that death is an everyday occurrence in a big hospital like King's Mill. I don't like bringing work home with me, spoiling your day.'

'But you talk to me about work all the time,' I say, refusing to be sidelined. She spends the first thirty minutes after returning home from her shift telling me about patients and staff and generally getting things off her chest over a cup of coffee.

'But the stuff I talk to you about isn't *death*, is it? Amusing little anecdotes that make you smile aren't the same thing as telling you about a patient who was admitted after a fall and ends up dying of a massive cardiac arrest a few hours later. That's what happened four days ago. See your face right now? You don't want to hear this stuff. Nobody does.'

'OK, but why didn't you tell me about the internal inquiry? You could have let me know you were all called in for questioning. I kept asking you if anything was wrong.'

She looks wretched. 'I was afraid to tell you. I was in total denial myself, couldn't believe they suspected me of any wrongdoing. And … well, I knew Perry's reaction wouldn't be good. I know he's sick of me being here and I thought if I told you what was happening, he might ask me to leave.'

I feel a twinge inside at the truth that is laced through her words. Still, I have to keep this conversation on track, even if what she's saying about Perry is true.

'I accept you might've been worried, but the phone call you got at the park … you must've known it was serious, and yet you just passed it off as a minor inconvenience, a rota change. How long did you think you could keep it all hidden?'

She huffs with frustration, her hands forming loose fists at her sides. 'I was trying to protect you from worrying, can't you see that? You're still not completely yourself. Things get to you more these days; you'd only have fretted if I'd told you the truth.'

I dismiss her veiled reference to the past. As far as I'm concerned, it's not relevant here.

'Not telling me has saved me a couple of days of worry, that's all. Now I'm *fretting*, as you put it, more than ever.'

'Well that's what I thought would be best,' she says a little petulantly. 'I'm sorry if I got it wrong.'

I shake my head, incredulous. 'Did you honestly think the best policy would be to ignore the problem? Did you think it would just go away?' I feel irritation whipping up inside me. 'What's Perry going to say to the fact that you've been arrested "pending further investigation"?' As I say the words, I can hardly believe the situation she's in. A couple of days ago we were eating ice creams at the park without a care in the world, and now today, it's Armageddon. It all just seems totally surreal.

'I was arrested but they couldn't charge me because there's no evidence. That's because I haven't done anything wrong.'

'I know that, Carrie!' Of course I know that. But does it really matter what *I* think? The hospital and the police are the ones who will decide Carrie's fate, and for some reason that isn't remotely clear yet, they are obviously convinced that she had something to do with the unexplained deaths.

'I'm not expecting any support from Perry,' she says, jutting her chin forward. 'It will suit his agenda that I've been suspended and arrested. He's been spoiling for a fight with me for a long time, wanting me out of his hair. Well, he might get a bigger scrap than he expects if he wants to start something.'

I didn't realise she was so aware of Perry's desire for her to move out. But the last thing I want right now is to be dragged into a discussion about that. To be fair to Perry, I think any normal man would probably be hoping a relative wouldn't outstay her welcome, and Carrie's silly playground threats just sound trite.

'Perry doesn't know anything about what's happened yet,' I say, feeling bilious again at the thought of it. 'But he's not going to be impressed when he knows you were aware of the implications days ago and you never said a word to warn us of what might be coming.'

'Do you think I knew it would come to *this*?' Her cheeks blaze with indignation. 'What Perry thinks is the least of my worries right now, and here's a thought, Alexa: you might be best not involving him at all at this stage. What can he do? He's four hundred miles away in Aberdeen.'

'That may be so, but he's also my husband, Carrie. He's got a right to know what's happening.'

'What if it all comes to nothing? I believe all of us on the ward are innocent. None of my colleagues are capable of doing anything so dreadful,' she says, her hands shaking as she pushes a tissue against her damp eyes. 'You know I've given that job everything. Jeez, Cameron even cited me as a workaholic in the divorce papers. I neglected him, apparently, put my career before our relationship. Ha!'

'I know, and he was totally out of order trying to shirk account-ability for what he did. But your marriage aside, I know you've put the job and your patients before yourself plenty of times over the years.'

'I consider it my duty to give everyone who comes onto the ward the best treatment I can. It would be easy for me to leave it to others, but every patient is important so I give each one a little of my time. I want every single person to feel valued, and that means I often have more interaction with them than usual in terms of medical duties. Should I be punished for that?'

'Look, you don't have to convince me, Carrie. I know you'd do anything for the patients in your care.'

'Samina Khalil was a six-month-old baby girl! Can you believe they think I'd harm her when my own niece was only eight months old back then?'

I shake my head sadly. 'And the other patient was an old man, I read.'

'Angus, his name was. Lovely old fella.' She pushed a knuckle to her front teeth. 'They must think I'm a monster.'

'Don't, Carrie. You can't think like that.'

She looks down at her hands. 'I can't even talk to Marcia or Roisin about it. The police said one or two things that make me wonder if the two of them have stabbed me in the back. I feel so alone. Thank God I have you and Florence. If I didn't, I might just …'

I grasp her hand, not wanting to hear the rest of the sentence. 'You'll always have us, I promise,' I say, fighting back tears. A flood of guilt and remorse fills my chest when I think of how she supported me unconditionally in my hour of need. 'Have the police told you that it's Marcia and Roisin who've said things about you?'

'Not as such. But they had statements from various colleagues, and it might have been one or both of them. They've got a promotion out of this, after all. I feel like my trust for everyone who works there has just dissolved.'

'What did they say? In the statements, I mean.'

'Stuff that means nothing on its own. Circumstantial evidence, like I apparently told a nurse to get on with other duties and that I'd monitor Samina myself. I think that person could be Marcia, though the whole time period seems like a blur. But if Marcia stuck the knife in like that, then she's the last person I want to turn to for support.'

If it's true, if Marcia and Roisin have turned against Carrie, she really has only got us. 'We're your family and Perry will support you too,' I say. 'I know you couldn't have done those wicked things, but while they're trying to pin the blame, we do have to take the accusations seriously.' It's the easiest thing in the world to try and bury your head in the sand, but trouble finds you anyway. I should know. At some point you have to face it. 'Have you got a solicitor? You need some good legal advice.'

'I'll have to apply for legal aid to get anything other than the duty solicitor. The guy they assigned me at the police station is next to useless. I've no savings, nothing to fall back on, so I can't afford a decent lawyer, even for a couple of sessions.' She stands up and brushes down her jeans, as if she might brush away her troubles as easily. 'Look, my head's thumping and my chest feels like it's going to explode. I'm not going to be able to rest like this so I'm going out for an hour or so to try and walk a bit of the pressure off.'

'I'll come with you. If you give me fifteen minutes, I can wake Florence and get her dressed.'

Carrie waves my offer away. 'No, no, honestly. Don't take this the wrong way, Alexa, but I'd rather be alone. I want to try and work through all the crap in my head, you know?'

I stop myself insisting we accompany her, because really, I don't want to drag Florence out into the damp drizzle after she's just got over a cold and cough. So I nod and Carrie leaves the room, squeezing my arm as she passes.

I hear her putting on her shoes and jacket in the hallway, and then the front door clicks open and closed.

Sitting there in the quiet house, I close my eyes and try to think.

Carrie's right. Perry is a long way from home, and thanks to the tensions of us all having to live together, there's no love lost between the two of them. But this is his house too, and I can't let him find out from someone else what's happening on his own doorstep. I just can't.

On top of that concern, Dermott, who Perry car-shares with, lives in Nottingham. His wife could easily get to hear about what's happening and alert Dermott up in Aberdeen. The whole rig would be buzzing with the news. Perry would rightly be furious if he found out about what's happening through that particular channel.

I have to speak to him as a matter of urgency, whether Carrie likes it or not.

19

The police station

Adam sat in Della Grey's office. While she took a phone call, he stared at the framed photo on the wall of the superintendent and the Sheriff of Nottingham at some star-spangled charity event last year. It was another world altogether, away from the often uncomfortable realm of policing he lived in.

'Partridge?' Grey barked, and he realised that she'd finished her conversation and was looking at him expectantly.

'Sorry, ma'am. I came to report that we're making good progress in the King's Mill case but there's nothing concrete as yet, I'm afraid.'

Grey frowned, her salt-and-pepper eyebrows knitting together. 'You interviewed Carrie Parsons at the hospital yesterday and then again today, and you've *still* not got what you need from her?'

'She's a tough one to break,' Adam replied. 'She's the type that's got an answer for everything. I thought we'd cracked her in the last five minutes, she faltered a bit when we mentioned we were searching her sister's house, but she recovered. We had to let her go.'

'I can't keep authorising you to put her through the wringer, Adam, you know that.' Della tapped her short, functional nails on the desk. 'What's your next move?'

'They trawled some stuff from the search. We've got officers going through that as we speak, and I'm hoping for an update from them before the day's through. Tomorrow morning we're driving over to West Bridgford to speak to Beth Streeter.'

'She's Angus Titchford's daughter?'

'Yes. In the afternoon we've got a Zoom call booked with Samina Khalil's parents. They're on an extended break in Karachi, staying with relatives there.'

'And as far as we know, they're not yet aware that Samina's death may have been unlawful?'

Adam shook his head. He was dreading the call.

'Tricky. OK. Do your best, but do it fast.' She dipped her chin and looked up at him. 'What does your gut say, Partridge?'

'Honestly? I'm still not sure. Carrie Parsons is a strange one, but I'm not sure she's got a killer's edge.'

'Whatever that means.' Grey sniffed. 'I understand she lives in the same house as a one-year-old child. Her niece?'

'Yes. PC Butler had a useful chat with Alexa Ford – she's Parsons' sister, and the owner of the house. Seems Parsons spends a lot of time with the child, sometimes alone. Mrs Ford's husband is away at the moment, working on a North Sea oil rig.'

Grey's expression instantly darkened. 'That child is our priority. Get one of the agencies on the case. We can't take any chances, Adam.'

'Already sorted, ma'am. I'm speaking to social services later.'

20

Dr Nathan Mosley

Dr Nathan Mosley packed his gym bag, thanking his lucky stars that so far his name as whistle-blower in the A&E deaths hadn't been leaked to the press. He prayed it stayed that way.

Reporters had been lurking around the hospital entrance today, asking probing questions about the criminal investigation. They were jackals who didn't really give a toss about the patients whose lives had been lost. Nor did their concern lie with the victims' families, who were suffering and in turmoil, trying desperately to find out the truth of what had happened to their loved ones in the hospital. Anyone who'd ever lost someone could understand that, Nathan included.

Even though they pretended they were fighting for transparency for the sake of the families, the press were only really interested in the unpleasant details. There was one main question they seemed to want answering, preferably in as much gory detail as possible: what exactly had happened to the two patients … how had they died?

Nathan's head was full to bursting over his part in all this. The inquiry was like a juggernaut, flattening everything in its path, and it wasn't going to go away any time soon.

He knew he'd acted correctly in reporting the cases, but he'd seen how his colleagues were being treated, and that wasn't pleasant to witness. There was little he could do about it now, but it had occurred to him he could help himself by finding a coping strategy. He realised that, thanks to his crazy shifts at the hospital and his main meal of the day usually being fast food eaten on the go, his underused gym membership would be the perfect distraction when he was off duty. It was vital he kept his mind off the investigation when he wasn't working, otherwise there was a really good chance he'd soon be taking time off with anxiety.

So despite feeling more like binge-watching a box set on Netflix, he packed his trainers, then scooped up the gym bag together with his phone and car keys and opened the front door.

The package was sitting on the welcome mat in front of the door. He was surprised, as he hadn't ordered anything online for a couple of weeks. His name was written on it in black marker pen – big bold capital letters – but there was no address, so it must have been hand-delivered.

He looked up and down the long second-floor landing, but there appeared to be nobody around. Picking up the package, he carried it back inside.

He took a knife from the block and cut through the brown paper the package was wrapped in, then peeled it back to reveal a plain brown cardboard box taped securely closed with masking tape. It looked as if there had once been an address label on there that had been torn off, leaving the stringy remnants of the glue behind. He opened the lid and sniffed cautiously. There was an overpowering smell of perfume but also something unpleasant beneath it that he couldn't identify.

The back of his neck prickled a little but he steeled himself and pulled out a couple of layers of tissue paper before the contents finally revealed themselves to him.

Nathan cried out and jumped back from the box. Clapping his hand over his mouth, he rushed out of the kitchen into the small hallway, fighting the nausea that threatened to overwhelm him.

Inside the package was a decomposing fish, too far gone to see what type it was. Its partial eye stared haplessly, its flesh rotting and oozing with maggots and flies.

Once the shock had abated a little, he strode over to one of the kitchen cupboards. Pulling out a black bin bag, he took a deep breath in and swept the box and its vile contents into it. He tied a knot in the top and marched out of his apartment without locking the door, heading for the refuse bins outside.

21

Alexa

Perry and I have a routine that works for us when he travels back up to Scotland. He always texts me on the journey, usually when they reach about halfway. He'll ask how Florence is and give me an updated estimate for when they're expecting to arrive at Aberdeen harbour, just like he did earlier. When he eventually gets there, he'll sometimes call me if he has to wait for transport out to the rig, but if he's taken straight out there, he'll normally wait until the next day before contacting me.

We keep in touch throughout his absence via email. It might not sound enough, but it is; we never go more than a couple of days without one or both of us sending a message. So long as I know he's safe out there, an email update is fine.

Although it's possible to speak to him, it was made clear to us from the beginning that it would only be acceptable in an emergency. As his next-of-kin contact, I have a nominated number to call, but even then, I'd have to go through several intermediaries to reach him. If I was to call that number right now and ask for Perry to ring me back as a matter of urgency, his colleagues would no doubt twig something was amiss when his boss approached him.

Although I definitely consider Carrie's situation to be a family emergency, it's the kind of situation I wouldn't want everyone gossiping about. The last thing I need is to put Perry in a difficult position, particularly when he's trying to make his mark in his new role. It's far better to send a considered email, as I know he has access to Wi-Fi most days. He has always complained that the signal isn't strong enough to download Netflix films or even books and music – he has to do all that before he leaves home – and the management ask that families avoid sending photographs or videos on email because their server can't cope. But a message from his wife? It can cope with that.

I sit down and compose the email. It's far from easy. I've got to try and convey the gravity of the situation to him but avoid making it sound so serious he feels he has to come home. Such an interruption would be a disastrous start to his new job, and if I'm honest, I could do without the aggravation of having him and Carrie at loggerheads. Perry can't make a difference to Carrie's plight, but he does need to know about it.

Hi Perry,

I wish I could have waited until you got back home to give you this news, but it's important you hear what I have to say directly from me and not through some other channel.

Carrie is in terrible trouble at work. There have been some unexplained deaths on the A&E ward. It's all over the media if you want to know more, but a lot of it is sensationalist, so please don't panic. The truth is, she has been suspended from the hospital on full pay and arrested and questioned by the police. She hasn't been charged yet as the investigation is still ongoing. As Carrie says, they clearly haven't got any evidence and won't find any because she's done nothing wrong!

I'm talking it all through with her and trying hard to get to the bottom of exactly what's happened. Obviously she's completely innocent and it's important she feels supported by us.

I'll keep you informed of what's happening every step of the way, but there's one more thing I need to ask you. As you know, Carrie hasn't got any savings and she really needs the advice of a criminal lawyer. I think a good brief will wipe the floor with the allegations against her and clear her name quickly. Are you OK for me to pay for a couple of sessions from our savings account?

Perry, I'm so sorry to lay bad news on you just after your arrival in Aberdeen. Email's not the ideal medium to receive this unexpected information, I know, but it's the quickest way of reaching you. And it's confidential, at least.

Please let me know you've got this message by return, and if you're OK about the money. I'll be in touch again soon.

I love you.
Alexa

22

District Child Protection Team

Amanda Botha looked at the pile of case files on her desk and sighed. With another working weekend looming if she had any chance at all of clearing her backlog, she'd finally admitted to herself she was well and truly overwhelmed with work.

She'd already got a full-to-overflowing roster, and then, on top of everything, she'd opened her emails to find a serious allegation from a member of the public that now had to take priority.

Her mobile phone rang and the screen lit up with a familiar name, someone she'd not heard from in a good while.

'How's things with my favourite social worker?' Adam Partridge said by way of greeting.

'She's busy, Adam,' Amanda sighed. 'Very busy. I take it you're working late too?'

'Funny you should mention that, and sadly the answer is yes, because our jobs don't just fit nicely into the nine-to-five slot, do they?'

Amanda snorted. He could say that again. She couldn't remember the last time she'd been able to stick to reasonable working hours.

Adam continued. 'Actually, I'm calling to see if you might be free for a little chat.'

She laughed in spite of herself. Her life had become one long stretch of work, more work, watching a bit of television with Basil, her trusty mongrel, on the sofa and then early to bed before the cycle started all over again the next day. She didn't have free time any more and she knew where the exchange with Adam was leading.

'I can always find time for a chat with you, Adam but I'll tell you now, I'm too busy to get involved with a new case.'

'That's a shame. Got an unusual one I reckon you could make a big difference to. But if you're sure, I can pass it on.'

'Go on then, tell me more.' Her interest was piqued in spite of herself.

'King's Mill Hospital are undertaking an official inquiry into two suspicious deaths on the accident and emergency ward. Both patients had a fairly straightforward prognosis and were expected to make a full recovery.'

Amanda frowned. 'I saw something about that.' She usually made it her business to keep abreast of the local daily news as part of her role in the wider community, but her workload had scuppered that plan too, recently. King's Mill was the major hospital in the area, and was an important place for the people who lived around here on both an employment and a community health level.

'The media don't know too much about it yet. The hospital has gone to great pains to keep it hush-hush and it's been entirely internal until now. But a criminal investigation was opened yesterday and yours truly is the senior investigating officer.'

'No surprise there,' Amanda said drily.

'The story's going to break in full tomorrow. Sherwood Forest Health Trust and Nottinghamshire Police are making a joint public announcement that the two patient deaths – a six-month-old baby girl and a man in his eighties – are being treated as suspicious, and they will confirm at the press conference that a criminal investigation has been launched.'

'Any ideas so far about what happened?'

'We've got someone who looks good for it, the A&E ward manager. We arrested her and interviewed her at length today, and we've done a house search, although it doesn't look like they found much there, sadly.'

'You haven't charged her yet?'

'Not yet, but we've made a promising start. We just need more time to delve a bit deeper, plus the hospital are going way back to see if these are the only two suspicious deaths and to do some extra testing on the two possible victims so we can definitely confirm cause of death. The suspect has worked there for over ten years in total and she's also got ten years under her belt at the QMC in Nottingham.'

Amanda was torn between telling Adam again that she hadn't got the time to take it on and wanting to know more.

'Tell me a bit about the victims,' she said, pulling a notepad towards her.

'So, we've got Angus Titchford, an eighty-two-year-old man admitted to A&E after a fall. Confirmed broken hip. They'd placed him on the A&E ward to wait for a bed to come up in another department when he had a massive cardiac arrest out of the blue. The other case happened four months ago. A six-month-old baby girl, Samina Khalil, was admitted with a severe viral infection. Doctors had stabilised her on the A&E ward and kept her in to monitor her progress when she suddenly experienced respiratory problems. Both victims admitted with straightforward conditions; neither made it off the emergency ward.'

'And two very different victims,' Amanda said. 'With no doubt two heartbroken families but I still don't get why you need my help, Adam.' Her forte was working with specific families, not groups of different people.

'The families of the victims are not what I need your help with. The ward manager is strenuously denying all charges. The hospital board has suspended her and today, we arrested and interviewed her. But here's the worrying bit.' Amanda heard the shuffling of paperwork at Adam's end of the line. 'Carrie Parsons, the ward manager, lives with her younger sister, Alexa Ford. Also living in the house are Alexa's husband, Perry, and their one-year-old baby girl – that's Carrie's niece – who Carrie is often left in sole charge of.'

Amanda gasped. 'I've had an email from a member of the public this morning who's concerned that a one-year-old child may be at risk from a family member called Carrie Parsons.'

Adam sighed. 'Now do you get why I'm asking for your help?' he said.

23

The North Sea, off Aberdeen

Perry took a sip of coffee from his thermos flask as he stared out over the railings. The North Sea whipped around the rig like a dancing devil, waiting for its chance to consume any living thing that dared to stray in reach of the wicked waves. During his three years of working here, he'd never seen one day yet where the sea was placid and restful. There had been episodes of calm, but at some point it always reverted to its relentless rumbling, as if something deep beneath were lashing out in pure fury.

He'd been working for hours on a potential problem with pipework near the south drill corner. It had kept his mind focused and clear of negative thoughts, but now that he'd taken a break, he couldn't get the two emails he'd received out of his head.

Both emails had been about the inquiry at King's Mill Hospital but Alexa's was far more detailed in terms of what had happened to Carrie because her suspension and arrest wasn't out in the public domain yet. He knew his sister-in-law would be trouble once she'd got her feet under the table in the house and boy, he hadn't been wrong.

While on the one hand he had been initially grateful when Carrie had moved in and was there to support Alexa after their terrible ordeal, he had become increasingly concerned over the past few months that his wife was relying on her sister far too much. It had now got to the stage where Alexa wouldn't leave the house if Carrie was at work, which meant Florence was stuck in with her. She'd always been a bit naïve when it came to Carrie, but now she seemed to defer to her sister for all child-rearing advice, despite Carrie not having any children of her own.

Infuriatingly, Carrie always knew more about Florence's developmental milestones than the health visitor. She knew the most 'progressive' playgroup to take Florence to, exactly what Alexa should cook for their daughter's meals and when she should take her naps. Perry had no doubt that Alexa's recent decision that he should sleep in the spare room if Florence seemed at all fractious during the day came directly from Carrie's spiteful logic.

While some people might think it was nice for the sisters to be so close, Perry felt it had reached unhealthy proportions. In his humble opinion Carrie had a sinister edge lurking beneath her supposedly 'caring' nature – a type of control she exerted over Alexa.

Some might say that was an overreaction, but then he remembered that neither sister had any other friends, nor did they appear to want any. Carrie saw colleagues at work regularly, but Alexa often saw no one else unless she and Carrie took Florence out together.

Things had been so different three or four years ago. Alexa had been like any other woman: enjoying her job helping kids with learning difficulties, popping out to the shops, the library, the gym … just getting on with life, really. Then everything had changed. He understood why, of course he did. He just hadn't thought it would last so long, and in fact get worse.

This lengthy phase of sadness and upheaval had culminated eight months ago with Carrie coming to their door late one evening, broken-hearted after the breakdown of her marriage to Cameron when she'd discovered he had someone else. He and Alexa had sat up with her while she relayed a litany of appalling tales about her ex's conduct and his questionable morals.

Alexa had swallowed every aspect of Carrie's sob story and begged Perry to let her sister stay with them for a couple of months, 'just until she can get her own place again'. He'd foolishly agreed, completely believing Carrie's assurances that it would only be a short time before she got on her feet.

That had been eight months ago and there had been no sign at all that she would be leaving any time soon.

Shortly after Carrie's marriage had broken down, Perry – without the knowledge of Alexa or Carrie – had met Cameron for a drink for old times' sake. The two men had always got on well and had even played the odd game of golf together during the five-year marriage.

Cameron had confided stuff to Perry that was straight out of a horror story. He said Carrie would sometimes lock herself in their bedroom for days, refusing him access. She'd cut the arms off two of his best suits when he'd arrived home a day late from a European conference due to a delayed flight, but the scariest incident was when she'd stood over him one evening as he lay soaking in the bath.

'She'd plugged the hairdryer into an extension cable and held it over the water while she demanded I name everyone who'd sat on my table at a work dinner the previous night,' he told Perry, shaking his head, still in disbelief. 'She had this crazy look on her face that I still think about to this day. I swear to God she was seriously considering electrocuting me. You want to watch her in your home, mate, she can be a proper psycho.'

'She's fuming about this so-called debt you left her in, though; what's that all about?' Perry had asked him.

'The debt's a real thing, but she knew all about it. In fact, it was her idea.' Cameron frowned, downing the last of his pint. 'We'd carried on like idiots for a couple of years, living beyond our means after I got a promotion. I should have put my foot down but she wanted more, more, more all the time. New cars, holidays abroad, a new kitchen … My credit cards were already maxed out so she got herself a couple and also a loan from the bank, all in her name. We were living off them just to pay bills at the end, and we left each other in a mess. I'm still paying debt off too.'

Carrie was already a walking disaster, it seemed, and now this hospital drama had exploded seemingly out of nowhere. Perry scanned through Alexa's email again. Now that he knew the truth about their indulgent lifestyle from Cameron, he'd be damned if Carrie thought she had licence to work her way through his and Alexa's modest savings while she tried to wriggle out of this latest fix.

When he'd first read the email, he'd gone straight online and googled *King's Mill Hospital deaths*. The search results were shocking. An old guy and a tiny baby, both dead at the hands of an as yet unidentified killer … was it possible that it could be his sister-in-law? She was crazy enough and he had it on good authority there was plenty of circumstantial evidence stacked up against her.

He wiped the sea spray from his face with the back of his hand and screwed the flask lid on tight before heading back down to his cabin. He had thirty minutes before another lengthy stretch out on the south corner of the rig. It was important that he got this dealt with and conveyed the strength of his feelings to Alexa. He'd foolishly allowed Carrie undue influence over his wife and 24/7 access to his precious daughter when he was working away. Despite him half-heartedly trying to encourage Alexa to speak to Carrie about moving out, there had been no progress in the matter. How had he been so stupid to let it come to this?

The thing was, Carrie's influence over Alexa had the potential to tear their lives apart if she so desired. Although he wanted her gone, he didn't want to make an enemy of her for his own reasons. It had to come from Alexa. Still, this was a real chance now to get her out of their lives once and for all, and he was determined not to waste it.

Back in the cabin, he opened up his laptop, pressed the message reply button and began to compose his email to Alexa. He had to be clever how he worded it, but this time he wouldn't be taking no for an answer.

24

Alexa

I glance at the clock, wondering where Carrie could have got to. She said she was just going for a little walk to clear her head, but she's been gone an hour and a half.

The laptop is open on the coffee table and my head jerks towards it when an email pings in from Perry.

Hi Alexa,

It was a shock to get your email. I've looked online like you suggested at a few of the news reports. What the hell is happening at that hospital? Did you know that one of the victims was a six-month-old baby?? I can't believe that Carrie said nothing at all to us about what was kicking off at work. She's the ward manager … she had to know about the deaths and yet never thought to mention it!

The thing that really bothers me is how she insisted we went out for tea while she looked after Florence last night. I find that troubling. I mean, doesn't she realise the severity of the situation? What people might say about us as parents? They'll assume we knew all about the hospital deaths when we decided to take ourselves off out, leaving our daughter with a potential killer!

Sorry. I know you keep insisting Carrie is completely innocent, and that may or may not be so. The fact remains that you just don't know.

Anyway, our first priority must be securing Florence's safety. Surely you can see that? It's natural you want to support your sister, but Florence has to come first.

It's difficult to get things over in the right way in an email, but I need to speak to you before you touch our savings. I'm going to ask the boss if I can phone you in the morning.

In the meantime, please make sure you don't leave Florence unattended with Carrie. Not even for a moment. Can you promise me that?

Love,
Perry

I close the lid of the laptop and sink back down on the sofa. Perry's email is not the response I was hoping for. It sounds to me like he's already tried and convicted Carrie. I expected sympathy and outrage that she could be accused of such a heinous crime – the feelings I myself am struggling with. But this reaction, almost blaming and accusing her … this I did not expect even from Perry.

Florence pulls herself up on the chair, clutching a soft velvety rabbit in her chubby hand. I lean forward and clap as she turns towards me.

'Come on, Florence! Can you walk to Mummy?' Her face breaks open in a wide grin and she lets go of the seat cushion and wobbles on the spot. 'Come on, princess, you can do it!'

She takes a step towards me and promptly plops down on her backside. I clap manically anyway. 'Good girl! Won't be long now!'

I get down on the floor and start posing her plastic animals around a stack of Lego bricks. Delighted, Florence crawls towards me at a rate of knots and I kiss her on the top of her head as she knocks the figures down again.

I'm not ready to respond just yet to Perry's disappointing rant. Here I am, back in my appointed position of piggy-in-the-middle. My husband on one side and my sister on the other. Just when I hoped we could all fight from the same corner because I love and care about them both.

I hear a key in the lock. I pick Florence up and walk into the hallway as the front door opens and Carrie appears.

'Where have you been?' I say, struggling to contain a wriggling Florence, who's immediately reaching for her auntie. 'You were out longer than I thought.'

'I've just been for a walk, like I said.' Carrie purses her lips. 'Had to get some fresh air. What's happening, it's … well, it's surreal. I needed something to ground me.'

I nod. Surreal is right. 'You must have walked quite a way,' I say.

Not to be ignored, Florence lets out an excited yelp.

'Come on, give Auntie Carrie a big cuddle, that's what I need right now.' Carrie steps forward and lifts Florence out of my arms. I think about what Perry said in his email and instantly push it away. I refuse to think like that. Yet his words keep bouncing back.

In the meantime, please make sure you don't leave Florence unattended with Carrie. Not even for a moment.

'I'll make us a coffee,' I say, turning away and leaving Florence and Carrie alone in the living room. I won't allow Perry to brainwash me against my sister. Florence adores her aunt and I completely trust Carrie with her. To think anything else would be utter madness.

Five minutes later, I bring the coffees in and sit down, watching Carrie on the floor, patiently helping Florence to match coloured shapes to the shallow spaces on the wooden board. Each time she fits one correctly, Florence looks to her aunt for praise and gets it in spades.

I can't bear to think of the suffering little Samina's family are enduring right now. It makes me feel almost guilty that our baby is safe and bathed in so much love.

'I've decided I'm going to look for a better solicitor,' Carrie says, sipping her coffee.

I nod. 'You need someone good. If the hospital and police are looking for a scapegoat, we have to make sure it's not you.'

'I think it's clear they've already decided on that one.' She lets out a bitter laugh. 'But good means expensive. I'm applying for legal aid, so we'll see how that goes.' She pauses for a moment before carrying on. 'Did you speak to Perry about what's happened?'

'I've sent him an email. Haven't received a reply yet,' I lie, praying my face doesn't colour up and betray me. 'Let's look at getting you a reasonable lawyer first. I'll fund it from our savings account, no arguments. I know Perry will want to support you as much as I do.'

'Alexa, no, I—'

'It's not up for negotiation,' I say firmly, opening up my banking app. 'That's what's happening.' I press a few buttons and transfer a thousand pounds to Carrie's account. It feels good to do it, like I'm making a difference despite Perry's disappointing reaction.

'I don't know what to say … thanks so much to you both, I—' Her words are drowned out by an ear-piercing squeal from Florence.

I laugh and reach down to scoop her up, but she gives a throaty growl of protest and launches herself across the floor straight into Carrie's arms.

25

Carrie comes into the kitchen while I'm still in my pyjamas having a sneaky coffee before Florence wakes.

'I heard you up with her in the night,' she says, pouring herself a coffee from the pot. 'What time was it?'

'About four o'clock. I think she's got another tooth or two coming through.' I cover my yawn with a hand. 'She was gnawing on her knuckle and her cheeks were hot. I'm just grateful she went back off.'

'I tried to drag myself out of bed to help out, but honestly, I felt drugged.'

'Not surprising with all the stress of yesterday,' I remark. 'You're up and ready early.'

'I've been online and got myself a list of possible solicitors,' she says, sipping her coffee. 'If you and Perry are good enough to help me out with the cost, I figured the least I could do is make the effort to find someone who knows their stuff.'

She seems upbeat and positive and I feel more optimistic that maybe we can stop this witch hunt before any real damage is done to her reputation.

She finishes her coffee quickly. 'Right, I'm off. Got my phone if you need me. I should be back around teatime.'

I nod and let her go. I was hoping we might pop out to the supermarket this morning – I'm desperate for basics – but I suppose it'll wait until she gets back.

I sit down at the breakfast bar to finish my coffee and jump out of my skin when my phone rings, the shrill tone seeming to echo around the kitchen. I snatch it up, expecting it to be Perry, but see at the last moment that it's an unknown number. But I can't risk not answering; it could be he's ringing on a secure line or something.

'Hello?'

'Hi, am I speaking with Alexa Ford?' a friendly-sounding female voice enquires.

I pause for a moment before answering. I realise I need to be on guard for people calling to find out information. Like journalists or local gossip-mongers.

'Yes, this is Alexa Ford,' I say cautiously. 'Who is this?'

'Mrs Ford, my name is Amanda Botha. I'm a social worker with Nottinghamshire County Council. I wondered if I could pop over for a chat? Today, if possible.'

'A chat about what?' I say, trying not to sound nervous.

'I'll explain everything when I get there. It's quite complex, you see. It concerns the King's Mill Hospital inquiry.'

An ice-cold trickle of dread starts at the top of my head and traces its way down the entire length of my spine.

'My sister's out for the day,' I say quickly. 'I can tell her you rang.'

'It's actually you I need to speak to, not your sister.'

It would be so easy for her to say she's a social worker when she's really a journalist trying to get an interview.

'Sorry, but how do I know you're not press?'

'I'm going to text you the number of my office. It's known as MASH: the Multi-Agency Safeguarding Hub. You can call them directly to check my visit is genuine.'

I feel suddenly cold. I've heard of this hub locally. It's for social services, child protection, that sort of thing.

'I could drop in later this morning, about ten thirty. Would that be OK with you?'

'Yes,' I hear myself say. 'That time is fine.'

The text comes through with her office number within minutes of our call ending. I immediately google MASH and discover the head office is just a few miles away. I check the number on the website and it's the same one she's sent via text.

I ring the number and explain to the receptionist in a rather garbled fashion that I'm checking the validity of the phone call and subsequent social services visit I've agreed to.

'Yes, Mrs Ford, it's genuine,' she assures me. 'Amanda Botha is a child protection social worker with the hub. If you just bear with me …' I hear her tapping a keyboard. 'Yes, here we are. I can see she's entered a ten thirty visit at your address into the linked team diary.'

I swallow. Child protection social worker? It's the sort of title that would make any caring parent's heart skip a beat. I thank the woman and end the call, instantly feeling like a bad mother. Good parents don't have dealings with this hub. It's only concerned with dysfunctional families, where children could be in danger.

I feel like crying. At this exact moment I wish more than anything I could bury my face in Perry's broad chest and hear him tell me that he'll take care of everything. But Perry isn't here. It's just me and Florence – and soon, the woman from social services.

There's a twisty feeling in my stomach when I think again about how Carrie kept quiet about everything that's happened until she couldn't conceal it any longer. Perry's right to be annoyed about that. If she'd been honest with us then maybe we could have been better prepared, instead of firefighting calls and visits from social services and the police.

Florence wakes up about nine thirty. I wash and change her and then bring her down for her breakfast. I can't face eating anything myself; unsurprisingly, my stomach is burning as if it's full of acid.

Despite this, I make another strong coffee and sit next to Florence in her high chair. She picks up a piece of banana and throws it on the floor with an angry yelp.

'I know, sweetie, Mummy feels a bit like that too at the moment.' Although I'm trying to encourage her to feed herself as much as possible, I take a spoonful of the apple and pear purée I made a couple of days ago and lift it to her mouth. She looks at me suspiciously before eating it. 'It's pretty lonely here without Daddy and Auntie Carrie around, isn't it?'

With my anger now dissipated, I'm wishing Carrie was here with me after all. Anything would be better than facing social services alone.

Another squawk and the sloppy piece of ripe mango I've just carefully peeled and chopped hits the wall, leaving a wet splodge.

26

The police station

Craning over Nell's shoulder, Adam read the joint Nottingham-shire Police and Sherwood Health Trust's press release about the hospital investigation.

'They don't name Carrie Parsons as the suspended member of staff,' Nell remarked. 'But it doesn't take Hercule Poirot to work out that she's the only senior nurse not at work in the A&E department. It won't be long until they cotton on to that.'

'I wouldn't like to live in the Ford household right now,' Adam murmured. 'Once the press work it out, they'll be relentless.'

Adam was still miffed about the results of the Section 18 search, which he'd been updated on late last night. They'd found precisely nothing to further incriminate Parsons.

Nell closed down her computer. 'Ready to go when you are, boss.'

The appointment with Angus Titchford's daughter had been scheduled for 10 a.m. They left the station and Adam drove the pool car while Nell read from her notes.

'OK, so Beth Streeter is forty-four, married to Daniel, who works as a banker, commuting to London during the week. They have five-year-old twins, Josh and Jemima, who were very close to their grandfather.'

'Beth's mother died a few years ago, right?'

Nell nodded. 'That's what the hospital notes say. Apparently Angus was in good health up until the fall that landed him in A&E, although he had slipped once before and suffered a sprained wrist.' She scanned the page. 'On the day of his fall, the paramedics called Beth to tell her they were taking her father in and she dashed straight to the hospital.'

'Good. Well, we'll try and keep it nice and light,' Adam remarked. 'The last thing we want to do is cause her any more distress, but it's vital we speak to her.'

The journey to West Bridgford, a leafy suburb on the outskirts of Nottingham, took them around twenty-five minutes from the station. Adam turned the car into a quiet, tree-lined street.

'This is Priory Road,' he said, peering through the windscreen as the car rolled slowly forward. 'We're looking for number ninety-nine.'

'There.' Nell pointed to a large detached Tudor-fronted house with a generous front garden and a black Range Rover Evoque on the driveway.

'Very nice,' Adam murmured as he locked the car and appraised the house.

Beth Streeter answered the door before they had a chance to knock, with a friendly if sad smile. She was a tall woman with ruddy cheeks and shoulder-length wavy brown hair that looked as if it had been washed and left to dry naturally. She reminded Adam of one of the horsey set from the farms that surrounded Saskia's parents' house in Leicestershire.

'You're from the police, I take it?' she said. Adam smiled and nodded. 'Come on in.'

'Thanks for seeing us at short notice, Mrs Streeter. I'm DI Adam Partridge and this is DS Nell Tremaine.' He held up his warrant card for inspection but she waved it away.

'Call me Beth. Come through to the living room; the kids hadn't *quite* managed to destroy it when I left them to answer the door.'

She led them through the first door off the hallway into a traditional front room with a large bay window. It was comfortably furnished in neutral shades of beige and coffee, with red cushions adding a splash of colour on the brown leather suite. In the middle of the space sat two young children, focused on building an impressive tower with coloured bricks.

'This is Josh and that's Jemima,' Beth said. 'Say hi to the detectives, kids.'

'Hello,' they said in unison.

Adam immediately spotted a large framed photograph of a smart young soldier, obviously taken some years ago.

'That was Dad when he started his National Service in 1950,' Beth said proudly, following his gaze.

'Are you the police?' Josh asked, his eyes wide.

'We're police officers, yes.' Nell smiled. 'Looks like you're doing a smashing job of building that tower.'

'It was bigger the first time, but Jemima knocked it down.' Josh frowned.

'By mistake,' Beth added gently.

Josh sat up straight, turning his back on the brick tower. 'Have you got any handcuffs?'

'We haven't. Not today,' Adam said, and the boy looked disappointed.

'Our grandad died,' Jemima said.

Adam opened his mouth and closed it again, nonplussed.

'We're so sorry to hear that,' Nell said kindly. 'It's very sad.'

Beth clapped her hands. 'Right then, you two, remember what we talked about? You're going to play nicely with your bricks and I'll just be across the hall in the kitchen with the officers. I'm leaving the door open and there's a chocolate chip cookie in it for both of you if you behave, OK?' She turned to the detectives. 'Come on, I'll make us a drink.'

The kitchen overlooked the long, narrow back garden. It was mainly laid to lawn, with the odd pot of colourful planted flowers dotted around the patio area. Various brightly coloured toys including a mini-trampoline littered the grass.

The instant they stepped into the kitchen out of direct view of the twins, Beth's face crumpled. 'I'm sorry, I'm trying so hard to keep how I feel from the kids. I really didn't want to get upset, but you being here brings it all into sharp focus.'

Adam reached under the glossy white units and offered her the box of tissues sitting on a shelf there. Beth took one and held it over her face before dabbing her eyes.

'We're so sorry for your loss,' Nell said softly. 'I realise it's a very difficult time for you and your family right now, and the last thing we want to do is add to your distress.'

Adam nodded. 'But it's crucial we speak to you about what happened when you got to the hospital to see your father. I hope you understand.'

Beth sniffed into the tissue. 'I'm so glad I got there in time. He was all right, you know. He was making jokes to the nurses about being a Clumsy Clarence, and then out of the blue, after I left, he …' She caught her breath as words failed her.

Nell lowered her eyes in sympathy and took out her rough book and pen. 'Could we start at the beginning, Beth? When did you last see Angus at home, and how did you know he had been taken into hospital?'

'I'd popped over there with the kids on Easter Saturday. They took him a chocolate rabbit and it was a nice day so we sat in the garden to chat while Josh and Jemima ran off some steam.'

'And he seemed in good spirits then?' Adam said.

'Oh yes, he was on top form. Teasing the kids – he called them the Troublesome Twins – and laughing because they said he wasn't allowed to eat his chocolate until the next day.' She looked out of the window, her eyes dull and vacant. 'The next morning, I got a call really early, about seven fifteen, seven thirty at the latest. I was still in my dressing gown and had only just turned my phone on. It was Dad's number and I just had this horrible feeling, you know?'

A loud shriek sounded from the living room and Beth broke off from what she was saying and dashed out of the kitchen. She stood in the doorway to the living room and had a sharp conversation with the children before returning.

'Sorry. Just brick-building politics,' she said.

'You were telling us about the early-morning phone call,' Adam recapped. 'Did you think Angus was calling you because something was wrong?'

Beth nodded. 'My first thought was that he'd had another tumble, maybe hurt his wrist again. But it was far worse than that; it was a paramedic telling me Dad had had a very bad fall and they were taking him to King's Mill. Fortunately, because it was Easter weekend, Daniel was home, and I just pulled some clothes on and set off for the hospital.'

'So you got to the hospital about what time?' Nell asked.

'Just after eight. There was hardly any traffic so there were no hold-ups. The paramedic had told me to head for A&E and said they'd instruct me where to go from there if Dad had been transferred. As it was, he was still in A&E waiting for his X-ray. They'd put him on the ward, though, and I remember feeling glad he hadn't been left in the corridor on a trolley. You see that, don't you, on the news?'

Adam grimaced. 'Can you describe how he was in himself? You mentioned he was joking with the staff.'

'Yes, he was being quite jolly, that's his nature. But I could see in his eyes that he was in pain. He looked pale, too, but when I asked him how he felt, he just said he was a bit bruised and shaken but that he'd be fine. He did say that the panic button I'd suggested seemed like a good idea now. I felt glad he'd come round to the idea of having one fitted.'

'Back to the staff,' Nell prompted her. 'Can you remember who you saw, any names or descriptions, and their manner with your father?'

'Ironically, they all seemed brilliant,' Beth said, and Adam glanced at Nell. 'There was a young doctor, he'd already ordered the X-ray to be done. Then there were a couple of nurses I saw rushing around.'

'What interaction did you have with the staff?'

'When I first got there, a senior nurse, Marcia, took the time to explain what had happened, why Dad had been brought in. I had a few questions about his injuries and she answered everything really patiently, I never felt rushed or a nuisance.'

'And did your father seem at ease with the staff who were around?'

'Oh yes. One of the nurses said to Dad, "We'll soon have you back home, Mr Titchford," and he joked that he rather liked the fuss and might just stay where he was for a couple of days. Her name was Nurse Kenny ... Roisin, I think.'

Nell made a note. 'Anyone else who stuck in your mind?'

'There was the woman in charge. She was a bit more no-nonsense, but then she was very busy ... they all were, to be fair. She brought Dad some pain medication and then had to take it away again as she'd got the wrong tablets.'

'That sounds like it could be the ward manager, Carrie Parsons,' Nell said.

'That was her. I didn't see her name badge but I remember I heard Nurse Kenny call her Carrie.' Beth frowned. 'I heard someone had been suspended ... do you know who?'

'Sadly, we're not at liberty to disclose any details at this early stage in the investigation,' Adam said. 'I'm so sorry. I appreciate it's torture for you, not knowing, but we mustn't compromise anything at this crucial time.'

'It's OK, I understand. It's just … so frustrating. I mean, it's so unfair. My dad was getting on but he had a good life. He was just starting to enjoy life again after Mum died.' Beth looked beaten. 'My husband reckons it's going to be difficult for them to prove if there was any wrongdoing. Like he said, they could just say his ticker gave up on him with the shock of the fall. I can't bear to even think they might get away with it. As far as I'm concerned, they're all to blame if anything awful happened to him. Someone should have noticed …'

Adam watched her battling her emotions in order to try to deal with her father's sudden death. He didn't like to push, but this was their only chance to ask her some questions.

'How long did you stay with your father on the ward?' Nell asked.

'I was actually with him probably' – Beth pursed her lips – 'thirty minutes or so. They're all very busy, you kind of feel you're getting in their way a bit.'

'Beth, I've one more question to ask,' Adam said gently.

'Go ahead,' she replied, seeming to steel herself. 'Anything that helps …'

Adam nodded his thanks. 'When you went in to see your father, did you at any point notice anyone alone with him?'

She thought for a few moments. 'No, I was with him all the time. I didn't see anyone else with him apart from when I left.'

'When you left?' The hairs on the back of Adam's neck prickled.

'Yes. I got to the end of the ward and looked back to wave to him, but he was already talking to a member of staff and she started to draw the curtains around his bed, blocking his view of me.'

'And did you recognise that member of staff?' Nell asked, keeping her voice level.

'Yes,' Beth replied, looking first at Nell and then at Adam, as if she was trying to weigh up why it might be important. Her face darkened. 'It was the ward manager. Carrie Parsons.'

27

Alexa

Florence and I both start when the doorbell rings. I glance at the clock, standing up in panic. If this is Amanda Botha, she's early.

I slip Florence out of her high chair and pick her up. She's clutching a small piece of softened rusk in her fist, but I don't have time to wipe her face and hands clean now.

I walk down the hallway and look through the security spyhole. A slim woman in her forties is standing on the step. She has short brown hair and a friendly face. I open the door, still on the chain, and peer out.

'Hello, Mrs Ford.' She flashes a lanyard at me. 'Amanda Botha. Sorry I'm early, but …' I'm already closing the door to take off the chain and miss her reason for arriving early. I open the door fully and step back.

'Come in. Sorry about the state of Florence here, she was in the middle of decorating the kitchen with her breakfast when you rang the doorbell.'

I'm babbling like I always do when I'm nervous, but Amanda just laughs and closes the door behind her. She seems so laid-back, not like the sort of judgemental official I expected. Then I realise with a jolt that I've let her in without inspecting her lanyard.

'Sorry, I didn't get a good look at your ID.'

It feels uncomfortable to raise it when I've already checked her out by phone, but I have Florence to think about.

'Oh, sorry. There we go.' She lifts her lanyard up and I see that it gives her name, her title and some abbreviated qualifications that don't mean much to me. While I scan the details carefully, she smiles and coos at Florence, who has gone very quiet and seems intent on burying her hot face in my neck. 'And I also have this.'

She dips into her shoulder bag and produces a laminated card. It's an officially stamped and verified ID from Nottinghamshire County Council identifying her as a MASH district child protection social worker. I think I can safely say she's checked out fine now, but I still feel panicky when I see her title again.

'Come through,' I say, leading her into the front room. 'Sorry, I just … I wanted to be sure who you were, that's all.'

'Please don't apologise. I wish more people were as careful as you are.'

I feel bad that I doubted her now; she seems quite nice. I leave her in the living room while I make coffee but I take Florence with me. In the kitchen, I put my daughter in her bouncy chair and soon she's happily squealing and bashing the row of attached toys in front of her.

My phone rings and my heart jumps into my throat when I see Perry's emergency rig number lighting up the screen. I can't take his call, not now. He'll know something's wrong and he's already riled about Carrie. I've yet to tell him social services are involved, but it has to be done in the right way at the right time. My heart flutters when I realise that the list of things Perry doesn't know is growing by the hour.

I turn my phone off and push it in a drawer before taking our coffees through. When I double back for Florence, it's easier to pick her up chair and all and carry her through that way.

'She's adorable.' Amanda sips her drink and smiles as Florence regards her curiously. 'How old is she?'

'She turned one last month and she's crawling like a dart. Pulling herself up on the furniture, too.' I smile proudly. 'I think she's going to walk soon; she keeps having a go.'

'Ah yes, she'll get there. They're all different.'

On the face of it I probably appear relaxed and confident, but inside it's a different story. I feel hot and clammy at having a stranger in the house, and my mind is racing, wondering exactly why she's here, plus I've now got a headache starting. How am I going to explain this visit to Perry? He won't need much more evidence to order Carrie out of the house.

I look at Amanda, sitting there all calm and collected. However nice she seems, I'll do well to remember she's a social worker; not only that, but child protection specifically. These are the people who whip children away from their parents in an instant if they believe they're being neglected. They work closely with the police, too … the same officers who have already arrested my sister in connection with two crimes she didn't commit.

I need to cut through all the pleasantries and distractions.

'You haven't actually said why you're here,' I say lightly, in the hope that it doesn't sound too blunt. 'Why it is you want to speak to me and not my sister.'

'Yes, I was getting to that.' Amanda carefully places her mug down on the coaster I provided and opens up her large tote bag, pulling out a small stack of papers that she puts on the seat cushion next to her. 'I wanted to come and introduce myself in the hope that I can offer you some support. I've brought some information about how an intrusive inquiry like the King's Mill Hospital one can affect a much wider circle than the person directly involved.'

I nod and take a breath. 'I'll level with you, Amanda, there's no doubt in my mind that my sister is innocent. I know you probably hear this all the time, but on this occasion, it's true.' I can hardly say out loud that Carrie is being made a scapegoat by the hospital and the police, but I can shout from her corner.

'She's given everything to that job – over ten years of service – and then, on the word of some junior doctor who's been there five minutes, they're willing to suspend and arrest her. She hasn't been charged because they haven't got enough evidence, did you know that?'

'I'm not involved in the actual police investigation, Alexa, but the thing is … well, there's another issue I'm obliged to address. It's the reason why I've come here to speak to you today.' She laces her fingers in front of her. 'You see, we've been contacted by a member of the public about Florence's safety, and—'

'A member of the public? Who exactly?'

She presses her lips together. 'Sorry, but I can't give you any more details than that due to data protection. Suffice to say that the person was concerned enough for Florence's welfare to alert us.'

As if on cue, Florence starts to grizzle.

I can feel my face burning as I reach down and lift her out of her bouncy chair and sit her on my knee.

'So let me get this straight,' I snap. 'Any coward hiding behind anonymity can say what they like about my family and bring social services down on us, but if I want more details about who they are, I can sing for it?'

Amanda looks taken aback by my vitriol, and to be honest, I've surprised myself with the strength of feeling that's showing itself. I put Florence down on the floor near her small pile of toys.

'I understand it's difficult for you to hear, but please understand we are legally bound to conduct a thorough investigation in these cases. When someone makes an allegation of this nature, we don't simply take their word for it.'

I bite my lip. 'Investigation?'

She presses her lips together. 'That's the wrong word for me to use, really. In view of your current situation, with your sister living here in the family home, we'll need to carry out what we call a family assessment.'

'And you'll be assessing *what*, exactly?' If my heart beats any louder, I feel sure she'll hear it.

'We'll need to establish whether there's a risk posed to Florence by Carrie living here.'

Florence's own aunt, a *risk* to her? It's almost too ridiculous to acknowledge, but I press on anyway.

'This assessment, what does it entail exactly?'

I look down at Florence, who is happily sitting on the floor now, bashing together the brightly coloured building bricks in front of her and periodically glancing up and smiling at us both. She looks so happy and well adjusted. Surely Amanda is experienced enough to see that without a lengthy assessment procedure?

She pats the paperwork by her side. 'If you're happy for us to go ahead, I have a few documents I'll need you to sign. These basically give us permission to contact your health provider and childminder or nursery if you use one. We'll also share information with the police and interview other members of your family. We'll visit your home to ensure Florence's basic needs are met.'

I can't speak. Can't she already see in the short time she's been here that Florence is much loved and well cared for? I know a few signs that indicate a child might be neglected: if they're withdrawn, unresponsive, unusually quiet … Florence isn't demonstrating any of those things.

'It sounds invasive, I know, but we try and make it as painless as possible. If we get access to all the information we need, the process can be quite swift and straightforward.'

Sure. I bet she uses that line on everyone to get them to sign the paperwork. Before it turns into an absolute nightmare. Before you've realised you've agreed to a social worker having free rein in your home, looking in your cupboards and drawers. The next thing you know, other people are suddenly in charge of your child's life, their care.

I don't notice my shallow breathing until it's barely there and I'm gasping. Amanda is suddenly sitting next to me, her

hand on my back. 'Just breathe, Alexa. That's it. And again …
in and out. It's going to be fine, really. I'm not here to hound
you; just to support you and your family. Please believe me
when I say that.'

I'm vaguely aware of her standing up and leaving the room.
Thirty seconds later, she's back with a glass of water. I take it and
gulp some down.

I want to believe her, I do. But …

'I'd have thought it's Carrie who will need the support,' I say,
still pulling in short, sharp gulps of air. 'She's devastated by what
they're accusing her of.'

Amanda nodded. 'I understand. But as I hope I've made clear,
I'm actually here to support you and Florence.'

I sip my drink so I don't have to speak. This all still feels very
weird. She must know what's happening with the police and
Carrie. If I tell her my sister kept me totally in the dark up until
yesterday, she'll think even worse of her.

'If you like, seeing as I'm here, we can make a start just by
having a chat about your personal circumstances, your family life.
DI Partridge told me your husband works away. Is that right?'

I nod. 'Perry's a senior production operator on an offshore rig in
the North Sea. His usual shift pattern is two weeks on, two weeks
off, but this time there's a special job he's involved with, the first
one since he's been promoted, so he's away for three weeks. He
left yesterday morning at six, before the police came for Carrie.'
My fingernails carve into the fleshy part of my palm. 'I've emailed
to tell him about the hospital inquiry and he's really worried, but
… well, he's hoping to call me later today to chat. He has to get
special permission to use the rig telephone.'

'He's concerned about leaving you and Florence here with
everything that's happening?'

I nod. 'We're both concerned. Florence is our number one
priority, but we also want to support Carrie.'

Amanda nods distractedly, pulls a sheet of paper from the stack of paperwork and glances at it.

'I understand Carrie has lived here with you for about eight months now. Is that correct?'

'Yes.' I sigh. 'It wasn't supposed to be for this long, but ... well, you know how time passes without you realising sometimes. I love having her here; she's a great help with Florence and we're really close.'

'And your husband, Perry ... does he feel the same?'

'He gets on well with her, yes.'

She smiles. 'I meant does he love her living here like you do?'

'He was happy to help her out, of course he was, but he's ... well, he's had enough of her being here now, I think.'

'I see. Has Carrie expressed any intention of moving out any time soon? Have you broached the subject with her?'

'I was supposed to speak to her while Perry is away. She's my sister, so I'm fully comfortable with her staying as long she needs, but Perry thinks we need time on our own as a family.' Something about Amanda's easy, laid-back manner makes me feel safe talking to her, although I know I have to be careful. But if I'm open, maybe she'll see I've nothing to hide. 'I know he's right, but ... well, it's awkward, isn't it? Finding the right words to tell someone you love to just go?'

Amanda nods sympathetically. 'It's not easy. I'd imagine you'd feel a real pull of loyalties.'

I look at her. 'That's *exactly* how I feel, yes. And now that all this has kicked off with the police and social services, I suppose Perry has all the ammunition he needs to insist Carrie leaves.' I don't mention that he's *already* kicked off about it. I don't want to give Amanda the impression we're always arguing.

'OK, I have a few more questions, and then if you can sign the assessment forms, we can get the ball rolling. Do you have any close friends who play a part in helping you care for Florence?'

The only people I really have are Carrie and Perry. And both are inaccessible right now, at opposite ends of the problem. But my aim is to convince social services that everything is fine so they can do their assessment and leave us alone.

'I'm very careful who I leave Florence with,' I say. 'I trust Carrie completely with her and Florence adores her.'

It's important Amanda knows that. We're happy, Florence is happy. 'Whatever some twisted, bitter troublemaker might be saying, my daughter is in very safe hands.'

Amanda writes something down before looking up at me again. 'Is there anything else you'd like to discuss with me today that affects your family life?'

I don't know how I manage it, but I push away the horrible pictures of two years ago that spring into my mind. I look her in the eye and I say, 'No, there's nothing else I can think of.'

She takes me through the forms and I sign in the areas she's marked with a cross.

'I'll initiate the assessment on our system and be in touch again soon.' She hands me a small printed business card. 'Any questions you or your husband might have, or if you need any other support, just give me a ring on that number. My mobile number is on there too.'

'Thank you,' I say in a small voice.

She gathers her stuff together and stands up.

'I'll show you out,' I say, picking Florence up. She rubs her eyes and gives Amanda a gummy smile.

'You really are lovely, aren't you?' She tickles Florence under the chin and I lead her to the front door.

Just as she's about to leave, I feel a jolting need to reason with her. 'I hope you've seen today what a happy child Florence is,' I say. 'I think the world of her and I'd never let any danger come to her.'

'I'm sure that's the case, Alexa.' She smiles, taking Florence's fingers and jiggling them by way of goodbye. 'But with respect, it's not you we need to worry about. Your sister, who has access to Florence, has just been arrested in connection with two unexplained deaths and suspended from her workplace. While she's living under the same roof, we have to take steps to ensure your daughter isn't at risk. I'm sure you want to be certain of that more than anyone.'

'Yes,' I say, my voice flat. 'Of course I do.'

I watch her as she walks down the path to her car and it feels as if someone just turned a powerful spotlight on in my head.

Perry is in Scotland and Carrie is busy fighting for her job and her reputation. That leaves just one person to look after my daughter. One person who has to step up and take responsibility for her.

That person is me.

28

The North Sea, off Aberdeen

Perry tried Alexa's mobile once more before replacing the cordless office phone in its cradle.

He'd had to go through official procedure to get permission to make a phone call to shore in the middle of his shift, and Alexa hadn't been ready. He'd been unable to give her a set time in his email, but he'd told her it would be during the morning. His guts felt like he'd swallowed a bucket of eels and he hadn't been able to sleep properly, so he felt thick-headed, as if he'd been drinking the night before.

At the end of his shift yesterday, after he'd emailed Alexa, he'd only just showered and changed into clean clothes when he'd been called back out on an emergency job. He'd braved the icy wind and the rotten-egg stink of the hydrogen sulphide that was always present out here, his mind's eye filled with the happy face of his beautiful daughter. He could almost feel the warmth of her chubby cheek next to his, the grip of her tiny fingers on his own. She smelled of talcum powder, strawberries and fresh milk. How he loved her.

He'd felt grateful for the wind on his face as his eyes prickled. He would not allow anything to happen to Florence. Despite Alexa's misplaced loyalty, he promised himself he'd do the necessary, whatever it took. He had one priority and that was to keep his daughter safe. He was even willing to put his own happiness aside to ensure that.

Up on deck with a cluster of weathered, tired men looking to him for guidance, he forced himself to push the vision of Florence to one side as he was faced with a nightmare scenario. There was the serious threat of a borehole collapse, caused by the drilling fluid pressure being too low. A major part of his new job was to troubleshoot such problems and come up with speedy solutions that would save the drilling company both time and money.

The emergency had taken all his focus and powers of concentration, but ultimately he'd managed to avoid the loss of a well. His manager, Ade Tinker, had been delighted with his efforts.

'It's clear we chose the right man for this job,' he said, patting Perry on the back as he returned to his cabin, exhausted. 'Very well done. I'm impressed.'

It was one in the morning and Perry had felt so weary he could barely put one foot in front of the other. Again he dragged himself under the shower and got changed; then, instead of going up to the mess to get a bite to eat, he lay on his bed and waited in vain for sleep to come.

After twenty minutes of staring at the ceiling, still wide awake, he'd picked up his laptop and begun a thorough search of the latest on the hospital inquiry.

It was probably the worst thing he could've done, feeling so helpless and remote out here, but he couldn't help himself. And what he found meant he was unable to sleep at all. There were unregulated forums and comments, people second-guessing what might have happened to the hapless patients who'd died. Carrie was named in many of them, and there was even gossip about her marriage, plenty of which Perry happened to know was completely untrue.

Now, following his failed phone call home, he walked into the outer office and over to his boss's desk feeling like a fool.

'Sorry, Ade, she's not answering.'

'Oh dear, that's a shame,' the other man said, frowning. 'Didn't you tell her to expect your call?'

'I did, but she must be busy with the baby.'

'Ah yes, unpredictable little bundles at times, aren't they?' Ade grinned. 'Well, not to worry. If you want to try again later, when you've finished your shift, just come up. Keep me up to date on that pipe sticking issue.' He dropped his gaze to a stack of paperwork on his desk.

Rather than leaving, however, Perry sighed and sat down opposite Ade uninvited. He was usually one of the most private members of staff on the rig, but this was different. He had no choice but to level with his manager.

He cleared his throat. 'Can I speak to you confidentially?'

Ade looked up from his paperwork in surprise, but when he saw the look on his senior staff member's face, he immediately gave him his full attention again. 'Go ahead, Perry. I'm all ears.'

29

Dr Nathan Mosley

The whole unexplained deaths situation at the hospital had blown up beyond anything Nathan had envisaged.

He'd been naïve, of course; what had he expected really? Blowing the whistle on the two deaths was like dropping the H-bomb in the middle of the hospital. The board of trustees had scrabbled to contain the damage as much as possible and, after a cursory medical audit, the police had been called in almost immediately.

In the throes of deciding whether to report the situation, he'd supposed there might be an initial quiet internal inquiry that might even prove there had been no wrongdoing. There was always the remote but possible chance the deaths would be found to be natural after all.

But it wasn't to be, and the inquiry and the criminal investigation had both exploded. The A&E department was functioning as usual, apart from the fact there were some new supervisory staff now in place appointed by the trustees. This had caused palpable tension, but two people had been temporarily promoted to acting ward manager in the light of Carrie Parsons' suspension.

Unsurprisingly, gossip was rife. An anonymous note had been sent to the board by an individual claiming to have witnessed a senior nurse administering potent cardiac drugs to Angus

Titchford. The board had duly reported this to the police and the senior investigating officer was frantically interviewing staff again, stressing that the person who wrote the note had an obligation to come forward to give an official statement. So far, nobody had, but then Nathan only knew what he'd overheard on the ward and in the canteen.

There was a clear, visible hierarchy in the hospital. The doctors and consultants were on one level, the junior doctors below them. The qualified nursing staff occupied the rung under that, and the auxiliaries and medical assistants were on yet another level. He tried to hover between the divisions and get on with everyone, but it didn't surprise him when he saw the ward staff gossiping in little clusters that dissipated the moment he arrived. Another few months and he'd be a fully qualified doctor. When that moment arrived, he'd have to demand a bit more respect from his subordinates.

Amongst the doctors, Nathan's formal complaint hadn't been mentioned specifically. He knew they were all aware, but doctors operated on a professional level where it was possible to simply act as though something hadn't happened, and there were several cliques in the doctor/consultant realm that he didn't feel part of yet.

His superior officer and senior cardiac consultant Javeed had told him straight away that he'd done the right thing but warned him of the consequences.

'You've proved you are a moral, professional man,' he'd said approvingly. 'Too many junior doctors are concerned with popularity with the general staff. This, you have shown, does not matter to you. You've put the safety of the patients first and it won't go unnoticed.'

It was a bit of a backhanded compliment, Nathan felt. Javeed was basically saying he'd be despised by the ward staff for what he'd done. But if that was the case, then so be it. As far as Nathan was concerned, he wasn't in a popularity contest. He just wanted to get his job done and qualify.

He parked the car and reached over into the back to haul out his rucksack. When he stood up straight again, his eye caught movement over by the small wall that bordered the apartment foyer. There was an alleyway running alongside, and he was almost certain someone had just dashed in there as he pulled up.

He locked the car, walked across the road and peered into the alleyway. His mouth was dry and his heart racing. Ridiculous! It was broad daylight, for goodness' sake. He was becoming far too jumpy.

He squinted as he scanned the full length of the alley. He could see light at the end where it opened up to the back of the apartment block. It was dim down there but he could make out several refuse bins dotted along one side. It would be very easy for someone to dash behind one of them to hide.

He shifted his feet. He wasn't sure whether to go down there. Ordinarily he wouldn't have bothered, but since he'd received that vile fish delivery yesterday, he'd been unsettled. Although he couldn't swear to the fact, he had nevertheless somehow convinced himself that somebody was watching him, and despite his racing heartbeat, he was the kind of man who preferred to face his fears head on than turn the other way.

'Hello? Is someone down there?' he called out more confidently than he felt, but the alleyway remained silent, with no discernible movement.

First there had been the unpleasant delivery. Then, last night, when he went to bed and pulled down the blind, Suzy had spotted a figure loitering across the road. She'd looked at him, her eyes full of fear. He'd turned off the lamp and opened the window to get a better look, but by that time the person had disappeared. Now this. Someone had definitely rushed into the alleyway when he'd got out of the car.

He took a few steps forward and the smell of stale urine and garbage assailed his nostrils. The very air felt thick and hostile here. He'd dealt with numerous stab wounds since starting work at the hospital. Some of them fatal but all of them nasty. Generally the victims were people in exactly this type of situation: getting themselves involved in something rather than just walking away.

Persuaded by his own cautious thoughts, he turned to leave the alleyway. Suddenly he heard a shuffling noise. He whipped around again to scrutinise the space just as a mobile phone rang the other side of the refuse bins.

The ringing abruptly stopped and silence fell again, but now Nathan was riled.

'I know you're there, so you might as well come out and tell me what's so fascinating about watching me park,' he said, keeping his voice steady in the face of possible attack.

He heard the shuffling noise again, and then a figure emerged from beside the second refuse bin.

Nathan squinted as the person walked towards him.

'Carrie?' he said in disbelief.

She continued walking until she was just a few steps away from him. He stepped out into the open air, but she lingered inside the alleyway so that she was concealed from the street.

'Why did you do it? Why did you have to speak up?' Her mouth twisted into a tight knot of loathing as she fixed her eyes on his. 'My life has been ruined and it's because of *you*. You and your wild, crazy accusations.'

'Carrie, I …' Nathan stepped back again. Composed himself. 'This is a conversation we shouldn't be having, you know that.' The police and the hospital board had clearly instructed all staff that no one was to contact the suspended ward manager.

'Ten years I've given to that hospital. Ten years and they make *me* the scapegoat. Thanks to you.'

Something occurred to him and his face darkened. 'Did you send that filthy package to my door yesterday?'

Carrie smirked. 'I don't know what you're talking about.'

'You'll only make things worse for yourself if you carry on like this, you know.' He frowned. 'I know you've been watching me.

My girlfriend has seen you, and I spotted you last night on the street, too. What do you want from me? I have no sway with the inquiry.'

'I just want you to know you'll not get away with this. You can't just ruin someone's life and walk away smelling of roses. Sounds like the nasty package you received is well deserved.'

He looked at her again, this time from a medical viewpoint. Her eyes were wild, pupils dilated. She looked very pale and he wondered if she was taking some kind of prescription medication.

'I'm sorry about what's happened, Carrie, I really am. But you must know I have no control over the police investigation.' According to the hospital rumours, the evidence against her was pretty conclusive, so he was surprised she hadn't been charged yet. Shift rotas, inventory of medicines and patient one-to-one contact had swiftly pointed to one person who had had consistent contact with both victims: Carrie Parsons. 'I'm afraid you've left me no choice but to report this interaction with you. I shall also tell the police you've been watching my flat.'

'I wouldn't do that if I were you.' She stepped forward again and stumbled. She looked menacing and unstable and he had to force himself to stand his ground. She was shorter than him but of quite a sturdy build, and if she'd been drinking and medicating, as he was beginning to suspect might be the case, she was likely to be unpredictable. 'Your mother's in the Willow Tree care home, isn't she? Sutton Road?'

His mouth fell open. 'How did you—'

'It would be a terrible mistake on your part to underestimate me,' she hissed. 'I'll do anything it takes to pay you back if I lose my job over this. Anything.'

'It's out of my hands now,' Nathan said boldly, even though he felt nervous of the interaction. He shouldn't be talking to a suspended member of staff. Period. 'I'm not in a position to help you, I'm afraid. All I'll say is that if you're innocent, then you've nothing to worry about.'

'You could speak up for me, tell them you've worked with me for nearly a year. Tell them I've always been conscientious and efficient.'

This was getting out of hand and Nathan knew he needed to bring it to a quick end.

'I have to go now. Don't contact me again, Carrie. It's for your own good that you adhere to the rules.'

'Don't imagine you'll get away with this,' she hissed as he walked away. 'You'll pay one way or another, I'll make sure of that.'

He tried to reassure himself. There was no need to get rattled; she was just a desperate woman full of empty threats.

Yet there was something unnerving about her. Something chilling that made his blood run cold, and when he lifted his key fob to the apartment's security door, he saw that his hand was shaking.

30

The police station

On the way back to the station, Adam and Nell discussed their conversation with Beth Streeter.

'She didn't seem to make the connection between that last chilling glimpse of Carrie Parsons closing the curtains around Angus and her father's death at all,' Nell said.

'I think people have a hard time doubting medical professionals,' Adam said. 'It's like you grow up trusting them from childhood – teachers and policemen too – and the thought that one could be a bad egg ... well, it's a big jump for some people to make.'

'True. When are we going to pull Carrie Parsons in for interview again? She said she was never alone with Angus Titchford, and it turns out she very much was.'

'We'll see how the call with Mr Khalil goes. The rest of the team are collating the witness statements from hospital staff and medical experts. We've seized most of the paperwork from the hospital now including the shift rotas and the drug and medical administration paperwork. We'll need a good chunk of time to go through all that, and then we'll get Parsons back in.'

Nell let out a long breath.

'That was a heartfelt sigh,' Adam said. 'The investigation getting to you already?'

'Just from the point of view of seeing families in shock and suffering. It's pretty tough. Your loved one goes into hospital, a place they're supposed to be safe and cared for … a place that's supposed to make things better, you know?'

Adam made a noise in his throat to show he understood. 'And then you find out something terrible happened in there on top of the grief of losing them.'

'What time's your Zoom call with Mr Khalil?'

'Two o'clock. Pakistan is four hours ahead of UK time, so we didn't want to make it any later than that.'

'Samina's family don't know about the hospital inquiry? They still think it was a natural death?'

'As far as I know they don't. I just said the call was in connection with her death. His brother emailed him and set it up.'

'Don't envy you that conversation,' Nell said. 'What a mess.'

'Yeah.' It was Adam's turn to sigh. 'You got that right.'

Detective Superintendent Grey offered Adam her office to take the Zoom call with Asmin Khalil. He sat behind her desk and she sat over the other side of the office with Nell. Sitting in Grey's chair felt like when he'd once gone on a trip to Kensington Palace with school and for a dare had sat on one of the roped-off thrones. He'd got a week's worth of detentions and his mum had stopped his pocket money for a month.

Asmin Khalil joined the call and Adam braced himself. He'd been hoping there might be connection problems and he wouldn't have to look at Mr Khalil's face when he told him the bad news, but the man's image was crystal clear. He had a neat black beard and wore a white shirt open at the neck.

'Good afternoon, Mr Khalil, thank you for joining the call. I'm Detective Inspector Adam Partridge of Nottinghamshire Police. I'm recording this call so we can refer to it at a later time, are you happy with that?'

'No problem, DI Partridge. What's all this about?' There was an impatience about the man. 'My brother said something about Samina's death. We've come to Karachi to stay with my parents to try and put the tragedy behind us.'

Adam got that the Khalils didn't want everything raked up again. When he found out why he was calling, Adam felt sure he'd understand.

'In December of last year, Samina was admitted to King's Mill Hospital in Sutton-in-Ashfield with a suspected serious viral infection. She was severely dehydrated and subsequently—'

'DI Partridge. I don't wish to appear rude, but I really don't need to hear all this again. My wife remains severely depressed over Samina's death and she is unaware I'm taking this call. So please, just get to the point.'

Adam glanced at Grey, who gave him a nod.

'I'm very sorry to have to tell you, Mr Khalil, that Nottinghamshire Police are currently investigating the circumstances surrounding the deaths of both your daughter, Samina, and also one other patient who died on the same ward at the hospital just a few days ago. We are trying to establish whether any criminal offences may have been committed in relation to either death.'

There was a stunned silence as Mr Khalil stared unblinking at the camera.

'It's regrettable that I've had to give you this upsetting news via a video call, but—'

'I … I don't understand. Samina died from breathing difficulties. My wife and I were there when they tried to resuscitate her. I can assure you they did everything they possibly could to save our daughter. How can her death be *unlawful?*'

'The investigation is ongoing, Mr Khalil, but the hospital board were satisfied there was enough evidence to open their own internal inquiry, which has resulted in a member of the senior ward staff being suspended.'

The man dropped his head and cradled it in his hands. 'This will destroy Fareda,' he muttered. 'What will I tell her?'

'I realise it's a terrible shock, Mr Khalil, but we are pulling out all the stops to get to the truth. Could I possibly ask you a few questions in relation to Samina's admission to the hospital?'

There was no response. Mr Khalil sat with his head in his hands and let out a long, agonised groan. For an awful moment Adam thought he was going to refuse, then he seemed to come to his senses. 'Yes, yes, of course. If I can help, I will.' When he looked up at the camera again, Adam saw that his eyes looked sore, as if he'd rubbed them.

'Can you tell us, sir, how Samina came to be taken to hospital?'

'Yes. She took ill the night before. I'd been away for two days – I'm a senior project manager for British Gas – and I got home late. Fareda was in a terrible state. Samina was vomiting, had diarrhoea … she couldn't keep anything down, even water.' His voice seemed to get fainter as he spoke, but Adam didn't interrupt. 'We made the wrong call, said we'd see how she was the next day. In short, she deteriorated, became much worse, and the next morning we took her to A&E in the car.'

'Can you take me through what happened when you got there?'

'They were very good. I checked her in and they fast-tracked her past the triage stage and directly onto the ward. A doctor saw her and diagnosed a severe viral infection, with the main problem being that Samina was extremely dehydrated. Within twenty minutes they had her hooked up to a drip and assured us she'd be picking up in a relatively short time.'

'You felt she got good treatment?'

'The best,' Mr Khalil said without hesitation. 'I think you must be mistaken in thinking anything was wrong. Samina was obviously far more poorly than we thought.'

31

Alexa

In the afternoon, Carrie returns home from her trip out to the solicitors' offices.

Florence immediately crawls towards her holding up a bright orange building block, as if she's trying to tempt her auntie to play with her. But instead of slipping off her jacket and giving Florence her full attention as she'd usually do, Carrie starts pacing around as if she's looking for something.

'How did it go at the solicitors' offices?' I ask her.

'Fine,' she says distractedly.

'So … have you made an appointment with someone?'

'What? Oh, not yet. I have to go back to sort things out properly.'

Go back again just to make an appointment? Carrie seems very vague, but maybe that's just my imagination. Besides, her mood is the last thing I'm concerned about right now. My head is full of social services.

'Carrie, I need to talk to you,' I say, not sure how I'm going to break the news. 'While you were out, I got a call from—'

'Can't it wait, Alexa?' She's downcast now, and irritable. 'I'm really tired and I'd like a rest for half an—'

'Sorry, but it can't wait, no!' I blurt out. 'I've had a visit from social services while you were out. Here, at the house.'

'What?' She sits down heavily. 'What did they want?'

'They've had an anonymous tip-off from some busybody – a member of the public – that Florence could be in danger.' I swallow, my throat suddenly parched. 'They've got to carry out a risk assessment.'

'What kind of danger do they think she might be in?' Carrie says slowly.

There's an uneasy silence and I feel irritation rising in me. What does she think the danger might be? It's not rocket science to work it out. 'I suppose they think it's relevant that one of the patients who died at the hospital was a baby.'

'They can't just walk in and demand to do an assessment!' Carrie raises her voice and Florence looks up from her bricks, alarmed.

'It's OK, sweetie,' I soothe her before turning to Carrie again. 'They *can* demand it, apparently. The social worker said they're legally bound to do so when there's been a tip-off like this.'

'A tip-off by who, exactly? Someone too cowardly or too sly to identify themselves?'

Her face burns with indignation, and again I feel a new irritation at her blatant refusal to take any responsibility whatsoever.

'I know what you're saying, Carrie, but the social worker made it perfectly clear I haven't really got a choice in the matter. I had to sign paperwork to agree to it.'

'You shouldn't have done that, Alexa,' she says sternly. She often talks to me like that and usually, I accept it, barely notice it. But today, I really don't feel like being treated like a kid. 'You should have refused to sign anything until I've seen it.'

'And how would *that* have looked?' I snap, and she looks taken aback. 'If I'd refused to sign the papers it might have seemed we had something to hide. When it involves my daughter, I'm going to do the right thing, not wait for you or anyone else to give me the all-clear.'

She winces as if I've slapped her, but I haven't finished yet.

'I've already told you I trust you, Carrie, and that I'm here for you. I hope you believe that. But Florence has to be my top priority. You have to promise to tell me everything from now on, OK? No more secrets. I want to know the truth about the hospital and the police inquiry as it happens, not weeks later. I can cope with the truth; there's no need to hide it any more.'

'Are you calling me a liar?'

'No. I'm saying that keeping key information to yourself is a deal-breaker. I need to know what I'm up against. I don't want to hear new developments from anyone but you. Do you understand what I'm saying?'

My heart is thumping on my chest wall but my words come out clear and uncompromising, and the relief I feel is akin to walking in the fresh air after being locked in a fusty basement.

Carrie folds her arms. 'You've made yourself crystal clear. Does Perry know about the social services visit?'

'Not yet, but I have to tell him.'

Frustrated, she throws her arms in the air and takes a step towards me. 'Why do you have to tell him? What can he do from the middle of the North Sea, for God's sake?'

'That's hardly the point, Carrie. Florence is his daughter too and he has a right to know about the assessment.'

She juts out her chin. 'Well, you can tell him when he's back and all this crap is behind us.'

I stare at her. 'Whatever you think of Perry, he's my husband. If I don't tell him, social services probably will.' I soften my voice a little. 'We'll all get through this together, I know we will. But there are some things we can't wriggle out of and the assessment is one of them.'

'You're living in a fantasy land.' Carrie screws up her features into a tight knot. 'The nicer you are to these people, the harder they'll push. Don't you realise that?'

'Carrie, I—'

'Don't waste your breath, Alexa. I know the real reason you're telling Perry; it's because you don't trust me to be around Florence.'

'That's ridiculous! Of course I—'

'You don't trust me because you think I'm guilty.' She talks over me and the old feelings of doubt and reliance start to take a grip again before I push them away. 'You think Florence isn't safe here when I'm around.' Her eyes are shining with malice, her lips sucked back into her mouth. Just for a moment, she doesn't look like Carrie. She looks hostile and vindictive, and she clearly hasn't finished with me yet. 'I kept my mouth shut for *you* when it mattered, didn't I? I never breathed a word to anyone about what happened. About what you did.'

I feel the blood drain from my face like someone just pulled a plug. My legs wobble and I grope behind me and sit on the arm of the sofa.

'I'm sorry. I didn't mean it like it came out.' She walks over and slides her arm around my shoulders. 'I shouldn't have said that; you know I didn't mean it, right? Christ, what are these people doing to us, Alexa? Making us say terrible things, turning us against each other. That's what they want … to come between us. Can't you see that?'

The doorbell rings and she jumps up. 'I'll get it,' she says, leaving the room.

A few moments later I hear voices at the door and then in the hallway. Florence looks alarmed when I stand up. 'One second, poppet,' I tell her as I move to the doorway to crane my neck out.

'It's the police,' Carrie says stonily, leading them into the living room.

DS Tremaine makes a few cute sounds to Florence and DI Partridge smiles and nods at her.

'Sorry to interrupt; we won't be long,' he says, and turns his attention to my sister. 'Carrie, we're here because Dr Nathan Mosley contacted us this afternoon. He says you've sent him an unsolicited package containing a rotting fish and that you've been following him.'

'Today, apparently, you actually approached him and made a threat against his elderly mother, who's currently residing in a care home,' Tremaine adds.

I shake my head in disbelief and stare at Carrie. Nathan Mosley is the junior doctor who, rumour has it, blew the whistle on his fellow staff.

Carrie looks aghast. 'Why would he say that? I've been here all day, right, Alexa?'

Three pairs of eyes turn on me.

'Yes! Well …' I can't believe she's put me in this position. Why doesn't she just tell them the truth? That's what I need to do. 'Apart from your trip out to the solicitor's.'

'And what time was that?' Partridge asks her.

'About one thirty this afternoon. I've completely lost track of time today.'

'That's about the time Dr Mosley said you approached him in the street,' Partridge says.

'What's the solicitor's address?' Tremaine asks.

'Hang on, I'm not a prisoner, am I? I'm not banished to the house and not allowed out?'

'No, of course not,' Partridge says in a measured tone. 'I'm asking before I check the CCTV on Dr Mosley's street. So if you were outside his apartment rather than at the solicitor's office, now's the time to tell us.'

'OK, I did see Dr Mosley. By accident, that's all.'

'Where is your solicitor's office?' Tremaine asks again. 'Because Berry Hill Lane, where Dr Mosley lives, is about two miles from the town centre, where most solicitors have their premises. It's unlikely you'd bump into him outside his home as you were leaving your appointment.'

I look at Carrie in confusion, but she won't meet my eyes.

'I didn't do anything wrong. I didn't threaten him and if that's what he says then it's a lie.'

'Why did you turn up outside his home, Carrie?' Tremaine asks.

'I just wanted to talk to him. Ask him why he framed me for the patient deaths.'

'I can't emphasise strongly enough how important it is for you to stay away from Dr Mosley,' Partridge says gravely. 'If there are any more complaints from him, we're going to have to bring you in again. Is that clear?'

'Yes,' Carrie says moodily.

I show the detectives out, and when I get back into the living room, Carrie is busying herself tidying up Florence's coloured bricks.

'What the hell was that all about?' I say.

'I'll make us a drink,' she says, letting her arm drop away from stroking Florence's hair. 'Then we can talk properly.'

'There's no milk,' I say. 'And we've nothing in for tea.' I look at her and realise she's exhausted.

'Look, I did see him, OK? But he's lying about me threatening his mum, Alexa. He wants to ruin me and I don't know why. He can say what he likes about me but I can't even speak to him? How is that fair?'

'It isn't fair.' I shrug. Carrie wouldn't threaten someone's elderly mother, that's just absurd. 'But if the rules say you have to stay away from him, you can't flout that, or you'll find yourself in even more bother. And you can't afford for that to happen.'

She hangs her head and nods. 'You're right. I'm sorry, it just adds to the pressure on you too.'

'You go and rest upstairs while Florence and I go to the supermarket and get something nice for tea,' I say. 'How's that sound?'

'You mean you'll go out on your own?'

'Yes,' I say. 'I'm ready to do it. I know I can.'

Carrie looks at Florence, who is now happily crawling half dressed around the living room floor, chattering nonsense to herself. 'I've got a better idea. You go shopping and leave her here with me. We can practise our farm animal noises. What do you say, Florence? Want to play with Auntie Carrie while Mummy pops out?'

Expertly, Florence pushes herself up to sitting and claps her hands in delight, obviously approving of Auntie Carrie's plans.

But Perry has forbidden me to leave Florence alone with Carrie. 'I don't think I should leave Florence here. You look exhausted.'

'Nah, we'll be fine, won't be, chubs?'

Another squeal of approval from Florence.

I stand there dithering. If I leave Florence here I'll be able to get the shopping done in half the time. Plus she gets someone else to play with after being with me all day. I keep thinking about what Perry might say, but he needs to realise that Carrie can still be trusted with our daughter.

'OK, if you're sure.' I take Florence's cheeks in my hands and kiss the top of her head, then, before I can change my mind, I grab my handbag and jacket and leave the house.

It actually feels good, taking control again. As I reverse the car off the drive and turn Heart radio on, I exhale and realise just how much tension I've been holding in my neck and shoulders.

At the end of the road, I slow and indicate to turn right. Three people I don't know, standing in a close group on the street corner, turn to look as I pull up alongside them. They all stare in at me, hungry and wide-eyed. They don't look particularly friendly, and as I pull away, one of them says something and the other two glare harder. Press.

I can't deny that it unnerves me a bit. Maybe they recognise me as Carrie's sister. She's on her own in the house with Florence … I should warn her in case they knock at the door. I call on hands-free, but she doesn't pick up. I try the landline and it goes through to answerphone.

'There are some dodgy-looking people hanging around at the end of the street, Carrie. Make sure all the doors are locked.'

It's in my nature to think of all the bad things that could happen, because that way, I reason to myself, you can keep yourself and the people you love safe by being proactive.

I switch to BBC Radio Nottingham for the four o'clock news. A clammy dread washes over me as the presenter's voice rings out.

'Following on from the internal inquiry into two unexplained deaths at King's Mill Hospital, a source has informed us that a female member of staff has been suspended. The woman, thought to be a senior member of the A&E ward staff, has been arrested pending further police investigations. A spokesman for the hospital board of trustees told BBC Radio Nottingham, "King's Mill Hospital has an excellent safety record and we are well known throughout the country for our first-class patient care. We are determined to fully cooperate with the police investigation into the unexplained deaths but we are unable to comment about individual members of staff at this point in time."'

I slow down and pull into a bus stop lay-by. Our near neigh-bours and people who live in the vicinity all know that Carrie is 'a senior member of the A&E ward staff'. It's only a matter of time before the press get hold of her name, and it will be plastered all over social media well before that. She'll probably have one eye on the news at home too and will be as shocked as I am that the staff suspension has been leaked. Honestly, she must feel like the whole world is against her. Even Dr Mosley is kicking her when she's already down, it seems.

I turn off the radio and focus on my driving. It's been a long time since I've been out in the car on my own. I often drive Carrie and Florence if we go somewhere, but when Perry's home, he seems to do all the driving, which I'm happy with as it's one less thing to worry about.

The car is automatic and shifts smoothly through the gears as I pick up speed a little on the wider roads. I forgot how calming and therapeutic driving alone can feel. The car acts as a barrier to the outside world so I get to be out and about safely yet still see other people and the scenery. With fear always uppermost in my mind, I'd forgotten how much I'd missed this.

I pull up at the perimeter of the car park so that I can log some extra steps on my Fitbit, and use the central pedestrian walkway to head for the shop.

Inside, the supermarket is pleasantly busy. Piped muzak plays and it feels warm and welcoming. I come here often, but it's always with Florence and Carrie or Perry. So even though this environment is familiar, it feels like I'm hitting a personal milestone today.

I glance at the clothing section as I walk in and I'm actually tempted to browse a little, maybe get myself a new top or something. It seems ages since I treated myself.

I feel a bit shaky and I glance down to see my hands clutching the shallow trolley hard enough that my knuckles are white. It's a strange feeling being out on my own, but I keep reminding myself I'm trying to break free of the invisible chains I've wrapped myself in. I'm doing it for Florence, and that's the only thing that matters. I have to trust myself to keep us both safe now.

I carry on walking. I can't spare the time to browse clothing today; I need to get back home to my daughter. I'm feeling increasingly guilty that I've done the one thing Perry made me promise not to do – leaving Florence in Carrie's sole care – plus Carrie and I have got lots more talking to do, especially now the fact that she's been suspended has hit the media.

As I head for the cook-chill aisle, a middle-aged man approaches from the other end and stops to watch me. I feel a familiar rush of agitation, but try and squash it before it can explode and have me abandoning the trolley and heading for the doors. I focus on the array of products on the refrigerator shelves in front of me, but the more I strive to ignore the fact that he's behind me, the more the items morph into a blurry mess in front of my eyes,

I tell myself there are lots of people around. I tell myself I'm quite safe in here. But you hear about predators in shops and bars all the time, don't you? Striking up a conversation, following people out to their cars. Next thing you know, they're outside your house tracking your movements and—

'Oh, there you are, Peter!' I spin around to see a woman walk over to him and put a cauliflower in the shopping basket he's holding. Quite obviously his wife. She looks at my alarmed expression and smiles. 'No rush, love, we'll wait until you've finished.'

They're just waiting to look at the ready meals. That's all it is. He was waiting politely, giving me a bit of space. I don't have to terrorise myself like this anymore. I can choose to stop.

Forcing myself to breathe, I move further down the aisle. I feel like a fool, but there's no harm been done. I've dealt with it and that's what matters. I'm doing OK.

I select a Chinese takeaway bag for two and grab a spring roll and prawn toast selection pack. Not the healthiest choice perhaps, but it'll be tasty and easy to just shove in the oven while I bath Florence and get her ready for bed so Carrie and I can talk.

On the next aisle I pick up milk and some mild cheddar for Florence, who adores cheese with a few peeled chopped grapes. On the way to the checkout, I see that Carrie's favourite Sauvignon

Blanc is on offer, so I put a bottle of that in the trolley too. It won't do us any harm to unwind with a glass later.

It's different being on my own, and now that I've calmed down a bit, it's actually nice! No Florence wriggling and screeching in the trolley, no Perry moaning that he has to get back for the big footie match starting, no Carrie telling me what I should and shouldn't be eating if I want to shed the stubborn half a stone I'm always complaining about.

There's no queue at the checkout and the lady who serves me is pleasant and efficient.

'Ooh, I could just eat that for my tea,' she says as she scans the Chinese food through. 'And I wouldn't mind that bottle of wine either. You've got a good night ahead.'

'I promise I'll only be having a glass, not the whole bottle,' I say, and we laugh. How refreshing just to pass the time of day with someone again!

As I start to pack the items into my canvas shopping bag, my phone rings. I pull it out and see immediately that it's Carrie. She's probably calling to tell me about the news report. I can't answer right now, so I reject the call. A minute later, the phone rings again. This time it's Perry's mobile number.

He must've moved heaven and earth to make a call from the shore, the only place his mobile will work. I think about the strict procedure he'd have had to follow. I can't ignore him again.

I say to the checkout lady, 'I'm so sorry but I have to take this call.'

'No worries, love.'

'Hello? Perry?' Silence on the line. The reception in the harbour area is notoriously temperamental. 'Perry, are you there?'

'Where are *you*?' he says curtly.

I remember the promise I made to him about not leaving Florence alone with Carrie. He can't know I've done just that.

'I'm … at home,' I stammer and the lie is out of my mouth before I can stop it. Taken aback, I immediately trip myself up. 'Well, almost home. I had to pop out and—'

'I told you not to leave Florence with Carrie.' He sounds cold, and I can tell his voice is straining with the effort of keeping calm. I wonder how he's so certain Florence isn't with me.

'Listen, I'm just at the checkout, about to pay. Do you want to hold the line for a couple of minutes?'

'I told you not to leave Florence,' he repeats stonily.

'Florence is fine; stop worrying,' I say, aware that the checkout lady is watching me, waiting for me to complete the transaction. 'Carrie's bearing up well and she offered to—'

'I know exactly what state Carrie is in, because I'm here at the house with her now,' he snaps. 'You'd better get back home as soon as you can; there's something wrong with Florence.'

I drop the carton of milk I'm holding. 'What? What's wrong with her?' Silence. 'How come you're back from Scotland already? Perry?' My voice rings out loud and shrill. 'For God's sake, tell me right now! What's wrong with Florence?'

It's only when I stop shrieking that I realise he's already put the phone down.

32

The checkout operator looks at me as if I've lost the plot when I push my phone and purse back in my handbag and announce that I have to go.

'Sorry,' I wail, leaving a heap of scanned items in the packing area. 'My baby is ill, I have to get back.'

Customers at the surrounding tills stare curiously, nudging each other.

'Would you like us to keep your items until …' Her voice fades into oblivion as I run out of the store to the car park. The fresh air hits my hot face and for a horrible moment I can't remember where I parked.

There's something wrong with Florence.

Each one of Perry's curt, critical words is like a dagger in my heart as I repeat them silently again and again in my head. What did he mean? Is she listless with a temperature? Is she screaming and in obvious pain? Why didn't he explain before he rang off, and what on earth is he doing back from Scotland so early?

I step off the pedestrian path and a car horn beeps furiously, jolting me back into the moment. I meet the eyes of the irate driver, who's had to swerve to avoid me and narrowly missed hitting another passing car. He mouths something I'm glad I can't quite discern, and without responding, I move on, bewildered.

Remembering that I parked way up at the top, I break into a clumsy run. I jump in the car and reverse blindly out, earning myself another prolonged blast of a horn. I ignore it and drive, too fast, out onto the main road.

I told you not to leave Florence.

When I hit the first set of traffic lights, I connect to the car's Bluetooth and call Perry's phone. No answer. I try Carrie and then the landline. No answer from either.

What if the ambulance is there and the paramedics are trying to resuscitate Florence right at this very moment? I grip the steering wheel so hard I fear I might snap it. I feel like I'm going to be sick, and everything I see through the windscreen seems unreal … irrelevant.

What if my baby has a breathing problem? Or she's choked on one of the small model farm animals she's only allowed to use with an adult present? I know Carrie was planning to practise animal sounds with her, and maybe she got distracted by the news report and … Oh God, please no. What if there *is* truth in what the hospital and police are saying about her? What if—

A blaring of horns starts behind me and I realise the traffic lights have turned green while I sit here torturing myself. I put my foot down and drive as fast as I can. I don't care about speeding tickets. I don't care about annoying other drivers. I just care about getting home to my baby.

'Please God,' I pray out loud. 'Please let Florence be OK.'

My top has ridden up, and the bottom of my back is damp and sticky against the faux leather of the car seat. I think about what happened two years ago and swallow down bile. Lightning doesn't strike twice, that's what they say, isn't it?

The rest of the journey is a blur, but somehow I manage it without causing a major accident. There's still a group of people standing on the corner of our street as though they're waiting for someone. I drive straight past them, and as I near the house, I can see there's no ambulance outside. Thank goodness.

But … maybe the ambulance has already left!

I pull up outside the house, two wheels clumsily mounting the pavement, then run inside, shouting out as I burst through the front door.

'Hello?' No one answers. 'Perry? Carrie?'

I rush into the living room, where Perry is cradling a whimpering Florence in his lap and Carrie is standing stock still over by the front window with a sour face and folded arms.

'What is it?' I cry, and as I rush over to my baby, I address Carrie. 'What's happened?'

I bend forward to lift her out of her daddy's arms, but as I do so, Perry turns in a protective gesture, so my outstretched hands can't quite reach our daughter.

'She fell,' Carrie croaks.

'She's really hurt her left arm,' Perry says, sending an accusing glance over at Carrie. 'She can't bear for me to touch it and she keeps rubbing it.'

'Let's see.' I sit down next to him and he allows me to take Florence into my arms. She looks up but barely seems to register it's me. I can see she's in a different place. She's in pain.

'I've called an ambulance,' Perry says grimly. 'We need to make sure she gets properly checked out.'

'An ambulance probably won't arrive for hours for a minor arm injury,' Carrie says in a small voice.

I look over at her. She hasn't moved from the window since I walked in. Wide eyes and hugging herself now. 'What happened, Carrie?'

'Like I just told Perry, we went out into the garden for a little nature hunt. You know, gather a few flowers and leaves to make a picture. But within minutes, that kid next door started up with his drone.' She means our other neighbour's sixteen-year-old grandson. He's a bit of a nuisance with his various pieces of kit, as Perry calls his drone and his model aeroplanes, but he means no harm. Carrie rubs the bridge of her nose. 'I decided to come back in again but Florence started stropping for a little go on the baby swing and I thought it wouldn't hurt as the drone wasn't above our garden or anything. I heard my phone ringing in the kitchen and I thought it might be the hospital or … Anyway, I ran back inside to get it.' She hesitates when I squeeze my eyes shut. 'I know, I know. I shouldn't have left her, but I was gone literally ten seconds, Alexa, I swear to you that's all it was.'

'Ten seconds is all it takes,' Perry hisses behind me.

'And what happened?' I say faintly, cradling my injured daughter as close as I can without adding to her discomfort.

'I was already heading back outside when I heard her scream, and when I got to the kitchen door I could see she was on the floor. I thought I'd strapped her in properly! She was wriggling, but—'

'But you were too busy trying to get to your bloody phone,' Perry says caustically, and I find I can't reprimand him because he's right. Carrie didn't take due care and attention because her damn phone was ringing. She's let Florence down badly.

'She took the weight of the fall on her arm?' There's a floodgate holding back my emotions and I wonder how long it will hold. 'Is it broken?'

'I don't know for sure what happened because I didn't see her fall. She was already … she'd already fallen out when I got to the door. But I had a little look at her arm when I picked her up and I think it might just be badly sprained.'

'Jeez, she must have come a real cropper,' Perry snaps. 'There's a bruise there already, look.' Gently he pushes up Florence's sleeve and shows me an angry blue-black shadow on her upper arm.

My heart seems to fold in on itself and I let out an involuntary sob.

'Alexa, you know how much I adore Florence. I love her so much.' Carrie's voice shakes with emotion. She lets her arms fall to her sides and walks over to us. I look up and see a desperation to be forgiven on her wet face, her eyes pink and swollen. 'I'd do anything to keep her safe. I—'

'You didn't, though, did you? You didn't keep her safe at all!' Perry stands up and Carrie instantly shrinks back, intimidated. 'Is that what happened to the poor baby at the hospital?'

'Perry, please don't!' I wail, and Florence jumps, alert and startled in my arms. She starts to properly cry. 'Just sit down. Please.'

Perry seems to realise what he's just said and he does sit down. Elbows on his knees, he pushes his face into his hands and lets out a long, weary sigh.

'Alexa, I think you're better taking Florence to A&E,' Carrie says gently. 'She needs her arm looking at as soon as possible.'

'She's right, Perry,' I say. 'We could take her there now and she'll be seen much quicker than waiting here for the ambulance.'

'She's better waiting here at home than in some packed A&E department, not to mention one her auntie has just been suspended from,' Perry says firmly, as if there's no discussion to be had.

Carrie seems to shrink into herself and Perry looks resolved.

I look at my baby's face. Her cheeks are red and blotchy and her eyes half open as she quietly cries. She looks so sorry for herself, and sleepy. I don't like the look of her; she could have hit her head when she fell. It might not just be her arm that's hurt.

But the A&E department that Carrie is under investigation at … I can't think of a worse destination. But really, who cares about any of that? Florence is the priority here, not what people might say, or how they might stare at us there.

A dull thud starts inside my skull as a debate rages in my head. I'm Florence's mother and it's down to me to do what I think is best for her. I don't need my husband or my sister to make the final decision on whether we take her to King's Mill Hospital.

'I'm taking her in,' I say, and stand up. They both look at me in surprise and I get ready to tackle their objections, but there aren't any.

Perry takes Florence from me while I fish for the car keys in my handbag. He turns to Carrie as she takes a step forward, his voice cold. 'I think, under the circumstances, it's best you stay here.'

She nods and steps back to the window again. And this time I say nothing.

A couple of minutes later, we're in the car and heading for the hospital. Perry drives and I sit in the back next to Florence in her car seat, holding her hot little hand and trying to soothe her the best I can. It's only a ten-minute drive, but as soon as we get properly moving, Florence starts crying and then screeching.

'Her arm is obviously really hurting her,' Perry says through gritted teeth as he negotiates the roads like a Formula 1 driver. 'I bloody well told you not to leave her on her own with Carrie. I had a feeling something like this might happen.'

'Just drive carefully, Perry. We don't want to add a car accident to the list of things going wrong.'

I talk to Florence in gentle soothing tones, and after a few minutes, thoroughly exhausted, she quietens down. I feel so disappointed in myself for leaving her with Carrie. It would never have happened if there had been two of us to supervise her out in the garden.

But I'm not going to start apologising and telling Perry he's right. Not this time. I had no way of knowing this would happen; nobody could have. Since we bought the swing in early spring, Carrie must have strapped Florence safely into it a hundred times or more. I did nothing wrong in trusting her to look after my daughter while I popped to the supermarket. Or at least I thought I didn't.

The thoughts start whizzing around my head until I can barely think straight.

Perry falls into a moody silence and I know he's biding his time, waiting to have a proper go at me when we get back. I can sense the fury bubbling away behind his expression of grim concern, the tight mask he's donned to get him through the visit to the hospital.

When we finally get there, park up and carry a now sleeping Florence in, still in her car seat, my heart sinks. The A&E waiting area is crammed, just like Perry feared. There aren't even two vacant seats together. Perry gives our details at the desk and I sit down with Florence on my knee. She chooses that exact moment to wake and begin screaming and thrashing around. This exacerbates her sore arm and her screams seem to get louder and louder. My skull is soon thumping along in perfect synchronicity with her yells of protest and frustration.

The people nearest to us shrink away. I receive sympathetic glances, frowns and tuts of disapproval and ignore them all. After ten minutes of continuous screeching, a healthcare assistant walks over and says something to Perry. He nods and she discreetly beckons me with her head, leading us down a corridor to a small treatment room.

'You can wait in here; it's cooler and quieter for her. The nurse should be with you in five or ten minutes.'

I feel relieved there's no recognition on her face. It's not surprising really; I hardly know any of Carrie's shift colleagues. With the different surname, there's no reason anyone will recognise us.

Florence calms down almost immediately and Perry takes her from me while I reach for her free-flow cup out of the changing bag and give her a little water.

'I don't need to tell you how serious this is, Alexa,' he says, stroking Florence's forehead as she sips the drink. 'Something really bad could have happened. As it is, she might've broken her arm, despite what Carrie says. How do you think that will look?'

I close my eyes and try not to think about Amanda Botha and the social services assessment that Perry is still unaware of.

'I just popped out to the supermarket,' I say. 'It wasn't as if I left her with Carrie for hours on end.'

'I understand that,' he says, looking as if he can't grasp my attitude at all. 'But this can't go on. Surely you know that? Carrie shouldn't be anywhere near our family home while all this stuff is happening.'

I take the cup from Florence and stare at Perry.

'Carrie's her auntie and she's looked after Florence all her life. Whatever the hospital board and the police say she's done has no bearing on her love for Florence. She'd never hurt her and nothing you can say will change my mind.'

But even as I say the words, a tiny sly part of me is thinking *what if* … I feel an absolute witch for even allowing the thought to enter my head, but what if Carrie has got something to do with those two deaths at this hospital? What if I'm fighting my husband to keep someone in the house who is a danger to my daughter?

I look at the medical trolley in the corner of the small room, laden with surgical bandages, plasters, antiseptic and cotton wool. Materials stacked and ready for patching people up, putting right accidents caused by ignorance and a failure to take proper care and attention. Accidents can be patched up, but it could have been so much worse. I could have allowed something tragic to happen to my child all for the sake of getting in something nice for tea.

What if something terrible happens to Florence in the future and I find myself looking back at this very moment? Today. Right now. Is it possible I might recall how easily I could have made a different choice, to move from backing Carrie to taking heed of what Perry was trying to get through to me? Will I be haunted about how easily I could have avoided tragedy in these crucial moments of decision-making?

Perry hands Florence her favourite rattling toy and looks at me. He seems to sense I'm in turmoil inside.

'Look, I know this isn't the time or the place to tell you, but … the stuff Carrie told us about her marriage to Cameron? It was all lies, Alexa. She did some terrible things to him: threatened to electrocute him in the bath, slashed his suits and—'

'What are you saying?' My body floods with damp sweat as Florence shakes the rattle with her good hand. Again and again until I feel like my head is full of dried seeds. 'Who told you this stuff?'

'I went for a drink with Cameron when they first split up.' He puts his hands up when my face floods with colour. 'I knew you wouldn't approve, but it was just a drink, that's all. To draw a line under everything.'

'I can't believe you did that after everything he did to her. Don't you dare tell me he's the victim in what happened, because I absolutely don't want to hear it.'

'I'm not saying that. But you should know that it wasn't just him that did stuff. She very conveniently left out the details of her own craziness.'

'Just leave it. Please. We're not here to analyse Carrie's marriage.'

He shuts up immediately and we sit in terse silence. Questions begin to flood into my head then. What if Perry is right? What if my sister is unstable and everyone can see it but me? What if Carrie has a severe mental illness I don't know about? Confused and racked with guilt, I try and push the doubts away. How could I even think such things about my own sister, and after everything she's done for me?

The door opens and Roisin Kenny walks in.

She freezes for a second in the doorway, stares first at Perry and then me. To her credit, she quickly clicks back into work mode and smiles at Florence.

'How are you both? OK I hope?'

It's a statement rather than a genuine question. Her manner is professional but brisk. She looks on edge.

After placing a folder on the table, she crouches down next to Perry so she's on Florence's level. She has delicate features and she smells faintly of a pleasant floral fragrance.

'Oh dear, have we been in the wars, Florence?'

'It's her arm, Roisin. She … fell out of a swing and hurt herself.'

Perry throws me a look and I clamp my mouth shut.

Roisin leafs through the folder and takes out a piece of paper. She studies what's printed on there for a moment before laying it back on the desk, face down.

'Let's take a little look, shall we then, Florence?'

I take the rattle and Florence snuggles into Perry's side. Roisin moves closer to Perry and his face colours slightly. After a few moments, Florence allows Roisin to gently touch her hand. When she presses her upper arm, she flinches and cries out.

'Do you know how she fell out of the swing and exactly how she landed?'

I shake my head. Roisin raises her eyebrows and looks at Perry as if she knows this is not the case.

'We weren't home when it happened,' he says, and far from responding from a place of spite, he sounds beaten and tired. 'I came home just minutes afterwards.'

'I see,' Roisin says. 'So who was looking after Florence at the time?'

For an instant the world seems to stop. Perry is looking at me; Roisin is looking at me. Even little Florence fixes her big blue trusting eyes on me. If I could say I was with Florence when it happened, there would be no awkward questions asked. Usually I'd never try and cover for my sister over something serious like this, but she's at an enormous disadvantage. Because of the hospital's allegations against her, people are bound to jump to conclusions. But Roisin is her *friend*. Surely Roisin knows Carrie is innocent of the charges made against her.

But it's wishful thinking even if it had occurred to me before we checked in at the A&E desk. I can't say I was there because Perry knows. And now he's blabbed it out to the Roisin.

'Alexa?' His voice cuts into my thoughts. 'You're being spoken to.'

'Sorry!' I look at Roisin.

'I have to ask who was looking after Florence if you weren't there. It would be useful to ask them exactly what happened.'

Her face looks taut and slightly hostile when she turns to look at me. She knows full well Carrie lives with us. Is she forcing me to name her?

'It was my sister, Carrie. You know … Florence's auntie,' I say unnecessarily. 'But she told us exactly what happened. She thought she'd strapped Florence into her baby swing, and she'd just run inside for her phone when Florence must've slipped and fell out. When Carrie came back outside, Florence was already on the floor.'

Roisin nods slowly and I get the impression she's studying me … my expression. I feel like I have to elaborate further. 'I mean, Carrie wanted to come to the clinic, but we told her to stay at home. I could call her if—'

'We might need you to do that, yes, but I'll take a look at Florence first.' She turns to Perry. 'Could you possibly remove Florence's top and vest, please, Perry?'

Her clear green eyes fix on to his and he looks away and starts to pull clumsily at the neck of Florence's stripy top.

It's no surprise when our daughter kicks off, screeching and wriggling for England. I help Perry get the top off and then slip off her vest. Her beautiful smooth little torso looks so exposed, I want to wrap her up again, but then I see the nasty bruise on the inside of her arm, such a dramatic contrast to the rest of her unblemished white skin. 'Oh,' I gasp, pressing my fingertips to my mouth.

It's blossomed horribly since I first saw it at the house and is now a swollen mass of red and purple. I look at Perry and he too is staring at it, his face pale and tight. But thankfully he keeps a lid on the thoughts about Carrie that I know are playing constantly in his head.

'Remove her leggings too, please,' Roisin says. 'Just leave her nappy on.'

Is it my imagination, or is she acting a lot cooler than when we started?

'I'm afraid it's going to be a little uncomfortable for her,' she says. 'Don't worry if she's vocal; I'm not causing any further damage to her arm. I'll be as careful as I possibly can.'

She presses down gently, easing the tiny swollen limb slightly forwards and backwards. Florence shouts, squeals and yelps, but she isn't hysterical. 'Such a brave little girl,' I croon softly into her ear.

Roisin checks her head, pushing her hair aside so she can determine if there's any swelling or bruising there, I presume.

'Doesn't look like she hit her head in the fall,' she murmurs, and I breathe a sigh of relief.

Then she does something strange. Using the pads of her fingers, she traces methodically up and down Florence's torso and down each leg, pressing gently. She asks Perry to turn her over and examines every inch of her back, bottom and legs, even wiggling each tiny toe and finally her fingers.

Seemingly satisfied, she sits back and turns over the sheet of paper, and I feel reassured that she's at least given Florence a really thorough examination. A bubble of emotion bursts up from my throat.

'You know Carrie better than most people, Roisin,' I blurt out. 'You know she wouldn't hurt Florence.'

'I'm sorry, but I'm not allowed to discuss it, Alexa,' she says coolly, referring to her paperwork. 'Right, I think Florence's arm might be fractured, but she'll need an X-ray just to be on the safe side.' She pauses and glances at us both in turn. 'If you stay put, I'll get the ball rolling and send someone through to collect you when we're ready. Perry, while Alexa stays with Florence, could I trouble you to sign some paperwork in the other office?'

'Sure.' Perry stands up and brushes down his jeans.

'What happens with a fracture?' I say as they head towards the door. 'Will it heal fully, or might she have problems with it as she gets older?'

'Let's wait for the X-ray results, shall we? A doctor will take a look and come here to speak to you about it.'

Roisin turns and wiggles her fingers goodbye to Florence.

I glance up as they leave the room and catch Roisin looking back over her shoulder at me. I smile, but it isn't returned.

33

Almost as soon as Perry has left, a healthcare assistant comes to escort us to Florence's X-ray in a room at the end of the corridor.

It's a quick procedure and apart from the odd spurt of crying when the radiographer has to place her arm in a certain position, Florence is really brave.

When we're back in the small room again, I sit with Florence on my knee, gently rocking and reassuring her.

I think about texting Carrie to give her an update but to be honest, I don't know everything yet myself and I can't help feeling a bit resentful towards her. After all, she's the reason we're here. My phone is in my handbag and I've no wish to start looking at it.

Perry comes back in after about ten minutes.

'You've been gone a while,' I say.

'I used the bathroom. Is that OK?'

He sits, moodily scrolling through his phone. It's obvious he still hasn't forgiven me for leaving Florence alone with Carrie.

'What did you have to sign?' I ask him, jiggling a colourful teething toy in front of a disinterested Florence.

'Just something reception should have asked me to sign when we arrived,' he says without taking his eyes from his phone screen.

'Did you … say anything to Roisin? Did she ask about Carrie at all?'

'No and no. She's made it quite clear she's not allowed to discuss it.'

I sigh. We can't go on like this.

'I know what you think about Florence's arm, but give me some credit, will you? I know my own sister.' I keep my voice low just in case the walls in the clinic are paper thin.

'You keep saying that, but you didn't know about the problems she was having at work, did you? She kept all that very well hidden.' He glances at an incoming text, then pushes his phone into his pocket and runs his fingers through his short, gelled hair. 'Look, Alexa, I'm not saying that Carrie is a monster. What I *am* saying is that she might be teetering on the edge of something we're not aware of at the moment. She might not be in her right mind. We just don't know. All this stress would get to anyone, right?'

He's right about the stress thing, but I'm not about to agree with him.

'The stuff Cameron said … it's really serious, Alexa. She could have *killed* him in that bath!'

'Oh for goodness' sake, he's probably just saying that for effect!' I snap, thinking about the police visit to Carrie earlier that I won't be sharing with him. 'The day I start believing anything that comes out of that lying rat's mouth is the day I might as well give up.'

He shakes his head as if I'm a hopeless case.

'Stressed or not, Carrie will cope far better with what's happening with the support of her family. Florence will comfort her, distract her from what's happening. I can't just take that away from her; it could send her right over that edge you're talking about.'

But he's having none of it.

'Which is worse in your opinion? Carrie slightly more stressed, or the possibility that Florence is in danger?' His expression is one of frozen determination. 'We're waiting in a clinic for an X-ray to see how badly our daughter's arm is injured after she was left in the care of a woman accused of two unexplained deaths.' His face looks like it's etched in granite. He is utterly convinced he's right to the exclusion of any other possibility, and frankly, I don't know why I'm wasting my breath.

'If you can't put up with it, why don't you …' My words fade out as I speak without thinking.

'Why don't I what?' He sits up a bit straighter.

I grit my teeth and turn away from him. I wish he'd just go back to Aberdeen. He should never have turned up here without giving me prior warning. I can't stand this stress on top of everything else that's happening.

I change tack. 'All this bickering between us, Perry … it's killing me! I need your support. Carrie needs your support.'

I lower Florence back into her car seat and pop her dummy in.

'*Florence* needs my support!' He gives a heavy sigh. 'You and Carrie both have my support, Alexa, and I think you know that deep down. But it's simple: she can't stay in the family home. Not until this case is properly resolved, and as far as I understand it, that could be weeks … months even. We *have* to put Florence first.'

'I always put Florence first, but Carrie would never hurt her.'

'Florence *is* hurt and it happened on Carrie's watch.' He turns in his chair, his expression grave. 'Carrie has been arrested for two unexplained deaths and one of those victims was a *baby*. We'd be guilty of wilful neglect, having known that, if something happens to Florence. Jeez! Wake up, Alexa.' He bangs the heel of his hand on the desk and Florence stirs in her sleep.

'But Carrie didn't do anything!' I cry, and immediately clamp my hand over my mouth, but of course, it's too late. I pray the people waiting outside didn't hear us barking at each other. I bring my voice level down. 'Carrie is the victim in all this; she had nothing to do with the hospital deaths.'

Florence opens her eyes and looks around the strange room with a bewildered expression. Her bottom lip wobbles.

'Come on, sweetie. Come to Mummy.' I reach down and pick her out of the car seat, cradling her in my arms.

'Say what you like, but I'm telling you this. Hospitals don't just suspend people over the natural deaths of patients. The police don't begin a criminal investigation unless there's good reason for it.' I feel myself close off to what I know on one level is perfectly logical reasoning, but on another, assumptions I simply cannot accept about my own sister. 'Hopefully Carrie will be cleared of any wrongdoing, but until that time comes, we have to be sensible and put Florence's safety first.'

'There's no *hopefully* about it, Perry. Carrie is innocent. If *we* don't believe that, who will?'

Perry doesn't reply, merely raises an eyebrow. We sit in silence a while longer. Florence starts making little mewing sounds to comfort herself as she lies listlessly in my arms.

I think about all the other people working on Carrie's ward. All people who probably had contact with those patients but haven't had their lives ruined like she has.

Perry stands up and stretches. 'Christ. How much longer are we going to be stuck in this shoebox?'

I glance at my watch. We've been waiting for twenty minutes to hear about the X-ray. I jut out my bottom lip and blow air up onto my face. 'It's so hot in here,' I complain.

Perry reaches over to the wall to turn on a fan. He presses a button and cool air soothes me.

'Thanks,' I say.

'Welcome,' he replies dully, sitting down again.

What has happened to us? How on earth am I going to tell Perry about the social services assessment? I close my eyes and allow the fan to blow away my thoughts for a few moments before I have another go at convincing him.

'She's always been there for me through thick and thin,' I say quietly. Call me stupid, but I have to try and make him see. 'She's never let me down, even in my very darkest times.'

'I'm not disputing that, Alexa,' he sighs. 'I know she supported you fantastically when you needed it most. But that's irrelevant when it comes to her current situation. It's Florence's safety that's paramount, not repaying your sister's loyalty.'

He reaches out to touch my arm, and before I can stop myself, I stiffen. Wordlessly he removes his hand. It's a long time since we've felt a real emotional closeness, longer since we last made love. It didn't happen overnight; drifting apart has been a long process. We've had stuff to deal with, Florence coming along after such a terrible ordeal and then Carrie moving in with us. Often, if Florence is off-colour or a bit fractious, it's just been more practical for Perry to sleep in the spare room. He sometimes snores, and if I'm really tired, I might suggest we sleep separately so he's not constantly waking me and I'm not constantly prodding him to change his sleeping position.

Sleeping apart probably happens more times than I've realised. I don't know.

Perry's talking again. He's returned to his 'Carrie is cracking up' theory.

'I mean, look at the state she got herself into when her marriage broke down and she discovered all the debt Cameron had apparently left her in. How long was she off work with anxiety and depression? Nearly two months! And according to Cameron, *she* was the one who wanted a lifestyle they couldn't afford and bought more and more on credit.'

'According to Cameron?' I glare at him. It was actually six weeks she was off work, and any normal person would have been completely crushed after what she had been through. Her husband betrayed her in the cruellest way and ruined her financially too, and nothing Perry can say will change that fact.

'I told you, I went for a drink with him when they split up, OK? I got on well with the guy, so shoot me.' He glares at me, silently daring me to challenge him.

I open my mouth to do just that, but he's already off on his rant again.

'At least acknowledge the fact that Carrie has been under massive strain in her job, pressure we didn't even know about. Nobody's saying she's killed anyone on purpose, but she might have made errors, and she clearly doesn't confide in you about everything. Remember that.'

I can feel my temper rising into my throat and I swallow it down and speak normally.

'So you're basically saying she's guilty as charged, even though she *hasn't* been charged precisely because there's not enough evidence?'

'No, that's not what I mean. Don't put words in my mouth. She's been arrested and suspended and that's bad enough.' He leans forward and strokes Florence's hair and I see that her eyes are nearly closed again. All the upset has exhausted her. Exhausted me too. 'I don't know what happened on that ward, Alexa, and if you're honest, neither do you. But I'll tell you one thing I'm certain of: the hospital board and the police have to be accountable for their actions and decisions, and I'm sure they must have *some* evidence or information to back up what they've done so far. Agreed?'

He's trying to trick me into saying there's at least a possibility Carrie has done wrong. We don't generally argue an awful lot – probably due to the fact that he's away working for long periods at a time – but when we do, he often waits for me to become flustered and then bulldozes me into saying something damning that he can throw at me after the event.

But I've got used to his tricks.

'All I know is that Carrie's told me she's innocent, and that's enough for me.'

He makes a disparaging noise. 'Well then you're a fool.'

'Don't you dare speak to me like—'

'You're a fool because you won't even consider there may be a risk to Florence, and as her father, I find that unforgivable.'

Stalemate. We glare at each other.

The door opens without warning and Roisin Kenny steps into the room. I smile with relief that things are moving again.

'Have you got her X-ray results?' I ask hopefully.

She doesn't answer but stands back as another person appears in the doorway. A short woman with a now not-so-friendly face stands there, her brow furrowed with concern.

Perry looks at her and then back at me. I stare open-mouthed at the door.

'Who's this?' he asks, clearly fed up of getting the silent treatment.

I say nothing. I can't. Instead, I lower my eyes to the floor, dreading the moment the woman opens her mouth and gives me an enormous problem.

'Hello, Mr Ford, pleased to meet you at last. I'm Amanda Botha, Florence's social worker.'

Perry jumps to his feet, ignoring her outstretched hand. 'What?'

She turns to me and waits a second until I'm forced to meet her eye. 'Hello again, Alexa.'

34

Perry appears to have been struck mute. His face is puce and he's actually trembling as he continues to stare at Amanda Botha. I decide it's best not to look at him as I try and work my way out of an impossible situation.

'I'm sorry,' I say, and it sounds pathetic even to me. 'With coming straight here from the supermarket, I didn't have a chance to tell you. I only met Amanda this morning. She came to the house to explain—'

'She's been to our *house*?' He's incredulous and his arms look tense and awkward, held straight at his sides as they are. 'I'm Florence's father. I should have been told about this.' His voice quivers with emotion, and I want to crawl away and hide.

'I suppose this is down to you?' I glare at Roisin. 'Call yourself a friend of my sister and then you—'

Amanda Botha shakes her head. 'When you registered Florence's details at the desk, I received a direct alert. Our computerised systems are all linked to aid multi-agency efficiency. Nurse Kenny had nothing to do with it.'

'Are you allowed to do that?' I frown. 'Sounds a bit dodgy data-protection-wise. A bit Big Brother.'

Behind Amanda, Roisin leaves the room and quietly closes the door behind her.

'Oh, well done, Alexa,' Perry murmurs under his breath.

'One of the forms you signed gave us permission to collaborate with other agencies, Alexa,' Amanda states simply.

I signed everything she put in front of me without reading a thing. I just wanted to get rid of her. The copies of the documents were still in my bedside drawer, untouched since her visit. I look down at my sleeping baby, tears pricking my eyes.

Amanda walks towards us and addresses Perry directly. 'I'm happy to answer any questions you might have, Mr Ford. I was under the impression you were working away in Scotland and that your wife had told you about my house visit. Let's sit down, shall we?' She plants herself on a chair and I do the same, but Perry remains standing. 'We've been contacted by a member of the public concerned about Florence's welfare in light of Carrie Parsons' suspension from King's Mill Hospital. Alexa has agreed to us visiting your home and speaking to various individuals in order to conduct an assessment of your circumstances. This will enable us to ascertain whether Florence is at risk.'

Perry shakes his head. 'There's no assessment required. I don't want social services in the house.'

'I'm afraid we're required by law to carry out an assessment in these circumstances. It's better you agree to it, otherwise we will have to take action to force the issue.'

'Who *is* this member of the public?' I demand, so that Perry understands I'm with him on this point. 'Anyone could do that out of spite; it's ridiculous that you'd just take their word for it.'

Perry sits down. He looks dazed.

'How is Florence?' Amanda asks.

'Florence is fine,' I say tersely. 'She's been very upset and so it's knocked her out.'

Amanda pulls a large notebook from her bag and rests it on her knee.

'Can I ask what happened to her? How she injured her arm?'

My heart is thumping, my cheeks burning. I'm exhibiting all the signs of guilt. I have nothing to feel guilty for, but somehow I feel I have to try and protect Carrie. But Perry speaks up before I can stop him.

'I flew back home from Aberdeen earlier today and discovered Carrie alone in the house with Florence. I—'

'I can tell Amanda what happened, Perry,' I say, throwing him a look. I wish again that he'd stayed in bloody Scotland.

'But you weren't there, Alexa. You were at the supermarket.' He's playing hardball. He's not giving me an inch in which to defend Carrie.

Amanda chips in. 'It would be really helpful, Mr Ford—'

'Perry.'

'Thank you. It would be helpful, Perry, if you could tell me exactly what you found when you got back to the house.'

'I didn't bother telling Alexa I was on my way home early; I just got a cab from the airport. When I walked in the front door, I heard Florence screaming. Carrie was trying to soothe her but Florence wasn't having any of it. She was far too upset.'

Amanda writes something down on a fresh page of her notebook.

'Just to confirm, Florence was already injured when you got to the house?'

He nods. 'I took her from Carrie straight away and demanded to know what had happened. She said the two of them had been out in the garden and Florence wanted to go in the baby swing. Carrie strapped her in but then heard her phone ringing and realised she'd left it in the kitchen.'

'She ran back inside to get it and was gone all of ten seconds,' I add. 'While she was inside, Florence must have wriggled her way out of the swing and fallen to the ground.'

Amanda looks up from her notes. 'Did Carrie actually see Florence fall from the swing?'

'She says not. When she came back out of the kitchen, she said Florence was already on the ground.'

Amanda scribbles away. 'And what happened then, Perry?'

'Like I said, I took Florence and she stopped crying so hard. It was like she didn't want to be held by Carrie.'

'You don't know that, Perry,' I counter quickly. Trust him to embellish the facts. Doesn't he understand that social services are like terriers once they have a scent that something is wrong? This isn't the way to play it at all.

'I know she calmed down after a few minutes when I held her.' Perry shoots me down and addresses Amanda again. 'When I touched her arm, she squealed in pain, and then I knew she'd been injured.'

Perry's face darkens and it feels to me like he's trying to portray the situation as negatively as possible. *She'd been injured.* She fell out of the swing. It was an accident! Yes, Carrie made an error of judgement in running to get her phone, but the circumstances were hardly normal. She was worried it was an important call from her solicitor or the hospital, or even the police.

Perry wants Carrie out of the house so badly he'll do his level best to portray her in a bad light any chance he gets. Ironically, he doesn't seem to realise he's making it sound as if Florence is at constant risk in her own home.

'We haven't been told much about her arm apart from that it's probably fractured,' I say, not giving him a chance to put his foot in it again. 'We're still waiting for the X-ray results.'

'Well, it *is* fractured.' Amanda looks up from her notes. 'The doctor has viewed the X-ray – you'll have a chance to speak to her before you go – and has diagnosed a spiral fracture. This particular injury is referred to informally as a "toddler fracture" in pre-school children.'

'Poor darling,' I say, looking at Florence.

Amanda pulls out a piece of paper from between the pages of her notebook and regards us both before reading out loud from it. '"A spiral fracture is consistent with a child's arm being twisted or pulled hard. It is often seen in the case of non-accidental injuries in young children."'

'Christ almighty!' Perry growls.

'What are you saying?' I whisper, my voice almost inaudible. I'm dreading her reply, but I have to know. I have to hear her say it.

'I'm saying that as neither of you saw the accident actually happen, and in the unusual circumstances of your sister being under arrest and caring for Florence, we can't completely rule out that the injury wasn't inflicted on purpose.'

'That's preposterous,' I say, pressing my throat with my fingers as if I'm scared what might come out. 'Carrie would never hurt Florence. *Never.*'

Amanda raises a hand to calm me down. 'I understand how you feel, Alexa, and I'm not saying that's what *did* happen. But given that none of us was there at the time of the accident, I'm obliged to flag up the possibility.'

'Exactly. Which means you don't know either way.'

'So what will happen now?' Perry sounds nervous.

'Florence's assessment is now being given the highest priority. We've already rescheduled and will be starting it tomorrow.'

35

The police station

Adam Partridge's phone rang in the incident room.

'Roisin Kenny here to see you, Adam,' the desk clerk said brusquely.

Adam stood up and called over to the other side of the office. 'Nell?' He beckoned her, grabbing his jacket from the back of the chair and slipping it on.

'You look pleased.' Nell sniffed. 'Saskia agreed to let you rub her feet tonight, has she?'

He gave her a caustic smile. 'You really are hilarious, Nell, but this is even better. Roisin Kenny's here.'

Nell raised an eyebrow. 'That's good timing with the alert that's just come in about Florence being seen at A&E.'

Adam nodded. 'We'll have to speak to the hospital directly about that one due to data protection but Roisin can certainly answer some of the other questions we have.'

As they walked down the corridor, Nell sorted through the sheaf of notes she'd scooped off the desk on her way out of the office. 'So, Roisin Kenny has been appointed acting ward manager in Carrie Parsons' absence. She's job-sharing with Marcia Hunt.'

'What's interesting is that Roisin and Marcia were Parsons' two closest colleagues on the ward.' Adam straightened his tie and smoothed his quiff with a careful hand. 'She seemed very tetchy about that during her interview.'

'When I rang Roisin Kenny to ask her to come down and make a statement, she told me she'd had no contact with Parsons since she was suspended.'

'To be fair, we did ask the hospital staff not to contact her.'

'True enough. But if you're really good friends with someone, that would be quite difficult to adhere to, I'd imagine.' Nell paused. 'Something about the way Roisin said it made me think that the dynamics might have changed in their relationship.'

Adam pulled the corners of his mouth down, interested. 'Well, now's our chance to find out. We'll record the interview so the conversation flows rather than stopping and starting to write it down. You can transcribe later and get her to sign the statement,' he said, and opened the door to the foyer, where Roisin Kenny sat waiting, staring blankly at the wall.

In the interview room, Nell did the honours with the recording while Adam sat back in his chair and studied Roisin.

She was a slim, striking woman with pale freckled skin and green eyes. Adam knew from her staff record that she had turned forty earlier that year. She wore her dark red hair pulled back in a tight bun. When she unbuttoned her mac he saw her hospital lanyard was still in place and she wore a thin grey cardigan over her blue nurse's uniform.

She caught Adam's eye and she said tightly, 'I've come here straight from my shift. My last patient was little Florence Ford but I'm guessing you already know about her A&E visit.'

'We've received the alert,' Adam confirmed grimly. 'We'll be contacting the hospital about that in due course.'

Roisin gave a curt nod. It was clear she didn't want to be there, but there was an officious manner about her that seemed to suggest she liked to do things properly and by the book. He'd imagine she was doing a reasonable job as Carrie's replacement.

'We appreciate you coming in, Ms Kenny. We wanted to talk to you about the initial police interview you had at King's Mill Hospital on Wednesday the fifteenth of April,' he began. 'You were asked some questions then about your colleague, Carrie Parsons, and I'd like to revisit one or two of your answers.'

Nell consulted her paperwork. 'So, the first thing was that you said Carrie had made a couple of mistakes with patients' medication the Sunday before?'

'Yes. She brought out the wrong type of painkiller, and if I remember correctly, she got mixed up with the beta blockers.'

'And this was on Sunday the twelfth of April?' Nell clarified.

'Yes.'

'Beta blockers. Now they're used to treat heart conditions, is that right?' Adam said.

'That's right. Conditions such as angina, atrial fibrillation and high blood pressure,' Roisin said. 'There are different types depending on the patient's symptoms.'

'Could the wrong type of beta blocker cause a heart attack?'

Roisin shook her head. 'They're normally used to *treat* heart attacks. I've never heard of them causing one, although they can have unpleasant side effects.'

'Angus Titchford died of cardiac complications,' Adam stated.

'Yes, but I didn't attend to Mr Titchford on that day; I was looking after other patients.'

'Are you aware of who *was* attending to him?' Nell asked.

'I believe it was Carrie Parsons,' Roisin said.

Nell picked up her sheet of notes again. 'You also mentioned in your initial interview that Carrie Parsons relieved you of your monitoring duties of Samina Khalil on the twenty-seventh of December last year.'

'Correct. I'd initially been assigned to carry out Samina's general monitoring; that's taking her blood pressure and temperature and overseeing her drip.'

'But Carrie Parsons moved you from those duties?'

'Yes. She asked me to do the medicine trolley run and she took over the monitoring of Samina.'

'That seems a strange swap of duties when Carrie was the senior member of staff,' Adam remarked. 'You'd think she could find something more important to do.'

Roisin shrugged. 'That's Carrie for you. Since she found out her ex-husband is getting remarried, she's been unpredictable and moody. We never know how she's going to be on any given shift; we're all fed up of it.'

Adam sat up a bit straighter. 'This was something new, was it? She got moodier after discovering her ex had been carrying on with her old school friend, which was …'

'About four months ago,' Nell provided, after checking her notes.

Roisin nodded. 'In my opinion she got much worse then, yes. We used to be really good friends, saw each other after work for the odd drink or maybe an exercise class, but … well, she stopped doing all that when her marriage first fell apart. She only wanted to do things with Alexa and her niece, Florence.'

'And what about Perry, her brother-in-law … do he and Carrie get on, do you know?'

Roisin laughed. 'I'd like to say they do, but basically they can't stand each other. Well, that's what Carrie used to tell me, anyway. She'd often say life was so much better when he was working away. But I know Perry and he's a lovely guy, so I took what she said with a pinch of salt.'

'Just out of interest, would you say Carrie and Alexa's relationship is unusually close?'

'Oh, definitely. Carrie told me they were always really close growing up, and it's really ramped up a notch since … since Alexa's personal problems. So for the last couple of years.'

'When you say "Alexa's personal problems", can you clarify what you mean?' Adam pressed her.

Roisin looked at Nell and then back to Adam as if she was trying to gauge how much they knew. She sighed and folded her arms.

'I think you'd better ask Alexa that. It's not really for me to say.'

Adam leaned forward on the desk. 'Now that sounds interesting. If you know anything about the family, anything that could be relevant, it would be an enormous help if you could enlighten us, Nurse Kenny.'

Roisin thought for a few moments as if considering her options. Then she took a deep breath and began to speak.

When she'd finished, the two detectives turned to look at each other and Adam let out a low whistle.

'Bloody hell!' he murmured. 'I wasn't expecting *that*.'

36

Alexa

We wait at the hospital for another hour while they put a cast on Florence's tiny injured arm.

Perry is finding lots of excuses to keep away from me. Making the odd phone call, tapping out texts, getting coffee or fresh air … I'm dreading the journey home, wedged together in the car.

'If we're lucky, she won't need an operation,' the doctor tells us just before we leave. 'With a spiral fracture, we find the younger a child is, the quicker they tend to heal. Bring her back in a week to see how the fracture is mending.' Again Perry falls completely mute, and I can feel renewed fury over what's happened rolling off him in waves.

We get back to the car and the silence between us is like a toxic glue that keeps us from communicating. For a full five minutes neither of us speaks a word.

Florence is asleep in her car seat, her arm in its white cast secured across her narrow chest. My entire body is racked with guilt at seeing my baby in this state. I feel so bad I wasn't home when it happened. But equally, I can't feel malice towards Carrie. It was a spur-of-the-moment response to run inside to get her phone, one I can understand under the circumstances. She'd never have done it if she'd known what would happen. I'd probably have done exactly the same thing. Perry too, if he'd only be big enough to admit it.

Nevertheless, I feel really bad that he had to find out about social services' involvement by Amanda Botha turning up unannounced. She was so friendly this morning, but now I feel like she's been deliberately sneaky and her friendly support was just a smokescreen to get me to sign their invasive assessment paperwork without making any fuss.

'I'm sorry I didn't tell you about social services,' I say quietly, seized by a sudden bolt of remorse. 'Somebody's out to make trouble for us. That's all it is. Amanda says the assessment could be over really quickly if we cooperate.'

His head whips round long enough to issue an outraged glare at me before he turns back to the road. 'Sometimes I'm staggered at your naïvety, Alexa,' he says with barely concealed distaste. 'Someone may well be out to make trouble for us, but the *real* reason they're sticking their nose into our lives is because your sister has been accused of killing people and it's plastered all over the internet. The exact same sister who's sleeping in the room next door to our one-year-old child.'

I gasp. 'Carrie has not *killed* anyone!' Just that word is shocking. It cannot and shouldn't be applied to the flimsy accusation against my sister.

'Call it what you like. We hadn't got a clue two patients had died on her watch under suspicious circumstances, because she never breathed a word to us about them. On both those days she came home as usual, had her tea and said nothing, like it had just been a normal day.'

'She didn't want to worry me, Perry.' It might sound pathetic to him, but I believe it to be true.

'She's brainwashed you, Alexa, and you're the only person who can't see it!' He raises his voice and bangs the steering wheel with the heel of his hand. I look back to check on Florence, but she's still

sleeping soundly. 'Imagine this was another family on the news …
you'd be shouting, "Wake up, you idiots!" at the television.' He pauses
a moment as if he's grappling with his anger. 'You have to refocus.
This is not about your relationship with your sister; it's about our
daughter. It's our job to keep Florence safe and protect her however
uncomfortable that makes us feel. However hard it is to do.'

I take in his beetled eyebrows, the thin, colourless lips, his
cheeks flushed with ill-disguised rage, and for a brief moment I
actually despise him. For a few seconds I even consider screaming
at him, 'I've got an idea: why don't you leave me and Carrie and
Florence to work this out together? We don't need you!'

Instead I say calmly, 'Do you really think I could sleep at night
if I thought Florence was in any danger? Do you think I'd let Carrie
live with us if I had the slightest doubts about her?' The car slows
and stops outside the house. I see a man and a woman walking
towards us, but no one else is around. No gaggle of reporters. 'I'm
Florence's mother, for goodness' sake!'

Perry turns in his seat and stares straight at me. 'And I'm her
father. Do you really think I can let you carry on putting our
daughter in danger like this? Do you actually realise that social
services have the power to take her away from us?' His voice wavers
slightly but his tone is firm and unerring. 'Carrie can't stay here,
Alexa, and if you don't tell her to go, I will.'

Inside the house, it's quiet. Carrie's boots and handbag are in the
hallway, so I figure she must be up in her bedroom. Since all this
trouble started, she doesn't seem to stay downstairs for any length
of time. I can't imagine what's happening inside her head: a terrible
mix of fear, anger and worry, I should think.

Perry carries Florence inside still sleeping in her car seat and
sets her down on the kitchen floor. We both visibly jump when
the doorbell rings a moment later.

'That's all we need,' I sigh, pressing the heel of my hand against my forehead. 'I can't face seeing anyone at the moment.'

'I'll get it.' Perry walks into the hallway.

'Whoever it is, just send them away,' I say, following him. 'This isn't the time for visitors.'

I hang back in the alcove under the stairs while Perry opens the door. I can't see any faces but I can see two sets of jeans-clad legs.

'Mr Ford?'

'Yes?' I can hear the suspicion in his short reply.

I hear some mumbled names that I can't quite catch. 'We're from the *Sentinel* and we want to speak to you about the accusations against your sister-in-law, Carrie Parsons.'

'Not interested.'

I dig my teeth into my knuckle. Even though she's not been officially named by the hospital, the press have obviously worked out Carrie is the suspended member of staff now, and they know she lives here. It was only a matter of time.

As Perry begins to close the door, one of the reporters puts a booted foot out to stop it closing completely. I take a step towards them and realise it's the couple I saw when we parked.

'Perry, this is your chance to tell your family's story,' the woman calls out. 'There's a lot of negative press breaking and we can help—'

'Move your foot or I'll do it for you,' Perry growls, and a moment later the door slams shut.

I rush forward and look out of the hall window at the retreating journalists. There's another figure loitering across the road. It's the woman with the stringy brown hair. I turn to Perry.

'Soon as those journalists are safely down the road I'm going out to speak to that woman.'

'What woman?' He looks out of the window and peers at her. 'Who is she?'

'I don't know but I don't think she's press. I've seen her out there before … she looks, I don't know, sort of *lost*.'

Perry shakes his head but says nothing. I know he's thinking I'm naïve again. Too trusting by far and I suppose he might be right.

A minute or so later I open the front door, check the reporters are definitely gone and then dash down the driveway. The woman is startled when she sees me and I witness the split-second dithering I know so well. She looks around, wondering whether to dart away.

'Hello,' I say, not too friendly but not challenging. 'What is it you want? I've seen you before, waiting around out here.'

'I … is your sister home?' she says, looking across at the house.

I swallow. 'She might be. Do you know her?'

'Yes … well, I know all *about* her.' She presses her lips together. 'I need to speak to her.'

She can't be press; she looks far too nervy.

'You said you knew her … but then you said you knew *about* her,' I say, hoping to encourage her to start talking. 'Which is it?'

'Could you ask her to come outside for a minute?' she says, staring at the house and ignoring my question.

'Look, I'm not being funny but I don't know who you are. You might be a reporter, or—'

'I'm not.'

'But how do *I* know that? I'm not asking Carrie to come out here for you to start asking her about the hospital case.'

'It *is* about the hospital case but' – she looks up the street – 'not in the way you think.' Her words emerge softer this time and her eyes darken as her attention is taken by something else. I follow her stare and see a silver car cruise slowly past the top of the road. And then suddenly she's moving. Walking briskly away in the opposite direction.

'Hey, hold on!' I call out. 'Tell me what it's about and I'll—'

'Sorry, I've got to go. Tell Carrie I want to speak to her … please tell her!'

'But what's your na—' I stop calling abruptly as she breaks into a run and swiftly moves out of earshot.

I should just discount her as some eccentric woman who's just interested in getting involved in all the drama but I can't. There's something about her that makes me want to know more.

'What was all that about?' Perry cranes his neck out of the door to look down the street when I get back inside. 'Who is she?'

'I don't know but she wants to speak to Carrie about the hospital case.'

'Ha! Don't they all.'

'No, she's not press.'

He looks at me. 'Then who is she?'

'I don't know and now she's just run off.' I slip off my ankle boots again.

Perry shuts the front door. 'You shouldn't give people like that the time of day.'

'How did those two reporters know your name?' My entire body pulses with adrenaline after my encounter with the woman. 'How come every man and his dog seem to know where we live and who we are?'

Perry makes a disparaging noise. 'You just don't get it, do you? Don't you realise how they work? This is just the start of it,' he says darkly, his eyes flicking to the door. 'They'll know everything about us soon. The second Carrie is formally charged, our lives will be plastered all over the internet to be judged by strangers who've never even seen us in the flesh. They'll dig up everything they can get their ruthless hands on, and I mean *everything*.'

I give an involuntary shiver, realising the implication behind his words. Our personal, private business … and Perry seems so certain that Carrie *will* be formally charged with the deaths. I put my hand on the wall to steady myself. I can do this. I can get through it.

'I only want to protect you, you know that, don't you? Going out and speaking to strangers like that woman … it's got to stop.' Perry places his strong, firm hands on my shoulders and looks into my eyes. 'The reason they're all coming here is simple. It's Carrie they're interested in and that's why she has to move out, *now*. There really is no other choice if we want to keep Florence safe. If she goes, we won't have this problem.'

'I don't need you to tell me what to do, Perry,' I say, shrugging out of his grip and taking a step back. 'I can look after myself and my daughter just fine.'

'*Our* daughter,' he says, narrowing his eyes before turning and walking away.

37

As Perry stands and stares morosely out of the kitchen window, I unstrap a still sleeping Florence from her car seat and, being careful not to knock her arm, carry her into the living room to lie her on the sofa. She stirs slightly, lets out a tiny whimper and then sinks back into rest.

I hear the stairs creak, and moments later Carrie appears in the doorway. I press my finger to my lips.

'How is she? Did they – oh my!' She creeps over to Florence and clamps her hand over her mouth, staring at the cast on her niece's arm in disbelief. Her eyes brim and she shakes her head. 'I'll never forgive myself for this. Never.'

'Carrie, don't. It could've happened to any one of us,' I say gently. 'Roisin took care of her at the hospital.'

She looks up, startled. 'Really? Did she say anything about me? Send a message?'

'Sorry, no. I did try to bring the conversation around to you but she said she's not allowed to discuss the case.'

Carrie pulls a face. 'Sounds like Roisin. Probably frightened of tripping herself up or saying something she shouldn't.'

I hear Perry sniff at the doorway and turn around to see his flinty eyes watching us, his mouth stretched tight. If he truly thinks Carrie is this good an actress then he's deluding himself. I'm relieved when he turns silently away and walks back into the kitchen.

I close the living room door and perch on the edge of a sofa cushion. Carrie sits on the chair and folds her hands between her knees, rocking back and forth.

'Did you hear those people at the door?' I ask her. 'They were reporters from the *Sentinel*.'

She drops her head and nods.

'There's someone else that's been hanging around. A woman, looks to be in her mid-twenties with long, lank brown hair. She's a scraggy thing, like she lives on her nerves. Have you seen her?'

Carrie hesitates and for a second, I think she's going to say she *has* seen the woman. But then she pulls down the corners of her mouth and shakes her head.

'I've seen her hanging around outside the house before,' I continue. 'When Perry just got rid of the reporters I saw her again, across the street. I ran over to ask what she wanted and she asked me if I could bring you outside to talk to her.'

'She'll just be another one of the jackals who are after a story. The ones posting lie after lie about me online.' When she looks at me again, I see her face is grey and her eyes look haunted.

'Hmm. She could be but … there's just something about her. Something that tells me she's not after a story like the others. Anyway, if I see her again, I'll give you a shout.'

'I'm so sorry about what happened with Florence, Alexa,' Carrie blurts out. 'I'm sorry that this is affecting you and Perry. I can see how furious he is with you for supporting me,' she whispers.

'Take no notice of that,' I say. 'I'll deal with Perry.'

She regards me doubtfully before speaking again. 'If I had the money I'd move out tomorrow. I feel like everyone but you already thinks I'm guilty, even though I haven't even been charged.'

'Well, people have no right to think that,' I say. 'The truth will out, that's what I say.'

She looks unconvinced, but nods. A tear slides down her cheek. I walk over, take her hand and sit on the arm of her chair.

'The police seem to be gunning for me with a vengeance they don't have for anybody else who works there. I read online that they're interviewing some of the hospital staff again. Somebody there's got an axe to grind against me but I haven't a clue why.'

'Maybe the police have realised they're going after the wrong person and that's why they're interviewing people again?' I say hopefully, but she shakes her head.

'It didn't read like that. It sounded as if it's all in connection with "the suspended member of staff". *Moi*.'

'Anyone can write this stuff on social media, Carrie. It's all fake news.' My nostrils flare with indignation. 'You're a sitting duck at the moment, just waiting to be charged. We can't go on like this; it's time to fight back.'

Carrie lets out a hollow laugh. 'Fight back *how* exactly? The hospital and the police think I'm guilty, and now the press do too … I'm starting to think the charges can't come quickly enough, because at least then I'll be away from it all. And you three will be able to get on with your lives.'

'This is not like you, Carrie! You can't give up.'

She looks at me but her eyes are dull and distant. It feels like someone took my confident and capable sister, who always takes charge of a situation, who always knows what to do in a crisis, and replaced her with … well, with someone like *me*. A ditherer, someone who expects the worst and acts like a kicked dog around authority.

'It's not a case of giving up,' she says quietly. 'It's a case of knowing when you're beaten. And right now, I definitely feel beaten.'

'I think that's a natural reaction. But indulge me.' She looks at me blankly. 'How many staff work on your shift? Is it reasonable to say that any one of them could be to blame?'

She sighs. 'There are a good few, but to be fair, only a handful have the authority to get up close and personal with the patients and administer medical treatment. And two of those are my closest work friends, so it's not as possible as you might think.'

'Marcia and Roisin,' I say, and she nods glumly.

'I know how this sounds, Carrie, but is there any chance at all that either one of those two could have—'

'No,' she says, cutting me off. 'I'd trust them both with my life. We've worked together for years, as you know. I was at nursing college with Roisin.' Her face darkens. 'We're not as close as we used to be, granted, and I'm not keen on some of her life choices, but over the years we've both gone above and beyond, on occasion, in order to save lives. This inquiry is an insult to the whole shift.'

'That doctor … the whistle-blower …'

'Nathan Mosley,' she provides. 'He just reported the deaths. He thinks they're suspicious, and I suppose, if he really believes that, then he did the right thing. He did what you're meant to do.'

'But he's only a junior doctor, right? What if he got it wrong?'

'That's what they're investigating now. They're going back years and combing the patient death records. They're also looking into the two deaths and … everything that entails.'

I nod, showing that I know what she's referring to. The first death, the baby, happened four months ago. The press have reported possible plans to exhume her body. I shudder and glance again at Florence sleeping peacefully.

'Do you think Dr Mosley suspected you from the start?'

'I don't know. He had no reason to, and the police didn't say that he'd mentioned me.'

'So what *did* the police say, Carrie? They must've given you some evidence … solid reasons to explain why they arrested you. They don't carry out house searches unless they believe they'll find something; that's the only way they'd get a warrant, and we still haven't heard if they found what they were looking for. You seem to think Dr Mosley has acted reasonably, but if that's the case, why did you go to see him?'

I see her start to close down in front of me. She folds her arms and tucks her chin down towards her chest, and for the first time, doubt flashes through my head. Why would she act like this if she's innocent? The instant this occurs to me I reject it, unable to handle the feelings that stir inside me.

It's just the stress tightening its grip, that's all it is.

Carrie is thoughtful for a few moments before she speaks. 'There was some circumstantial evidence and someone on the shift had made a comment about me ...'

'What circumstantial evidence?'

'Oh, just about who did what. I got someone's medication wrong which really isn't that big a deal on a busy ward.'

'And what did your colleague say about you?'

She sighs and shakes her head. 'I'd been in the interview for what seemed like ages. I can't remember everything.'

'It's vital you tell me all the facts, Carrie. Look, can I come with you to see the solicitor? I know it's easy to forget the detail when you're stressed. If I know the facts, then I can—'

'Thanks for the offer, but you don't have to get involved,' she says. 'I know Perry won't like it.'

'I don't care what Perry thinks! We have to fight back. In my view, you're making it all too easy for them to pin the blame on you.'

I want to shake her, make her stand up and fight for her innocence. It's the strangest thing, like our personalities have been switched. I'm the sister who's taking control, who isn't afraid to face the enemy. It feels odd but empowering.

With each minute that passes, my conviction grows that maybe we can do something. The police seem focused on Carrie being the culprit, but we can try and find out the facts ourselves. Carrie might not be allowed to speak to her colleagues, but *I* can. I'm not an employee of the hospital. I'm not under arrest.

It occurs to me then that I don't actually need Carrie's permission to do it. She's worrying about the effect all this will have on me and what Perry will say about it. That's not important to me right now.

I feel stronger than I've done for years and I'm determined to fight not only for my sister, but for my family. If I can uncover something that helps to prove Carrie's innocence, then finally Perry will see he's been wrong all along. And our life can get back to some normality.

Carrie yawns. 'I think I might just take myself off up to bed,' she says. I nod and don't challenge her. She places a gentle kiss on Florence's head and lays her hand briefly on my shoulder as she heads for the door.

As soon as she has gone, Perry appears again, looking grim.

'I've just had a text,' he says, pressing his fingers to his forehead. 'It's Ade, my boss. He's got a real crisis going on up on the rig and he's asked if I can go back up there just for two days.' He shakes his head. 'It's typical, but one of the worst scenarios has happened – a full borehole collapse. It's dangerous for the men and could threaten the whole operation. I'd refuse to help out, but … with the promotion and everything, I—'

My heart flutters. 'It's fine, Perry. You go.'

He holds his hands out as if to show he's not hiding anything. 'I'll be back again on Monday, but I feel bad leaving you like this with everything that's happening. The social services assessment and—'

'It's fine,' I say again, relieved that this work emergency has somehow enabled us to talk again. 'In some ways having fewer people around here might be better with tensions running so high, if you know what I mean.'

He nods. 'It'll give you a chance to speak to Carrie about moving out, too.'

I blink. 'When do you have to go?'

'There's a flight at four thirty tomorrow morning from Birmingham.' He sighs. 'Ade's waiting to hear back from me whether I can make it up there that quick.'

'Do it,' I say. 'Get it over with, and hopefully a few things might resolve themselves while you're away.'

'Thanks,' he says bashfully, as if he's thinking about our earlier disagreements. 'I know things are tough for you right now, and this is yet another thing we could do without.' I expect him to leave the room then, but he doesn't. 'We don't talk about *us* much, I know. But I do care, you know. I wish things were different, Alexa. I'm guilty of neglecting you and I'm ashamed of—'

'Perry, I know. We're both to blame in different ways.'

He's standing so close I can smell the orange and bergamot aftershave he applied this morning. I wonder fleetingly if we can recapture some of our emotional closeness when all this is over, or if it's too late for us. Either still seems possible, but at least I know now he's not happy to just let our relationship slide into oblivion.

He squeezes my hand and kisses me on the cheek.

'Thanks for understanding but the same rule still applies, Alexa. Under no circumstances must you leave Florence alone with Carrie.'

He holds my stare until I feel forced to give him a curt nod and then he goes back upstairs to pack.

Perry being away for two days will give me a chance to speak to a few of Carrie's colleagues and try to get a picture of what happened on that ward. I feel hopeful, confident and determined that I can do this.

As far as I'm concerned, my husband's trip back to Aberdeen could not come at a better time.

Perry wakes me leaving for the airport at one o'clock.

He slides carefully out of bed and I can tell he's trying to move around lightly, but I've been awake on and off since getting into bed at about nine. We decided on an early night after all the drama of the day and the news of Perry's early-morning flight, but Florence has been restless, waking twice already. I gave her the pain relief the clinic prescribed at about 11.30 and I'm praying that might last her a few more hours before the next dose is due.

'I've agreed with Ade I can call you later today,' Perry whispers when he sees my eyelids flutter. 'To check how Florence's arm is and also to find out how the social services assessment goes, although I obviously haven't mentioned that detail to him.'

'OK.' I yawn, my stomach turning at the mere mention of social services. 'Hope you get the borehole problem sorted.'

'Well I'll be back in two days whether it's sorted or not,' he says firmly and kisses my cheek. 'Text you when I land.'

When I hear him leave, I tiptoe downstairs and make myself a cup of tea to take back up to bed. On my way back, I push open Florence's door just to check she's not lying awkwardly on her arm. A shadowy figure bending over her cot jumps back as I shriek, spilling hot tea down my dressing gown and over my hand.

'Carrie!' I gasp when she spins around, pressing her index finger to her mouth. 'What are you doing in here?'

She steps back from the cot and I see Florence stirring, but mercifully she adjusts her position slightly and seems to settle again.

'Just checking on her!' Carrie presses a flat hand to her chest. 'You scared the life out of me. I heard Perry leave and thought you were fast asleep in bed.'

'Are you OK?' I peer closer in the half-light from the illuminated landing. She looks like a rabbit that's been caught in headlights. She obviously didn't hear me creeping about downstairs in the kitchen. 'It looked like you were going to lift Florence out of bed.'

'What? Not at all. I was just checking she wasn't in any pain.'

We both know Florence would let the whole house know if she was in pain, but I let it go. Maybe Carrie is still feeling guilty about what happened in the garden and just wanted to make sure she was OK.

'I gave her some medication just before midnight,' I say. 'So she should sleep for a bit longer.'

Carrie walks past me to the door. 'I'll leave you to it then,' she says lightly. 'Night, Alexa.'

38

I can't sleep. At all.

I'm swamped by awful thoughts, problems that seem to grow bigger every minute I lie here staring into the dark. What is it about the early hours that magnifies everything that's bad and swells it until your head is on the verge of bursting?

Everything I've done for the past year to keep my baby safe, almost smothering her in the process because I feared letting go even slightly, and *still* this has happened. She's injured and the authorities are suspicious that she isn't safe here, in her own home, with the people who love her most in the world.

The thing that tortures me most is that it's my fault it happened. I decided to leave Carrie alone with Florence when she's quite obviously distracted and trying to get through the worst time in her life. I put doing the food shopping ahead of keeping safe the most precious thing in my life.

But of course, this is not the first time I've been in this situation …

I turn my head and look longingly at the headache tablets and the day-old glass of water on the bedside table. I have some stronger medication tucked away at the back of the bathroom cabinet. It's probably out of date now, but who cares? If it still works half as well, I'll be much improved. 'Magic tablets' I used to call them, with the power to wrap me in a bubble and temporarily numb the pain.

As I lie there in the darkened room, that two-year-old buried pain slices through me, as devastating and agonising as any knife. And I remember. I remember how I grabbed blindly to anything that could lessen it. Prescription drugs, alcohol, days spent in bed lurching between the pain of wakefulness and the shallow, anxious half sleep that was almost worse. I don't want to return to those dark, dark days.

Yet as I lie here, that old pain is just as terrible as it was back then. In fact, it seems even bigger, stronger somehow. It fills up my insides, swelling and seeping into every pore. It's pain that has grown too big to be hidden away any more.

I curl up into a ball on my side and a long, low groan escapes my lips.

'My baby,' I whisper, the pillow already wet beneath my cheek.

I feel the pain, endure its sharp edge as it rushes through me like a scythe. This pain is bright, cobalt blue shot through with blood red. It's vibrant and still brand new and it's almost a relief to let it come.

I don't know how long I lie there, my eyes screwed shut, holding my breath as long as I can. But the bright colours are muted now, the sharp pain reduced to a dull, thudding ache that throbs from my head to my feet.

I know then that I have to tell Perry the truth of what happened that day. Despite everything else that's happening, he has a right to know.

'It's my fault,' I'll tell him when he comes home. 'It's all my fault that Daisy Mae died.'

39

2018

My newborn daughter was so perfect. Seven pounds two ounces of perfection. I held her in my arms straight after delivery and looked down into her blue eyes, and I thought, *This is it. This is the happiest moment of my life.*

That moment turned into minutes and hours and days, and still I couldn't believe I had her in my arms.

Daisy Mae came two weeks early, while Perry was still working his final week on the rig before coming home for the birth. So Carrie ended up as my birthing partner and she couldn't have been more brilliant, although, just like when we were kids growing up, a bit of work was needed on her bedside manner. Everything that came out of her mouth was an order: 'Breathe, Alexa, breathe!' or 'Push, push now!'

'I'm not a midwife; I think I did quite well considering,' she protested when we had a good laugh about it afterwards.

Daisy Mae was born without drama, even though my labour was long. She had a head of fine, downy dark blonde hair with a hint of russet. She was perfect in every single way.

At the time, Carrie lived in a brand-new house in the next town with Cameron. She confided later that her marriage was already in trouble, but her commitment to me was unwavering. She took two weeks' holiday from work and came over every single day. She'd get to us about nine and sometimes, depending on how Daisy Mae was feeding, she'd stay until seven or eight in the evening.

'We can manage the baby ourselves now, can't we?' Perry grumbled after a while. 'It would be nice to spend a bit of time alone together when Daisy Mae sleeps.'

That was the problem, though: Daisy Mae hardly slept at all. Day after day, week after week … it really got to me. I'd already be shattered by the time Carrie arrived in the morning, and Daisy Mae would be screaming her head off, her face and body hot and red like a little skinned rabbit.

Perry took a week off work, but the time seemed to whizz by. To be honest, it was a relief when he went back to the rig, because I felt unable to deal with the unspoken animosity between him and Carrie on top of the horrible, burgeoning feeling of doom that I hadn't told anyone about.

I didn't know what was wrong with me. The pile of mother-and-baby magazines at the side of my bed largely featured perfectly groomed, radiant mothers and their adorable, peachy-skinned cherubs who lay peacefully in their baskets and stared adoringly up at them with big blue eyes.

I didn't match the pictures and I knew this wasn't how a new mother should be feeling, so I just kept smiling. I smiled when people from my old job at the college called round with thoughtfully chosen cards and presents, I smiled when I took Daisy Mae out in her pushchair and old ladies stopped to declare she was the prettiest baby they'd ever laid eyes on.

When Perry telephoned home from the rig every day, a special perk for new fathers, I smiled as I spoke into the phone so he wouldn't sense the dark misery that lurked inside of me. And most of all, I positively beamed when the health visitor called round and made notes on how Daisy Mae and I were doing.

The only person who knew that smile wasn't real was Carrie. And after a couple of months, it was Carrie who forced me out of bed to get showered and dressed and personally delivered me to the doctor's surgery.

'A textbook case of postnatal depression,' the GP said cheerfully as she tapped at her keyboard. 'These will soon have you feeling better. You'll feel brighter, better able to cope, even on the worst days.' She printed off the prescription and signed it, explaining how and when to take the concoction of medications. There seemed to me to be quite a list of them back then but on reflection it was probably only two or three. 'Come back and see me in six weeks,' she added as I left the surgery.

What she didn't mention was that it would take four to six weeks for the drugs to take effect.

If she'd told me that, things might've been different.

Four weeks and two days after my initial doctor's appointment, I'd had a particularly bad night. I was alone in the house and Daisy Mae had woken each and every hour. I changed her, tried unsuccessfully to feed her, held her, sang to her … but nothing worked.

We both fell asleep in the chair as dawn started to break, her soft, warm body cradled in my arms. We slept for a couple of hours like that until she woke at 5.30.

It's hard to say this now but I remember looking down at her and feeling nothing. Three months ago, I'd thanked my lucky stars to be blessed with the gift of a healthy beautiful baby girl. Our lives were complete; Perry and I were a family. Now when I looked at her she felt to me like a changeling child, not like my own flesh and blood at all. I just couldn't control my dark, illogical thoughts; it was as if they had a life of their own.

Had someone swapped my baby for this one in the hospital and that was why she wouldn't settle with me? That russet shade in her hair … neither Perry nor I had even a hint of that colour. What if … what if my real baby was somewhere else this very moment, in someone else's house?

I couldn't cope with the thoughts. I set Daisy Mae down in her cot and went downstairs, where I took an extra tablet. I could hear her screaming and I turned off the baby monitor but I didn't go back up. I made a coffee and then couldn't face it, so I poured it down the sink.

I sat at the table and cradled my head in my hands. I could still hear Daisy Mae crying, so I got up and turned the radio on, increasing the volume until I couldn't hear her at all. Then I curled up on my side on the small sofa in the kitchen, pushed in some earplugs I found in the drawer and fell deeply asleep.

I woke up to Carrie shaking me roughly.

'Alexa, wake up!' she shouted above the music on the radio. I opened my eyes. 'Wake up, for God's sake! Where's the baby? Where's Daisy Mae?' She looked frantically around the room.

'She's … she's upstairs in her cot,' I said, sitting bolt upright and then jumping to my feet so fast I felt dizzy and had to hold onto the worktop. 'She was crying. I couldn't stand it.'

Wordlessly Carrie rushed past me, out of the kitchen and upstairs. I broke into a run and followed her.

'She's been awake all night. I just … I just needed a short rest, but I fell asleep!'

On the landing, Carrie rushed into the baby's bedroom, but I hung back. It was strangely silent up there … too silent. I leaned against the cool wall and closed my eyes.

I convulsed as Carrie let out a strangled cry then started to whimper, calling out Daisy Mae's name again and again. She stumbled out of the room carrying my tiny daughter, her niece, pale and limp in her arms, and stood there in the doorway, her mouth braced in a silent scream.

Dreamlike, I tiptoed over to the two of them and touched my daughter's face. Her skin felt cool like alabaster. Her lips were tinged with blue.

'She's gone, Alexa. She's … gone,' Carrie whispered, her voice catching in her throat.

I felt sure I could hear the ticking of my bedroom clock, the walls of the house creaking and straining, the roof beginning to crumble.

'The house!' I cried out. 'It's about to fall down. Run!'

I rushed outside into the garden. It was cold and raining and I was shivering all over.

When I looked down, I only had my pyjama top on, with my knickers. I ran back inside and closed the door. Carrie was still standing in the bedroom doorway, holding the baby, tears rolling down her cheeks.

'If we get her warm again, she might still be OK,' I told her.

'Alexa. We need to call an ambulance,' Carrie whispered. 'Your baby is … she's gone.'

But she wasn't gone, she was there. Right in front of me.

'I'll make up a bottle,' I said, turning away.

Much later, I don't know how long afterwards, Carrie told me a story.

'So let's go through this once more. Daisy Mae was restless in the night and you sat up with her and tried everything to calm her, didn't you?'

'Yes,' I said.

'Eventually you both fell asleep in the nursery chair and she was still sleeping soundly when you put her back in her cot and came downstairs. That's right, isn't it?'

'Yes,' I said.

'You fell asleep too, and when you woke up you went upstairs to get her and you found her floppy and listless. I came round to visit and found you here in the kitchen, holding her. Yes?'

'Yes,' I said.

'Good. Now, tell me the story back.'

It took half a dozen tries, but eventually I got it and could relate it flawlessly and by rote. In my head I called it 'The Story of How Daisy Mae Died'. I told it to the ambulance driver and the doctor. I told it to Perry, and most of all I kept telling it to myself. Again and again and again.

Daisy Mae's cause of death was recorded as Sudden Infant Death Syndrome. Cot death. Afterwards, I couldn't stop thinking how she suffered from blocked sinuses, which could have exacerbated matters and could have contributed to her breathing difficulties.

I've tried not to think what might have happened if I'd brought her downstairs instead of leaving her to sob.

Every single morning I battle with the question that's waiting for me as soon as I open my eyes to start the day: Is it my fault my baby died?

40

It's 6.30 when I hear Florence grizzling, properly awake now. I sit up, push off the quilt and sit on the side of the bed for a few seconds until I feel fully awake again. What a night.

I was up another couple of times in the early hours with her. I gave her another dose of painkiller the second time, and mercifully, she went back to sleep.

Swirling images of shadowy figures in her bedroom have haunted me most of the night. In my last dream, I walked in and Carrie was there, smiling down on my baby, but the next time I looked it wasn't Carrie at all but a slavering demon with sharp teeth, about to pluck her out of her cot and take a bite. Me and my hyperactive imagination.

I shake the last remnants of dream fear off and pick up my phone. There's a text from Perry telling me he's landed at Aberdeen airport. My guts feel like liquid when I revisit my decision to tell him about how I feel I'm to blame for Daisy Mae's death.

I've pushed her death away for so long, burying the guilt and horror of the memory deeper and deeper and yet still it resurfaces every single day, colouring my mothering of Florence. Robbing me of joy. Even though the thought of truly facing the past terrifies me, I know I can't ignore it any longer.

Florence seems to sense I'm awake and ramps up her yelling.

I've already got the beginnings of what promises to be a banging headache, partly through reliving that old guilt and partly from the numerous worries stacking up in my head: whether Florence's arm will heal without an operation, Carrie's arrest and possible charge, the social services assessment today and Perry's increasing anger about my sister still being in the house. The worst thing is, I can't see instant solutions for any of them.

I walk onto the landing and look at Carrie's bedroom door. Usually, on the rare occasions I sleep a bit later, she is in Florence's room like a shot when she wakes up, picking her up and sometimes even taking her into her bed to play and to give me an extra half an hour. But her door is firmly closed, so it looks like it's all down to me this morning.

'Hello, beautiful!' I walk in and open the curtains and Florence manages a small bounce, but she's definitely subdued compared to the normal bright smile she greets me with. She looks hot and she thrashes around, her good hand gravitating to the cast again and again as she grumbles softly. She's obviously in some discomfort.

It makes me want to cry when I see her cast. It must have been so painful and frightening for her when she fell, and although Carrie would have been there in an instant, it wasn't the same as Mummy being there to comfort her.

I lift her gently out of the cot and smother her with kisses. She looks down at her arm as if she's wondering where the plaster cast came from.

'Let's go and see Auntie Carrie, shall we?'

She flaps her good arm half-heartedly as we walk next door. Usually she'd be chanting her version of Carrie's name – 'CaCa … CaCa …' – but she's a bit grumpier this morning.

I tap on Carrie's bedroom door and wait for an invite.

'Good morning, Auntie Carrie, can we come in?' There's no response, so I push the door open. 'We came to say hello, didn't we, Florence? And we wondered if Auntie Sleepyhead would like a nice cup of …'

The curtains are closed and the bed is unmade, but there's no Carrie here. It's still only 6.40; where can she have gone so early? I wonder.

I carry Florence down to the kitchen, looking around for a scribbled note, but there's nothing. Carrie knows Amanda Botha is carrying out her assessment this afternoon, so maybe she's made herself scarce because of that, but it doesn't make sense that she'd have rushed off so early, and without speaking to me first.

I gingerly put Florence in her walker, not sure if it's going to be possible for her to use it. Luckily, the rigid cast sits just above the tray, but I'm still nervous she's going to catch it and cause herself more pain. I walk slowly to the front door so Florence can follow me. Usually she'd be barrelling along, yelling happily. But today she's much quieter, seems more cautious.

Carrie's warm jacket has gone, and her ankle boots. Maybe she's just headed out for a walk to clear her head; that makes more sense. She doesn't say much about how she's feeling – she's always been the same – but she must be feeling the pressure. She's a pariah at the hospital, with nobody contacting her now she's been suspended, and my heart goes out to her.

I make coffee and cut some pieces of apple and mango and chop a few grapes for Florence's breakfast. I lift her out of her walker and lower her gently into her high chair. Usually she wriggles as I'm trying to get her in there, making it a difficult task, but today her chubby little legs just dangle passively. She loves to feed herself with finger food and usually objects to any attempts to help her, but today she seems to realise she's less able.

I sit next to her and drink my coffee, oohing and aahing at how clever she is at using her left hand to pick up the fruit. When she's either eaten or squashed the fruit pieces, I spoon-feed her a mini-size fruit yogurt.

It's hardly a surprise that I can't stomach any breakfast myself. Much to Florence's loud consternation, I wipe her face and hands and slot her into her walker again. Every time I see that cast, my heart aches. I'm so proud she's taking it all in her stride.

She's a bit more needy, I think, and a little grouchier than usual. The doctor at the clinic told me to give her a dose of Calpol if I think her arm is hurting her, but I decide not to do that so early in the day.

As I fill her cup with water, I catch sight of the calendar on the wall and remember something useful. Carrie used to keep her shift rotas for coming months on her laptop diary. She got the laptop out of my car boot a day or so ago, and if I can get into it, that will tell me when her colleagues will be at the hospital. The shift rotas are worked by the whole team for a block of time, and then they change to another shift pattern after a couple of months. That way all the shifts get to vary their work pattern and share the awkward times fairly. Before the inquiry, Carrie was on what she called the 'nice shift', working nine until five each day.

Gently I pick Florence out of her walker again. She looks at me as if I'm mad.

'Sorry, pumpkin. Mummy's messing you about a bit, isn't she?' She grins and lets out an ear-piercing squeal. It's a good sign. 'I know it's sneaky, but we're going to have a poke around in Auntie Carrie's bedroom. You won't tell her, will you?'

'CaCa … CaCa!' Florence yells as I carry her upstairs.

Sneaky is right, but what choice have I got? I'm doing this for Carrie's own good as well as mine. I tried to reason with her yesterday about speaking to her colleagues, trying to get an overview of what happened on the ward, but she seemed so closed to the possibility and was quite negative. That's my justification for getting the information I need from her laptop, and while I'm at it, I'll see if there's a record of Roisin and Marcia's home addresses.

I sit Florence on the floor and close the door so she can't escape onto the landing. Even with her injured arm I'm sure she'd find a way. I toss her a couple of soft toys that Carrie keeps on her bed and she seems quite happy playing with the rabbit I bought Carrie last Christmas from her niece.

I open the laptop and immediately hit a numerical pad asking for the password. I enter Carrie's date of birth and it rejects that. I feel certain it must be Florence's date of birth, but that's rejected too. I bite my lip and think.

'What could it be, Florence?'

She looks up at me wide-eyed, busily chewing the rabbit's ear. I reach down and touch her soft downy hair, let my fingers linger over her peachy cheek. And then another date of birth comes to me. I tap it in and feel a chill in my bones as the computer unlocks.

I close my eyes and for a few moments I remember her.

My beautiful girl, Daisy Mae Ford.

Carrie is quite organised with her computerised files. She's one of those sorts of people who can't bear for her emails to stack up. While my unopened emails are left sloppily somewhere in the region of 1,500, Carrie has to open and either reply, file or delete as soon as she can get to them.

So I'm not surprised when I see a clearly marked icon on her desktop that says *Shift rotas*. I open it up and scan down the dates. I can see that if she hadn't been suspended, she'd have remained on the nine-to-five shift pattern until the middle of next month. That suits me perfectly, because it means that if I get to the hospital for about 8.30 this morning and hang around the entrance, I should catch her colleagues coming into work. It's also convenient because I will get back home in good time for Amanda Botha's visit at 2 p.m.

I close the rota spreadsheet and, seeing no need to hunt for Roisin and Marcia's addresses now I know when they'll be working, am closing the laptop lid when the icon below the shift rotas catches my eye.

I bend forward and squint at it: *Mosley.*

Isn't that the name of the doctor who reported the deaths and started up this whole sorry mess?

Glancing at Florence and seeing she's engrossed in pulling over a stack of paperbacks next to Carrie's bed, I double-click on the icon. The screen fills with pictures of Dr Mosley, obviously taken without his knowledge or consent.

They're taken paparazzi-style, in quick succession. Shot after nearly identical shot: Mosley getting out of a car, opening the back door for a bag, walking into a building … a building I know. It's the block of new apartments that have garnered lots of attention for their modern steel and glass design, on the outskirts of Berry Hill in Mansfield.

I think about the number of times my sister has made some excuse – needing air, or popping into town – and disappeared for a couple of hours or more.

Is this what she's been doing with her time? Stalking Dr Mosley and taking covert photographs of him? She's lied to me and the detectives, claiming to have merely innocently bumped into him. She was also adamant she hadn't made a threat against his elderly mother.

The back of my neck suddenly feels damp, my throat dry and scratchy. I look over at Florence, sitting there so innocent and vulnerable, and my eyes settle on her incongruous cast. My hands start to tremble. What else might Carrie have lied about?

Do I really know my sister as well as I think I do?

41

The police station

Adam Partridge knocked and walked into Della Grey's office. He sat in the chair she indicated to him.

'I hope it's good news, DI Partridge,' she said, tapping the end of a biro on the desk.

'It is, ma'am,' he said, unbuttoning the jacket of his maroon suit as he sat down. 'We think we've got enough to charge Carrie Parsons with the two deaths.'

Della shuffled to the edge of her seat.

'Good news indeed!' She brightened. 'Explain.'

'Well, we've strong circumstantial evidence. Parsons was present on the ward on both patients' dates of death, plus she had direct involvement with both. We have various witness statements including the one from Roisin Kenny, who told us about the so-called medication mix-up and the fact that Parsons took her off monitoring duties for Samina Khalil and took over herself.'

'This medication mix-up … surely staff can't just go in and help themselves to dangerous drugs? There must be some procedure.'

'Well, there are various medications that need a two-nurse check, including potassium ampoules, but it's not counted daily like morphine-based tablets, for example. It would be fairly easy for Parsons to get some if she so wished as she holds the ward keys.'

Grey nods. 'I see. What else?'

'We have the injury to Florence Ford, sustained when she was in Parsons' sole care. It's been diagnosed by a doctor as a spiral fracture, which can be consistent with yanking or pulling the arm.'

'That's certainly a lot of coincidences,' Grey remarks. 'Promising, but I hope there's more.'

'Oh yes, there's lots more.' Adam was on the edge of his seat now, gesticulating with his hands. 'We have CCTV footage of Parsons re-entering the ward at the exact time she said she was on her break. Plus new medical evidence from the pathologist who carried out the post mortems of both patients in addition to blood samples taken prior to their death. Angus Titchford was unlawfully killed with a lethal injection of a drug called ajmaline that can be used to test arrhythmic contractions. In an older patient, its presence wouldn't necessarily cause alarm. Also, we just received confirmation that buried in a blood sample taken thirty minutes before Samina Khalil died are unusual and unexpected levels of potassium, again most probably injected. This will avoid an exhumation of the body.'

'Thank goodness for that.' Grey's features tightened. 'If the evidence is there, why wasn't it picked up way before now, in the case of the baby at least?'

'Apparently an experienced medic – like Carrie Parsons – could effectively disguise the evidence, and unless you were specifically looking for it in a blood sample, it would be easily missed. Mr Titchford was in his eighties and little Samina was very ill with a virus that can become quickly life-threatening in a baby.'

'OK, all that sounds plausible, but what about motive, Adam? Why on earth would Carrie Parsons, a nurse for over twenty years, choose to kill two innocent patients?'

'Well, that's the unknown thing, but we've got statements from colleagues to say that the end of her marriage destabilised her. Then, a few months later, she discovered her ex – Cameron

Kingsley – was marrying an old school friend of hers … well, that possibly tipped her over the edge.'

'Are you saying she had a mental breakdown?'

'Nobody's actually used that term, but the hospital's HR department have confirmed she was off work for six weeks following the break-up, and … wait for it, Kingsley said once she tried to electrocute him while he was soaking in the bath.'

'Heavens!' Grey exclaimed, her neat eyebrows shooting up.

Adam nodded. 'He's working over in Dubai at the moment, but I spoke to him by phone this morning and he's put down what he told us in an email. He's coming in to make a formal statement as soon as he's back; that'll be in a week to ten days.'

'Good work, Adam. You've moved mountains in a very short time. Instruct DS Tremaine to speak to the CPS, get their lawyer into the station if possible. We'll go for murder and/or manslaughter … whichever we can get to stick.'

42

The North Sea, off Aberdeen

Dermott Morgan stood at the window of the canteen, enjoying the quieter surroundings after the breakfast mayhem had largely passed. He watched as Perry Ford climbed from the transfer vessel to return to the rig and felt a twinge of regret.

Dermott and Perry had been tight from the day they'd started working here together, three years ago now. They'd bonded over coffee and toast on their first morning, as soon as they realised they both lived in the East Midlands area. Dermott was already a dad then, to his toddler son, and Perry had told him he and his wife were trying for a child. Both men hoped to forge a career here that would give their families a good life.

Dermott watched now as Perry walked along the upper deck and took the first flight of steps he came to. He drained the last of his tea and plonked his chipped mug down with a loud clunk, causing one or two of the dozen or so blokes in there to look up from their food.

When Perry had left the rig the day before for a 'personal emergency' at home – as Ade had told them all at a staff briefing – Dermott and the rest of the team had been concerned. Apparently Perry would be gone for two whole weeks.

He had left quickly, without saying goodbye or giving an explanation to his friend, and Dermott had emailed him after his shift saying he hoped everything was OK. He'd said that if there was anything Zara could do to help, Perry or Alexa only had to call her, and he'd copied Zara in for good measure.

The men had all felt a little unsettled by the development. They were painfully aware that each and every one of them stood at the mercy of fate and could do little but hope and pray that things remained well with their loved ones back home while they were temporarily stranded in this foul-smelling but well-paid bubble in the middle of the tumultuous North Sea.

Now that Dermott had a bit more information, he felt like a fool. Perry hadn't replied, of course, and since Dermott had read Zara's latest email with the news back home ... well, he wouldn't be car-sharing back and forth with the man any more, put it that way.

They had an emergency situation at the south corner of the rig, and Perry was one of only three men who had the specialised skills to help get it sorted. Ade had told Dermott late last night that Perry had agreed to return for a couple of days.

'Perry Ford's back.' Dermott turned to the others in the canteen with a furrowed brow. They all looked up, but nobody said anything. 'Let's give him a friendly welcome back, eh?'

The men frowned and muttered to each other. One or two of them stood up, nodded to Dermott and left the room.

Dermott took one last look out of the window, tracking Perry's confident swagger to the secure entrance. As the metal door swung open and his colleague disappeared inside, he turned and walked out of the canteen.

There was no place here for a man like that.

*

Finally, over on the starboard side of the rig, Perry got back to his cabin and closed the door. He sat down on the single chair in the corner and put his head in his hands.

He'd had to keep it all together at home in front of Alexa and also on the journey back here. He'd called into Ade's office on the way up here and put a brave face on, not wanting to tell him the awful details of his life back home but now he felt exhausted and completely depleted of energy. It was all really getting to him now.

God only knew what would happen with the Carrie situation. He hoped and prayed Alexa had the sense to give her sister her marching orders before he got back or he was going to have to take control whether his wife liked it or not. It was time for him to stop saying and start doing, even though that would bring its own problems.

When it came to Carrie, Alexa was utterly blinkered. Yes, Carrie had been a good friend to her sister and had stuck by her in hard times, but there was a limit to how far you could repay loyalty when it involved the heinous crimes Carrie was currently being accused of.

Yet Alexa just would not have it, wouldn't even *consider* it. Truthfully, he didn't feel he knew his wife at all any more. For the first few years of their marriage she had relied on him, turned to him for advice and support when she needed it. They had been so close … both in the bedroom and out of it.

He'd been truly happy for a while until life had dealt them such a terrible blow with the death of their first child; something he tried not to think about because Alexa was still unable to discuss what happened. There had been joy and light when they were blessed with Florence, of course, but then Carrie had come onto the scene with a vengeance eight months ago, moving in and casting her long shadow on all three of them.

Now he felt like a stranger in his own home, had done for months and months. Distracted by his job, by the upcoming promotion, he'd managed to largely push his marriage concerns out of his head, resolving to leave it to Alexa to do the right thing and tell Carrie to move out so they could start rebuilding their relationship. But now … now it might be too late for all that.

Perry sat upright in the chair, laced his fingers and stretched his arms high above his head. He could feel the rigidity in his neck and shoulders and there was no chance of the tension easing yet.

He knew all about Carrie Parsons and who she really was. He knew there was certainly a possibility she'd probably done what they were accusing her of. She was poison and he didn't want her around his precious daughter a moment longer than necessary. Neither would Alexa, if she knew the truth like Perry did.

The problem was, his hands were tied. He couldn't possibly tell Alexa how it was he knew about these things …

He sighed and forced himself to his feet. He felt so weary and heavy. All he really wanted to do was sleep, fall into oblivion and forget his problems for a couple of days if he could.

Perry unlaced his boots and took off his thick woollen socks. He set the shower running and stripped off his clothing, luxuriating in the cool air on his clammy skin. He stayed stock still under the scalding arrows of water for a good five minutes, allowing the heat to penetrate his taut shoulders and the soreness at the back of his neck.

He towel-dried his hair and patted his skin down, feeling fresher and a little better already. He opened his laptop and rattled off a hasty email to Alexa.

Back on rig and having a rest before late shift. Please don't leave Florence alone with Carrie, not even for a short time. She has to move out asap. This thing has gone too far and we need to talk. Will call you later. Hope the assessment goes well.

He stared at the email before pressing send. He could barely believe social services were assessing his daughter's safety in her own home. The shame of it … and all because of Carrie Parsons.

What had he been thinking of when he'd agreed she could stay in their family home? The lads at the gym had laughed at him when he'd told them. 'You'll be pushed out in no time, mate. Get rid of her, sharpish, I say,' one of them had bluntly advised over a pint later. Perry wished now he hadn't dismissed his words as easily. Still, it was too late to do anything about that now. Getting his sister-in-law out of the house pronto was the crucial thing and all he could currently focus on.

Ade had suggested he take an hour's break before continuing work at the borehole site and Perry knew exactly how he was going to spend it: napping. He set his phone alarm for 45 minutes' time, turned off the light – which guaranteed pitch dark in his inner cabin without windows – and pulled back the sheets. He climbed into the single bed, relishing the opportunity to sink into a restful sleep for an hour or so. But instead of closing his eyes and relaxing into the comfy mattress, he yelped and instinctively jumped out of bed twice as fast as he'd gotten into it.

He pressed his hands down on the bed and the cold, sodden sheets stuck to his hands. He snapped on the light and looked up at the ceiling, expecting to see water dripping through from a leak above, but it was dry as a bone. He crouched down and sniffed the sheets before recoiling back, the understanding of what had happened finally dawning on him like a flash of blinding light.

It wasn't water that had soaked the sheets through; it was a scenario far worse than that. Someone had urinated in his bed.

43

Alexa

I arrive at the hospital at 8.21 a.m. I pull the car into a vacant bay, tucking the payment ticket into my handbag before sitting Florence in her pushchair and heading towards the main building. I veer off to the left as I move closer so I can enter the building via the less busy reception area I know Carrie and the other staff use.

Florence would usually be happily singing and clapping her hands, but she's quieter today. Still, she seems comfortable enough, so her arm can't be aching too badly. I look around me as I walk, which is a bit of a novelty. I'm not often out on my own with Florence, and on the very rare occasions I might wait alone for Carrie or Perry outside a shop or something, I will huddle into myself, looking down and hoping to disappear.

Even though it's still early, there are lots of people milling around the smaller reception entrance. Ambulance staff in uniform, visitors standing outside having a smoke, a patient still hooked up to an IV, and a couple of people in suits looking up at the building and referring to clipboards.

The powerful realisation hits me that for the first time in years, I'm not afraid. I'm not nervous that someone might strike up a conversation; I'm not frightened that someone could grab Florence. Let them try! I'm stirred up inside from finding Carrie's worrying stalker snaps, quietly simmering with rage at the thought that life here is continuing as usual here while my family is falling to pieces.

My mind is racing at double the usual speed and I long for just an hour of peace, away from our mounting problems.

I stop walking and sit on a bench under a tree just a stone's throw from the entrance. From here I can see everyone coming and going. There's no chance of me missing one of Carrie's colleagues as they enter the building.

I haven't texted Carrie to ask where she is. I'm too annoyed with the discovery that she's lied to me about where she's been going. She's disappeared again this morning … is she out taking more photographs of Dr Mosley? She doesn't seem to have considered how bad it could look if Amanda Botha finds out from the police that she's been harassing him. Also, she didn't bother leaving me a note before she left, even though she knew I was bound to worry. I understand she's massively stressed right now, but she has to think of the bigger picture and acknowledge that we're all bound together in this mess.

I dig around in the changing bag under the pushchair and pull Florence's drink out. I offer it to her but she bats it away, squealing in mischief.

'Are you playing games with Mummy?' I tickle her tummy and she folds up in glee – as best she can with the cast in place – over my wriggling hand.

'Alexa?' I look up to see Marcia standing in front of us. After all the effort to get out early, I might have missed her. 'Hello, sweetheart!' She touches Florence's cheek. 'Oh no, what's she done to her arm?'

'Marcia, hi!' I stand up and think about hugging her, but it doesn't feel quite right, and I wouldn't want any of the management to read something into it. 'I was hoping to catch you before you went in. Florence had a little accident on the swing, but she's OK.' I'm aware she's probably heard all about it from Roisin anyway but I'll get it out of the way early on.

'Is everything all right with you?' She frowns, her eyes fixed on Florence's cast. Then, 'Is Carrie OK?'

'I wouldn't go so far as to say she's OK,' I sigh. 'She's just about coping. Understandably, she feels totally betrayed.'

Marcia's face colours up a little. 'I wanted to contact her, to come round for a chat, but … well, they've made it crystal clear that that's not acceptable.'

'I know. Carrie told me she's not supposed to contact you; that's why she hasn't come with me this morning.' I push the incriminating photos of Dr Mosley swiftly out of my mind. 'To my knowledge they haven't specified you can't talk to her sister, though?'

Marcia shakes her head but looks nervously towards the building, and I seize the opportunity, not wanting her to get cold feet.

'Marcia, please just level with me. What do you think about all this … this mess? Do you honestly believe Carrie had anything to do with it?'

'No!' she says without hesitation, and I feel my tight chest loosen a touch. 'But … well, it's not quite as simple as that, is it?'

'I know what you mean, but what in particular do you think is so damaging?' My question is deliberately ambiguous. Marcia is obviously under the impression that I'm aware of certain details, and I don't want to scare her off by revealing Carrie's told me next to nothing about the case.

She sighs. 'Where do I start? There's the CCTV evidence; that needs explaining.' She stares at my blank face. 'You know, when Carrie claimed to go on her break but the CCTV shows her returning to the ward?'

'Oh yes, of course,' I say. I'm starting to feel sick.

Marcia shrugs. 'I mean, how is she explaining that to the police?'

'I think she's … Well, we can talk about that later, but just tell me about the other things you think are putting her under suspicion first. See if we agree.'

She checks her watch. 'I can't be late. They've put extra management in since …'

'Just five more minutes,' I plead. 'Knowing what you think will really help me to help Carrie. She's feeling so low about it all.'

She hesitates and looks around her again before speaking. 'Rumour has it she insisted on being the one to monitor the baby, Samina Khalil. A nurse was already starting her checks when Carrie took over.'

I nod. 'She'd want to make sure the baby was OK. You know how much she loves children.'

'I know,' Marcia agrees. 'But why did she keep going to the drugs room and getting the patients' medication wrong? She'd been seen in there several times that morning. I'm sure she had a perfectly good reason, but you have to think how it looks, don't you? To the police, I mean.'

I nod mutely. I feel as if I've had the stuffing knocked out of me. All the times I've tried to talk to Carrie in detail about the case and all she ever says is that she's being made a scapegoat and that someone's framed her. But this stuff Marcia is reeling off sounds like serious evidence to me. Evidence that my sister – who I've given a home to, who I've defended countless times to Perry – has deliberately kept from me.

A familiar figure behind Marcia catches my eye.

'There's Roisin!' I say, waving my arm.

'I wouldn't—'

'Roisin!' I call. 'Over here.'

Roisin stares stonily ahead and continues into the reception area. She must have heard me; other people who were right near her were glancing over at my hollering. I look at Marcia, puzzled.

'She … she's been in a bit of a funny mood lately,' Marcia confides, biting her lip. 'I wouldn't bother trying to talk to her if I were you.'

I stare at the reception doors, nonplussed. If anything, Carrie was closer to Roisin than to Marcia. She's been to my house before, eaten my food … why would she just blank me like that? Especially since she's just examined Florence at the A&E department. Maybe it's because I accused her of reporting our visit to social services but surely she understands I'm under a tremendous amount of stress.

'Anyway, how are you, Alexa? Worrying after everyone else as usual, I see.'

'Oh, I don't know, Marcia.' I sigh heavily. 'I'm trying to keep positive, but there's so much crap happening right now. You wouldn't believe it.'

She nods sympathetically and glances at her watch again. 'Listen, I'm really sorry, but—'

'I know, you'll be late. Thanks so much for speaking to me, Marcia. I appreciate it.'

'I can't contact Carrie,' she says regretfully. 'But please give her my love and tell her I'm thinking about her. We all are.'

Not Roisin, I think mean-spiritedly. She couldn't even be bothered to give me two minutes of her time, and I still haven't managed to work out why. I understand she had to be professional while she was working but out here she has more leeway.

'One thing before you go, Marcia,' I say, and she stops walking. 'This doctor who reported the unusual deaths. Dr Mosley?'

She nods. 'Not really everyone's favourite colleague at the moment,' she says.

'Did he put the blame specifically on Carrie's shoulders? I mean, did he tell the police he thought she'd had something to do with it?'

'Nobody knows what he did or didn't say in the complaint. But he has apparently said that Carrie is making his life a misery outside of work by hanging around his apartment building.'

My throat contracts as I think about the photographs on her laptop. 'Has he said what she's doing there?'

'Look, Alexa, I'm sorry, I really am, but I have to go. I've got stuff to do before the shift starts.'

'Please, Marcia …'

She looks at me cryptically. 'Maybe you and Carrie need to have a conversation,' she says softly. 'It seems there are a lot of things she's not telling you.'

And with that she walks away and disappears into the building. I stand there for a moment trying to figure out what she means.

How come everyone but me seems to know so much about my sister?

44

After everything that's happened this morning, the last place I feel like going is Saturday playgroup, but I owe it to Florence. And if truth be known, I can't stand the thought of going back to the house after speaking to Marcia at the hospital. I feel too hyper.

It's a popular session, the only playgroup in the area that runs on a weekend. We usually attend during the week but we have been on a weekend a few times, too.

I'm hoping our trip there will settle my mind down, give me something else to think about other than all the mounting evidence against Carrie. Evidence she's effectively kept from me, and why? I can only think of one reason right now … she's got things to hide from me.

I park the car a good way from where the playgroup is held so we can walk and get some fresh air. Five minutes later, Florence has had a dose of her pain medicine and is sitting in her pushchair. She looks pale and lacklustre, but she finds a smile for me as she cuddles her soft Benjy Bunny with her good hand. She must be missing our old routine.

'Florence?' She looks up. 'Shall we go to playgroup? See some of your little friends?'

I'm not sure if she understands or not, but her face lights up and she gives a half-hearted bottom bounce. We don't have to stay for the whole session – I'll see how she goes with her arm – but she needs to be around other kids, have a change of environment and escape the invisible stresses we have at home, even though more will be piled on us in a few hours in the shape of Amanda Botha.

Carrie and I have taken Florence to the Tiny Tots playgroup most weeks – when Carrie's shifts allowed – since she was just a few months old, and I've got to know some of the other mothers there. There's one group who are a bit cliquey, but there are other mums, like me, who are more laid-back about the whole thing. We don't sit with one particular group or anything; we gravitate towards whoever looks friendly.

So far as I know, the media still haven't officially named Carrie as the member of hospital staff who's been suspended but, as the only member of her A&E team who isn't working right now, her name is being spread wide on social media and we've obviously had some interest at the house.

Nobody I talk to at playgroup lives on our street but they can easily find out the facts about the hospital inquiry online and a whole lot of damaging speculation on top of that … but why does that mean Florence should have to hide away in shame? She's the innocent in all of this.

It's a pleasant ten-minute stroll through a small local park to Tiny Tots. I point out birds and flowers to Florence as we walk. It takes slightly longer than going via the street, but we see plenty of nice doggies out for their walks, and when Florence gives a little squeal of excitement and points her finger, she alerts me to a cute grey squirrel scaling the trunk of an enormous oak tree.

'Well spotted, sweetie!' I praise her, and her little face lights up and melts my heart.

I don't know why I turn around, just a feeling, I suppose. When I do, I see a figure loitering behind us, perhaps fifty yards down the street. When I slow down walking, so does the figure. I stop walking and stare. It's the same young woman … long brown hair, skinny and wearing jeans and a fitted walking jacket. The one I spoke to outside the house.

She looks around furtively and for a moment I think she's going to approach me but she quickly turns and starts walking away.

'Wait!' I call but that only seems to spook her more. I wait and watch her but then she turns a corner and so I set off walking again. I haven't got time to worry about our close encounter on top of everything else but she's starting to irritate me big time.

Now that we're on our way again, I'm glad I made the effort to come to playgroup, and Florence's attentiveness to the things around us tells me she's enjoying being out of the house too. It's easy to get trapped into thinking the worst when you're stuck inside. Out here, things seem brighter and more manageable. Who knows, it might all work out in the end.

The village hall is buzzing when we get there. I take a breath, put my smiley-happy face on and march into the foyer, I hope I look confident and relaxed even though a thousand insecurities are racing through my head.

What if I don't know anyone, what if someone asks me about Carrie, what if Florence's arm starts to really hurt and—

STOP! I shout the word in my head two or three times, and the insecurities fall silent.

I can do this. I *am* doing it.

I take Florence and her changing bag out of the pushchair and park it up alongside the others. I nod to a couple of familiar faces and walk into the large hall, heading for the far corner, around where we usually sit. There is a group of mums sitting there already, heads clustered together, some bouncing their babies on their knees.

As I walk, I see people turning to look at me, but then I often do that too, watching who's arriving, in case it's someone I know.

'Hello, everyone!' I say brightly when I reach the group. Nobody looks up, everyone still rapt in their conversation. 'Looks like we're late to the party, Florence!'

A couple of the women shift guiltily in their seats and sit up. When they see it's me, there are wide, surprised smiles on some of their faces.

'Oh, Alexa! We didn't think you'd be here this week …' Vanessa, who started attending the playgroup at about the same time as I did, speaks a little too enthusiastically. An uncomfortable lull settles over the group momentarily, as if she's said something she shouldn't have. 'Budge up, everyone, make room for one more.'

'Why didn't you think I'd be here?' I ask, pushing Florence's changing bag under a chair and sitting down.

'I just …' She shrugs. 'I don't know really. Don't do that, sweetie, it's dirty!' she calls out to her small daughter, who is about to gnaw on a grubby-looking soft toy.

I catch the surreptitious glances between one or two of the women.

'So, how are you, Alexa?' Another mum smiles tightly, bouncing her ten-month-old on her knee. 'How's the family?'

Several pairs of eyes watch me intently. I look around the hall and I could swear it's quieter, heads turned my way, people muttering to each other as they regard me with interest.

My stomach starts to cramp and I feel like running out. I really don't want to be here.

Everyone knows when they're being talked about, don't they? It's a feeling that creeps up from your guts into your throat and just sits there. Biding its time, waiting for its chance to choke you.

These women are pretending everything's normal, and my unspoken role is to pretend I don't know that *they* know something's very wrong in my life.

Sounds double-Dutch, but it's true. Even though Carrie hasn't yet been named officially as the suspended member of staff, everybody here seems to know exactly what's happened. And they don't look happy about it.

45

District Child Protection Team

For the second time, Amanda Botha rang the doorbell at the Ford family home.

There were a handful of journalists at the gate, suddenly her new best friends, it seemed, judging by the probing questions they were calling out to her.

'Are you a friend of the family?'

'Are you here to speak to Carrie Parsons?'

It was uncomfortable to be the object of their scrutiny. They'd pointed their cameras her way and taken pictures of her car. Goodness knows how Alexa and her husband were dealing with it, being just ordinary people as they were. It must have been hell to be plunged into this nightmare scenario with little or no warning.

The door opened and Alexa appeared, looking flushed and a bit hassled.

'Amanda! Hi, come in.'

'Gosh, where did that lot come from outside?'

'They were here when Florence and I got back from playgroup.' She dabbed her forehead with the back of her hand. 'They seem to have worked out it's definitely Carrie that's been suspended now rather than it being a popular rumour.'

'Must be hard to deal with.'

'It's … *really* hard to deal with. I'm just turning a blind eye to it at the moment but I'm dreading going out.' Alexa was being rather philosophical about it on the surface but her face looked tired, washed-out.

'Apart from that, how are you? How's Florence?' Amanda asked, bending forward to remove her shoes.

'No, please, leave your shoes on. Your feet aren't dirty and the carpet's covered in spills from Florence's cup, it's fine!' Alexa babbled nervously but she led Amanda through to the lounge and said brightly, 'Florence, Amanda's here to see us again!'

Amanda couldn't help but admire Alexa's clever framing of her visit as a pleasant event, to help put the toddler at ease.

'Hello there, Florence!' She crouched down to speak to the child in her walker. Florence was pale and a little quiet, but that was only to be expected after her recent hospital visit. 'Are we going to have some fun today? Play with a few toys?'

Amanda looked up at Alexa and caught a familiar look of resentment on her face before she could convert it into a wide smile. Amanda couldn't blame her and parents often reacted like this. It wasn't Alexa's fault her sister had been arrested. She hadn't asked for this awful situation to descend on her family. All families usually detested social services' involvement, feared it, too.

'Perry's been called back to the rig, annoyingly,' Alexa said. 'He was hoping to be here, but there's been an emergency out there and they need him back. It's just for two days.'

'Oh dear, that's unfortunate for him, and for you too. I'm sure you could do with his support right now with what's happening outside on top of everything else.'

For a moment, the other woman's face drooped and Amanda thought she was going to cry.

'Would you like a drink?' Alexa said instead. 'Coffee, tea, water?'

'A glass of water would be lovely, thanks.'

She watched as Alexa visibly dithered between leaving Florence with Amanda and taking her into the kitchen with her.

'Could you watch Florence for me while I get our drinks?' she said eventually.

'Of course! We can play together for a few minutes, can't we, Florence?' Amanda turned back to the child, and a few moments later she heard Alexa pottering around in the kitchen. It was a good sign that Alexa trusted her. She'd initially thought the woman was far too nervous, paranoid even. Unfortunate flaws that could easily rub off on small children. It was incredible what infants could pick up on subconsciously. But Alexa seemed to have grown calmer and more confident in her motherhood role just lately and it was encouraging to see.

Amanda picked up a few brightly coloured bricks and placed them in front of Florence. The child used her uninjured arm to good effect and began bashing a brick on the plastic tray.

Amanda looked around the room. It was comfortable and well furnished. She could tell that Alexa wasn't a clean freak but it was fairly tidy apart from a scattering of toys everywhere, which was always nice to see. She'd done a family assessment last year in a big detached house on the outskirts of Worksop where there were no visible signs at all that a child actually lived there. Toys were firmly shut behind cupboard doors and the toddler in question was only allowed to play with them in his sterile-looking bedroom. Money had no relation to love and affection, and it had been a powerful red flag to Amanda during that particular assessment.

Her first impression in this house was that Florence was very much wanted and at the centre of the family. If anything, there had already been clues that Alexa was a little *too* protective of her daughter, rushing to assist her in small tasks when it would be better to let her do them herself, to allow Florence to fail and try again.

But Amanda considered these things to be positive negatives, to coin a phrase. She didn't know why Alexa had such hang-ups, didn't need to really; nobody was perfect. But on balance, she was confident they came from a place of love and caring for Florence.

But with an aunt who had been arrested in connection with unnatural deaths at her place of work, it didn't take much to figure out that little Florence Ford's apparently ordinary and loving family home might not be the safe, nurturing place it initially appeared to be.

And it was Amanda's job to find out whether that was indeed the case.

46

The North Sea, off Aberdeen

'You've got a nerve coming back here.'

On his way back from the drilling shaft, Perry stopped walking as Dermott, followed by a group of five or six other men, stepped out onto the top deck. Eyes were narrowed and collars pulled up as the sea mist whipped around their faces, the greasy smell of oil hanging in the air like a witness to the confrontation.

'Why's that then?' Perry used a belligerent tone but his heart pounded. In that split second, he knew without doubt that the men must be aware of what Carrie had allegedly done. 'If it's confession time, maybe the person who pissed all over my bed wants to own up?' He glared around the group, meeting every pair of eyes.

'What kind of man harbours a murderer in his house?' Dermott challenged him.

'Yeah, how can you support someone like that? A baby killer?' one of the other men growled.

Perry squared up to Dermott, the man he still thought of as a good friend. Had he made an error of judgement in failing to confide in him? He'd had to make a call and he'd decided not to say anything to Dermott in the hope that the situation back home could soon be resolved. With Zara living back in Nottingham,

K.L. Slater

he'd been foolish to think Carrie's suspension and arrest wouldn't get back to Dermott.

Perry was aware of the eyes of the other men on him, and the back of his neck felt hot and sticky. He felt grateful for the sudden blast of biting sea air that tunnelled through the group, causing some of the men to shiver and stuff their hands in their pockets.

They all had wives, partners, kids; they knew how complicated family life could be. Perry wanted to reason with them, explain how from the beginning he'd tried to insist that Alexa kick Carrie out. But he knew that would make him sound like a complete sap.

They didn't know about Alexa's fragile mental state. He couldn't adequately explain just how completely she believed Carrie to be innocent and how she was holding onto that like a lifeline. Anyway, why should he pander to this lot? Some of them barely had a brain cell between them, and his family business was his own.

He stepped closer to Dermott, jutting out his jaw so his face was only inches from his colleague's. 'Keep your nose out of my business,' he said from behind clenched teeth. He was a full half-foot taller than Dermott, and broader across the shoulders and chest. 'You know nothing about what's happening, so zip it.'

Dermott swallowed but stood his ground. 'My Zara knows a friend of the family of that old fella your sister-in-law snuffed out. His daughter's in pieces, man. His grandkids too. It's ruined their lives and you're protecting the lowlife who caused their grief.'

'It's not been proved yet. She's not been charged.' He glared around the faces, his cheeks burning with the irony of what sounded all too like a defence. 'Anybody here heard of the phrase "innocent until proven guilty"?'

Feet were shuffled but nobody commented. Then Dermott piped up again.

'She's been questioned, suspended, *arrested*.' Disparagingly, he counted off the actions on his fingers before turning to the men gathered behind him. 'It's all over the internet; the only reason she hasn't been charged is because they're still investigating and gathering forensic evidence. That little baby died four months ago. They say they might have to exhume the poor mite to try and work out exactly what the murdering bitch did to her.'

A murmur went around the group; jaw muscles flexed and foreheads folded into deep creases as menacing clouds rumbled furiously overhead. The sheer crested waves rose in unison around the rig and seemed to hover there watching them for a couple of seconds before crashing down thunderously again. The water appeared slick and black in the fading light of the day. Perry was always aware of how the sky and sea looked so much closer out here, and there was barely any colour. Everything looked dark and menacing.

A couple of the men took their hands out of their pockets and flexed their fingers before forming loose fists. There were rarely violent incidents out on the rigs, but it wasn't unheard of. There had been a case here a couple of years ago where one man had attacked another with a metal pipe, accusing him of having an affair with his wife. Over the years, the odd man had plunged into the icy depths of the unforgiving waters, either through suicide or a terrible accident.

'That wind's getting up,' one of the men snarled. 'Waves are building fast too. Be easy to get too close to that edge.'

Most of the rig had safety panelling, but there were a few hazardous areas where an exposed thousand-foot drop into the water was necessary for drilling access. They were perilously close to one of those areas right now, and it would take no more than a few seconds, a moment of madness, for Perry to cease to exist. This was no time for misplaced pride.

'I hope none of you find yourself in this position,' he shouted above the roar of wind and water. 'But if you do, I hope you get the same treatment.' Then he turned and walked briskly away in the direction of Ade's office. His head felt light while his bones were like lead.

*

An hour later, he'd texted Alexa that he was on his way back to Aberdeen airport.

He'd just joined the check-in queue for his flight home when his phone rang. His face lit up when he saw who it was.

'I'm on my way back from Aberdeen; tell you about it later. Can you meet me at the airport in two hours?'

'I'll be there, I've been waiting all day for you to call,' she said, her voice full of warmth. 'I've missed you so much. I hate having to pretend like this.'

'I know, it's tough. We'll talk later, there's lots to discuss.' His phone beeped with another incoming call. 'Listen, I've got to take this. See you at the airport. Don't be late.'

When she'd gone, he tapped on the screen to answer the next call.

'Hi, Alexa,' he said. 'Did you get my text? I'm on my way home.'

47

Alexa

When Amanda Botha finally leaves, about an hour and a half later, I feel as if I've been five rounds sparring in the boxing ring. I'd got an expected email from Perry when he arrived at the rig but then received a completely unexpected text saying he was on his way home again! I called Perry to find out what's happened.

'How did the assessment go?'

'Amanda's only just gone, so my head's spinning. It went as well as expected, I suppose. How come you're coming home so soon? Is the problem sorted?'

'I'll tell you all about it when I get back,' he said, sounding hassled. 'I'm getting a cab from the airport, so no need for you to pick me up.'

We said our goodbyes and all I could think was that it was a relief I didn't have to go to the airport. I needed to come down a bit after the assessment.

It was all very cordial of course, conducted in Amanda's easy-going manner. She asked me lots of questions, now I come to think of it, as part of our general conversation. What sort of thing does Florence like to eat? What meals would you give her in a typical day? Does your sister help a lot with Florence's care? Does she prepare Florence's food and bath her? Do you leave them to play together while you get other stuff done? How does Florence act when Carrie's around?

When I brought our drinks through, Amanda looked around the room. 'I thought Carrie might be here, actually.'

'No, no, she's got an appointment with her solicitor,' I said confidently. 'He's convinced they haven't got enough evidence to charge her and that will emerge quite soon, we hope.' Where on earth Carrie can have got to, I can't imagine.

Amanda nodded but didn't appear overly convinced.

Under different circumstances, it might have been easy to believe she was just interested in Florence. A bit of a giveaway when she seemed so interested in Carrie and wrote down everything I said, though.

When we went into the kitchen so I could warm up Florence's food, she watched me like a hawk.

'Have you thought about letting Florence feed herself?' she asked.

A curl of discomfort unravelled in my stomach. 'I've always been worried in case she chokes on something,' I said. 'You read about it happening all the time, don't you?'

I was surprised when she agreed with me. 'Choking is a real hazard. But I'm not talking about leaving her alone to do it. Sit next to her, eat something yourself or read a magazine, perhaps. That way you're there if Florence needs you but you're allowing her to experiment how to consume different types of food and develop her spatial skills. You're giving her the confidence that she's capable instead of passing on your fear.'

It was as if someone had turned on a light bulb in my head. It made perfect sense. Why hadn't I thought of that? I'd never considered that Florence, at her young age, would pick up on me feeling unsafe and being on red alert all the time.

'Do you plan on having another baby? Or do you think you'll stick with just the one?' she asked and for the first time I felt really vulnerable. She saw my expression. 'Sorry, I can be a bit blunt sometimes. You don't have to answer that.'

'It's fine,' I say, feeling far from OK about even thinking about it. What do I say? *I'm a mother of two girls but my first baby died.* 'We … haven't really talked about it at length.'

Amanda nodded, made a note and moved on.

So, the assessment was a mixed bag in the end. I'd rather it hadn't happened, but I can't deny I learned stuff about myself and about Florence. I'm sure Amanda picked up plenty about us, too.

'We usually do three visits in fairly quick succession before switching to a weekly one,' she explained before she left. 'That means I'd like to come back in a couple of days' time if possible.'

She didn't really phrase it as a question and so I didn't feel I had any choice but to agree. She has this way of just taking you along with what's expected. But I also felt a sense that we were best getting the assessment done and out of the way as soon as possible.

'That's fine by me,' I said.

'And it would be really useful if your husband could be present at our next session.' She hesitated a moment. 'Carrie too, if you're able to arrange that?'

I swallowed. Perry and Carrie in the same room, talking about taking care of Florence? It was a disaster waiting to happen. I'd texted Carrie to ask where she was when I returned from playgroup. In the end, I'd decided not to stay. There was more negativity in the room than there was here at home. Weirdly, nobody said a word about the situation or asked me anything outright about what had happened at the hospital, but their veiled stares and gossipy nudges were as bad as if they'd asked me to stand up and give a statement about Carrie's case. As it was, I'd had no reply to my text yet. I'd heard nothing from her at all.

'I'll try my best to get them both here next time,' I said, walking Amanda to the front door with Florence in my arms.

I watched from behind the curtain as she drove away, and that was when my body seemed to fold in on itself and I realised I'd been holding myself rigid for the last ninety minutes. Now, though, I feel thoroughly exhausted. Florence is ready for her nap and I'm in desperate need of a lie-down before I collapse.

I take Florence to her room and lay her down in the cot, stroking her head and humming her favourite lullaby. Within seconds, she's out like a light. But instead of heading straight to my own room, I stop at Carrie's door, hesitate and go in. I sit on the bed and open her laptop again, putting in the numerical code, the date of birth that tugs my heartstrings, and retrieving the contact details on the staff list she's got.

I take a photograph of the information and close the laptop again.

Marcia was really helpful at the hospital this morning. She spoke to me willingly even though she was really nervous about getting into trouble with the hospital management. It was obvious she cares about what happens to Carrie, albeit she's confused about some of the things she disclosed to me. The CCTV, Carrie's insistence that she monitor the baby herself, not to mention unusually frequent visits to the drugs room.

But Roisin? Roisin's cold-shoulder reaction when I called out to her really bothers me. She and Carrie have been good friends since their nursing college days. Both Roisin and Marcia have been over to the house on occasion over the last few years, and they even bought a beautiful broderie anglaise cot set between them as a gift when Florence was born. It doesn't make sense that Roisin would blank me like that, doesn't follow that she's not concerned about Carrie. Unless … unless she knows something I don't about the inquiry and wants to keep it that way. Maybe she has even told the police things that helped them decide Carrie was worth arresting and investigating further.

There's only one way I'm going to find out.

I wait until the start of the staggered afternoon breaks at the hospital – the time of which I'm familiar with thanks to Carrie frequently talking about it – then pick up my phone and call Roisin's mobile number from Carrie's contact list. It takes me by surprise when she answers on the second ring.

'Hello?' she says suspiciously.

'Hi, Roisin, this is Alexa … Carrie's sister.' Silence. 'I wondered if you'd mind talking to me for a few minutes? I know you're probably on your break but it won't take long.'

'I've got the afternoon off,' she says defensively. 'Talk to you about what?'

What does she think it's about? I almost say this, sarcastically, but that will only serve to annoy her. So I say, 'About Carrie. I was at the hospital earlier, talking to Marcia. I called out to you but you didn't seem to hear me.'

I give her the benefit of the doubt even though I know she couldn't have failed to hear me calling her name. It seems to do the trick and her tight tone relaxes a little.

'If this is about the fact that I'm doing Carrie's job temporarily, I felt I couldn't say no. And someone has to do it while she isn't here.'

'No, no. It's nothing to do with that, Roisin.' She sighs, as if I'm taking up her valuable time. Under the circumstances I thought she'd be more open to talking, particularly if she's got the afternoon off. 'It's just … well, Carrie's suspension doesn't make any sense. Look, do you want to pop round here for a coffee later? Or we could meet somewhere else, a café or something?'

Roisin gives a hard laugh. 'I don't think that's a good idea, Alexa, I really don't.'

'You seem … annoyed or irritated in some way, Roisin. Has Carrie done something to upset you?'

I remember Roisin as a happy, easy-going kind of woman. A couple of years younger than Carrie, she's never married or had kids, and Carrie said she loves to amuse herself by boasting at work about her long weekends away with girlfriends, and the fact that she only has herself to worry about when her colleagues are run ragged, worn out with working and coping with family life. That aside, she was obsessed by her nephew, Jay, of course.

'I'm on my way out,' she says coldly. 'Trust me, at some point you'll understand that I've done you a favour not getting friendlier.'

'What? How will that help me? I need Carrie's friends to talk to me about the case, tell me what their opinion is. Otherwise how am I ever going to help *her*?'

'It's a shame your sister hasn't shown you the same loyalty, Alexa, it really is. My advice is to stop being so gullible and focus on what matters to you. That should be your daughter. Precious Florence is the only one who deserves your efforts, trust me on that one. Now, I have to go.'

'Roisin, don't go! Roisin, please … tell me what you mean, I—'

The line clicks dead and I cry out and throw my phone onto Carrie's bed in frustration.

What the hell was Roisin trying to say? That Carrie is guilty of hurting those patients and everyone can see it but me?

Before closing Carrie's laptop down, I stare again at the name of the street where Dr Nathan Mosley lives. After my unpleasant interaction with Roisin, trying to speak to him face to face like I did with Marcia seems like a much better idea than calling him and trying to introduce myself.

I know the doctors work a slightly different pattern to the core shift staff. That might mean there's a chance he's at home. If he sees how desperate I am, he might open up and tell me exactly what he told the police about the patients' deaths.

I hate the doubt that's creeping into my conviction that Carrie is totally innocent. The clandestine photographs of Dr Mosley and him complaining to the police, her lies about being out of the house, several worrying things Marcia told me this morning and, finally, the cryptic phone call to Roisin, all point to a darker picture of my sister.

The more information I uncover, the more I'm finding it increasingly difficult to recognise the Carrie I know and love. But I'm not quite ready to give up on her yet.

48

I feed Florence and nibble at a cheese salad sandwich myself. Florence is grizzly; I think her arm is aching as she keeps gripping her cast. I give her a dose of medication and in a short time her eyes become heavy.

I carry her up to her bedroom and lay her in her cot. I sit in the comfy chair next to it and hold her hand through the white bars, singing her favourite nursery rhymes softly. She's asleep within minutes and I gently release her hand and, after checking the baby monitor is turned on, I tiptoe to the door.

I just get to the top of the stairs when I hear a key in the front door. I run down and meet Carrie in the hallway.

'Is Florence sleeping?' she asks, taking off her boots.

'Where have you been?' I put my hands on my hips. 'I was worried about you.'

'Worried? Why?' Her nonchalant tone ignites a spark of annoyance.

'Well … because so much is happening at the moment!' I snap. 'I thought you might've left me a note at least. You knew about the assessment, the last thing I needed was something else to worry about.'

'You know, you've changed, Alexa,' she says, shrugging off her coat and looking at me. 'You used to be so laid back and now … it seems you're always looking for a fight.'

'Oh really?' I laugh. 'Well, I like to think of it as facing up to reality and trying to deal with it. A change that was well overdue for me, I think.'

She blows out air. 'OK, well … I'm guilty as charged for not leaving a note, so if it helps, I apologise.'

She's got a really bad attitude for someone who's under arrest, suspended from her job and reliant on continuing to live under this roof. I don't expect gratitude but I do want a bit of respect.

'I'm going up for a shower and then—'

'Not yet,' I say shortly. 'I need to ask you something.'

She mutters something under her breath that has a definite *here we go again* ring about it and heads for the living room. I sit on the sofa and she sits down in the chair with a weary sigh.

'When we were waiting for Florence's X-ray results at the hospital, Perry told me something I need to ask you about.'

'Oh what a surprise! Is dear old Perry trying to shaft me yet again?'

'Carrie! What's got into you? You should be firing on all cylinders to try and defend yourself but you've just developed this really unhelpful attitude instead.'

'I'll tell you why, shall I? Because I've lost hope, simple as that. It seems everyone and their dog can say what they like about me … my colleagues, my bosses, the police … and now, another left hook from Perry, it seems. But don't let me stop you. What is it?'

'He told me that after you and Cameron split up, he went out for a drink with him.'

She lets out a cynical laugh. 'Why am I not surprised at that?'

'I know. And I'm so annoyed he did that. *But* I have to ask you something and I want you to be truthful with me.' She says nothing and I take a breath. 'Cameron told him you cut up his suits over some minor disagreement and … more worryingly, that you threatened to electrocute him with a hairdryer while he was in the bath.'

Carrie throws back her head and laughs.

'Carrie! It's not remotely funny.'

'No … it's hilarious! Seriously … you're asking me this stuff with a straight face?'

'It could be relevant,' I say carefully. 'If this was to get out, the press would have a field day.'

'Oh yes, course it could. I forget. If they rake up anything bad at all about me, it proves I must have murdered two patients in my care.'

'I never said—'

'You didn't need to. But I'll answer your question.' She looks me straight in the eyes. 'Yes. It's the truth that I cut the arms of the two expensive Italian suits he couldn't afford in the first place because when I complained about him being so late back from his trip for about the third time that month he said, "And what are you going to do about it? Go get a life, you sad little cow." And yes, it's the truth that I stood over him in the bath with a live hairdryer.'

'I can't believe … you were actually going to drop it in the bath?'

'Was I heck! It was a sick joke, granted but, before you judge me, I'd just found out through the wife of one of his colleagues that he was openly playing around, Alexa. When I asked him about it, he laughed in my face and said I was losing my marbles. In that moment I felt so utterly powerless, so inconsequential to him.'

I'd seen him talk down to her before and rile her publicly when he'd had a drink.

'He shut the bathroom door in my face but didn't lock it. I heard him running a bath and in a mad moment, I plugged the hairdryer into an extension and waited a full five minutes before walking in with it blowing hot air.' She grins. 'I thoroughly enjoyed seeing the fear on his face for all of five seconds before I walked out again. It's one of my best memories of our faithless marriage, if I'm honest.'

I might have even shared a little snigger with her if she wasn't under arrest pending further investigations but as it stands, I'm disappointed it's the truth.

'Him telling Perry all about that is probably the only time Cameron's told the truth about our marriage in all the years I've known him,' she says icily.

Carrie embarks on a rant about some of the other stuff Cameron did during their marriage and I stare out of the window, her voice fading out. The only thing I can think about is that she hadn't told me any of this stuff during the hours and hours we'd chatted about their break-up. All I got to hear was all the bad things *he'd* done or *he'd* said.

There seems to be a worrying recurring pattern. Carrie is extremely selective in what she's telling me now and what she has told me in the past. What if she's doing the same with the awful events at the hospital?

Am I the biggest gullible fool out to keep giving her the benefit of the doubt when other evidence – like this – stacking up against her is growing by the day? It would be easy to laugh at Cameron getting his just deserts but what if the hairdryer had fallen from her hand that day and entered the water, electrocuting him? Would that not have been her fault, either?

Above all the stuff currently whooshing around in my head, one question continues to loom large: Is my sister a danger to Florence?

Carrie's phone rings.

'What is it?' she demands urgently.

I snap out of my musings and sit up to attention.

'But … when? I mean, are you sure about this?'

Her face drains of colour and her eyes meet mine, dark and spooked.

She ends the call and I'm too afraid to ask what's wrong.

'That was my lawyer,' she says in disbelief. 'He says the police are intending to charge me with the deaths of both patients later today.'

49

Alexa

Perry's voice echoes in my ears: all those times he's issued warnings about leaving Florence alone with Carrie. All the times I've defended her to the cost of my marital relationship, and it turns out he was right all along … she can't be around Florence. With the imminent police charge against her, the number of occurrences is now overwhelming.

I have to do this. I have to find the courage for my daughter.

'This is the hardest thing to say, Carrie, but … you need to pack your things and go.' I feel like sobbing. 'I'm so sorry but we have no choice now. I'm shocked, I honestly never thought they'd actually charge you …'

Her jaw drops and she stands there for a stunned moment without reacting. Despite everything she's kept from me – the circumstantial evidence Marcia shared, the incidents during her marriage, her stalking of Dr Mosley – I still can't bear to see the hurt etching her drawn features.

Then, 'Go where? I *have* nowhere to go, Alexa, you know that.'

'You can't stay here or we're going to lose Florence, you must see that? Arrested is one thing but … I'm sure social services will have no hesitation in taking her into care when they find out you've been charged with the patient deaths and you're still here, in the family home. At the very least they'll be doubling up on their assessment visits. That's no way for Florence to live. Just book into a B&B somewhere until the dust has settled and we know exactly what's happening. I'll pay.'

'I didn't do it, Alexa. I didn't kill those patients,' she says in a small voice, her bad attitude now vanished.

'I know,' I say and despite everything I've found out that she's kept quiet from me, I do still believe my sister is innocent of the charges. 'But there are other things too. Worrying things that you're doing, like stalking Dr Mosley.'

'I'm not stalking him, I just—'

'The police may have believed your story that you just bumped into him, but … well, if you must know, I've seen the photos on your laptop.'

'What?' Her face darkens. 'Have you been snooping in my room?'

'I wanted to find your rota. You didn't have the courtesy to tell me where you were going before you left the house, so you gave me little choice.'

'You've no right to—'

'You've been told not to contact anyone at the hospital, but you've been hiding in the bushes and taking photographs of Dr Mosley without his knowledge.'

'I've been monitoring him, watching his movements, that's all. Someone has to.'

She's obviously in total denial, creating some ridiculous story in her head about Nathan Mosley because she can't handle the fact that he started this whole thing by doing his duty and reporting the suspicious deaths. But there's something else I want to quiz her about.

'While we're on the subject of your colleagues, have you any idea why Roisin blanked me at the hospital and then basically refused to talk to me when I called her?'

Carrie opens her mouth, closes it again. Looks at her hands.

'Obviously you *have* got an idea. Are you compiling a photo album of her too?'

She narrows her eyes. 'You need to stop poking around, Alexa. Trust me. You need to back off.'

'No!' I yell without thinking and listen for a second for the baby monitor to alert me that Florence is awake. It stays silent and I lower my voice to a hiss. 'This has gone too far. You promised you'd stop keeping secrets when it came to the investigation. You gave me your word.'

A strange look settles over her face but she says nothing at all.

'I hate to say this, Carrie, but you've proved that Perry was right all along. I've backed you every step of the way and you've failed me.' Her cheeks flood with colour, but before I can bite back the stinging words, more of them tumble from my lips. 'I'm the first to admit Perry has his faults, but we have a right to know what's happening and your secrecy stops us doing that. We have to protect our daughter.'

'You really want to know what's happening under your nose, do you? Well, let's start with Perry, the man who's been "right all along",' she mocks me and I stand up to leave the room because the last thing I want right now is to get into a slanging match about Perry.

But what she says next knocks me off my feet.

'Here's the little nugget of truth you want to hear so badly. Your husband is having an affair.'

'What?' I actually laugh as I collapse down again on the sofa. 'What are you talking about?'

'He's been having an affair with Roisin Kenny. *That's* why she wasn't keen on speaking to you outside the hospital, no doubt.'

I can't speak. Marcia's reaction, trying to dissuade me when I called out to Roisin this morning. Roisin herself on the phone reacting to my suggestion to meet her for coffee: *I don't think that's a good idea, Alexa, I really don't.*

I turn her words round and round in my head, but they still don't make sense.

'*That's* why Perry had to agree to me moving in, *that's* why he's tried to get you to kick me out of the house instead of doing it himself,' she says breathlessly.

'But you … *you've* been lying to me all this time, to protect Perry and Roisin?' My voice sounds distant. Faint.

'No! It wasn't like that …'

Roisin's voice plays over and over in my head. *It's a shame your sister hasn't shown you the same loyalty, Alexa, it really is.*

'How long has it been going on?' I say faintly. 'How long have you been protecting them?'

'Ten or eleven months, a year, tops. You'd just had Florence when it started. It's just a fling, Alexa. I – I didn't tell you at first because I didn't think you could handle the truth,' Carrie stammers. 'Roisin has had countless affairs with married men ever since I've known her, and she always gets bored and moves on. I guess I hoped the affair would just run its course, fizzle out without you having to get hurt. Foolish. I know that now.' We both hold our breath. 'The fact remains. I didn't hurt Florence on purpose and I never harmed those patients.'

But Perry … having an affair with *Roisin*? Scenes flash into my head. The two of them talking at Florence's christening. The way she'd insisted on helping me carry the buffet items through at Florence's first birthday party, dressed up to the nines in a short skirt and towering heels while I still felt bloated and depressed after Daisy Mae's death and then having Florence quite quickly afterwards.

'Is that why you and Roisin aren't friendly any more?' I say, pieces slotting into place now of why the three colleagues no longer met for after-work drinks and the odd night out.

'Yes. It seems Roisin has tried to stick the knife in with her statements to the police because she saw this as her chance of getting me out of her hair for good. She and Perry know I hold their secret and could tell you at any point, spoil their nice little arrangement.'

'But you've chosen not to, not because you were worried about my wellbeing but because you've been able to hold it over Perry's head and stop him kicking you out of our home when you overstayed your welcome.'

'No! That's not how it was.' She chews her inside cheek, her eyes wild and restless as she tries to talk her way out of it.

'Do you think Roisin knows anything about what happened to those patients?'

Carrie shakes her head. 'I don't think so, no.'

I sit there staring into space for a moment, thinking about the ongoing lack of intimacy between me and my husband. How I've consistently blamed myself for being the one with the problem, piled on the guilt for never being totally honest with him about what happened two years ago, and it acting like an invisible barrier between us …

But Carrie, too! My sister, the person I've trusted most of all, keeping something like that from me because in her opinion I'm not strong enough to know the truth. I can't help but think that it has suited her to stay quiet, to hold it over Perry's head and keep her in a strong position. My sister is a liar, a manipulator. Can I even believe she cares for my daughter, or is Florence a pawn in her plans like the rest of us are?

I've been such a gullible fool. I feel hot with shame.

Well, no more.

I walk out of the living room and upstairs, into Florence's room. She's still asleep, her feet bare, her neat little toes capped with nails that look like tiny shells. Everything about her is so perfect in this rotten, deceitful world we live in. I feel like I'm all alone in this world apart from my daughter. Florence is the only thing I care about right now, and I will fight tooth and nail to protect her.

I leave her sleeping, reassured now I've seen she's resting and getting some reprieve from her painful arm injury.

Downstairs, Carrie is still dithering, pacing up and down the living room.

'Carrie, go. Please, just go.'

'Alexa, wait … please don't do this.'

'Just go. Now.'

She storms out of the room crying and I hear her footsteps thudding up the stairs. I have to get some air or I might keel over.

I walk into the kitchen and open the back door. Leaving it ajar, I walk a little way down the garden. Our neighbour's sixteen-year-old grandson, Remy, is out next door, and judging by the sounds emanating from the other side of the hedge, he's playing some sort of computer game. I've watched him before from the upstairs window. He's always got some new technology at hand, and he will often sit there for hours, a slave to the brightly coloured graphics on the screen, until his battery eventually runs low.

I sit down on the wooden seat near the bottom hedge and think back to when we were younger, back when it seemed Carrie and I would never let anything come between us. She's always been my big sister, my guardian angel, and I couldn't possibly have envisaged the day when we'd be at loggerheads like this.

I look up at her window and see her walk across her bedroom. She'll be packing some bits together, leaving the place that has been her home for the last eight months and checking in to some soulless B&B during the worst time of her life. I've nothing left to give her but it breaks my heart to send her packing in her hour of need.

A head pops up over the fence. Remy.

'Oh, hi, Mrs Ford.'

'Hello, Remy,' I say dully, willing him to go away.

'I asked Gran if I could come round to show you something, but she says you've got a crisis on and not to bother you.'

Thank goodness for her common sense. Obviously she knows everything that's happening, thanks to the media. 'She's right that we've got a lot on at the moment, Remy. Maybe next time you're over.'

He frowns. 'I wanted to show you today, because I'm going home tomorrow.'

I stand up and start walking back towards the house. 'I'm sorry, Remy. Like your gran says, it's just not a good time.'

He watches me. 'You'll be sorry!' he shouts good-naturedly before disappearing again.

'Probably,' I call back with an air of disregard. I'm losing count of the things I'm sorry for.

I pause at the top of the garden and marvel at how much the Japanese acer has grown since last year. Last year, when life was normal and everything was calm and as it should be. I bend forward to sniff the rosemary and thyme in my scrawny herb garden. I had such plans for it a couple of years ago, but never got past three or four herb varieties before I abandoned my efforts.

I walk back into the house, my head hanging. I wish I could say I feel relieved but I feel wretched and so bone tired of it all. I glance at the door and see Carrie's jacket and boots have gone. The house already feels empty and cold.

Upstairs, I tiptoe into Florence's room, astounded she isn't yelling the house down with all the noise that's happening.

I see immediately her cot is empty.

'Carrie?' I call out in shock, even though Carrie's obviously gone. There's an almost imperceptible sense of alarm in my voice as my brain immediately leaps to the worst possible conclusion. But I've only been away from the house for a few minutes, and the kitchen door was open the whole time, so I'd have heard if she had woken up.

I stand on the landing and call out. 'Carrie? You there?'

There's no answer.

Panic infects me as I rush into the other bedrooms and then downstairs into the hallway and then the living room.

'Carrie? Florence?' I call, trying and failing to keep my voice from rising. I bound back upstairs, shouting, 'Carrie? Carrie! Where are you? Florence?'

I run into my bedroom and look out of the window, down to the road, and the room starts to spin.

Carrie's car has gone. Of course it's gone.

I'm trying to get more air in my lungs, but the breaths come shallow and rapid. I stare out of the window, my mouth open, my eyes wide. Carrie has taken Florence. She's taken my baby.

With a shaking hand, I pull my phone out of the back pocket of my jeans and press Carrie's number. Again and again I call, but each time I just get her voicemail. I end the call and this time I press 999.

'Hello? Please help me. My child is missing. She's just been taken without my permission by a member of my family.'

The voice on the end of the line says, 'You say she's been taken by a member of your family. So you know who this person is?'

'Yes,' I say, my voice breaking. 'Her name is Carrie Parsons. She's my sister.'

'Oh wait!' My head jerks up in frantic hope as the front door opens, but it's Perry who walks in.

He stares at my face, then at the phone in my hand, and his face darkens as he looks around the room.

'Where's Florence?' he demands.

'Get out!' I scream, and then my legs give way and I'm falling.

50

I open my eyes. I'm lying on the sofa in the living room. I feel like I'm waking up to the worst hangover in the world. I can hear the blood thundering through my head and I'm sweating, heat bubbling away under my skin.

'Thank God,' Perry says, his face looming above mine.

'Leave me alone,' I whisper, my voice hoarse, my throat feeling raw, like it's been scraped completely dry. 'I don't want you here.'

'You're confused, Alexa. You collapsed. Dropped the phone and went out like a light,' he says.

Two paramedics, a woman and a man, arrive. They tell me their names but everything sounds muffled and meaningless. My mind is full of Florence's sweet face, her rosebud mouth, her chubby rosy cheeks. 'Where's my baby?' I cry out.

The woman speaks to me gently. 'Let's just focus on getting you sorted,' she says. 'Your husband has everything under control.'

'I hate him!' I wail, and they all look at each other.

Silently I curse myself for telling Carrie to leave. I should have waited, discussed things properly with her. Even though I hate to admit that Perry is right, Carrie might be very fragile mentally. If that's the case, the thought of her having sole responsibility for the most precious thing in my life fills me with pure horror.

Did she even take Florence's changing bag with her? I'm not sure. What about the Calpol? Florence can't tell her whether her arm is sore and aching; she needs to be cared for, protected from bumps and too much movement. What will Carrie give her to eat? All the fresh, nutritious meals I've lovingly prepared are in the freezer … and Benjy Bunny, who sleeps in her cot … did Carrie remember to take him with her too?

'I need to check,' I mumble, trying to sit up.

The paramedic speaks to Perry in a low voice. 'We're going to take her into hospital. Her blood pressure is dangerously low and her heart is erratic. She needs an ECG.'

Perry is on the phone now. He's talking about Carrie to someone, giving her name, her description. Her telephone number. Then details about Florence, and about me being out in the garden when …

The sound in my head grows louder, like rushing water. My mouth is bone dry, and when I try to stand up, I start to wobble.

'She's going to collapse,' I hear the female paramedic shout out.

And after that … well, I don't really remember anything.

I wake up in a hospital bed. I pull an oxygen mask from my face and struggle to sit up.

'Florence!' I call out.

A nurse immediately appears. 'It's OK, calm down now. Lie back and relax, that's it.'

'I want … to … see my baby,' I say, those six words exhausting me beyond anything I've ever experienced.

'I know you do, I know.' The nurse reattaches the mask. 'I just need you to pop this back on until I've done your readings, is that OK?'

I lie back and close my eyes. My blood feels like it's on fire, my heart wrung out and hollow. I've always said Carrie would never hurt Florence; I believed it with all my heart. It happened so quickly, the way she managed to whip my daughter away in the time it took me to walk down the garden and back. Had she planned it all along? She couldn't have been thinking straight. If she had, she would have considered Florence's injured arm, the fact that she'll be in pain … I squeeze my eyes tighter, tears spilling out of the corners. I can't bear it, can't bear not knowing if Florence is safe.

The Carrie I know and love would never let any harm come to her, but who is this new person who seems to have emerged? The person who lies and behaves completely out of character might be distracted, might not be thinking straight. What if she has had some sort of breakdown and fails to properly care for my daughter?

The heat under my skin dissipates and I start to shiver, as if I've been plunged into an ice bath. The disturbing thoughts bounce around wildly in my head until they feel like a kind of weird dream. I must drift off again, because the next time I wake up, the oxygen mask has gone and Perry is sitting at my bedside. His expression is grim. I turn away from him because I can't bear to look at his cheating, lying face.

'The police want to speak with you,' he says. 'They want to know about Carrie, whether she's shown signs of personality disorder.'

He clamps his mouth shut and a muscle flexes in his jaw as the two detectives dealing with the case walk over to my bed. I know he's probably trying not to explode. I've lost count of the number of times he's tried to speak to me about Carrie not having one-to-one contact with Florence. How many times he's tried to warn me that Florence may be in danger. Privately I wonder how I can have been so naïve. But now I know he's in no position to judge me.

'I feel like it's my fault.' The words exit my mouth in a wail. 'I asked her to move out. I should never have taken my eyes off Florence for a second.'

'Did your sister exhibit any worrying behaviour today, Alexa? Did you notice anything unusual compared to her normal demeanour?' Partridge asks me gently.

'She's spent more time than usual in her bedroom over the last few days,' I say haltingly, battling the exhaustion that keeps hitting me like a wave. 'She wouldn't talk much about work, or about anything. But on the other end of the scale, she'd go missing for hours without telling me where she was going or how I could get in touch with her.'

'She concealed everything from us about what was happening at the hospital, lied, in effect,' Perry added. 'I wish I'd just kicked her out from the off.'

You lied too. I glare at him and he looks at me questioningly, not understanding my obvious animosity towards him.

'Has she spent more time than usual with Florence in the last few days?' Tremaine asks.

I shake my head. 'Less time than usual, I'd say.'

'I've told Alexa again and again not to leave Florence on her own with Carrie. I thought, under the circumstances, we should be cautious. In fact I asked her numerous times to tell Carrie to move out of the family home.' Tremaine nods, but Perry hasn't finished. 'That didn't happen, and now we've got a social services intervention on our hands.'

If I had the energy I swear I'd jump up and claw at him.

'Well, we're trying to locate your sister,' Partridge tells me. 'Your husband's given us the salient details, including her car registration, but do you have any ideas where she might have gone?'

'I told her to pack her things and get out. I said to book into a bed and breakfast and that I'd pay the bill.'

Perry rolls his eyes but doesn't comment. I know he'll be thinking about our financial situation. He doesn't know yet that I've given Carrie money for a solicitor.

'We're not classing Florence as missing as such yet,' the detective says. 'Although we're extremely concerned, she's Florence's aunt, a blood relation who often had sole care of her. It's possible she has every intention of returning her safely, but we can't ignore the fact she's under arrest. We'll want to locate her today. If this leaks to the press, it could get nasty and out of control very quickly. We've got a trace out on her mobile phone and also her bank cards. Hopefully that will shed some light very soon.'

The press attention is bad enough as it is. Goodness knows how interest would balloon if they realised this had happened. *Killer nurse abducts one-year-old niece*. I can see the headlines now.

I can never forgive Carrie for this. And on top of everything, I've been stupid to so readily defend her when Florence hurt her arm. What if her patience snapped, or she grabbed her in frustration? It's time to admit my trust in Carrie has been shattered into a million pieces that can never be put back together.

When the detectives leave, I turn my back on Perry.

'What's wrong with you?' He storms over to the bed. 'Why are you looking at me like *I've* done something wrong? You're the one who let that mad witch walk off with our injured daughter!'

'And you're the one who's been having an affair with Roisin Kenny for the best part of a year,' I say evenly. 'So you can drop the holier-than-thou act, you lying rat.'

51

Alexa

Back home, I'm lying on the sofa covered with a blanket. Perry keeps trying to strike up conversation, to explain himself and tell me why he did what he did, but I'm having none of it. I don't want to talk to him about Roisin Kenny. I don't want to hear his pointless excuses. I only care about where my daughter is. That's it.

Despite this, we look at each other in alarm when there's a rapid knock at the front door.

'It could be something to do with Florence.' I start to move.

'You stay here,' he says. 'I'll go.'

Feeling wobbly, I stand up and listen as he walks down the hallway. I still feel light-headed and out of it.

'Oh, bloody great.' I hear him sigh, obviously not impressed by the caller he can identify through the glass panels of the front door. But he opens it anyway. 'Hello, Remy.'

I close my eyes. Dammit. *Don't invite him in, Perry, not today.*

'My dad's picking me up from Gran's soon and I wanted to give you something before I go,' I hear Remy say. 'I mean, you might not like it, but it kind of belongs to you and—'

'You'd better come in, Remy,' Perry sighs wearily.

I can't believe Perry's actually doing this, inviting the kid from next door in when our daughter is out there, missing. I turn back to the sofa, and when Perry walks into the room, I'm sitting down again. I can't even raise a smile at the lad.

'Remy's brought us a … a gift, is it, Remy?'

I look at his hands; he's holding a laptop.

'It's not really a gift.' He sits down next to me without being asked and opens it up.

I give Perry a look. 'Remy, I'm sorry, but can this wait until another time? I'm tired and worried and I'm really not interested in seeing your new computer game.'

'Alexa!' Perry scolds my blunt manner.

'It's not a game I'm showing you,' Remy says, seemingly oblivious to my irritation. He sweeps his fingers over the monitor and the screen lights up. Perry walks over and stands looking over his shoulder.

Suddenly a clear image of our garden from above fills the screen. A surge of annoyance rises up and I shift in my seat to face him.

'Remy, this is not on. That drone is an invasion of our privacy and I'm going to have to—'

'Alexa … look,' Perry whispers, pointing at the picture.

The date in the top right corner is the day that Florence injured her arm.

'There's no sound,' Remy says apologetically as we peer closer at the screen.

The drone drops a little closer, and Carrie appears out of the kitchen door. She's carrying Florence down the garden, talking to her, pointing things out. I see Florence clap in that adorable excited way she does when she sees a new flower or a bird.

We went out into the garden for a little nature hunt.

Carrie is looking this way and that. She glances sharply up in the air as if she's detected the drone, but is then distracted again by Florence, who is wriggling and pointing at the swing.

I thought it wouldn't hurt as the drone wasn't above our garden or anything.

I take in a sharp gasp of air, then press my lips together, trying to stop myself from crying out. I watch as they get to the swing and Carrie looks around again. With the new suspicions about my sister at the forefront of my mind, I wonder if she's trying to ascertain if anyone is watching. I feel like I'm going to throw up. I can feel tension rolling off Perry in waves, his hands forming tight fists as he watches intently.

Carrie sits Florence in the swing and fiddles around awkwardly as if she's trying to strap her in; then she straightens up quickly, like she's been spooked, and looks towards the house.

'Her phone's started ringing,' I say faintly.

She looks down at Florence and back at the house. Then she bends forward as if she's saying something to her, and the next thing, she's haring off towards the kitchen door. Carrie is out of shot, but the drone stays in place. Florence bats her hands on the swing bar. Her little mouth opens and closes and I know she's probably shouting, objecting to the fact that Carrie isn't there pushing her. She bucks and rocks in the swing, sort of levers herself up and out, and then, in a split second, she's falling and on the floor, squirming awkwardly.

I shouldn't have left her, but I was gone literally ten seconds, Alexa, I swear to you that's all it was.

Literally seconds later, Carrie is running down the garden, swooping down and picking Florence up. Checking her over, kissing her head. Her hand comes up to her forehead in distress as she rushes back towards the house with my baby in her arms.

Alexa, you know how much I adore Florence. I love her so much. I'd do anything to keep her safe.

The screen turns blank and I look at Perry.

'She was telling the truth,' I say, and he has the grace to look confounded.

'Yes,' he says, as if he doesn't know where to go from here. 'She was.'

*

Perry asks Remy to email the video clip to him and gives him a tenner for his trouble. The boy is delighted with his reward.

'Thanks for letting us see this, Remy,' I say quietly. 'I'm sorry I didn't listen to you when you tried to tell me about it before.'

'That's all right, Mrs Ford.' He beams, closing his laptop.

Perry shows him out and comes back in looking sheepish.

'I knew it,' I say acidly. 'I always knew she'd never knowingly hurt Florence.'

He bites his lip. 'I'm sorry. I just didn't know what to believe. Can't you understand that, Alexa? After the two patient deaths and her arrest, I ... I didn't know what to think.' He pauses. 'Listen, can we talk about—'

'Carrie is far from perfect, I know that. But I believe with all my heart that she would never hurt Florence, just as she'd never knowingly hurt one of her patients.'

I swallow, trying to forget the weight of the doubt that filled my mind before viewing Remy's drone clip. I'm starting to feel a little stronger now.

'That doesn't answer the question of why she's taken her now though, does it?' he says grimly, changing tack again. 'She fully knew the distress it would cause you. So why?'

'I think it's because she's telling the truth and nobody will listen,' I say more out loud to myself than to Perry. 'A guilty person would never take Florence. She'd keep pretending everything was fine, try to convince us all she was innocent. Carrie probably truly believes that we're going to stop her seeing her niece. Me asking her to move out, social services' involvement, the police on the cusp of charging her ... it all fits with her probable assumption that she won't be allowed contact with Florence.'

And then my thoughts start to travel down a different path. One that hasn't occurred to me before. I stand up slowly so I don't feel dizzy, and make my way into the hall.

Perry follows me. 'I really don't think you should be getting up just yet. Why don't you lie down and I'll—'

'Why don't you just go?' I say, infuriated by the fact he's trying to slot nicely back into his caring husband role. 'Go away and don't come back. That's the best idea.'

'I'm going to go out and look for our daughter,' he says in a spiteful voice. 'Try and find your crazy sister and repair the damage you've both done.'

'Fine by me,' I call, clutching the banister and walking upstairs. My voice raises another couple of octaves as I climb higher. 'And if you need a shoulder to cry on, I've heard Roisin Kenny's are nice and broad when it comes to married men.'

52

I hear the front door open and close and I breathe out. I don't for a minute think Perry has gone for good, but him leaving will give me some space, and that's a great start.

I've got to take it easy because I still feel weak but I can't stay here when there's so much at stake. I know what it is I need to do.

The first thing I do is call DI Partridge. He sounds hassled when he answers.

'Any news, Mrs Ford?'

'Nothing,' I say regretfully. 'I wanted to tell you I have to pop out for a little while. But I have my phone with me, so if you hear anything—'

'No problem. We'll call you right away,' he says briskly before ending the call.

I wonder if he thinks me a bad mother, 'popping out' when my daughter has been unexpectedly taken away by her aunt. But after seeing Remy's drone footage, I'm back to trusting my sister implicitly. At least when it comes to Florence. And what I'm about to do might just help with the other charges about to be made against her, too.

I grab what I need and set off in the car. I'm heading out to Mansfield, a town just under five miles away and about a ten-minute drive from our house.

Berry Hill is an affluent area on the outskirts of the town. The new apartment block I recognised from Carrie's photographs of Dr Nathan Mosley is a steel and glass tower of luxury apartments built just a couple of years ago.

I don't know if he'll be home, I don't know if he'll speak to me if I do manage to see him. But I have to try. For Carrie's sake I have to try.

On the way, I call Carrie's phone on hands-free. It's still off but I leave a message.

'Carrie, it's me. A lot's happened since I last called. The lad next door, Remy, he's got drone footage of Florence's fall. We know you're telling the truth now. Bring her back, Carrie, please. We can sort all this out, I promise. I'm driving to Berry Hill. I'm going to try and speak to Nathan Mosley, see if he'll tell me exactly what information he gave to the police. It's the only thing I can think to do now. Please bring Florence back, Carrie. I'm begging you. My heart's breaking.'

I turn off Nottingham Road and on to Berry Hill Lane. I can see the new apartment block shimmering in the near distance and I'm irritated to see all the road leading up to it has been newly marked out with double yellow lines meaning I can't park up right outside as I'd planned.

I turn down a side road with a small row of shops at the top end and find a space on the road there.

I'm reversing into the parking space when a familiar figure catches my eye. It's the woman with the straggly hair again who I saw again this morning before she scuttled off again. This time she hasn't seen me. Hastily, I complete my parking manoeuvre, grab my handbag and jump out of the car. But frustratingly, as I look around, she's nowhere to be seen.

Just when I think I've imagined seeing her, I spot the woman across the road, walking past the shops. She walks, eyes downcast, arms folded and hugging herself and then turns into the last door, a small café called The Coffee Pot.

I walk quickly over there and into the café. Inside, it's small, cosy and full of the delicious aroma of freshly ground coffee beans. There are a few customers in there and out of eight small tables, there are just two or three spare. I feel a twinge of nerves standing there alone and I immediately push it away.

The woman is standing near the counter behind a customer who's settling his bill.

'You OK?' A waitress carrying a tray of crockery stops as she passes me. 'Just get yourself a table and I'll be over in two minutes.'

The woman turns and stares at me. I thank the waitress and walk towards her.

'Hi,' I begin, stepping forward. 'I was just parking up and spotted you coming in here. I'm—'

'I know,' she says in a faint voice. 'I know who you are.'

I can see now she's not quite as young as I first thought. She's probably in her late twenties. Her hair is thin and her skin looks dry and parched. She looks generally neglected, as if she's forgotten how to properly care for herself.

'Look, I need to speak to you, just for a few minutes,' I say confidentially. She reacts like a startled doe, eyes darting around her. I recognise that feeling. 'I know how it feels to be scared to be out on your own but we can sit down together, if you like. Can I buy you a coffee?'

She hesitates, looks as though she's weighing up having coffee with me or running out while she's still got the chance. But then she nods and I lead her to a table at the back of the café where I hope she might start to relax a little.

'Grab that table at the back, it's nice and private,' I say. 'I'll get the coffees in.'

'They come to the table to take the order,' she says.

I want to launch straight into the questions I have but I'm nervous about scaring her off. So I make a point of looking around the traditional décor of the place with faux antique beams and brass kettles and pots hanging from them. 'Nice little place, this; do you know it?'

She shrugs. 'I often come here while I'm waiting for my boyfriend to get back from work and let me in.'

Strange. She's got a boyfriend but has no door key?

We sit down and the waitress comes over right away. 'Hello, Suzy. You OK, love?'

She nods. 'Fine thanks. I'll just have a latte please, Pat.'

'Make that two, please,' I add.

I wait until the waitress has gone before speaking.

'Sorry, I should've introduced myself properly ages ago. I'm Alexa Ford,' I say. 'And you're Suzy, I gather?'

She nods.

'How do you know Carrie? Or know *about* Carrie, as you said?' I see her stiffen at the mention of her name. 'Can you tell me what you need to speak to her about? I can pass a message on, if you like.'

She taps the sugar sachets straighter in their white plastic holder. Her fingers are slim with short, bitten nails and chipped burgundy-coloured varnish.

'I know about her because my partner goes on about her non-stop. Or did do before she got suspended. He hates her with a passion.'

I gasp. Hate is a strong word to use. 'What's your partner's name?'

'Nathan Mosley,' she says simply. 'He's a doctor at the hospital.'

My skin begins to crawl. 'You're Dr Mosley's girlfriend?'

It's easy to have an idea of what sort of person would be a good match for another one, sometimes unfairly. Surely any doctor could see that Suzy isn't in the best health? And why does she have to sit in a café waiting to be let into her own home?

But Dr Mosley is bound to feel annoyed with Carrie. She's approached him and even taken photographs quite clearly without his consent.

'Why does he hate her … is that what you want to tell her?' Her fingernail starts to carve into the wooden table-top and her chest is rising and falling with alarming speed. Now I've finally got to speak to her again, I have to do something before she just jumps up and takes off like a spooked deer. 'Look, I know Carrie has made a nuisance of herself with your boyfriend. She's been watching him, taking photographs. It's not on, I can understand him getting annoyed but … she's desperate, you see. She's about to be charged for the deaths of two patients at the hospital and Dr Mosley was the one who reported it to the authorities in the first place. If you know anything at all that might help us … you can trust me.'

Still, she stays silent. The waitress brings our lattes over and, probably unfairly, I curse her timing.

'What I'm trying to say is, you can tell me anything. Anything at all. I won't be shocked.' She looks at me with big, soulful eyes and I'm moved to say more. 'I can see you're nervous. I've been there myself, scared to go out on my own but I've got over it now, I've had to. Maybe we can even meet for a coffee again sometime, until you get your confidence up, I mean.'

'It's not going out I'm scared of,' she whispers. 'It's going *home* that terrifies me.'

'What?' I look down as she gently pushes up her sleeve to pull out a tissue and inadvertently reveals a fresh-looking bruise on her forearm. 'Has he done that to you? Nathan Mosley?'

Quickly, she pulls down her sleeve so it covers half her hand. 'Nobody knows what he's capable of,' she says. Her eyes dart to the window of the café and she scans the road outside, before letting out a breath.

I swallow, trying to keep the anticipation out of my voice, trying not to rush her.

'Outside my house you said you knew about Carrie … what did you mean by that? Why does Nathan hate her?'

'I … I can't …' Bag of nerves doesn't cut it. This woman is clearly *terrified*.

She knows something, I'm certain of that but I also feel that if I push too hard she'll just take off. So I ease up a little.

'Do you and Nathan live together?' I say casually.

'Yes,' she says and then adds, 'well, sort of, I suppose. We're engaged but it's complicated, depends what mood he's in. It's his flat.'

'Do you mind me asking why you don't have a key to his flat?' I ask her.

Suzy looks back down at the table and shakes her head. 'He's funny about stuff like that.'

Funny about stuff like *keys*?

I watch her. There are long moments where she appears totally unaware I'm opposite her. She's twitchy and seems tight as a drum, ready to snap. I'd taken it as a fear of being out on her own, like I've had but I'd say this is far more serious.

I remember a girl I went to college with. She had the same nervous disposition, as if she was always on the edge of something, expecting the worst. She had an abusive boyfriend who used to drop her off at college and pick her up. We'd sit in the library together sometimes in our lunch break because he didn't approve of her eating lunch in the canteen 'with male students drooling over her', she'd quote him.

I get the distinct feeling Dr Nathan Mosley might not be the nice, easy-going doctor he appears to be to the members of the hospital board and his colleagues. He's quite clearly physically abusing his girlfriend.

'You said Nathan hated Carrie. Is that why he reported the deaths? Did he point the finger at Carrie so they'd investigate her?'

'It's worse than that … he …'

Suddenly, Suzy stands up. 'I've got to go now,' she says, her eyes flitting around the room. A couple of nearby customers look up, their interest piqued.

'Suzy, please. Two more minutes and then I'm out of here, I promise. Please, I know he's hurting you and you're afraid of him but … tell me what he did. To Carrie.'

Reluctantly, she sits down.

Suzy bites her lip. Looks at me, looks away.

'What is it?' I say. 'Please tell me everything you know about the patient deaths. I'll help you get away from him, I promise.'

Her eyes flicker to the window again and I'm suddenly filled with urgency. I could call the police here but that could mean a lot of unnecessary drama for the café and for Suzy. And I don't actually know anything solid yet about Mosley apart from the fact he's abusing Suzy and has an axe to grind with Carrie for some reason. But she almost said it, I almost got her to tell me what she knows about the hospital case. And even if I find out nothing else, I have to convince her to go to the police to report Mosley's physical abuse of her.

I realise the best bet is for me to get Suzy somewhere quiet and private so she feels secure enough to talk. Understandably, she's far too jumpy here.

'Let's go.' I stand up and pull money from my purse to leave on the table for our coffees. 'We need to get away from this place and get you to safety. You can come home with me and we can talk more there, OK?'

She looks like she might object and then she nods. For the first time she looks a touch less tense.

The waitress appears. 'Is something wrong with the coffee?' she says, glancing at Suzy who's already heading for the door. 'Is she OK?'

I shrug. 'I'm not sure but she's very nervous. I'm getting her out of here.'

'Poor thing. She doesn't know whether she's coming or going with him, that's what it'll be. You finished with this?' She indicates Suzy's untouched latte.

'You mean her boyfriend, Nathan?' I glance at the door to see Suzy disappear out of it.

'Hmm, comes in here sometimes. Respectable doctor one side, psychopath on the other if you ask me. I've known a few in my time.' She picks up Suzy's unfinished drink. 'There's something really off about him. He openly treats her like dirt and she's a lovely girl.'

I make my excuses and rush out of the café. A fine drizzle of rain has joined the cool wind now. I look up and down the street but there's no sign of Suzy. She keeps slipping out of my fingers.

Frustrated, I start walking to my car which is parked near the bend. It will afford me a view of the whole street I can't see from here. A few paces on and I hear muffled sounds coming from an alleyway that runs alongside and around the back of the shops. A man has his back to me and facing me, her face a picture of terror, is Suzy.

'Hey!' I yell, running towards them.

He turns around and I see it's the man in Carrie's photographs. Nathan Mosley. He has a deep handful of Suzy's long hair. 'Leave her alone!' I screech.

A couple walking towards us slow and I shout to them, 'Call the police!' But instead of rushing to help, they promptly turn around and walk off.

He frogmarches her out of the alleyway. 'Mind your own business. She's coming home with me.'

'No!' Suzy cries out weakly. 'Let me go. Please, I want to go with her.'

I rush up and grab Suzy's other arm.

'Back off, bitch!' Nathan swings his arm and his fist smashes into my cheekbone. The pain ricochets through my head and I stagger back, clutching my face.

He's dragging Suzy away from me, out onto the street towards the parked cars. I'm yelling for help but nobody's helping … there's hardly anyone around.

I jump back as there's a screech of brakes and Carrie's car pulls up directly opposite. Carrie's driving but Perry jumps out of the passenger seat and rushes across the road.

He takes one look at me clutching my injured face and then barrels towards Nathan and a now sobbing Suzy. 'Let her go,' he yells but Nathan points keys at a car and unlocks a black Audi which he's just paces away from.

'Don't let him take her,' I cry out.

'Let her go!' Perry yells again and as Nathan pulls open the car door and tries to push Suzy in, Perry lets fly with a well-aimed punch at the doctor's head. Nathan staggers back and falls to the floor and Suzy runs to me. While Perry stands over a whining Nathan, I wrap my arm around Suzy's shoulders and help her as she staggers away.

Carrie gets out of the car, her phone pinned to her ear. 'Police please,' she says and looks at me as if she's trying to gauge my reaction to her but there's something more important I need to check.

Suzy sits down on a small wall next to the car and I run and wrench open the rear door.

'Florence!' I see my baby in her car seat and she beams at me. She's holding a toy I haven't seen before and she looks happy and relaxed. I open the door and kiss her face three or four times. Her favourite nursery rhyme CD is still playing in the car and her little feet are tapping away to the music. I'm desperate to take her out for a cuddle but she's safe and happy and I don't want her to see anything she shouldn't over the road.

I close the door again and turn to Suzy. 'You OK?'

She nods. 'Alexa … your face.'

The throbbing pain is increasing by the minute and when I gingerly touch my cheek I can feel it's already badly swollen.

Across the road, Mosley is still on the floor and Perry is looking over at me. 'Florence is fine,' he calls. 'Are you OK?'

I nod and turn to Carrie as she comes off the call.

'Police are on their way,' she says. 'God, Alexa, your face!'

Our eyes meet and I see the pain and regret on her face. But I don't want to talk about why she took Florence without permission right now.

People are coming out from the row of shops, standing and watching Perry and Nathan. I see Perry talking to them and looking towards our group.

'Carrie, this is Suzy,' I say, sounding as if I've been to the dentist as I can only move half my jaw now. 'She's Nathan Mosley's girlfriend.'

'I've seen you before,' Carrie says. 'At the hospital a couple of times, hanging around in the car park.'

'Waiting for Nathan.' Suzy nods.

'She says he hates you, Carrie,' I frown, waiting for her to explain why.

She shrugs, looking puzzled. 'Hates me? We've never had a wrong word at work!'

'It's because—'

Suzy's words are drowned out as a police car zooms around the corner, siren blasting, lights flashing. Close behind it an unmarked car pulls up and DI Partridge jumps out and heads straight over to us.

53

During the ten-minute drive home, Perry sits in the front next to Carrie and I snuggle up to Florence in her car seat, in the back.

She reaches for my hand and links her little fingers with mine and the spread of warmth inside me reaches from the top of my head to my toes.

Before we left the scene, I quickly explained what had happened to DI Partridge and DS Tremaine.

'She said Mosley hates Carrie but we still don't know why.'

They assured me they'd take good care of Suzy, who was badly shaken. They took Suzy and me aside for a few minutes and she managed to give them a brief history of what had been happening in her relationship with Mosley, but she said nothing about the hospital case.

'I can pick you up from the station after you've given a statement if it helps,' I told Suzy.

'That's kind of you,' Tremaine said. 'If it's OK with Suzy, I think it's really important we help her make contact with her family again.'

'I really want to talk to my mum,' Suzy said tearfully. 'But thanks for the offer, Alexa.'

There's not much conversation between the three of us in the car on the way home. Perry and Carrie speculate what's going to happen to Mosley and what information Suzy might have about the case, but I stay quiet, distracted by my throbbing jaw.

When we get home, I unbuckle Florence and carry her up the path. Perry beats me to the front door, unlocks it and opens it wide for us. I take Florence into the kitchen and Carrie follows us while Perry goes upstairs.

'Alexa, I just want to say I'm so, so sorry I caused you more worry and grief by taking Florence,' she says meekly. 'It was just … I don't know, *desperation*. That's honestly what I felt.'

I lower Florence into her high chair before turning to face my sister.

'Why did you do it?'

'Like I say, it was a moment of pure madness. I looked in on Florence before I left and she opened her eyes and smiled at me and I thought of all the years I'd tried for kids with Cameron and how it wasn't meant to be. I thought about …' she hesitates and lowers her voice, 'Daisy Mae and how we lost her. I couldn't risk losing Florence too. I love her like my own, you know that. I just panicked, right there in her bedroom. I realised that if the police charge me and put me in prison, I won't see her again for years. She wouldn't know me at all.' Her eyes glitter with tears as she looks over at her niece. 'It might not make sense to you now but taking her was all I could think to do.'

'But you knew it would kill me. How could you?'

'I admit I wasn't thinking about you.' She looks wretched. 'Something's changed between us, I know you feel it too. I've been guilty of keeping some things from you about the case and I'm truly sorry for that. But I told you the truth about Florence's arm and I told you the truth about the hospital deaths. I'm so sorry I kept Perry and Roisin's secret, but I did the right thing in the end and told you.'

'You're right that something's changed between us,' I say. 'I've discovered I can look after myself perfectly well. I'm grateful for everything you've done for me, I think you've always had my best interests at heart but since this has all happened, I don't need you or Perry in the same way I did before.'

'You didn't need me before, either,' she says sadly, touching my arm. 'You just didn't realise it back then and if I'm honest, it suited me. I felt wanted and important in your life; it was like being kids again. You and me against the world.'

'I blamed myself for Daisy Mae's death and I think the fact you tried to make me feel better by telling me the story of what "really" happened … it just compounded that fact in my head. I convinced myself I had to lie because I'd caused her death.'

She lowered her eyes and nodded. 'I'm so sorry. I've realised a lot of stuff about myself during these past few weeks and, mostly, I don't like what I've found.'

'Like what?'

'When Daisy Mae died I was still with Cameron, as you know. But I was unhappy. I knew our marriage was breaking down and I was scared. It was clear he didn't need me any longer and I was afraid of being alone. But you *did* need me. And Daisy Mae needed me. When she died I wanted to help you recover, of course I did. But on reflection, I think I wanted to help myself, too. I didn't consciously plan it but by constructing a story around her death where only you and I knew the truth, it sort of fed into that need for us to be bound together by something bigger. Like the feeling I had when Mum died. When it was just you and me, we had each other.'

I stare at her, stunned she's put so much thought time into not just the hospital case but other relevant events in our lives.

'Nobody will ever know about what really happened before she died, I promise you that. It was unforgivable of me to throw it in your face before. There's no need for you to be afraid of someone finding out or for you to feel guilty any longer. It will always be our secret.' She gives a weary sigh. 'I've been selfish, Alexa. I've inadvertently made it much harder for you to recover from Daisy Mae's death and I'm so, so sorry.'

'You did the best you could at the time. We both did,' I say sadly. 'But far from burying the truth again, the time has come for me to tell Perry the truth about Daisy Mae. No more secrets.'

54

The police station

Adam Partridge and Nell Tremaine sat opposite a clearly agitated Dr Nathan Mosley.

He had refused the offer of a duty solicitor. 'I've nothing to hide,' he'd said when Nell asked him, folding his arms.

The last time they'd met with the junior doctor was two days after Angus Titchford died. After initially meeting with management, he'd been the first member of staff they spoke to when the detective superintendent dispatched them to the hospital on that first evening.

'We meet again, Dr Mosley,' Partridge said. 'Last time we spoke it was to discuss your grave concerns that patients were dying unnaturally on the A&E ward.'

Nathan looked back at him steadily. 'You've made a mistake bringing me in here.'

'Interesting you should say that. Perhaps you'd like to explain why you assaulted your girlfriend, Suzanne Garton, in Taylor Street, off Berry Hill Lane. That's the reason you're here.'

'She's disturbed. Bipolar. When she's suffering one of her mood swings, she becomes very vocal, hard to deal with. Today was one of those days and I was just trying to get her safely back to the car before she lashed out at anyone.'

'I see,' Adam said. 'We have witness statements from several passers-by who said you restrained her against her will and used unnecessary force.'

'Well, they would say that, wouldn't they? They don't know what she's like, screeching and screaming when she wants some attention.'

'Is that something you see as your role, Dr Mosley?' Nell asked. 'To restrain and bully women who use their voice?'

'Not at all. She wasn't hurt, I was just encouraging her to get into my vehicle.'

'Would it be fair to say you control Suzy?' Nell pressed him. 'Don't even allow her a door key to your shared apartment?'

'You'll find it's my name on the lease, not hers. As such I'm well within my rights to decide who I give a door key to and I've certainly committed no offence in that regard.'

'Let's move on to something else a bit less contentious, shall we?' Adam said cordially. 'You trained as a doctor. Can you tell us how you ended up at King's Mill Hospital in your first post?'

'What's this got to do with my disagreement with Suzy?'

'I'm just trying to establish some background,' Adam said. 'We didn't get much time to chat that day at the hospital and I wondered what your path to working there had been.'

'Well, after my degree, there were several ward opportunities open to me and I researched them all. Decided on King's Mill. That's about it really.'

'When you say you "researched" them, what exactly did that entail?'

'Just the usual. Location, facilities, how it had performed in the past.'

Adam nodded. 'Did you consider the Queen's Medical Centre in Nottingham at all? That's a similar location, a teaching hospital with an excellent record of patient care.'

Mosley frowned. 'I didn't want to go there, didn't even consider it.'

'Why didn't you want to go to the QMC?' Nell asked. 'Did you at least visit the hospital?'

'No, I didn't. I had a bad experience there when I was a kid,' Mosley said. 'I didn't want to be reminded of that every day.'

'A bad experience?' Nell repeated.

'Yes. One I've no wish to discuss with you.'

'You lost your twin brother, Bradley, when you were both fourteen. Is that right?' Adam said.

Mosley's eyes flashed. 'Who told you that?'

'Is it true, Adam? That your brother died at the QMC in Nottingham?'

'I suppose this is Suzy running off her big mouth again.' Adam watched as a flushed pink colour rose in his cheeks and his hands tightened into fists. 'What's this got to do with me being brought in for questioning?'

'Your brother died and the nurse who was attending him at that time was' – Adam checked his notes for effect – 'Carrie Parsons. A twenty-seven-year-old nurse back then in her first job.'

'I fail to see—'

'And when you saw that name on the staff sheet of King's Mill Hospital, you elected to take the junior doctor position at King's Mill. Correct?'

'That had absolutely nothing to do with it.' Mosley gave a hollow laugh.

'Oh I beg to differ, Dr Mosley. According to your girlfriend, you'd tracked Parsons' every move over the years. Even when she married, she kept her maiden name for career purposes so it really wasn't that difficult for you to do so.'

'You're making a serious error if you're listening to anything that comes out of Suzy's mouth. You should check with her GP … anxiety, depression, she even self-harms on occasion.' His mouth twitched at the corner. 'Hardly a reliable source of information, DI Partridge.'

'Has she always suffered from those symptoms?' Nell asked sharply. 'Or did they appear when she met you?'

Mosley smiled laconically and didn't reply.

'I'll share my train of thought with you, Dr Mosley,' Adam said carefully. 'I'm thinking that someone who goes to the trouble of tracking a person obsessively for years, someone who blames a young nurse for the death of his twin brother … what might they do in order to exact that kind of hunger for revenge?'

Mosley's face remained impassive. 'Spit it out, DI Partridge,' he said, meeting Adam's stare. 'This tiptoeing around the houses is getting a little tiresome and I have patients to attend to.'

'Let me take you back to the twenty-seventh of December last year.' Nell shuffled her notes. 'The day Samina Khalil died on the ward. Can you tell me what your contact with her was?'

'I've explained all this to you before,' he sighed. 'I attended her on the ward and diagnosed a viral infection. The nursing staff took over after that.'

'A viral infection …' Nell said thoughtfully. 'Isn't that the exact condition you and your brother were admitted to the QMC with all those years ago?'

Mosley's calm expression cracked like a clay mask as he turned on Nell, hissing words through clenched teeth.

'I told you before, I don't want to discuss my brother. I *won't* discuss him.'

'I'm just saying it's a bit of a coincidence,' Nell said easily. 'I'm not sure why it's pressing your buttons, Dr Mosley.'

'Lots of people are unfortunate enough to suffer from serious viral infections, Nell,' Adam chided. 'Sometimes, sadly, they die and it's no one's fault. Wouldn't you agree, Dr Mosley?'

He remained silent for a few moments, his face seeming to swell with colour and fury.

'Sometimes they die through negligence, incompetent staff. In my opinion, that's what happened to Samina Khalil.'

'Let's talk specifics here. Who do you think was negligent and incompetent enough to cause her death?'

'I think Carrie Parsons killed her. She's incompetent. And that's not just my opinion, the trust suspended her because that's the conclusion they swiftly came to.'

Adam referred to his paperwork. 'The pathologist found it was highly probable that Samina died from an injection of potassium. Now, if administered in a certain dosage, that wouldn't kill immediately, would it?'

'Not as a rule, no.'

'There would be a delay?'

'Possibly a short delay, yes. Obviously a baby is much smaller and therefore the effects would be felt more rapidly.'

'So on the day Samina Khalil died, you made your rounds and got called back, I understand, when she took a turn for the worse.'

Mosley sniffed, sitting up straighter in the chair. 'That's right. I attended immediately and found Carrie Parsons with the baby. She was in a bad way.'

'And how long would you say it was since you'd examined Samina?'

'Oh, five, ten minutes tops. She'd been stable then and so I was immediately suspicious.'

'And yet you didn't report the death back then?' Nell prompted him.

'No. I couldn't be sure and it's a serious thing to do, to whistle-blow. It doesn't look good if you're wrong.'

'But when Angus Titchford died, then you felt bound to report both deaths?' Nell remarked.

'Yes, that's right.'

'So, on to Mr Titchford, then,' she said, glancing at the paperwork in front of her. 'I understand it was a similar case, according to the notes taken at your initial chat with us. You examined the patient, determined he'd probably broken his hip and ordered an X-ray. Fairly straightforward procedure, I'd imagine.'

'Entirely straightforward, yes.'

'After which, I presume, you went about your other duties?'

'Yes, I continued on my rounds.'

'You were paged by Carrie Parsons and had to return to Angus Titchford approximately fifteen minutes later,' Nell confirmed. 'The resuscitation team had already been summoned by Parsons and were attending the patient when you got back to the ward.'

'Yes, he'd already gone into cardiac arrest by the time I got there. He was alert and stable when I left him a short while before.'

'The pathologist found a lethal dose of a certain drug in Angus Titchford's blood, suggesting he'd been unlawfully injected to cause massive heart failure,' Adam said. 'Curiously, I understand your own grandfather died of the same thing.'

Mosley shuffled in his seat but didn't say anything.

'In both instances, you attended the patients shortly before they died,' Nell said. 'How do you explain that?'

'I'm the ward doctor. I see all of the patients so it's nothing unusual.'

'Dr Mosley,' Adam said, sitting up a little straighter. 'I put it to you that you engineered the deaths of both patients specifically to frame Carrie Parsons for the deaths. This was to avenge your late brother, whose untimely death you blamed on Ms Parsons thirteen years ago.'

'That's utter nonsense,' Nathan said, looking from Adam to Nell, his eyes wild.

'Dr Mosley,' Nell said. 'I'm arresting you on suspicion of the murders of Samina Khalil and Angus Titchford at King's Mill Hospital, A&E ward. You do not have to—'

'This is madness!' Mosley stood up, knocking his chair over in the process.

'Sit down, Dr Mosley,' Adam said firmly. 'Calm down.'

But Mosley was already too far gone to modify his behaviour.

'It's that bitch, isn't it? Suzy's told you all this … this crap. I should've silenced her when I had the chance.'

The door to the small interview room burst open and two uniformed officers dashed in and restrained Mosley.

'Parsons has no right to be a nurse, she's not fit to care for patients,' Mosley wailed as they escorted him out. 'She killed my brother. The bitch killed him and she thought she'd got away with it!'

55

Alexa

I sit with Carrie in the living room after DI Adam Partridge's call. The coffee I've made her sits untouched next to her.

'I can't believe it,' she keeps repeating. 'The boy whose death haunted me for years, nearly caused me to give up my nursing career, turns out to be Mosley's brother!'

I remember her talking about the teenager's death only vaguely. The overriding detail I recall is that it wasn't her fault.

'Didn't the consultant tell you he'd have missed the signs of sepsis too, that it was easy to do?'

She nodded. 'The symptoms for sepsis are better publicised now but back then, less so. The boy was confused, feverish and with a higher heart rate … all symptoms that could have been as a result of the viral infection he was fighting at the time. If it hadn't been for the paediatrician who assured me his death was not due to lack of care, I would have resigned there and then.'

'It must have been traumatic for the young Nathan Mosley,' I say. 'Him recovering and his brother dying.'

Carrie nods. 'He probably felt a lot of guilt because he was the surviving twin and naturally looked for someone to blame. I'd be the obvious choice and he was just a kid, after all.'

'And he's held that in his heart for all these years. It must have twisted him like a knife inside, making him angry and violent, as Suzy found out to her peril.'

Carrie nods. 'Usually, as they matured into an adult, the person would realise his brother's death was a sad accident. They'd probably come to the conclusion that it was nobody's fault. In Mosley's case though, he obviously internalised it and the fury and need for revenge just festered and grew ever stronger.'

'He was obsessed with you but when I saw the photographs on your laptop, I thought it was the other way around. Why did you spend hours hanging around outside his apartment and snapping pics?' I ask.

'I was trying to catch him doing something … I mean out of the ordinary, something dodgy. I just felt he couldn't be the person he portrayed himself as at work. Something felt off about him, so I just snapped away hoping I'd get something.' Carrie shakes her head. 'Sounds mad, I know. I made myself look even more guilty, but I was desperate. There was something about him that just jarred with me. I couldn't put my finger on it, and nobody would have believed me. Some part of my subconscious must have recognised him, but I genuinely hadn't a clue I'd treated the Mosley twins at a previous hospital. We only really get to know patients by their first name, and I must have seen thousands of faces in the last thirteen years. Although his brother's case haunted me, I could have never guessed Mosley was linked to it in any way.'

'Plus you only knew him as a child,' I remark. 'What happened to his twin brother was a tragedy, but to think he could sustain his hatred so much he'd track you down explicitly to try and ruin you? And worse still, to kill those two innocent patients in the name of his skewed obsession.'

Carrie shakes her head. 'He killed those patients pure and simple because he wanted to. Because he enjoyed having the ultimate power of life and death. Suzy's the proof he enjoyed inflicting pain on others, enjoyed the control. He probably felt a sense of poetic justice … that he'd suffered for the loss of his brother, so why shouldn't other families? After murdering the first one, little Samina, he realised it was possible to kill and blame it on me. The plan was hatched.'

'Yet the evidence seemed to show it was you who was always with the patient and not him.'

'He obviously used his medical expertise to inflict the fatal injections and overdoses at carefully planned times so he could make himself scarce in the meantime and be "summoned" when the patient took a turn for the worse.' She thinks for a moment. 'DI Partridge made an interesting observation that there are no psychiatric tests carried out on doctors. They go through the education system, go to university, and at the end of it, they're qualified for employment.'

I nod. 'How good are those psychiatric tests anyway? They can be faked easily by a psychopath and a trained doctor could easily rig their own answers to assure an acceptable test outcome. It's scary.' I pass Florence a piece of buttered toast.

'One mystery remains though,' Carrie says, frowning. 'Regrettably, it wasn't me who sent Mosley the parcel of rotten fish. I wish I'd have thought of that first! And I most definitely didn't report myself to social services as a person who could be a risk to Florence's safety. Which leaves the pressing question of … who did?'

56

Alexa

I text Perry and ask him to come over to the house, that there's something I need to tell him.

I'm standing at the window when he pulls on to the drive. He's crashing on his gym buddy's couch for a few nights until he can get something sorted. When he gets out of the car his face is bright and hopeful.

'Hey, little munchkin,' he sweeps a squealing Florence up into his arms. 'I've missed you so, so much.'

It's actually just been a couple of days since he took her to the park, but I can understand it's hard for him not to be around her when he's not working on the rig.

After a few more tickles and plenty of kisses, Perry sits Florence down in front of her pile of toys and she happily starts to play.

'You look well, Alexa,' he says, obviously noticing the few pounds I've lost and the effort I've made to style my hair and put on a little makeup. Mistakenly, he assumes it's for his benefit. 'I was so happy to get your text. It's high time we talked about us.'

'It's true I asked you over to talk, Perry,' I say. 'But it won't be the discussion you think.'

'Try me,' he says with a smile.

*

When I finish speaking, Perry sits in the chair, his head in his hands.

'I'm so sorry,' I say again. 'I had no right to lie to you about Daisy Mae. It was … the only thing that made any sense, because at the time I was ashamed and frightened of losing you. But I shouldn't have done it.'

'I don't know what to say,' Perry says quietly. 'It's a shock to think you ignored her when she was sobbing like that. And you shouldn't have lied; I had a right to know.'

'You did, but I was confused. I had postnatal depression. What's your excuse, Perry?'

'What?'

'What's your excuse for lying, for having an affair with Roisin Kenny?'

He drops his gaze. 'I haven't got one. I've lost count of the number of times I've said I'm sorry, Alexa. You and me, we'd been so distant. I just felt like I needed that closeness again, and Roisin was … well, she was a good listener. I made a terrible mistake but now it's over. When she picked me up from the airport on my last trip back from the rig, I told her I wanted to make a fresh start with you and Florence. Is that what you want, too?'

Instead of trying to work at our marriage and pour his energies into getting our closeness back, he'd taken the easy way out and turned to Roisin and her well-honed charms when it comes to married men.

I shake my head. 'I'm not ready to talk about us yet.'

'Take as much time as you like, Alexa.' He hesitates, keeps his voice light. 'I suppose Carrie will be moving back in here?'

'No. It'll be just me and Florence for a while. I need to let the dust settle again. The hospital have asked Carrie to go back, but she's got a little bedsit and she's looking for another job, possibly in a different area of the country. In the meantime, she's doing some bank nursing. Are you planning on going back to the rig?'

'Sounds like me and Carrie have got something in common for the first time,' he says. 'I'm not going back to Aberdeen. Not sure what I'm going to be doing yet; maybe find another rig, maybe find a new industry altogether.'

I've emerged from this ordeal with a new skill; I can shine the light of truth into the dark, murky areas of my life. When Roisin hinted I'd be better saving my loyalty, she spoke the truth. I do believe that in her mind, Carrie thought she was protecting me from their affair, like she's done since we were kids. Perry and I were going through tough times in our marriage and it was difficult for both of us. But he didn't *have* to have the affair; it was a conscious choice he made.

I can now look at the two most important adults in my life and see their reasons for making the decisions they did. I was always very good at that before I lost myself. But now, there's one big difference. My days of denial are over.

Ultimately, whichever way I try and soften the blow of what they did, I come to the same conclusion. They both betrayed me.

57

The police station

The desk clerk watched as the woman entered the police station reception area. She was tall, well-dressed but she had a hesitant manner, hovering around the entrance as if she hadn't yet fully decided whether she wanted to go through with something.

It was early in the day and there was nobody else currently waiting to be seen, so the clerk smiled and said in a bright, encouraging voice, 'Can I help you?'

The woman visibly jumped and clutched her neat cardigan across her chest. Slowly, she walked forward, her eyes skittish, searching the room as if to make sure no one was listening.

'I'd like to speak to DI Partridge, if possible,' she said in hushed tones. 'I need to tell him something important about the King's Mill Hospital case. Something very confidential.'

*

Adam's phone rang and his eyebrows shot up when the desk clerk informed him who was in reception.

Nell was busy speaking to a small team who were about to carry out a drugs raid on a local property, so Adam left her to it, slipped on his navy-and-grey-checked jacket and went through to the front of house.

'This is a surprise, Beth.' he smiled, wondering what could have brought Angus Titchford's daughter to the station this morning. 'Please, do come through.'

The press were having a very public feeding frenzy raking up everything they could find out about Dr Nathan Mosley and all had reported the innocence of ward manager Carrie Parsons. So Beth couldn't be under any illusion that the right culprit for her father's death hadn't been found. What on earth could she have to tell him that was so important?

Adam led her down the corridor to a small meeting room they used sometimes for 'pop-ins', as they called unexpected visitors. It was pleasantly furnished with comfy chairs and even a window that looked out onto the car park. A rare feature indeed in this place.

'Take a seat,' Adam said, sitting down himself. 'What can I do for you, Beth?'

'Firstly, I'd like to thank you and DS Tremaine for what you've done. Hopefully justice for my father can now be found.'

'I certainly hope that's the case.' Adam nodded gravely. 'Again, I'm so sorry for your loss.'

'Thank you. The reason I'm here is to come clean about my part in proceedings. I'm so sorry, so ashamed of myself. I don't know what came over me, it's not like me at all, not in my nature to—'

'Sorry, just stop there a moment.' Adam looked baffled. 'Come clean about what, exactly?'

Adam watched as Beth hung her head, her cheeks pink and hot.

'I sent Nathan Mosley a rotting fish, I sent an anonymous note to the hospital board and I reported a concern to social services about Carrie Parsons being in the same house as her baby niece.'

She gasped a little after getting it all out in one breath.

'That was all *you*?'

Beth sat a little straighter and forced herself to look him in the eye. 'If you have to arrest me, DI Partridge, then of course I understand. I've wasted police time and there's no excuse for—'

'There'll be no need to arrest you,' Adam said solemnly, trying to keep his face straight. 'But you could enlighten me as to why you'd have sent Mosley the package to punish him, when everyone initially believed he was the person who actually brought your father's death to our attention.'

'I suppose it was a measure of my temporary insanity. I blamed them all, you see. He was the doctor on the ward and Dad had died under his jurisdiction so it was a sort of knee-jerk reaction.' She paused to fan her glowing face with her hand. 'I engaged the services of a private investigator who revealed Carrie Parsons' home situation and also provided me with a home address for Mosley.'

Adam nodded slowly. He'd underestimated Beth Streeter; she was obviously a very resourceful woman. Still, this investigation had been full of surprises. He still hadn't quite recovered from Roisin Kenny brazenly telling them she was having an affair with Perry Ford when Adam had asked if she knew anything about the family that might be relevant.

'Well, consider your burden lifted, Beth. Carrie Parsons told us she was innocent of sending the package to Mosley and you've now confirmed that.' He wouldn't mention that Carrie Parsons had also threatened, stalked and harassed the doctor, quite understandably, as it turned out. 'I think anyone might've been concerned about little Florence under the circumstances.' Adam stood up. 'Thank you for coming in, I know it probably took a lot for you to do so.'

Beth looked shocked and remained seated. 'So you won't be charging me with anything?'

'No, Beth. You're free to go,' Adam said.

She stood up and looked him in the eye.

'You know, I wish you could have met my dad, DI Partridge. He was getting on a bit but he loved his garden, his bowls and his family; he believed in living life to the full. But justice will hopefully be done and I like to think he can rest in peace with Mum now. I thank you sincerely for your part in that.'

Adam nodded his thanks and showed Beth to the door.

There were some days – many days – this felt like the worst job in the world. But sometimes, on the odd occasion, he caught a glimpse into how people could begin to move on in their lives from very dark times when justice was seen to be done.

Today was one of those days.

58

Six weeks later

I lead Amanda Botha through into the living room.

'Hey, Florence! How are you?' She sits down on the floor to play with the coloured bricks, and earns herself a smile and a happy bounce from Florence. 'So pleased to see her cast is off. Six weeks and she's good as new!'

'Me too. What a relief when the doc said she wouldn't need an operation after all,' I say. 'Listen, I haven't had chance to say but thanks so much for getting Suzy some help.'

'No worries at all. Obviously I specialise in child protection but it only took a phone call to Women's Aid to get the ball rolling.'

'We're in touch, we're meeting for coffee tomorrow actually. It's made the world of difference that Suzy is back in touch with her family again. They thought she'd turned her back on them but now they know the truth, she's getting so much support from them,' I say, clapping when Florence manages to balance one brick on top of another.

'That's wonderful and there's more great news for you too. I can officially confirm the family assessment has been terminated.'

'That's fantastic.' I sigh with relief. 'We'll miss seeing you, though, Amanda, won't we, Florence?'

Florence lets out a yell that sounds exactly like 'oh yes', and both of us laugh.

'Well, I'm still here to support you, if you want it,' Amanda says. 'You and Florence have been through some pretty tough times through no fault of your own, and sometimes it helps just to get things off your chest. Plus I can help put you in touch with various support groups you might want to access, like I've done for Suzy.'

I nod; I know what she's referring to. I've already told Amanda about Daisy Mae, and over coffee, she now tells me she's done some digging.

'You weren't at fault in Daisy Mae's death, Alexa. Sadly, it was Sudden Infant Death Syndrome, nothing to do with her crying. It must have been such a shock, to wake up and discover your previously healthy baby had just slipped away like that. But it was just a cruel coincidence it happened when you fell asleep; it could have happened any time at all. You couldn't have done anything about that. You were ill yourself, remember that. In some ways Carrie took advantage of that to take control and look after you, just like she used to do when you were younger. It was still a terrible tragedy that Daisy Mae died. You would have handled it differently now, but you weren't in a good place so you blamed yourself.'

My body floods with gratitude at her words. I'm seeing a grief counsellor and she's helping me come to terms with my first baby's death, letting out my feelings in a healthy way like I should have done back then.

I always believed Carrie had fabricated the story of what happened during the two hours before Daisy Mae's death because she wanted to protect me from people saying I'd neglected my baby. Now I know it gave her some kind of control over me, too. The story didn't change the fact my baby died but it did provide a narrative about myself that meant I could just about live with the fact my child had died.

It was wrong of Carrie to do that. And it was wrong of me to agree to it.

59

The police station

Adam straightened the paisley Italian silk tie Saskia had surprised him with at the weekend to celebrate the end of the King's Mill Hospital investigation. He walked into the incident room to the customary round of applause that sometimes happened when a difficult case was brought to a conclusion.

'Thank you, thanks.' Smiling, he raised a hand. 'But this was a team effort as usual and I just wanted to give a little debrief before we head to the pub for a well-deserved drink. First round on me.'

Several officers cheered.

'Nell? Can you do the honours with a Nathan Mosley update?'

Nell stood up and looked around. 'So, as you know, Dr Nathan Mosley has been charged with the murders of Samina Khalil and Angus Titchford. He's currently pleading not guilty due to diminished responsibility.'

'There's a forensic psychiatrist on the case and Mosley will be undertaking psychological tests soon,' Adam added.

A rumble of disapproval fluttered around the room.

'Do you think he'll swing it in his favour, sir?' a uniformed officer called out.

'He's slippery enough,' someone at the back answered.

Adam shrugged. 'Who knows. I try not to torture myself with outcomes I can't control. We did our job and we should try to count that as a team success, whatever happens.'

'We got word this morning that the Khalil family are coming back to the UK this week,' Nell continued. 'Word is, they're planning to take legal action against the hospital for clinical negligence.'

'Can't really blame them,' a female officer called out. 'Sounds like Mosley had the run of the place. If he hadn't hated Carrie Parsons so much and reported the deaths to frame her, God knows how many more he could've killed before someone noticed.'

'Seems unfair though, if the hospital's hard-won reputation is ruined because of one bad egg,' another officer countered. 'All the people they help, all the lives they save on a daily basis … that could all be wiped out overnight.'

'Too true, and time will tell. In the meantime …' Adam stood up. 'Everybody ready? Let's go celebrate!'

A cheer of approval rose up around him as the officers pushed back their chairs and began to stand up.

Nell sidled up to him. 'Sometimes I wonder what happens to the people affected by something like the King's Mill case,' she said. 'Like, here we all are, putting it to bed … we've already moved on to other cases. I wonder about Beth Streeter, the Khalil family, Alexa and Perry Ford with little Florence and, of course, Carrie Parsons. They can't just shrug off what's happened, can they?'

'They'll all get there, they just need time,' Adam said, checking he had his wallet. 'They'll carve out new lives with varying levels of success, I'm sure.'

'I guess you're right,' Nell said, and she gave him a mischievous grin. 'Hope that wallet's nicely lined. I'm ordering one of those fancy cocktails with fruit and a sparkler in it.'

60

Alexa

'Alexa, come and get your coffee!' Vanessa calls. I help Florence into the little red plastic car and go back to the group. Within seconds, I've joined in with a conversation about a new kids' baking club that's opening next week.

The women have rallied around Florence and me, and nobody bats an eyelid now when we attend the weekly playgroup sessions. We never miss one! My friendships with a couple of the women have deepened. What's that saying: today's news is tomorrow's fish-and-chip paper?

The truth about my husband and sister has been a bitter pill to swallow, but on the bright side, I feel like I have a new lease of life. I make the most of everything now. My daughter and I are living life to the full.

We still see Carrie. We'll meet up at the park or she sometimes pops around to play with Florence if we're in. The dynamic between us has totally changed. I'm in charge of my own life now and Carrie fits around us.

Perry and I have agreed to keep the house for the time being, but that might change in the future. I just want some time for things to settle down, time to enjoy the blessing of raising my daughter without the crippling burden of the guilt and fear I've shouldered for the past two years.

We share the care of Florence; we haven't formalised custody yet or discussed divorce. But it's probably on the cards.

We've had a small stone set for Daisy Mae at the local cemetery, and Florence and I go now and again and take some flowers. It feels so good to celebrate my first baby's life and not hide her away like some deep, dark secret. She was too bright and beautiful. She existed, she was here and she will always be a part of me … part of all our lives.

No more irrational fear, no more hiding away or worrying that I'll hurt the ones I love the most because I can't be trusted.

I feel safe now, because I have the best person of all to take care of me and my daughter. Myself.

61

A letter to my daughter

My darling Daisy Mae,

Even though you weren't with us for long, I loved you so much, more than I'd ever loved anything in my whole life.

I'll never forget you, never try and leave you behind. You will always be with me in my heart. I'll always wonder what you would look like now, imagine how you would have grown into a beautiful girl. The sadness will always remain, but I wouldn't want it any other way, for a part of me died with you that day and my tears are part of my memory of you.

But now I know I need to forgive myself in order to be the best mummy I can to your sister Florence. To raise her without the shadow of fear tracing my every move, my every decision. I have to trust myself, trust my judgement and let Florence make her own mistakes in life.

As she grows older, I will be strong enough to let her fall and know that she'll get up and be better for it.

I don't know whether it's possible to fully forgive myself for failing you in those last few hours of your life, but I've realised now that I have to at least try.

I loved you more than anything in the world, you see, my darling. I would rather have taken my own life than hurt you. I wasn't myself, I was struggling so badly, I was so sad and bereft and I didn't even know it.

Where are you now? Somewhere happy I hope, with rainbows and sunshine. I hope you feel safe, my darling. Your sister will know you. I tell her all about you and show her your pictures. One day we'll be together again. Until that day, I make you a promise.

I will never forget you, Daisy Mae.

You were here, you were mine and you were loved.

Always know that you were loved.

A LETTER FROM
K.L. SLATER

I want to say a huge thank you for choosing to read *The Girl She Wanted*. If you enjoyed it and want to keep up to date with all my latest releases, just sign up at the following link. Your email address will never be shared and you can unsubscribe at any time.

www.bookouture.com/kl-slater

Fairy tales often begin with 'Once upon a time', but for me, story ideas often start with the two magic words 'What if …' This book started life with the dilemma 'What if your sister was accused of doing something terrible and you were the only person who believed she was innocent?'

So many stories explore the idea of how well we can really know someone. This may be because there are so many shades of grey between white and black, so many modes of behaviour and intention between good and evil.

No matter how well we know someone and for how long, can we really say we're able to predict a loved one's actions in every given situation? Of course not, and in that space, in that crevice of ambiguity, a story can turn and twist and sometimes surprise us. I hope you found a surprise or two in *The Girl She Wanted*, but readers are getting smarter and wiser, and alas, the job of the twisty thriller writer gets harder each time!

The book is set in Nottinghamshire, the place I was born and have lived all my life. Local readers should be aware that I sometimes take the liberty of changing street names or geographical details to suit the story. Although I use the names of real hospitals to add authenticity to the story, the events that occur within them in the book are entirely fictional and invented only for the purposes of this book. They are in no way meant to undermine the excellent care and first-class service patients receive there.

I hope you enjoyed reading *The Girl She Wanted*; if you did, I would be very grateful if you could take a few minutes to write a review. I'd love to hear what you think, and it makes such a difference in helping new readers to discover one of my books for the first time.

I love hearing from my readers – you can get in touch on my Facebook page, through Twitter, Goodreads or my website.

Thank you, dear readers ... until next time,
Kim x

 KimLSlaterAuthor

 @KimLSlater

 KLSlaterAuthor

 www.KLSlaterAuthor.com

ACKNOWLEDGEMENTS

I really am so fortunate to have such a wonderful group of competent and talented people around me.

Huge thanks to my editor at Bookouture, Lydia Vassar-Smith, for her wonderful insight and editorial support, which begins at the ideas stage of each book and culminates only when I write the acknowledgements.

Thanks to *all* the Bookouture team for everything they do – which, believe me, is an awful lot – especially to Alexandra Holmes and to Kim Nash, Noelle Holten and Sarah Hardy, who are all so diligent and a pleasure to work with.

Thanks to my writing buddy, Angela Marsons, who is always on hand to have a laugh, provide a shoulder to cry on or, since living in the country, give astute mole and wasp deterrent advice. And, of course, provide cute pics of her doggies when required.

Thanks, as always, to my incredible literary agent, Camilla Bolton, who is always there, and always in my corner. Thanks also to Camilla's assistant, Jade Kavanagh, who in a short time has become a tremendous support to me. And thanks of course to the rest of the hard-working team at Darley Anderson Literary, TV and Film Agency, especially Mary Darby and Rosanna Bellingham.

Special thanks must also go to Henry Steadman, who has worked so hard to pull another amazing cover out of the bag.

Huge thanks to Stuart Gibbon of The Gib Consultancy for providing the police procedural advice and a window into his extensive detective experience, and also to my old school friend Joanne Lewis-Hodgkinson for her most useful and knowledgeable medical advice. Any mistakes in translation or small tweaks in procedure are most definitely my own.

Big thanks to copyeditor Jane Selley and proofreader Becca Allen for sharpening up the prose.

Massive thanks as always go to my husband, Mac, for his love, support and patience, even when my writing schedule borders on crazy! To my family, especially my daughter, Francesca, and to Mama, who are always there to support and encourage me in my writing.

Thank you to the bloggers and reviewers who do so much to help make my thrillers a success. Thank you to everyone who has taken the time to post a positive review online or has taken part in my blog tour. It is always noticed and much appreciated.

Last but not least, thank you *so* much to my wonderful readers. I love receiving all your wonderful comments and messages and I am truly grateful for the support of each and every one of you.

Made in United States
North Haven, CT
09 April 2022

18071688R00198